Ryan leaped from his seat, fighting the jolt caused by the wag's halted momentum

He threw himself backward, barely keeping his balance as he reached the tail end of the wag. The sec door crushed the roof of the wag at the front, driving metal down onto the seat where he had sat a few moments before.

Ryan jumped from the wag and ran for cover, joining Krysty, Tammy and Mildred.

"Glad you could drop in, lover," Krysty said dryly.

"Just had a few things to do," he replied laconically.

He saw that the crushed wag—driven down with such force that the rear wheels had left the ground—held the sec door open for a gap of three or four feet. There was little indication of whether or not the Illuminated sec beyond were still in cover, or whether they had retreated.

Looking back, he could see through the open outer door, into the dawn light beyond.

The larger war party was advancing.

JAMES AXLER

DEATH LANDS®

Destiny's Truth

THE ILLUMINATED ONES BOOK II

A GOLD EAGLE BOOK FROM
WORLDWIDE®

TORONTO • NEW YORK • LONDON
AMSTERDAM • PARIS • SYDNEY • HAMBURG
STOCKHOLM • ATHENS • TOKYO • MILAN
MADRID • WARSAW • BUDAPEST • AUCKLAND

First edition December 2002

ISBN 0-373-62570-7

DESTINY'S TRUTH

Copyright © 2002 by Worldwide Library.

Printed in U.S.A.

Victory at all costs, victory in spite of all terror,
Victory however long and hard the road may be; for
Without victory there is no survival.
—Sir Winston Churchill
1874–1965

THE DEATHLANDS SAGA

This world is their legacy, a world born in the violent nuclear spasm of 2001 that was the bitter outcome of a struggle for global dominance.

There is no real escape from this shockscape where life always hangs in the balance, vulnerable to newly demonic nature, barbarism, lawlessness.

But they are the warrior survivalists, and they endure—in the way of the lion, the hawk and the tiger, true to nature's heart despite its ruination.

Ryan Cawdor: The privileged son of an East Coast baron. Acquainted with betrayal from a tender age, he is a master of the hard realities.

Krysty Wroth: Harmony ville's own Titian-haired beauty, a woman with the strength of tempered steel. Her premonitions and Gaia powers have been fostered by her Mother Sonja.

J. B. Dix, the Armorer: Weapons master and Ryan's close ally, he, too, honed his skills traversing the Deathlands with the legendary Trader.

Doctor Theophilus Tanner: Torn from his family and a gentler life in 1896, Doc has been thrown into a future he couldn't have imagined.

Dr. Mildred Wyeth: Her father was killed by the Ku Klux Klan, but her fate is not much lighter. Restored from predark cryogenic suspension, she brings twentieth-century healing skills to a nightmare.

Jak Lauren: A true child of the wastelands, reared on adversity, loss and danger, the albino teenager is a fierce fighter and loyal friend.

Dean Cawdor: Ryan's young son by Sharona accepts the only world he knows, and yet he is the seedling bearing the promise of tomorrow.

In a world where all was lost, they are humanity's last hope....

Prologue

"Jak... Jak, honey, time to wake up...."

Jak Lauren opened his red, sore eyes, feeling the earth spin away under him as he did so. A mat-trans jump always left him feeling weak and sick, his stomach muscles cramping to make him vomit substance where there was none. He spread his hands out to grasp the smooth armaglass floor of the chamber, expecting the cold and solid material to cool his fevered palms.

But there was no armaglass; instead, registering with a ringing alarm bell in his still befuddled mind, there was warm, clammy dirt beneath his hands. His instincts fighting the jump sickness, he tried to raise himself on his elbows, his vision clearing the fog before him.

Was it Gloria looking down at him?

"Hey, honey, don't look so startled," the Gate queen said before drawing back a little so that Jak was able to see that they were now in the open air.

The albino youth's senses began to cut into the confusion that had clouded him since awakening. He could smell the rich loam beneath him, soft and springy as Gloria stepped back. They were in a small clearing, surrounded by trees that looked like dwarfed and stunted elms, but in full leaf for all that. He could hear the hum of insects, and the rustles in among the undergrowth of small mammals—nothing big enough to be a threat, his senses told him. Normally, this would have made him relax, but in his bewildered state, his muscles remained tense, his attention struggling to focus as rapidly as possible.

Where he would normally spring to his feet with a lithe ease, Jak found himself struggling to hoist himself upright. His limbs were still tingling from the aftereffects of the jump, and refused to obey the impulses from his brain.

"Not right…" he said in a hoarse whisper. "Should be in mat-trans, not here. And Ryan? Others?"

He was now on his feet, clearing his head with a tentative shake that made his focus blur and the earth spin again for a second before it settled.

Gloria was now about twenty yards away from him, with her back turned toward him. There were marks on her skin that he couldn't identify from this distance, but it seemed like a patchwork of dark dots that randomly spread across her bared skin, disappearing under the long, flaming red tresses that hung down her back.

"You feeling better now, sweets?" she asked, her husky voice low and yet carrying that melodious note that he knew so well by now. It was good to hear her. The last thing Jak remembered was the Gate tribe entering the other mat-trans chamber in the redoubt before they were flung to who knew where. There had been no guarantee that they would end up in the same place, given the unreliability of the old tech.

But if they were here, where were the rest of the companions? And where was Gloria's faithful attendant, Tammy, and the rest of the Gate tribe?

Even as that flickered across his mind, Jak was sniffing the air, attuning his hearing to the slightest sound around, attempting to identify its source.

There was no one else around, no one human, that was, nothing but the smaller forms of wildlife that he had detected earlier.

"You're not talking to me," Gloria admonished. "Why not?"

"Not right," Jak repeated, almost to himself.

"What isn't right?" she asked. Jak prickled as she spoke. There was something in her tone that had suddenly—for no apparent reason—turned hostile, and he was sure now that something was very wrong.

The albino youth didn't reply. He steadied himself, trying to bring his still-rebelling body under control, his every instinct screaming that he was going to need complete control of himself, of his fighting capabilities, before too long.

He wasn't wrong.

"Not talking to me again," Gloria said, an angry hiss running through her tone. "That's not good, is it, sweets?"

"Mebbe," Jak replied with as neutral a tone as he could muster. It was hard, as his own hostility was rising with every moment, screaming at him that the whole situation was wrong, and that there was something even more perilous about the Gate queen than the threat of attack.

"Mebbe?" Her body tensed at that. He could see the muscles rippling beneath the dark lines of dots across her tanned skin. Her posture was still relaxed, but the muscle tone gave that as a lie. She was feigning her repose, preparing for attack.

Jak felt the rush of adrenaline through his body, washing the sluggishness from his system, tightening his muscles and tautening his nerves until he was ready for almost anything.

Almost...

"Mebbe, mebbe, mebbe..." Gloria muttered. "Mebbe it's time for you to die, then."

Jak was prepared. It was like a nightmare, or a time and place where this wasn't the real Gloria, but still it hit him hard. He hadn't quite realized how his feelings for the Gate queen had grown until the sense of betrayal hit him in the pit of the stomach. However, such emotion had been rare in the life of the albino teenager, and he had had the briefest of it snatched from him before, where his wife and child had been slaughtered. After that, this was easy to quell, to put into a place where he could ignore and concentrate on the immediate danger.

For danger he was sure there was. He knew with that instinct that had kept him alive for so long that he was about to be attacked.

But why?

There was no time for him to think about this—if, indeed, he could ever be bothered—as the need for action overtook the luxury of thought.

Gloria pivoted on her heel and sprang at him. Despite her pose of a relaxed posture, Jak had been able to see at twenty yards the way in which the corded sinew and muscle in her bare thighs and calves had tensed, ready for the sudden, explosive spring.

What he could not have been ready for was her face as she turned and leaped, her light red hair flying out around her, making her face visible to him as she soared through the stilled air.

The look of naked fury and aggression he would have expected from such an action: her face was contorted in a snarling scream of rage and explosive anger, her lips back over her vulpine teeth, sharp and gleaming. Her long nose was wrinkled by the tension in her face muscles, nostrils distended as she sought more oxygen to power her attack. Her eyes were sharp, pupils reduced to mere dots in the ocean of color by the adrenaline rush that also coursed through her as it did through Jak.

This was only to be expected. Any warrior in action would be reduced to the same set of facial characteristics, and Jak had faced this many a time in his life and—should that life continue—would face it many more times to come. But it wasn't that that, for the briefest of moments, froze him in confusion and fear—fear not of the warrior before him, but of what may be affecting her.

For Gloria's face was, like the skin on her back and—he could now see—the skin on the front of her torso, covered in a map of the black dots. Except that, as she got closer, sailing through the air in motion so slow to him that she almost seemed static, it was possible to see that those dots were more than just discolorations of the skin. They were the black-ringed holes of open sores, the centers red and raw and running yellow and green with discharge and pus. The crusts of these sores pulled at the skin of her face, seeming to stretch it out of shape, almost out of recognition the more that he looked at her. It didn't seem possible that this was the same woman whom he had joined in battle only a few hours previously.

It couldn't be. But whoever it was had only one thing now in mind: the chilling of Jak Lauren.

His attention had been so taken by the sight of her face that the bone-chilling scream, high-pitched and wailing, yet with a throaty undertone that gave it almost a dual-note quality of primal terror, had hardly penetrated his consciousness.

Now it did, leaving him with a sudden awakening and a thrill of terror that made the muscles ripple down his spine. It was a totally instinctive reaction, and it was a necessary one. It jolted him from the moment of frozen confusion and made him click into the fighting mode that operated only on an instinctive level.

Gloria was too close to him now for any attempt at an evasive maneuver. That would only make it easier for him to be chilled. Instead, Jak yielded to her attack, and began to fall back as she landed upon him, relaxing his muscles so that he hit the ground without damaging his thin, wiry frame. The earth was soft, but at speed and with the accelerating and falling weight of the Gate queen, to fall awkwardly could injure him and leave him easy prey for a follow-up attack. As it was, Gloria descended on top of him with her long-bladed panga in one hand and her other clawed, ready to lash out. She expected, at the back of her crazed mind, to drive him into the earth, knocking the air from him and leaving him vulnerable to a slashing blow from the panga.

It didn't quite work that way. Jak's hands attached themselves to her wrists as she landed on him, fastening on with an iron-tight grip, his elbows braced to keep those hands at bay. He fell back into the momentum of her fall, landing on his back and rolling as he did so, converting that momentum into a drive from his legs that flipped the woman over his head. He loosened his grip on her wrists as his legs began the drive up into her, so she was free to fly over his head and land a few yards away.

Before she had even hit the ground, Jak had already finished the backward roll, landing on his feet and pivoting so that he was facing her. Her face had been close to him for only a fraction of a second, but close enough for him to smell the decay on her skin, her rancid breath steaming into his nostrils. Her eyes had been bloodshot, with yellow around the iris, pinpoint pupils smaller than any he had seen on jolt, and the pus had been running from the sores on her face, disturbed from their crusted little pools by the motion of her attack.

Jak had been ready for her and ready for the recovery. Gloria hadn't, in her fury, expected such a maneuver. She had been nowhere near ready, and landed with a bone-jarring jolt on her back, the panga flying from her hand. Jak was surprised. The Gloria he had known would have recovered herself at least partially in midair, and been able to minimize the bad effects of such a landing. It crossed Jak's mind, in a fraction of a moment, that this couldn't be the real Gloria. How had she acquired such a disease—whatever it was that scored her skin—so quickly? Why had she so swiftly turned against he who had been her lover? And why was she fighting so badly when she had been the finest warrior he had ever met? None of this made sense to him in any way.

But there was scant time for reflection. Already, he was aware that in pausing he had allowed her to recover, as she had rolled on her side to recover the panga and was scrambling to her feet.

He couldn't make that mistake again. At any time it could prove fatal. From within his jacket, Jak withdrew one of his leaf-bladed throwing knives. He should finish this quickly if it was at all possible. He was acutely aware that it was the adrenaline that was keeping him at this pitch, and his body still hadn't recovered properly from the jump. Too long in combat, and it could start to fail him at a crucial moment.

With one fluid motion, the knife came from within the hidden recesses of his combat jacket, was palmed and then flicked between his fingers. Then his arm was drawn back and released in one simple motion.

The knife sped toward its target. Jak was already reaching for the next knife, to be certain; but usually there was little doubt that the sharpened and lethal piece of metal would fulfill its function.

Not this time. With a speed equal to that of the albino youth, Gloria swept her panga through the air, seemingly in a random motion. There was a flash of light as the weak sun caught the blade, a spark as metal met metal, and the leaf-bladed knife was deflected harmlessly into the trees.

"Have to do better than that, sweets," Gloria gloated.

Jak didn't answer. He wasn't going to waste energy and breath on idle words. Instead, he stood and waited. Every sinew and fiber itched to attack, but the cool hunter's brain that had made him wait silently for days on his prey back in the Louisiana bayou, where he learned to listen to his instincts, told him to let her make the first move.

Gloria stood, swaying, the panga held loosely in her fist. She laughed, a harsh, bitter gasp of breath, her lips drawing back over her teeth in a leer and her eyes—for one brief moment—returning to the Gloria that he knew.

Before this had time to register in his mind as anything more than the briefest of impressions, she was on him again. With a yell that cleansed her mind and galvanized her spirit, she flew at him, the panga weaving a pattern before her that cleaved the air with the razor-honed blade in such a way that to get past the defense would be the surest way to lose an arm.

Jak's answer was simple and efficient. The arc of the panga proscribed the air at a lowest point around the Gate queen's knees. It would take her only a few steps to reach him—she had already taken the first when Jak took action.

The albino flung himself down and forward, so that he was close to the ground. The warm smell of the loam rose up strongly, almost as a stench, and hit the back of his throat as he grazed the ground. Rolling, he was under the defense of the blade, looking up as the panga grazed the air above his face. It began to dip as Gloria's reaction clued in to Jak's offensive maneuver, but not enough to literally cut him off. Jak was past the arc of defense and took the Gate queen at the calves, sweeping them out from under her so that she fell forward.

Unable to keep her balance, it was all that she could do to stop herself from falling onto the panga blade as she pitched forward. Her arm out to one side, she caught it awkwardly as she fell, the blade jamming in the soil and acting as a sudden barrier to the free movement of her arm, the bone snapping as it was driven in two directions at once. The sudden pain forced a high-pitched scream from the woman, and her body jolted in the opposite direction, as though an electric shock had flowed through her.

Jak was on his feet and running toward her as she tried to recover from the pain and shock of the broken arm, which hung limply at her side. She looked up at him, the pain misting her gaze. Fumbling, she reached for the blaster that was holstered on her hip. Jak knew that it was a Vortak Precision Pistol, capable of incredible accuracy because of its lack of recoil, and that he had little, if any, time in which to act. But the pain and shock had dulled her reactions, and she was too slow. With his last stride, Jak took a flying kick at the Gate queen, his heavy combat boot connecting with her skull at the temple. It was too high to snap her neck, but enough to fracture the bone and to render her unconscious. With a dull grunt, the light went out in the woman's eyes, and they rolled back into her head as she slumped to the ground.

Jak was beside her before she hit, taking her head in one hand and pulling it back so that her throat was exposed. Like the rest of her, it was covered in a patchwork of sores. In his other hand, Jak had a leaf-bladed knife.

The blade pricked her skin, drawing a bead of blood. For a moment, Jak delayed his action. Usually, in such a situation, he would have no hesitation in cutting the throat of a foe and eradicating the threat. But this was Gloria....

He shook his head. Whoever this had once been, it was no longer the woman he had loved, and her only aim had been his chilling. He knew what he had to do.

And yet, still he looked away as he drew the blade across her throat, opening it up and draining her life onto the soil, which drank it in hungrily, absorbing the moisture in its rich depths.

Jak stood up and moved away from the chilled corpse, the knife—wiped swiftly on his jacket—back in its secret place.

It was then—with the prickling of the white hairs on the back of his neck—that he became aware that he was no longer alone. Whereas there had been nothing except small mammals within the range of his senses before, now there was something altogether more menacing.

Jak was on his feet and pivoting toward where he felt—rather than heard or smelled—the new threat to be. As he swung on the balls of his feet, he dropped into a crouch, palming one of his knives, his free hand reaching for the .357 Magnum Colt Python that he kept holstered at his hip.

By the time he had turned through 180 degrees, he had a weapon in each hand. But there was no way that he was prepared for the sight that met his bloodred eyes.

For in front of him was a detachment of the sec force from the Illuminated Ones, complete with one of their high-tech battle wags. The vehicle stood motionless at the mouth of the clearing, where a narrow trail cut through the dwarf elms. No sound had revealed its approach, which seemed nonsensical. Equally, no sound had announced the disgorging of the seven sec men who stood before him. They had the one-piece, shiny battle suits that he was all too familiar with, and the outlying pair carried the laser blasters that he had seen used to such devastating effect.

How had they arrived with no noise at all? Given that he could possibly have been distracted to some degree by his battle with Gloria to pay close attention to the slightest sound, the amount of noise made by a wag and detachment of sec would have cut through even the noisiest of hand-to-hand fights.

Jak's stomach flipped. This wasn't real; this was a nightmare like the one he had encountered on the last mat-trans jump. It was in some way precognitive, just as that had proved to be. The albino had no doubt about that now, as the likelihood of his having two such hallucinations during a jump was remote for any other reason. But what would it tell him?

More importantly, would he make it out of this nightmare alive? He didn't know for sure, but he had heard stories of dreams and nightmares that killed, bringing on fatal heart failure. He couldn't risk that there was any truth in these tales, he had to fight to the last.

But against seven lined up against him? With no cover? And with two of them carrying laser blasters that could obliterate him in a second? Why not? The albino hunter knew that he had no choice but to fight, and it was odd that they hadn't simply blasted him when he was facing away from them. Could it be they wanted to take him alive and not chill him?

If so, he had a chance.

As that flashed through his mind, he shifted his weight from side to side, giving no true indication of what his next move may be. He would wait for the enemy to make the first move.

And so they did. The two outlying sec men, their laser blasters trained on him, moved in a pincer movement, slow and steady steps carrying them over the springy loam. Jak's head moved from side to side, following their progress. The other five sec men strung themselves in a line and began to advance upon him. They weren't armed with blasters, but carried knives that looked like the Tekna favored by J. B. Dix. One of them carried a hypodermic syringe in his free hand.

Suddenly Jak's mind clicked the pieces into place. The syringe carried whatever had infected Gloria, whatever had made her that way, and he was their next target. That was why they hadn't simply blasted him with the laser rifles when they had him unaware. They wanted to take him alive.

It gave the albino an advantage, and one that he had to exploit fully. Testing their tactics, he moved lightly to one side. The sec man on the left sent a ray of light from the laser blaster that scored the earth beside him, leaving a smoking trench two feet in length.

Jak nimbly skipped aside, his lips drawing back over his sharp teeth in a humorless grin. As always, their tactics were predictable. Even though they shielded their faces—their eyes—from view, the thoughts that ran through their minds were always visible.

He focused on the center figure, the one who held the syringe, as well as the knife. He was their key man. Take him out of the hunt, and they couldn't fulfill their task. Then they would have to take Jak alive. That was his priority, to stay alive long enough to awaken from the mat-trans jump.

The albino fought to clear his head. He couldn't allow such thoughts to take him over, as they could so easily distract him from the task. He needed all his wits and reactions about him to carry out his next move.

As the line drew closer—hesitant as they could not work out why he seemed to be static—they arced even wider, so that they formed a semicircle around him. The sec team directly in front of him was now no more than a few yards away.

Time to move.

Jak crouched low, almost squatting and drawing as much power as he could from his whipcord calves and thighs. He had no run to gain momentum, and nothing to give him advantage in terms of height or drop, but he had no other option. This had to be as good as it got.

With a sudden yell that broke the unnatural stillness, causing a ripple of alarm in the sec ranks and unleashing the power of his strength and skill, Jak straightened in a leap that carried him over the gap between the advancing line and his position.

The sec soldier with the syringe and the knife saw Jak come toward him, the white hair flailing in the air, his eyes red like the blood he would spill, but could do nothing. For that all-important fraction of a second, the soldier was frozen in fear and confusion.

It was only that fraction of a second that Jak needed. He cannoned into the man and took him into a forward roll. Unlike Jak, just minutes earlier when Gloria had taken him in this fashion, the sec man wasn't ready for the assault. He fell heavily, making a muffled sound behind the visor of his helmet as the breath was driven from his body. Jak also heard the crack of bone as one of his adversary's arms hit the ground, the elbow shattering. A muffled scream, strangled by lack of air, also escaped Jak's prey.

Following through the roll and coming upright, Jak swiveled to face his opponent and took the arm that still grasped the syringe—the shattered elbow was on his knife arm. The albino stamped heavily on the forearm, the pain-deadened tissue causing the fingers to open. The syringe fell limply to the earth, and Jak stamped again, shattering the plastic vial and spilling its contents into the earth.

Whatever happened now in reality, in this nightmare he had forced them to take him alive.

This was the last thought to cross his mind before the butt of a laser blaster thudded against his skull, knocking him into unconsciousness. How the sec man had reached him without his noticing he didn't know, but then again, it didn't matter now.

JAK AWOKE with a pounding in the front of his skull, and a succession of bright flashing lights that whirled around his head. He tried to open his eyes and raise his head, see where he was, but that only made things worse, so he let his head fall back, closing his eyes until things began to settle.

"Oh, no, you're awake now," a harsh, guttural voice screamed. At least, that was how it seemed through the pain and the lights. Jak felt his head jerked forward by a hand that grasped his hair and pulled hard. He opened his eyes, ignoring the spinning and swirling lights that obscured a clear view of the bearded man clad in white who stood over him. The man held Jak's head in one hand, and in the other he grasped a syringe.

Jak tried to raise his arms to defend himself, despite the weakness that ran through his body. His muscles were slow and sluggish to respond, but even so it took him no time at all to detect the restraints that tied him down to the hard bed or table on which he lay.

"That won't do you any good," the voice rasped. "You're not going to get away from us this time. Just like that bitch whore, you're going to be our test sample. We'll see just how good this shit is, and how quick it travels. She was supposed to be our carrier, until you turned up and chilled her. Now you can be the carrier and we'll monitor you.''

''Why?'' Jak managed to croak through the blur of his head and his parched throat.

''Because we can use this to retain out rightful position in the world. The world as it is now, anyway.''

There were other questions Jak wanted to ask, but he couldn't marshal his thoughts, and his throat was too dry and cracked to force out any words at all.

He felt the pressure of the bearded man's hand on his arm, and the pricking pain of a needle, the pressure of liquid forced into the vein.

And then it began to fade....

Chapter One

Jak woke to find a similar pressure in his arm. Still halfway between conscious and unconscious, he yelled in pain and horror as he felt the needle spike him. Eyes wide-open but seeing nothing, he sprang upright, hitting out around him. He felt his wildly flailing arm catch something—someone—and he dimly heard a shout of surprise and pain mixed with the crash of a human body hitting a hard floor.

"Fireblast! He's freaking out. Hold him down!" Ryan Cawdor yelled, springing forward and grabbing Jak, pushing him down onto the bed in the redoubt sick bay.

"Got him," J. B. Dix gritted, approaching from the other side of the bed and joining the one-eyed man in pinning Jak to the hard surface. The albino continued to yell, but it was broken by a coughing fit as he began to choke on a stream of bile that rose unbidden into his throat and mouth.

Dr. Mildred Wyeth struggled to her feet, aided by Doc Tanner. She had fallen awkwardly and twisted her ankle, and the sudden pain as she put weight on it made her gasp.

"If you will allow me to teach you, as it were, the art of egg sucking, then I would suggest you let me spray that ankle and apply something cold to it before it begins to swell."

"Doc, you old buzzard, if you stop it hurting like hell on a hot day, then you can teach me anything you like," Mildred replied, seating herself gratefully on a chair. Doc smiled, his perfect white teeth giving his gaunt face a momentary resemblance to a grinning skull, before hurrying to a cupboard in order to obtain a painkilling spray.

Meanwhile, Jak had subsided from his fit of violence, the need to vomit out the bile taking precedence in his still clouded mind. J.B. and Ryan rolled him onto his side and stepped back, allowing him to release the toxin from his body.

"What the hell was all that about?" Ryan asked of no one in particular.

"I don't know," Mildred replied, "but I sure as hell wish he'd found a quieter way of coming to. Ah, that's better," she added as Doc sprayed her ankle, almost instantly deadening the pain.

WHEN JAK AWOKE, seemingly for the third time, the sick bay was in semidarkness, only one small lamp lighting the room.

"I see you've awakened a little more quietly this time," Mildred said, getting to her feet and walking to the bed. "Which is something I'm glad for, if nothing else."

Jak blinked, his albino eyes already accustomed to the gloom.

"Skip it," Mildred dismissed in answer to his unspoken question. "The point is, how are you?"

"Feel like shit," Jak croaked by way of reply.

"Yeah, and you look like it." Mildred grinned. "You've been out for a long time. I thought you'd fallen into some kind of coma. That's why we've been waiting here for some kind of sign from you.''

''Waiting?'' Jak was bewildered. It hadn't occurred to him up to this point, but it now registered with him that he was in a redoubt sick bay. How had he gotten here? He couldn't recall a time when Ryan would move his people out of a mat-trans chamber and into the main body of a redoubt without everyone being triple red and sharp.

''Gate?'' Jak asked suddenly, his guts lurching when he thought of Gloria and his bizarre dream.

In the semidark he could see Mildred's plaits move on her shoulders as she shrugged. ''Your guess is as good as mine. I've been taking a look at the computers here and reckon that the mat-trans computers at the other base must have had some kind of fail-safe device on them.''

''Eh?'' Still dazed, Jak was finding it hard to take in what she was saying.

Mildred came and stood over him as she continued. ''When we arrived, and it became obvious that you weren't going to come around, Ryan got Doc to stand guard over you in the chamber while the rest of us recced. As soon as we were out, we could see that there was only one chamber in the room, and we already knew that it wasn't as big as the one we'd used when we parted company with the Gate. And part company is exactly what we did.

''It was pretty obvious that whatever happened, we were nowhere where the Illuminated Ones had gone, and nowhere where the Gate had ended up. We divided up and searched the redoubt. It's small as they go, and still pretty well equipped. We haven't gone for the upper levels yet, so maybe it's been left alone because you just can't get in and out of it. Whatever, it's empty and safe for now, so we set you up here so I could examine and monitor you. Speaking of which…''

Mildred began to test Jak's reflexes and check his vital signs. The albino youth was silent while she carried out her tasks, waiting until she had finished before speaking.

''So we're on our own?''

Mildred nodded. ''Seems like the Illuminated Ones computers had an automatic reset to send the contents of the mat-trans to a random redoubt unless it was operated manually. We're here, God alone knows where the Gate tribe is, and the Illuminated Ones are safely wherever the hell they wanted to be. Which is just the way they wanted it.''

''And me?''

Mildred sucked in breath through her teeth. ''That's a good question. You know as well as any of us that you always take a while to come around from the strain of a jump. But this time it seems that you went into some kind of deep trance, almost like a coma. You were completely unresponsive and there was nothing I could do.''

''How long?''

''We've been here four days,'' Mildred replied, shocking Jak. He didn't realize that he had been unconscious for so long.

''Know where we are?'' Jak asked.

''Not yet. Not until we try and get out.''

Jak closed his eyes. He needed to get his strength back. Every fiber of his body was aching, and as he closed his eyes, leaving Mildred to exit the sick bay, he felt waves of sleep wash over him; sleep that was devoid of dream, good or bad.

"IT'S A BASTARD this has happened," J.B. muttered as he surveyed the armory of the redoubt. The walls were lined with racks where rifles, machine pistols, lightweight antitank blasters and grens should have stood. Instead there were only the remnants of trashed plastic-and-carbon fiber, the rusting remains of scrapped metal. The last scavengers or inhabitants of the redoubt had stripped the armory and then destroyed whatever was either too much to carry or simply surplus to requirements.

For the Armorer, the sight of deliberately destroyed weapons was like sacrilege. His obsession was to keep as much of this old tech as possible in good working order—not just because it was essential to survival in the Deathlands, but also because he could see beauty in the varieties of weaponry, and the ways in which they worked their art of chilling.

Ryan Cawdor stood by his friend, his single, piercing blue orb taking in the destruction.

"Whoever was last here didn't want to give any help to those who came next, that's for sure," he stated.

The armory was on a higher level of the redoubt than those they had been inhabiting since their arrival. The dorms, showers, kitchens and sick bay had been in fairly good condition, with enough supplies remaining to keep the seven companions alive, clean and fed while Jak recovered from his postjump trauma. His strength had returned quickly, and only a few days after his awakening they were ready to leave.

Which was just as well, as already the supplies of

self-heats were running low. Also, the heating of the water in the shower blocks was prone to be erratic, leading to a few scalding or freezing encounters. The heating and air-conditioning, which were also supposed to be comp controlled, had also shown some signs of falling into decay, with sudden switches in temperature, and the presence of dust in some of the rooms that should have been taken from the atmosphere by the air recyclers.

Although the companions had maintained a guard over the places on the lower level where there were points of entry for any foe, none of them had believed they were under serious threat of attack while they waited for Jak to recover. Not only did the redoubt seem to have been long since deserted, but there was also some doubt as to whether they could reach the surface level.

That was the purpose of this initial recce by Ryan and J.B.—they intended to scout the next two levels before bringing up the rest of their party. Despite his assertions to the contrary, Jak was still not at full fitness and alertness, so Ryan intended to leave him with a protective party until they were out in the open. From his own experience after being wounded or traumatized in some way, the one-eyed man knew Jak would come up to speed in the action of moving out, but would still need a degree of cushioning until he had attained full health.

So it was that the two men had ascended the levels of the redoubt until they were only one away from the top—and exit—level. There had been nothing to bar their way, and nothing to indicate that anyone had been there for a very long time. The comp system was failing to an even greater extent on this level, and it took them time to adjust to the dim lighting and the musty air.

And then they had found the armory.

"I wonder if they went out aboveground or used the mat-trans," the Armorer remarked, recovering from his anger at the sight of the armory.

"Only the one way to find out," Ryan replied. "If we find the exit level fucked, then we know the answer."

J.B. looked at his old friend. "You reckon we should recce that first, or bring everyone up?"

Ryan shrugged. "Doesn't seem to be even the remotest chance of things going triple red, but no point in moving them until we find out if we can actually get out this way."

J.B. nodded, pushing his spectacles back up his nose and setting his battered fedora on his high forehead. "Let's get to it, then," he muttered grimly.

The two men set off, adopting a defensive formation. Despite the quiet, still atmosphere of that level of the redoubt, and the vague notion that they would be absurd to anyone watching, both also knew that anyone watching would make such a formation a necessity.

But there was nothing, not the slightest indication of life in the upper reaches of the redoubt. Neither was it obstructed in any way. Despite the stale and dust-laden air, and the lights failing with an even greater regularity, there was nothing that would in any way be an obstacle to the companions leaving the redoubt via this route. When Ryan and J.B. reached the exit door, with the code scratched onto the metal above the key plate, the one-eyed man turned to his number two.

"Keep watch here. I'll get the others."

When he reached the lower levels of the redoubt, he found the rest of his party ready to move. Despite the fact that the way had been cleared in advance, they still adopted an attitude of caution and moved off in formation. Ryan took the front, with Krysty bringing up the rear in lieu of J.B. Behind them came Dean, Mildred and Jak—the albino moving with an extra caution brought on by the awareness of his slightly weakened state—then Doc.

At the exit doors, J.B. was waiting. He greeted them with a curt nod, and at Ryan's word they fanned out to cover the doors as they opened...if they opened, the one-eyed man added to himself as he passed on the lever that would raise the door, a chore that Dean had recently given up. There was no guarantee the mechanism would work.

His fears were allayed as the door rose with a squeal, the metal buckled slightly in its frame by the land shifts that had occurred around it in the previous century. When the door had lifted eighteen inches from the ground, Ryan stopped its ascent to take a quick look outside. No one ever got chilled by being cautious.

The entry to the redoubt was in a recess cut into the side of a small hill. A dirt-track road led away into an expanse of nothing—low-level scrub and vegetation, with no large outcrops or forestry to give the land any kind of definition. From what he could see of the hill they were standing within, it was soil and grass covered rather than rock. With the way clear, Ryan pushed the lever, allowing the door to continue upward.

Moving out cautiously, checking the surrounding area confirmed that they had been hidden within a low hill, similar to some others that were scattered around the landscape. The dirt road petered out, and there was little sign of habitation within view. The friends saw no signs of any large predators, as the land was undisturbed, with no real hiding places. There were some clusters of trees, but these were stunted and dwarf. J.B., taking a reading with his minisextant to try to determine their rough position by the sun, noted that the trees looked like mutie elms.

Ryan had ordered Mildred to stay back in the mouth of the redoubt with Jak until the immediate area had been recced. The albino youth hated the feeling of being protected, and of not being able to pull his weight within the group, but he also knew that Ryan was right. Until he was one hundred percent, he was a risk, a possible liability.

So he hadn't had a chance to view the full landscape until the area had been secured, and Ryan called both Jak and Mildred from the mouth of the redoubt.

When Jak took a look at the area where they landed, he felt his head swim for a second.

It was the area of his nightmare.

THEY TRAVELED for six days, with very little happening. On the first night, after J.B. had taken a sextant reading to confirm his initial estimate, they gathered around a campfire.

"Definitely what they used to call New England," the Armorer affirmed. "I figure that we must be about a hundred miles from the coast."

"The farther away the better," Krysty said with a shiver.

Dean gave her a quizzical stare, and the Titian-haired beauty told him about their previous visit to the New England coast, when Ryan and J.B. had been press-ganged into serving on the whaling ship led by the vicious Pyra Quadde, one of the ugliest and meanest women they had ever crossed, and far more dangerous than any of the mad male barons they had had to fight along the way. She was inclined to flog her crew for the sake of it, and drove them hard when they were on the seas. She also had a voracious and murderous sexual appetite, and had fixed on Ryan as one of her victims. It was a situation from which they had escaped by the skin of their teeth.

But despite that, the younger Cawdor found it hard to suppress a laugh at the thought of his father being cornered by a sexually rampant Pyra Quadde.

"C'mon, Dad, you know you really wanted it," Dean teased.

The one-eyed warrior didn't answer. Instead, he reached across the campfire to cuff his son around the head.

"My dear Ryan!" Doc exclaimed. "Surely you cannot blame your son for pointing out that which, to the rest of us, is nothing more than the obvious."

Ryan stopped and glared at Doc for a second before cracking his face with a smile. "Mebbe he's right there, Krysty. What do you think of that?"

She kept a straight face while replying, "Perhaps I should start rubbing myself with whale oil and get fat, eh, lover?"

They were making the most of such an opportunity. Chances to truly relax were few and far between. But Mildred, looking across to Jak, stopped laughing when she saw the expression on the albino's face. He was always stone-faced and impassive, but even he would usually have joined in with such ribaldry. However, he was distant, as though not even listening.

"Jak," Mildred whispered, plucking at the sleeve of his patched camou jacket, "what is it?"

The albino looked at her with eyes that, despite their fiery red, were as cold as ice.

"Know this place," he said simply.

The laughter ceased, all attention on Jak. Haltingly, he told them of his nightmare while in the semicoma. He gave them every detail he could remember, and was insistent about the landscape in which they now found themselves. And then he reminded them about his previous dream of Gloria.

When Jak had finally finished, there was silence while the companions pondered what Jak had told them. Finally, Doc spoke first.

"I think it would be unwise to discount this experience," the old man said softly. "After all, has not young Jak already shown himself to be in some way empathic to the Gate tribe?"

"That's a lot of long words, Doc, but I guess what you're saying is that Jak has some kind of link with Gloria, and that this dream was trying to tell him— and us—something," Dean added.

Doc nodded.

J.B. shook his head. "But the settings on those comps were random. How could it land us near both the Gate and the Illuminated Ones? Surely it'd be designed to spread anyone using those chambers after them as far apart as possible?"

Doc grinned humorlessly. "The ways of the whitecoats are not something that can be easily understood. Their minds worked in perverse manners, and the Illuminated Ones are nothing less than descendants of that foul breed."

Ryan agreed. "I figure that we should keep on triple red. Sooner or later, we're going to run into trouble."

"Tell me when we don't," Mildred added.

But despite this, and despite the aura of expectation created by Jak's nightmare, it was some days before they encountered any sign of life beyond that of the small mammals and birds that populated the area.

They crossed a vast region of sparsely wooded and vegetated land, with little in the way of outstanding landmasses, and the monotony of the vista before them was beginning to make them wonder if there was any population of note.

It was then, when their guard was lowered most by the drudgery of their trek, that violence suddenly hit.

J.B. had defined a course north by northwest, and they had just crossed the remains of what had once been a series of fields with large arable crops, when Jak stopped, his very being tense with sudden awareness.

"What is it?" Ryan asked.

"Listen," the albino replied.

The companions stopped. All ears were attuned to the silence, although none but Jak seemed able to detect anything. However, Ryan noticed that Krysty's sentient hair had begun to curl closer to her scalp, wrapping itself protectively around her neck.

A short time later a high buzzing noise became audible. It was like a swarm of insects, but somehow more alien.

"Look! Over there," Dean yelled, indicating a point to the northeast. Turning, the rest of the companions could see a distant dot that was approaching rapidly, growing into a shape that was recognizable, and yet...

"Holy shit," Mildred cursed, "I never thought I'd see one of those again."

Approaching them, growing larger with each second was a predark biplane, making good time and homing in on them.

"Some kind of sec scouting machine?" J.B. asked of no one in particular.

"Whatever it is, it's got us out in the open," Ryan replied. "Take cover. Spread and keep moving until you find it. Don't give them a chance to take us as a group."

He had no doubt that the craft would be armed, and this assumption was confirmed as they scattered. The whine of the aircraft was punctured by the staccato burst of a machine blaster, and the soil around them was ripped up by a hail of shells.

"Fireblast!" Ryan exclaimed, diving and rolling for the cover of a clump of bushes as the shells tore at his heels. Coming up for air, he could see that J.B., Mildred and Doc had found similar cover, while Krysty, Jak and Dean were headed for more outlying clumps.

The pilot of the sec machine had to be distracted while they attained that cover.

"J.B.! Try and take out the engine," Ryan yelled, taking the Steyr rifle off his shoulder.

"Okay, but wait until it drops a little more. Won't hit it otherwise," the Armorer returned.

Watching the craft turn and start to fire on the three still heading for cover, Ryan felt a gnawing impatience. He wanted to stop his people from being fired upon, but knew that J.B. was right. To fire now would be nothing less than wasting ammo, as the aircraft was still out of range.

Blasterfire strafed the ground around Dean, Jak and

Krysty, firing in a wide arc that still encompassed all three.

"Now!" J.B. yelled to Ryan as the biplane came closer to the ground.

The one-eyed man and the Armorer both stood up from their cover and took aim. J.B. had favored his M-4000, and both blasters roared almost simultaneously.

Ryan had aimed for the front of the craft and the engine; J.B., with a load of barbed metal fléchettes, had aimed for the body of the craft. Knowing it was made of fabric stretched over a metal skeleton, he reasoned that the fléchettes could rip through and take out the pilot.

Both weapons achieved their aim. The engine coughed and spluttered as dense clouds of black smoke began to rise, and the flight path of the plane dipped and swerved as though the pilot had momentarily lost control. The machine blaster also ceased.

The biplane turned and headed off shakily, the course erratic and the engine spluttering.

The companions regrouped, watching it recede into the distance.

"Well, at least we know there's a ville near here," Mildred stated. "We just need to follow the trail."

"And I'm certain we'll be assured a warm welcome," Doc added with more than a little sarcasm.

Chapter Two

They followed the direction of the retreating biplane, which took them away from the course they had originally planned. The prospect of finding some kind of ville, some kind of life, was too good to ignore, even though, as Doc had pointed out, they were unlikely to receive a warm welcome.

After an hour spent trekking over the rotting arable fields, they came to the remains of a two-lane blacktop road that stretched into the distance. The biplane was still visible, its oily smoke trail etched in the sky. J.B. looked toward the west, where the plane was headed, shielding his eyes from the glare of the sun.

"It's holding up well," he muttered, "and not dipping."

"Which means?" Dean queried.

"That the ville it came from is still some distance— good dozen miles, I reckon."

"Let's still head for it," Ryan suggested. "We'll try and keep good time, but stay triple red. Nearer we get—"

"—more likely to be sec patrols," Mildred finished. "We hear you."

They strung out in formation and proceeded along the side of the road, ignoring the smoothed surface in preference to a rutted drainage ditch that ran along the side. It provided cover for them in the event of hostility; and, more importantly, would do the same for any sec ambushes. So to prevent being taken by surprise, they would flush out this territory as they traveled along.

After the first four miles, the only sign they had of any kind of habitation were dirt roads that would lead off the blacktop at semiregular intervals. J.B. queried where they could lead, and both Doc and Mildred told him that they could be access roads to fields, or tracks leading to old farms from before skydark.

"Any chance of them being in use?" Ryan asked.

"Doubt it," Mildred replied. "Take a look at them."

Ryan cast his good eye over the state of the roads and tracks. They were rutted and cracked, with little sign of any use. Whereas the blacktop, despite the cracks of age and earth movement, had traces of recent use.

"Yeah. Anything that comes along this way only uses the main drag, and leaves the sides well alone."

"Which means we should find the ville the only populated place around these parts," Krysty added.

Progress was slow along the side of the road, and after six miles there were signs across the flat landscape that other old blacktop roads were beginning to converge in the distance.

Ryan eyed them speculatively as they took a rest. "J.B.," he said softly, "do you remember ever coming around these parts with Trader?"

The Armorer, removing his fedora to mop his forehead and then polishing his spectacles, thought carefully before answering.

"No, don't reckon I do," he replied, "but, thinking about where we are, I do remember something I heard about. There was talk of a trade route along the eastern trail that went through a ville called Crossroads, that had four old blacktop roads—still in good repair—come together from the four points of the compass.''

Ryan nodded. ''I can see three from here. Guess the other one wouldn't be visible until we were actually in the ville. That many blacktops isn't that common, and neither is a ville right in the middle. Remember anything said about it?''

The Armorer shook his head. ''Not that could help us. Good gaudies, good whiskey... The baron was a guy called Roberts, or Johnson, I heard. Pretty laid-back.''

''So perhaps we should not be too pessimistic about our reception after all?'' Doc asked, leaning heavily on his sword.

Ryan smiled wryly. ''I wouldn't bet on that, Doc. After all, we did blast one of his sec men, and a ville like that is worth a lot of jack, which means a lot of heavy sec.''

''Ah, well, so much for thinking it may be a trifle easy.'' Doc sighed. ''Shall we press on and face the inevitable?''

It wasn't until they were less than two miles from the ville, and could see the buildings in the distance, that the trouble began.

Ryan suddenly halted. Knowing there had to be a reason, the rest of the companions came to a halt and also drew their blasters. J.B. moved around the rest, keeping low, until he came to Ryan.

''What is it?'' he asked.

Ryan indicated three points in front of them—fanning out across the level of the blacktop—with the long barrel of the Steyr.

"Patrol, moving across the road. I just caught sight of a man keeping low to the blacktop. There's movement in the foliage there—" he pointed to the left "—and there—" pointing to the right "—and I don't reckon the moving man was the one I saw originally. I figure they're moving across from different posts in relays."

"Split into two parties and take them?" the Armorer asked.

"Yeah, but try not to chill them," Ryan advised him. "We don't want to piss the baron off by chilling some of his men, but we don't want them taking us out before we have a chance to say hello."

"With you there," the Armorer agreed. "How we gonna do this?"

"Me, Krysty and Dean will try and get across the blacktop and take out that side."

J.B. frowned. "What about Jak?" He was aware that the albino youth was the best suited among them to lead a raid such as this. Indeed, Ryan would normally have no hesitation in picking him. But now?

Ryan looked back to where Jak was waiting, aware that his words, although directed at J.B., could be heard by all.

"I don't want to risk Jak right now. I know it's been a while since he was out of it, but I won't risk a good man until he's sure, and I'm sure." Ryan looked back at Jak as he spoke, and was gratified to see the albino nod almost imperceptibly. "Jak can lead on this side."

J.B. assented. "We'll cover you... If it doesn't go off, signal when you're in position, and we'll advance in the meantime."

Ryan spared his old friend a wry grin and then indicated to Krysty and Dean to join him.

The chase was on.

The one-eyed warrior figured that they were far enough down the road to be fairly well covered if they kept low. There was a slight rise in the land, and it was only slackness on the part of the sec man that had allowed Ryan to catch a glimpse of him above that rise.

Going first, Ryan slung his Steyr over his back and slunk down onto the dusty and dirty blacktop. He crawled rapidly on his belly, his fingers making as much of a grip on the pavement as possible to help pull himself, the toes of his combat boots pushing him forward. He couldn't allow himself to rise enough to scramble or run at a crouch across the road. The only chance for any of them was to keep tight to the ground and not allow themselves to be seen above the rise.

While J.B. and Jak watched the far post for any sign of action—a closer look revealing a slightly thicker clump of vegetation that was the only sign of camouflage—Mildred and Doc watched the left-hand post, on their side of the blacktop. Meanwhile, Dean and Krysty watched Ryan make his progress with bated breath, only releasing small sighs of relief when he attained the cover of the other side.

Signaling he was clear, Ryan waited for Krysty to proceed next. The red-haired beauty dropped to the ground and began her journey across, aware of the danger not just by the adrenaline rush in her guts, but also from the way in which her sentient tresses clung to her neck.

She could smell the old tarmac and the scent of dead animals and ancient gasoline. It mingled with the excitement and fear in her belly, making her feel sick. She knew that she—like Ryan and soon Dean—was completely vulnerable in this position. If they were attacked, she would have no chance of saving herself.

It made her hug the road all the more, balancing this with her need for speed.

Ryan watched her progress, as he would watch Dean's, willing her to hurry. The others didn't dare to look, keeping their attention focused on the sentry posts. It was hard. Apart from the fact that there was a denser concentration of foliage, they had no idea what kind of defense the sec force may be concealing.

Krysty reached the other side of the road with a sigh of relief, and Ryan signaled for Dean to come across.

The younger Cawdor was keen to make rapid time, and set about his task with an almost reckless abandon. He crawled across the road with speed, almost heedless of the fact that he was sometimes rising above the tarmac in his haste.

"Fireblast," Ryan hissed to Krysty, "he'll be seen."

Almost as though he heard his father, Dean slowed fractionally and kept himself level with the road. But there was another peril to await him.

When he was three-quarters of the way across, he came face-to-face with a scorpion. Although not common in the predark New England, some of the creatures in captivity had escaped after the nukecaust, and had begun to breed, multiplying over the succeeding years.

It was just Dean's luck to find one right now, crawling from a hole in the road and coming up right in front of his face.

Dean froze. It wouldn't even realize he was there, or a possible enemy, unless he moved suddenly. Sweat beaded his brow, trickling into his eyes, stinging them and causing tears to prickle, misting his vision even more.

He was trapped. He couldn't stay there indefinitely, and yet any movement could cause him to be stung, possibly fatally.

On the near side of the road, in the ditch, Jak became aware that there was no movement on the road. He had been keeping it in the corner of his eye, and was alarmed at the sudden cessation. Indicating to J.B., Mildred and Doc that he would check it out, Jak slid back to a point where he could see Dean, still on the blacktop, and the creature that swayed before him.

There was only one thing Jak could do. Knowing that blasterfire was useless, and that Dean would be staying still to avoid being stung, Jak did the only thing that would resolve the situation. Palming one of his leaf-bladed throwing knives, he took careful aim and skimmed the knife along the surface of the blacktop—so close to the tarmac that it almost touched—until it slammed into the body of the scorpion. The razor-honed point of the knife penetrated the creature's armor and carried it away from Dean. The young man watched as the knife and the scorpion disappeared into the undergrowth at the side of the road.

Trying not to heave an audible sigh of relief, Dean began to move across the blacktop. When he arrived in the undergrowth at the side of the road, he was greeted by Krysty, holding up the scorpion, still embedded on the knife.

Jak had saved Dean and had also proved to Ryan his return to full awareness and peak condition, something that the one-eyed man acknowledged to the albino as he signaled across the road for them to continue.

The two parties now made rapid progress toward their prey. Each aimed for the sec post on their side of the blacktop, and each cut through the thin cover of the overgrown fields as swiftly as possible. Although they could disguise their progress by keeping low, the level of cover in the old fields was poor, and it was a balance between speed and keeping themselves unseen.

J.B. led the way for his party, with Jak taking point. Doc was just in front of him, and Mildred followed on J.B.'s heels. The Armorer slowed as they reached a sparse section, and Jak came around to crouch beside him.

"Not much," he said simply.

J.B. shook his head and spoke tersely. "No way we can all proceed. You reckon you can flank them without being spotted?" he asked, indicating a path around to the far side of the sec post. There was still a sparsity of cover, but possibly enough for someone with Jak's skill.

"Can try." The albino shrugged. "Better go—Ryan signal soon."

J.B. agreed, but before he had even had a chance to finish, Jak was gone.

OVER ON THE OTHER SIDE of the blacktop, Ryan had cut a swath through the undergrowth with ease, and he had now established a position within a hundred yards of the sec post. They were so close that Krysty could see the occupants: two men, drinking from a canteen and murmuring to each other, paying scant attention to the road, and especially to the undergrowth around them.

"Guess they don't get a lot of trouble, Dad," Dean whispered.

"Except mebbe today," Ryan replied wryly.

The one-eyed man cast a glance over to the far side of the blacktop, and cursed to himself when he realized that he was staring through foliage to an almost bare expanse of field on the opposite side of the road. There was no way that J.B. and the others could get that far forward. It gave them a harder task, no doubt about that.

It was then that he caught a shining reflection from the corner of his eye. Far-flung, it came from a metallic object to one side of the sec post and was shining in a regular pattern.

Jak.

Ryan allowed himself a smile. He should have known that they would have found a way to even the chances. He got ready to signal.

J.B. saw Jak settle and then direct a signal to the far side of the road. Looking ahead, he could see that the post was manned by a pair of sec men, neither of whom was paying too much attention to what was going on around him. One had wandered away from cover and was urinating onto a tree, while the other was resting his chin on his hands, staring at the road and seemingly daydreaming.

"It would seem that they are not used to regular traffic," Doc observed quietly in J.B.'s ear.

"Yeah, and they expect everyone to be using the road," the Armorer replied.

"I find that a satisfactory situation," Doc murmured.

Before J.B. could think of a suitable reply, his ears

pricked up at the sound of an owl hooting. It wasn't something that you would expect in the middle of the day, which was why it was the perfect signal for Ryan to use. It may perplex the sec men if they were listening, but it would also momentarily distract them while the companions burst from cover.

Which was exactly what happened. Ryan, Krysty and Dean came out of the undergrowth, moving across the ground at speed and fanning out to present a more widespread target. They were so swift, and the reactions of the sec men so slow that they were almost on them by the time that the sec men knew what was happening.

Ryan held his SIG-Sauer blaster in one hand and the panga in the other. As one man swiveled to cover Krysty, believing that his partner would take Ryan, and the other did likewise with Dean, Ryan leaped into the middle of the blaster nest, bringing the hilt of the panga and the butt of the SIG-Sauer down in a simultaneous motion on the skulls of the sec men, putting them out of action.

"That was almost too easy," he remarked with a touch of surprise in his voice.

On the far side of the blacktop, the others were finding their task just as easy. At the signal, Jak, Mildred and Doc had adopted a similar tactic, breaking cover and fanning out; meanwhile, Jak had skipped out from his position and taken out the urinating sec man with a blow from the heel of his hand to the base of the man's skull. He dropped without knowing what had hit him.

The daydreaming sec man had been jolted from his reverie and vacillated over which of the three advancing attackers to train his blaster upon: a decision that was taken from him by the feel of cold steel at the base of his neck.

"Drop or chill," Jak said quietly.

From here, it was easy for the companions to regroup on the blacktop with their prisoners, stripped of their weapons.

"Why haven't you chilled us?" one of the sec men asked sullenly.

"Because we want safe passage into your ville, and we don't want to make any more enemies," Ryan replied.

"Then why not just use the road like anyone else with decent business?" another complained.

"Because, my dear young man, after we had been attacked by that heinous flying machine and replied in a somewhat damaging manner, there was no guarantee of anything other than a somewhat warm welcome," Doc said, drawing a puzzled gaze from the sec man who had asked the question.

"Don't you worry." Ryan laughed. "Just— What was it they used to say in those old vids, Millie?"

"Take us to your leader," Mildred replied in dry tones.

So they did. The sec men led the companions through the center of Crossroads, right to the heavily guarded and opulent home of the baron—Jon Robertson, as laid-back as J.B. remembered from the old stories.

For when he saw the sorry state of his sec patrol for that blacktop route and heard Ryan's story, his only comment was: "Never mind that damn plane. You boys were just lucky these people ain't hostile. Shit, I'm gonna have to toughen up on you assholes."

HAVING PROVED THEIR WORTH by taking out the sec post, and their intentions by not chilling their captives, Robertson was more inclined to take their side of the story regarding the sec biplane.

"Well," he said slowly when Ryan had finished explaining, "I'd say that you had every right to try and bring that fucker down."

"By the Three Kennedys, it's not often that one comes to meet a man of such erudition and faith," Doc uttered, smiling broadly.

"What'd he say?" Robertson asked, puzzled.

"He means that we don't often come across barons—or anyone—who'd see our side of things over a firefight with their own sec," Mildred replied.

"Why in hell didn't he just say that?" Robertson murmured before brightening. "Anyway, who the hell says that I'd take your side?"

"But—" Ryan was about to speak, but was cut short from a gesture by the baron.

"Shit, I dunno if I'd feel so inclined if it was one of mine, but it wasn't. We don't have nothing like that around here. Yeah, people've talked of a machine like that, but we just put that down to jolt."

It was a startling revelation, but there wasn't time for the companions to think too closely about the implications of what the baron said, as he had already launched into a long, rambling discourse on the ville of Crossroads, with a number of asides about people whose names meant nothing to the companions, but obviously inspired great laughter among the baron's people.

The gist of his dissertation, as far as any of the companions could glean, was that the ville had been a small truck stop in predark times. As some kind of network and civilization had begun to build once more, the old blacktop roads that threaded across the country became invaluable trade routes for the convoys of traders that began to ferry goods and chattels across the remains of the land. So the population of Crossroads had grown and prospered, as they played host to a succession of convoys, many with jack and goods to spare for a good time.

The arable fields that the companions had come through on their journey were virtually useless. The same mutie-plant genetics that had caused the stunted dwarf elms had also affected the crops, with the result that some scrub farming was done near the ville in order to keep a basic crop going, and to grow grain for the ville's own potent brand of alcohol, but otherwise the whole economy of the town existed thanks to the convoys that passed through.

"So I guess I don't really have any objection to you folks staying on awhile," Robertson concluded, "but you know that you'll have to work for your keep."

"Never had it any other way," Ryan replied.

"Well, I'll tell you what. You can all spend some time with my sec—" he cast a glare at the sec men who had been taken "—and sharpen these stupe bastards up a little. Not taking anything from you, but they shouldn't have been taken that easily. Other than that, you can be bar sec—" he indicated Ryan and J.B. "—while you'se two can help on the farming," he added, indicating Dean and Jak. "'Cause I'll tell you what, we're shorthanded right now. There's some kind of sickness started, and our doc here ain't too sure what it is."

A coldness ran through Jak as he heard this, and he thought of his nightmare. Krysty and Mildred exchanged glances as the baron continued. "He could do with some help. You two women and the old man can help. I heard two of you addressed like you were halves."

"Yeah, guess we are," Mildred said softly. "But it depends what we find."

They were soon to know.

"THIS IS WHAT we're up against." Hector shrugged helplessly. "I've seen most of the things that get caught around here, and just about every type of clap that there is." He allowed himself a sheepish grin when Krysty looked at him questioningly "Hell, this is a trader's ville, with too many gaudies for its own good sometimes, the amount of trade they have to keep up to survive. But anyway, that's not anything to do with this, I'm sure of that."

Mildred, Krysty and Doc were standing in the middle of the large, one-room shack that constituted the ville's medical facility. There were twenty beds, lined ten to each side of the room. The healer, a thin, stooped man called Hector Murray, stood beside them. His face was drawn with worry, lined with too many sleepless nights. Large, limpid blue eyes held their gaze steadily, and he had a distracted habit of running one hand through his thinning hair while the other stayed firmly in his jacket pocket.

He reminded Mildred of interns she had known in her old, predark life, and she liked him instantly. He had acquired enough knowledge, and traded enough med supplies, to cope with the general run of problems in a ville like this, but was obviously baffled by something that he had never come across before.

"How long since this started?" Mildred asked,

moving to check some of the patients. There were sixteen in the shack, and two of them were victims of fights from which they'd come off worse, nursing broken bones and lacerations. But the other fourteen…

"Only a couple of weeks since the first signs." Hector sighed, joining Mildred at the bedside of a young girl. "She was the first, and she looks to be the most advanced. It follows a pattern that you'd expect."

"Which is?" Krysty questioned from the far side of the building, where she had been casting an eye over some of the other victims of the disease.

Hector looked across to her. "Starts like they've got some kind of cough, so you give them the usual. But it doesn't clear up. Then they have a day or so of shitting, and that goes. Eyes run. For the first couple of days that's all. Then they get the spots—kinda like when you see that old chickenpox. Don't get that often, but it's kinda like that. They get the fever, too."

"But the spots don't clear, obviously," Doc murmured, examining a sleeping man who was covered in the small blisters, red at the puckered edges of the liquid-filled sacs. The old man was a doctor of philosophy rather than medicine, but he was a man from another age, and he had a creeping feeling that he knew what was happening. He wondered if Mildred had reached a similar conclusion.

Unaware of this train of thought, Hector continued.

"No, they don't. They start to open and weep, then form a crust around the edge. I try to keep them clean within reason, but I can't risk infecting the already open—"

"You're doing right to leave them," Mildred interrupted. "There's not much you can do about them once they start. Tell me, have you lost any yet?"

There was silence. Mildred looked round questioningly, and her eyes met Hector's.

"You mean I'm going to?" he asked, but with a suggestion that he already knew the answer.

Mildred paused before answering. She couldn't be sure, and didn't want to commit herself before she'd had a chance to... To what? What else could she do here but observe?

"Guess that answers my question," Hector said softly. "You know what this is, then?"

"Not exactly," Mildred answered.

"Then I wish you'd share some ideas," Krysty interjected, joining Mildred, "because I've never seen anything quite like this before."

"I think I may have," Doc said quietly. "I think we should talk outside."

Hector agreed, and led them to his living quarters. It was a single-room shack, untidy and speaking of someone who spent little time there other than to sleep. He offered them seating, and all sat except Doc, who stayed upright—almost, it seemed, as an expression of his agitation.

"Ideas, Doc," Mildred said simply.

"I cannot be sure," the old man began, pausing before continuing. "I saw something like it once, but I was given to understand that it had been eradicated by the whitecoats before the nukecaust."

"You're thinking on similar lines, then," Mildred confirmed.

Doc raised an astonished eyebrow.

"It was during my youth that it was finally killed

off around the world. Trouble is, they kept some
strains to experiment on—''

"Typical whitecoat arrogance," Doc thundered.

"I'll agree with that," Mildred muttered. "Problem
is, it looks like a variant strain. And we don't have a
vaccine, or the time and facilities to search for one."

"Then we have no paddle, and are against the fecal
tide, as it were," Tanner said.

"'Scuse me," Hector interrupted, "but you people
should remember that I don't have the faintest idea
what the hell you're talking about."

"Me, neither," Krysty added sardonically.

For a moment, Mildred and Doc just stared at them,
then Mildred said, "Of course, you'd have no idea. It
was way before your time."

"What do you mean?" Hector was now beginning
to get agitated by what seemed to be nothing more
than riddles.

"No time to explain," Mildred said simply.
"You'll just have to believe us."

Hector shrugged. "I've little choice, have I? I've
got no idea what that is—" he gestured to the med
building "—and you have."

Mildred nodded. "Okay. Just trust us on this. Before the nukecaust, there was a disease that wiped out
vast populations. It was a virus that was transmitted
through contact, and it had symptoms very similar to
these. They managed to eradicate it, and I've never
heard of anything quite like it occurring during our
travels. But this…this looks very like it. It's fast, nasty
and fatal."

"What can we do about it?" Krysty asked.

"Without a vaccine or antidote, and not knowing
anyway if this strain has become mutie in any way…"

Mildred shook her head. "There isn't anything that we can do."

"Fuck! What is this thing?" Hector asked, a mixture of fear and helplessness grabbing at him.

Doc spoke quietly. "They used to call it smallpox."

OVER THE NEXT FEW DAYS, while Mildred, Doc and Krysty set to work trying to contain the outbreak of the disease and keep it confined—and also trying to avoid spreading panic—Dean and Jak set to work on the small patches of cultivated scrub that were on the outskirts of the ville.

The stunted vegetables and fruits that were grown there were stored and dried as reserve stock, and also used to ferment the alcohol that was sold in the ville's bars. The rich loam should have yielded strong, healthy crops, but somehow there had been a genetic mutation to all the crops in the area, and the farming was hard.

It was the time of year when the soil had to be tilled and the next year's crop sown. It was hard work. The farm crew had allotted Jak and Dean a horse and plow, along with the seed that needed to be sown along the trenches. There was little chance for them to interact or get to know their fellow workers, as only a handful of the ville's inhabitants worked on the farmland, and those that did were spread about the fields, too far apart to converse.

So it was down to the albino and the young Cawdor to prove themselves by work.

"This not good," Jak remarked, patting the bony flanks of the horse they had been given. The creature looked old, and although not starved, it seemed to be all bone and little muscle. The pitted and scarred, time-rusted plow that they had to attach to the beast seemed too heavy for it to manage.

Dean looked at the expanse of field they had to till.

"Well, we've got to get it done, Jak," he said simply. "So we'll just have to work out a way."

They harnessed the horse, and Jak went to the head and began to lead.

The plow stuck in the rich, thick soil. It began to turn, but was so damp and firm that the plow became bogged down, stuck in the grip of the earth. Jak whispered in the horse's ear, and the creature began to respond, pulling harder against the resistance of the earth. Dean followed behind, scattering the seed into the earth before it began to close again.

"Hot pipe!" he whispered to himself, then called to Jak to join him. When the albino left the horse and arrived at his side, Dean indicated the closing earth, and the level earth to their rear where there should have been a trench. "Have you ever seen anything like that?" he said.

The albino shook his head. "Like earth living. No wonder horse find it hard."

"Yeah," Dean agreed, "and I don't know about you, but I don't reckon that it'll get the whole field done."

Jak looked at the already tired and weak beast, then at the expanse of field they hadn't yet covered. He shook his head.

"Only one way," he said simply.

And so the farmhands in neighboring fields, who had deliberately given the young men the weakest of the beasts as a trial, stopped and watched in amazement as Jak harnessed himself to the plow alongside the horse, and began to help drag it across the field, cutting a furrow that Dean followed, sewing the seeds as he went.

About halfway across the field, the two young men changed places to spread the work. Jak followed the plow as Dean helped to pull.

When they had finished the field, they found that the farmhands from the neighboring fields had come across to watch them. Dean unharnessed himself and fixed them with a glare.

"Next time you want to palm us off with a dud, we'll break your balls," he said softly.

There was silence for a moment, until one of the farmhands burst into laughter.

"Everyone gets the old nag," he said. "Just means you've become one of us."

"All with hurting back?" Jak asked.

Dean wasn't sure if the albino—deadpan as always—had been joking or serious, but it had the desired result. They were surrounded by farmhands, clapping them on the supposedly aching backs in displays of camaraderie.

They had proved themselves to their new compatriots, which was always a vital part of survival in the Deathlands.

"WE AIN'T HAD MUCH in the way of trouble down here for a while. No big convoys going through. Kinda prefer it quiet, but then no one's getting any jack. I suppose you take your choice over which is best, right?"

The fat sec man they knew as Yardie scratched his balls and hitched up his pants, waiting for an answer.

"Sure," Ryan answered simply, not wanting to start the man off on another ramble.

The one-eyed man and J.B. had been assigned to

assist the bar sec on their nightly shift. The bar sec was a group of heavily armed sec men who also had unarmed-combat skills and were used to police the bars and gaudies frequented by the trading convoys. Their task was to stop trouble without it escalating, and not to alienate the traders by wrecking their crews otherwise they may not pass through again.

With no convoys in town at present, it had been quiet for the past few nights, and the fat man who was sec chief for the area had been telling them stories about the main drag—stories in which he was mostly the hero.

"Trouble is, all we get are horny men who just want to hit on any woman. They can do most what they like to the gaudies sluts, but when they get it wrong... See, there's this weird bunch of women live somewhere hereabouts—never can trail 'em—and when they come in to trade, they always get hit on. Tiny, no clothes...but real mean. I like to look after them, 'cause they shouldn't be treated like that. Had to chill a couple of mechanics once—just the one shot, clean through both of 'em. But then again, I seen one of 'em—red-haired thing that I'd crush if I fucked her—take out four men using nothing other than one of those big knife things like you've got."

Yardie indicated the panga that Ryan had strapped to his thigh, and the one-eyed man shot a glance at J.B. Could it be possible? The description sounded uncannily like Gloria and the Gate tribe. The Armorer's eyebrows shot up, but before he had a chance to say anything, both his attention and Ryan's were taken by a sudden outbreak in one of the bars.

All three men were standing on the boardwalk outside the bar, and through the open door came the sounds of an argument, followed by a staccato burst of blasterfire.

"Three blasters," J.B. said quickly. "Small-caliber handblasters."

Ryan nodded. "Okay, let's take them."

Almost glad of the opportunity to get away from the fat man, who was still standing, staring blankly at J.B.'s ability to determine the blasterfire, both Ryan and the Armorer were through the open doorway, opting to unsheathe their knives rather than use blasters.

Inside, the room was well lit. Most of the clientele had taken cover, and two men stood at each end of the bar, holding blasters. A third, with his back to the door, was slumping to the ground from a slug that had hit him in the stomach, blood dripping onto the floor.

Keeping low, both J.B. and Ryan exchanged a look, and by the subtlest of indications chose their prey.

Moving around the tables, J.B. circled his man, who was torn between turning to this new threat or taking out the opponent with the blaster. His indecision cost him both targets. J.B. leaped onto a chair and used it to launch himself at the man. The Armorer's Tekna knife speared through his blaster hand, momentum taking it down and pinning it to the bar. A scream of pain was killed in his throat by a chop across the windpipe from the Armorer's free hand. The man slumped to the floor.

Ryan, meanwhile, had come to his man from the side. His blaster-wielding opponent had no doubt about whom to fire on. He swiveled and took aim at the one-eyed man, who dived under the line of fire and felt the bullet pluck at his shirt as he reached his opponent. Hitting the man in the solar plexus with his full weight, Ryan drove him into the edge of the bar and heard two of the man's ribs crack under the pressure. His scream was high-pitched and ceased as the one-eyed man brought the hilt of the panga down on his head, hitting him on the temple.

"What the—?" Yardie stammered as he entered the bar, blaster drawn.

"Sorry. What were you saying?" Ryan asked him, unable to keep a twisting smile from his face at the sight of the fat man's expression.

Chapter Three

"Must do something—find them now, before too late!"

Jak paced up and down the length of the shack that had been given to the companions as a home while they were in Crossroads. He was agitated and upset, and it was obvious to Ryan that the albino wanted to move as soon as possible in search of the Gate.

"We have to wait, at least for a short while," Ryan stated.

Jak stopped and looked at him, red eyes burning bright in his white, scarred visage.

"Why?"

"Because the others know nothing of this as yet, and we need to know what they say, for one." Which was true. Jak and Dean had returned from their day's work in the fields when Ryan and J.B. had come off their sec shift and had told the albino about what they had been told by Yardie—albeit without his realizing the importance of one of his boastful stories.

Given the almost certain fact that the fat sec man had described the Gate, and the outbreak of the pox disease that Mildred, Krysty and Doc had been working on, matters seemed to be conspiring to confirm the veracity of Jak's mat-trans vision.

"Dad's right," Dean interjected. "It's not something I want to think about—and I know you don't—but we need to know more about the disease they might have before we go looking. Especially if it makes the Gate as wild as Gloria was in your dream.''

Jak paused and thought about that. All his life he had acted on instinct, but since his time with the companions had begun, he had learned the value of stopping to give a moment's thought, and how much time and triple-red danger it could save.

"Okay," he said finally, "wait and see what they say."

He sat down, brooding, and what followed seemed to be the lengthiest amount of time any of them had ever had to wait for anyone or anything. Eventually, Mildred, Krysty and Doc returned from the makeshift hospital they had been manning, leaving Hector and a couple of ville women to help him through the night shift.

"I hoped I would never have to see such things again, despite the horrors I have witnessed during my time here," Doc said wearily as he sat stiff and slow on the edge of his bed. He looked exhausted, as did the others.

"It's the fact that there seems to be nothing that we can do. That's the worst," Krysty added.

"There isn't," Mildred said softly. She, too, was exhausted, but not so tired that she didn't look sharply at Jak, sensing the atmosphere of tension in the shack. "What is it?" she asked him directly. When he failed to answer, she turned her attention to J.B. "John? What's happened?"

"Something that may have a bearing on what's going on here," the Armorer replied. And in a few short words, he outlined to the recently arrived companions what had occurred earlier in the evening.

"If that's true," Mildred said after he had finished, "then Jak's right. We should get after them as soon as possible. Not just because it would be good to see them, but because they may have something that tells us where this bastard disease has come from and what we can do about it."

Ryan agreed. "That makes a lot of sense, but we need to find out, at least roughly, where the hell they could be camped. We need to head in the right direction, after all."

It wasn't only true, but it broke the tension and caused a ripple of laughter. Certainly, the Gate had defended its position so well that their tribe's exact whereabouts was unknown.

The only one of the companions not laughing was Doc. He sat perfectly still, staring at the floor. It was only as the laughter died that he finally spoke. "There is one thing that we all seem to be overlooking," he said softly.

Mildred felt a shiver run down her spine at his tone of voice. "What?"

Doc looked her in the eye. "It's more than a trifling coincidence, wouldn't you say, that both ourselves and the Gate find it relatively easy to arrive in the same place, given that the mat-trans chambers were supposed to send us to random destinations? Not so random, would you not think?"

"You mean the comp settings didn't change that much?" Dean queried, and when Doc agreed, the young Cawdor exclaimed, "Hot pipe! Then that could mean that they didn't vary that much from the original settings!"

Doc nodded slowly. "And do you know what that could mean?"

Ryan answered before Dean. "It could mean that the Illuminated Ones are nearby."

"Exactly. And who better than a bunch of accursed whitecoat spawn to unleash such a vile disease, which was supposed to have vanished a long time ago?"

There was silence while everyone digested the import of this notion. Finally, Ryan spoke.

"If the Illuminated Ones are near, then we have two aims. First, we need to find the Gate to see if they're infected. Second, we need to track down the redoubt where those scumsuckers are holed up and finish what we started. In that order. But before we do that, we need to try and find out as much as possible for the people here."

The one-eyed man turned to Mildred. "How much time do we have?"

She shook her head almost imperceptibly. "Hard to say for sure, but certainly not long. The pox seems to run its course in about three weeks. We had the first two dead tonight. Their bodies seemed to be convulsed with muscle spasms, and they were running temperatures that shouldn't be possible." She closed her eyes, trying to shut out the picture in her mind. "The pox marks get worse toward the end, running alive and open. It's impossible to make them comfortable, I'd say. It must be a horrible way to die."

"And there is no cure," Doc prompted. "We could already be incubating. I agree with you, my dear Ryan, that we cannot rush into this. But be cautioned that we are on a finite time scale."

"He's right," Mildred agreed. "The clock is ticking…."

THE NEXT DAY, while they were in the med building, Mildred bided her time before asking. It had been a difficult night for Hector, and two more of the initial contractees had bought the farm during his spell on duty. The exhausted ville healer, who had no ideas on how to combat the disease, or even to alleviate the suffering he could see in front of his eyes, had retired to his shack to try to get some rest. The ville women who had assisted him had returned to their homes, sworn to secrecy. Chances were, they were too scared by what they had seen to raise the subject.

For a while Mildred, Krysty and Doc had been on their own in the med building, tending as best as possible to those who were ill. There were three new cases, all with the mildest of blisters and a high temperature. A casual observer would have put it down to chicken pox, and none was more surprised than the patients themselves when they had been detained.

However, the mounting problem was causing the conscientious ville healer acute anxiety, and it was only a few hours before he returned to the fray.

"You'll make yourself ill if you don't rest," Mildred said when he first returned.

He gave her a crooked grin. "Chances are I'll get ill anyway, being around here all the time."

"Fair point," Mildred agreed, allowing a silence to fall. On the far side of the med building, Krysty and Doc were arguing about the contents of a poultice that the red-haired woman wanted to use. Doc, despite his distrust of whitecoats, had an almost religious faith in the use of plundered medical supplies, and was arguing his corner while Krysty attempted to use her herbal skills, learned from Mother Sonja in her home ville of Harmony. From the corner of her eye, Mildred noticed

Hector deriving some amusement from the exchange between the two, and she judged that now was the moment for her to ask.

"Hector," she began in a tone that immediately made him look up, "I want to ask you something. We heard something about a tribe that camps near here and keeps itself to itself."

"Could be," he replied carefully.

Mildred pursed her lips. "A tribe where the women are the fighters—small, don't wear many clothes... beat the living shit out of men twice their size."

"Yeah, I'd be a liar if I said I didn't know who you were talking about," he answered, amused.

Mildred nodded. "We've come across them before. We were allies, but got separated. It'd be good to meet with them again, if we knew where they were camped...."

Hector shook his head. "I don't get out enough to know for sure, but I do hear they're in the more densely wooded parts, southwest of here. That's what I'm told."

"That's very interesting," Mildred said slowly. "Maybe we should check that out. One other thing. We were allies because of a group—real heavy blaster freaks—who lived underground. We got separated trying to follow them. I don't—"

Mildred stopped dead. Hector was looking at her with an expression that could only be described as fear.

"I don't— No, I know nothing about anyone like that. And if you don't want to find yourself having accidents in the middle of the night, I really wouldn't go around asking about things like that too widely."

With which the ville healer turned and walked away

from Mildred rapidly, leaving her staring after him with a thoughtful gleam in her eye.

THE MIDDAY SUN was beating down on the plowed fields. Dean, Jak and the rest of the ville workers who toiled the lands had broken for food and drink, and were gathered in the shade afforded by the side of the stables housing the plow horses.

"Best part of the day," one of them said as he took a long drink of water before passing the canteen to Jak.

"Now then, I always figured that the best part of the day for you was when you spent your paycheck in the gaudies by night," commented an older, more weather-beaten farmhand.

The first—a young man, little older than Jak or Dean, and as whip thin as the former—laughed. "That's the night," he said between bursts. "I was talking about the day."

The comment caused a general wave of good humor, and Jak gave Dean a swift glance. Was this the right time to raise the matter?

"Yeah, I hear it can get real wild here after dark," he said carefully. "My dad is on bar sec, and although he hasn't seen them yet, he's heard about these wild women that live outside and only come in to trade. Apparently they can stand up in a fight with any man and best them."

The young farmhand whistled. "Whoa, yeah. I seen them in action, all right. Real tiny, most of them. But they can chill any man that tries." He shook his head. "I heard they live down to the south somewhere, but—" he shrugged "—I'm just glad I don't have to deal with them!"

In the general good humor, Jak judged it was time for him to take things a stage further.

"Ryan and J.B. also tell us about fighters with weird shit clothes, wear helmets and fight with odd blasters. They hear these pass through—"

The good humor suddenly ceased, and a cold silence descended on the party. Slowly, all of the farmhands except Jak and Dean rose to their feet and headed off to their work without another word—with the exception of the young farmhand, who turned back for a second.

"Just a word, friend," he said to Jak. "You and your people shouldn't talk of that. There are those around here who would rather forget."

He left Dean and Jak to exchange glances and ponder the meaning of his cryptic words.

J.B. AND RYAN WERE ALSO finding it hard to get a reaction. On their sec duties along the strip of bars and gaudies that formed the main drag—and the main trade—of Crossroads, they had asked a few questions of both their fellow sec and also of passing trade convoy workers who had befriended them in the bars. So far, all they had asked about was the Gate, and the response had been the same as that received by their companions: the Gate tribe was looked on as an oddity, hard to best and fair to trade, but content to keep themselves to themselves. Consensus seemed to put their camp out to the south or southwest of the ville.

But things had been different when they had tried to bring up the matter of the Illuminated Ones. Deliberately keeping their descriptions vague, they had both noticed that those who passed through either knew nothing, or had only heard a few wild rumors, and those who came from the ville were quick to shut up and claim to know nothing.

"One thing for sure," Ryan commented. "If we carry on and we rattle enough bars to find out something...."

He said it on the third night, as he and the Armorer were patrolling the main drag. Now trusted to fulfill their task without his assistance, the garrulous Yardie had given them free rein—just when they could really have benefited from his inability to keep his mouth shut.

It had been a quiet night, with only a few drunks shooting off their mouths with nothing to back it up to trouble them, and they were looking forward to getting off shift and getting some sleep as the sun began to rise. So they were surprised when Yardie came barreling toward them, his dreadlocks swinging free in time with his fat man's walk.

"Why do you think he's here?" Ryan asked J.B.

The Armorer smiled. "Mebbe he's come to practice his famous fighting skills on those too drunk to throw a straight punch...or mebbe he just wants to talk."

"Which mebbe is just what we need," Ryan murmured, adding in a louder voice, "Hey, Yardie—what's happening?"

"Nothing much, by the looks of it," the sec chief grumbled.

"So why do we need the company?" Ryan asked.

The fat sec man looked the one-eyed man up and down, as though appraising him. "Y'know, I wouldn't have put you down as the stupe type," he said casually.

"Me?" Ryan queried.

"Yeah, you and your friends. You all ask a lot of questions."

Ryan shrugged. "Just a healthy curiosity about the area."

Yardie smiled without humor. "Yeah, sure. Trouble is, you ask the wrong sort of questions."

"Which are?"

"About people who pass through here, or people who don't."

There was something in the fat man's tone of voice that made both Ryan and J.B. get that tingling up the spine, the subtle raising of the hairs at the back of the neck that presaged some kind of danger.

Both immediately went for their blasters—Ryan the SIG-Sauer and J.B. his trusted Uzi—but were cut short by a gesture from the fat sec chief. Looking around, Ryan could see that they had been surrounded by bar sec, appearing from the insides of buildings all around them.

Ryan and the Armorer knew when they were outmaneuvered, and dropped their hands.

Yardie nodded in satisfaction. "Good move, Ryan. I really wouldn't have wanted anything to happen to you. Now you'll be good and follow me. The baron wants a word with you."

With which the sec man turned and headed toward the end of the ville where Robertson had his quarters. Ryan and J.B. exchanged looks, shrugged and followed. What other option had they at this stage?

No words were exchanged on the short walk, and neither Ryan nor J.B. was surprised to see that the rest of their companions were already in the baron's presence when they entered his villa. Robertson himself was seated on what passed as a throne, looking as laconic as ever. He dismissed Yardie and the sec men, despite the fat man's protestation, and waited until he was alone with the companions before speaking.

"I've been hearing things...things I don't like to hear," he stated.

"Such as?" Ryan queried.

"Well, you must have realized by now that I don't mind you asking questions about Crossroads—hell, it helps if you know a little about a place, as I figure it. But sometimes you can go too far."

"Like asking about the Illuminated Ones?" Ryan asked.

"That's what I like about you, Ryan," Robertson drawled. "You're sharp...sharp enough to cut yourself. And just mebbe that's what you're doing here."

"Is it?" the one-eyed man asked. "All we did was ask about a bunch of coldhearts we've come up against."

"Coldhearts is right," Robertson said bitterly, a shocking animation betraying a sudden depth of feeling.

"Something we should know?" Mildred asked gently.

Robertson looked at her. "Yeah. See, we'd heard about these bastards you call the Illuminated Ones, but they'd never come near us...not until one day when they rode in at sunrise in those armored wags of theirs, used those motherfucking weird shit blasters and took some of our people. Haven't seen them since."

"What about your people?" Ryan asked.

Robertson shrugged. "Don't really know. Yardie lost them out in the forest, and we never saw them again, which is why we don't like to talk of it." He stopped for a moment, as though considering whether to go on, before reaching a decision.

"There is one thing, though. Whatever happened, one of ours came back. A girl. She couldn't remember a damn thing, and she was the first to develop that weird shit disease."

"And the first to die from it," Krysty added in measured tones.

Robertson nodded. "And we don't talk of it for one simple reason."

"Which is?" Ryan questioned.

Robertson looked at him with a steady gaze that belied his usual manner.

"Because she was my only daughter," he said simply.

Chapter Four

It was a matter of biding their time, although time was the last thing they had to their advantage. On being sent back to their shack, none would speak of what had happened by a tacit agreement, in case they should be heard by any spying sec placed by Baron Robertson. It wasn't certain he would do that, but in order to carry out any plans they may have, it was necessary to make the baron and his sec men think that they were keeping their heads down and doing as requested.

But for all of them, the uppermost thought in their minds was when they would have a chance to discuss a course of action, and, more importantly, to take that course.

It made for a difficult couple of days, avoiding all mention of the Gate or the Illuminated Ones. In each of their allotted tasks, they carried on as usual, letting up on the question. For Ryan and J.B. it was easy, as on the bar sec patrols they were mostly on their own, and they kept the level of any conversations during the night at little more than passing banter. Likewise, out in the fields the only time that Jak and Dean had to converse with their fellow farmhands was during mealtimes, and then it was easy to keep the talk light, touching on nothing that could be misconstrued.

For Mildred, Doc and Krysty it was harder. In the med building, they were in the same environment as the ville women and Hector for most of the time, and at close quarters. But the ville healer, after being a little suspicious after the first inquiries, had taken their subsequent continuing silence on the matter as a lack of interest rather than a warning off. If he knew anything about their being taken in front of the baron, he neglected to mention it to any of them.

Besides which, both he and the companions had something more pressing to think about: the pox was spreading, and now six people had died. Every bed in the med building was now full, and Hector had others brought into the building from hotels along the drag. Without more staff, those he had were working overtime just to keep the patients comfortable; there was no time to think about searching for some kind of antidote or inoculation. Anyway, as Hector said to Mildred at the end of a long night, as he sat with his head in his hands, "Even if I had time, I'd have no idea how to go about it. I've heard that before the nukecaust they could do this, and things you've said have made me think this was possible... but I only know the little that I know. I'm the healer here because there isn't anyone else, and my mother was the healer before me. Doesn't mean that I really know anything."

"You're not doing so badly," Mildred said sympathetically. She could see in his drawn, pallid face and dark-ringed eyes a man who cared about what he did and felt helpless in the face of what seemed almost insurmountable odds. She could sympathize because she knew how he felt, and she knew that he would soon be left to cope alone. But it was the only way they could even hope to get to the root of the evil and destroy it—for evil was what she felt it to be. Since awakening to the vastly changed world of the Death-lands, Mildred had almost forgotten about such simplistic notions as good and evil...but this was another matter entirely. She could almost taste the evil behind this revival of a disease thought wiped out in another era.

Hector looked up at her as this went through her mind.

"But it's not enough," he stated flatly. "Just not enough."

They were words that stayed with her as she, Krysty and Doc returned to their shack.

Krysty, who knew what Mildred was thinking, was the first to verbalize what had concerned them all for some days.

"When we head off, Hector's going to have problems coping with this on his own. It's growing, and we've got to go soon."

"By the Three Kennedy's," Doc said sighing, seating himself wearily. "It's not a pleasant prospect, but something that must be done. And yet we have not talked of it yet. I fear we must go soon, or this will become an epidemic."

"I'm not so sure that it isn't already," Mildred said. "So far it's only people from Crossroads who've succumbed. But as soon as someone from outside starts to show symptoms..." She shrugged. "Then it gets really serious. If it travels—"

"Then there'll be nowhere left to hide," Krysty finished.

FATE WAS CONSPIRING to force their hand.

Ryan and J.B. were on patrol along the main drag of Crossroads, the dark night beyond banished by the glare of neon signs powered by generators, and the oil lamps from within the darkened bars and gaudies spilling out through open doorways.

It was a busy night as a new convoy had hit town, coming from the northeast and the coastal regions. It was led by a trader called Conroy, a tall, rangy man with a beard that was plaited halfway down his chest, old aviator-style shades and leather pants that creaked as he walked. His sec force was hired mercies, and his staff of driver, accountant and quartermaster were regulars who had been with him for some time. He used the East Coast trade routes frequently, which brought him through the ville of Crossroads on a regular basis.

Trader Conroy was a man who worked hard and liked to play hard. He had completed a successful trip, and he was ready to enjoy himself. To this end, he had immediately hired the sluts of two houses, and paid well to take over one complete bar on the strip for himself and his men. He had also invited Ryan and J.B. in to join himself and his men.

"Buy you a drink, boys—mebbe a woman if you want one," he told them as they entered the bar. "See, I can tell you boys are a little suspicious, and that's fine. You ain't been here long, and you don't know how I operate."

"That's not our concern, as long as there's no trouble," Ryan replied in a neutral tone.

Conroy slapped his thigh and laughed heartily. "That's a damn fine answer, but that's it, dontcha see? My boys have worked hard and deserve some fun, and mebbe they'll be a little high-spirited. Hell, if they get too boisterous, then you crack on them. I don't want to piss Robertson off, man, 'cause this ville is damn good to me. But—" he wagged a finger at them in a way J.B. found particularly annoying "—I don't want to get off on the wrong foot with you boys. Yardie's boys have never minded a drink or two, so why should you? After all, I give a little, you give a little…right?"

The Armorer turned to go, before he gave in to the temptation to smack the trader in the mouth, but Ryan stayed him with a hand on the arm.

"Won't do any harm, J.B.," he said quietly.

The Armorer shrugged. "Okay."

The barman gave them two measures of the potent brew in which the ville specialized. J.B. took his and wandered away, leaving Ryan with the trader.

"Your friend don't like me much," Conroy observed, indicating the departing J.B.

Ryan shrugged. "Mebbe he's just got things on his mind."

Conroy screwed up his face. "Yeah, right. I heard you call him J.B." And when Ryan assented, he added, "That would be J. B. Dix, would it?"

"That depends on who wants to know," Ryan answered.

Conroy laughed once more. "Right. A one-eyed man and a guy with glasses called J.B. You Ryan Cawdor? You must be," he added, answering his own question.

"And if I am?"

"If you are, then I've heard a lot about you. You wanna leave this place, go back to what you know?"

"And that would be?"

"You know…I reckon as every trader on the road has probably heard stories of Trader and his crew. The richest, smartest there was until he disappeared. And what a crew—the one-eyed man who was the meanest and smartest fighter in the whole of the wastes, and the guy with glasses, J.B., the one they called the Armorer, who supposedly knew more about blasters, plas-ex and grens than any man who ever lived. Hell, than any two men who ever lived.''

''You've given us a good buildup.'' Ryan smiled.

''Only the truth as I heard it,'' Conroy replied. All trace of previous humor had gone from his voice, and he was now deadly serious. ''Listen, Ryan Cawdor, you must know that I hire from trip to trip. That's because I've never found anyone I can trust to handle sec and keep their shit together. Just look at these guys.'' He indicated the drunken revelers around them. ''Fuck it, they deserve to party hard after this trip, but they're just mercies. Never found any yet that I could keep on between trips and trust not to try and rip me off or get themselves chilled. These are good boys for action if you pay them, but basically they're scum, right?''

''And me and J.B. aren't?''

''You're class of a different kind,'' Conroy said, leaning forward. ''We leave tomorrow. Come with us, you and the Armorer. I know he ain't taken to me, but I don't give a shit about popularity contests.''

''It won't bother him any, either,'' Ryan said slowly. ''Mebbe we will, at that. I'll talk to J.B., and we'll see you tomorrow.''

''I'll take a drink to that.'' Conroy smiled, ordering more of the spirit for himself and his companion.

Ryan took the drink from the trader. He had no intention of making the rendezvous, but it could be useful cover. If the baron and Yardie thought they were leaving with Conroy, then their absence wouldn't be put down to trying to find the Gate, and they should be left well alone.

Meanwhile, on the far side of the bar, J.B. was talking to a sec man whom he had seen only recently.

"Yeah, I was through here only a couple of weeks back," the sec man confirmed. "I was riding with a convoy that had come across from the west, trader called Malloy. He was supposed to meet up with trader Malone down on the coast, some pesthole little ville called Godot. But before we even got that far, he got into trouble with this baron called Estragon, who claimed Malloy was trying to rip him off."

"But that happens all the time," J.B. interjected.

"Ah, that was the problem, wasn't it? Malloy really was trying to rip Estragon, which was a fucking triple-stupe dumb-ass thing to do when you reckon on Estragon having just about the biggest stockpile of weaponry between here and the coast."

"So what did you do?"

"Only thing we could—me and some of the other boys. We jumped ship, dude. Got the fuck out as fast as possible and ended up trying to get work in the nearest ville, which is where I picked up with Conroy's crew. He pays well, and he gets rich by being hard but true—surest way for a trader to get chilled is to cheat. Play hard, but play fair if you want to survive, right?"

"I'll go along with that," J.B. said, his thoughts momentarily going back to his own days with Trader.

"Right. And besides, it landed us back here mighty quick, and this is just about the best damn ville in the whole land when it comes for getting drunk and getting laid."

The sec man downed the rest of his brew and banged his glass down on the table in front of him. He blinked slowly and heavily, then sat, missing his chair and falling to the floor. The revelers around him laughed, those who noticed in the confusion all around. J.B. was laughing, as well, a laugh that was stilled in his throat as he bent to help the man to his feet.

The sec man's skin was cold and clammy to the touch, although his face was flushed.

J.B. frowned. "You feeling okay?"

The sec man gave a short and unconvincing laugh as he rose unsteadily to his feet. "Should be able to take my liquor better'n that," he muttered.

J.B. examined him in the light cast by the lamp over the table. The man's face was flushed, but not in the way he would have expected from the alcohol. There were also signs of a rash on his forehead and under the growth of beard on his cheeks and chin.

The Armorer grabbed the sec man's arm and pulled up his shirt.

"Hey! What the fuck—" the sec man began, stopping dead when he saw the beginnings of pustules running up the inside of his forearm. "What the hell are those?" he whispered.

J.B. leaned in close to him. "You say you were through here a couple of weeks ago?" he questioned, and when the man nodded, continued, "I think you'd better come with me, my friend."

"Where to?" the confused and drunken sec man muttered as J.B. led him out of the bar. Ryan, catching the Armorer's eye as he moved past, made his excuses to Conroy and left the trader, joining J.B. outside.

"Trouble?" the one-eyed man questioned.

J.B. said nothing, but rolled up the man's sleeve. In the harsh glare of the bar's neon sign, it was easier for the two men to see the full extent of the infection.

"Fireblast," Ryan breathed. "Mildred's not going to like this."

"No one is," the Armorer replied. "This is where we move, right?"

"Triple sure on that," Ryan agreed.

RYAN WAS RIGHT. Mildred was far from happy when they led in the infected sec man.

"Go get Hector—and now," she said to Doc, who rushed to rouse the sleeping healer. Hector entered the med building in Doc's wake, and was grim-faced as Mildred showed him the infected sec man.

"If he's been carrying this to other villes," he began, but Mildred cut him short.

"No time to worry about that now. You need to get Robertson in on this right now. If outsiders are getting it, then not only is it being spread across the land, but your ville stands right in the line of fire for reprisals, 'cause it isn't going to take this boy's employer long to work out what's happening."

"Shit," Hector cursed, "all hell could break loose. You're right," he concluded, "I should go now."

The healer turned and left. Mildred looked stonily at Ryan.

"Time?" she queried.

Ryan nodded.

"Krysty," he said over his shoulder, "go and get Jak and Dean, and get them to gather everything then come over here—and triple fast. We're leaving right now."

"Should we run out on them at this precise point?" Doc asked. "They will need our help."

"They won't need anyone's help unless we get

moving and find the Gate, see what they know," Ryan snapped.

It seemed like hours but had to have been only a matter of minutes before Krysty returned with Jak, Dean and their collected belongings.

"Any chance you were seen?" Ryan asked.

"No chance. Time to take care," Jak answered decisively.

The one-eyed man nodded, then outlined the situation to the group. The knowledge that Hector was talking to Robertson—the knowledge that the first outsider had contracted the pox—would be incendiary. Chaos would break loose, and in this chaos was their chance to slip away unnoticed. The offer Trader Conroy had made Ryan and J.B. would only add to any confusion that would come in the wake of the notice of their departure.

Their route of escape wouldn't be easy. They wanted to go to the southwest, and the med building was situated to the east of the ville. They would have to negotiate their way around the edge of the ville without being noticed by the sec patrols.

Fate was to once again help them when they were in need.

With Ryan and J.B. now gone from the main drag, the bar sec was reduced—particularly the area where Conroy and his crew had taken over one bar for the night. The hired mercies had been drinking for several hours, and had pleasured themselves with the sluts they had hired. This was where it began to get difficult. The women were used to any kind of sexual act or kink, but when one of the mercies began to wave a broken bottle around and suggested its use as part of a floor show with one of the women, she could see herself not getting out alive, and retaliated by grabbing a bottle and breaking it over his head. Blood streaming, the sec man pulled a remade Walther PPK and chilled her on the spot. The sight of one of their compatriots being chilled caused the other sluts to forget they had been hired, and to fight back.

Before too long, the bar had become a battleground, with a firefight and hand-to-hand spilling out onto the drag.

A bar sec patrol who knew Ryan and J.B. should have been on duty went to what they assumed to be their assistance. They found themselves embroiled in a pitched battle that was already starting to attract revelers from other bars who were spoiling for a fight.

It was only a short while before word got back to Yardie, forcing the fat sec man onto the streets of the ville.

"Shit." He whistled through his teeth as he surveyed the pitched battle that had escalated along the main drag. "What the fuck is One-eye and Four-eyes up to?" he continued. Turning to his lieutenant, he snapped, "Halve the sector patrols and posts. Get them in here now, before we get outfought."

"Yeah, sure," his aide agreed, before adding, "What about the baron? He wanted you."

"Fuck," the fat sec chief swore. "What the hell is going on here tonight? And where the fuck are Ryan and J.B. when they should be sorting this?"

It was a question to which he would have found the answer incredible.

THE COMPANIONS DISTRIBUTED their belongings among themselves, took a few precious moments to check their blasters were loaded and ready and set off from the med building. Jak and Dean knew the outskirts of the ville better than the others, who had been confined mostly to the med building or the main drag during their stay in Crossroads, and guided them through the residential areas and past the tilled fields. In the distance, the sounds of the firefight going on along the main drag could be clearly heard.

"Sounds like Conroy's boys got a little boisterous," J.B. commented laconically.

"Yeah, shame we weren't there to stop it," Ryan added.

"Wait!" Jak said sharply, indicating that they get into the shadowed cover afforded by some of the dwellings.

Ryan had let Jak and Dean lead the way, with himself and the Armorer bringing up the rear. Mildred and Krysty walked each on one side of Doc, and they had traveled in a tight line, breaking only when they had to cross open ground, where they had traversed the distance singly, the others providing cover.

And now Jak's fincly tuned hunting senses had given them a warning. They melted back into the shadows of the shacks as three sec men came running past them, cursing and loading their blasters as they ran.

"Well, well, that is most interesting," Doc murmured after they had passed from earshot. "I would assume, from their direction, that they are from a sentry post."

Ryan agreed. "Looks like things have really heated up. The outsider with the pox and Conroy's mercies getting blaster happy. Guess that fat bastard Yardie doesn't know what to do except pull in all his sentries."

"Making it easier for us to slip away," Krysty finished.

Jak turned and looked at them, his white, scarred face highly visible under the moonlight, even in the shadows.

"Mebbe only some sec go in—still keep frosty," he commented.

Ryan nodded. "Triple red still, everyone. Lead on, Jak."

The albino said no more, but moved out into the moonlight, leading the companions along the edge of town. They skirted the tilled fields, with the southerly blacktop cutting across the lands to their left. As they left the built-up area of the ville behind them, Jak led them on a zigzagging path that took them through the scrub areas that had the most cover. Suddenly, with a gesture for them to stop, he pulled up.

"Sec post?" Ryan whispered.

The albino nodded. "Think deserted. Wait."

Without another word, the albino disappeared into the undergrowth, using the scant cover between their position and the sec post with such care that he was invisible even to the companions, who were trying to follow his progress.

Within a few minutes, Jak had returned.

"Empty," he said brusquely. "Must be in ville."

"Good," Ryan murmured. "This is what we need. Move out, but still keep low and on triple red."

Falling into the familiar formation, with Ryan in the lead and J.B. at the rear, they began to move through the scrub and out beyond the deserted sec post. The scrubland across the old, disused fields provided them with some cover until they were able to cross to the ditch at the side of the blacktop, and from there head south.

After a half hour's progress, Ryan called a halt and asked J.B. to take a sextant reading for their position. The Armorer complied, and then said, "We need to move over there—" he gestured across the blacktop "—if we're heading southwest. How far out do you think they're camped?"

Ryan shrugged. "Could be some way. I'd guess they'd put at least two days' distance between themselves and Crossroads, just for sec purposes."

"Gonna be a long haul, then," Mildred commented. "And what if we miss them?"

"They not miss us, if get close." Jak grinned.

Despite the fact that the area seemed deserted, and it was dark, they still crossed over the blacktop one at a time, keeping low while the others provided cover for whoever was making the trip. Vigilance couldn't be dropped for a moment.

Once they were all over, they headed into the scrub and the first clump of dwarf elms before establishing a camp. Ryan took first watch while the others tried to snatch some sleep. They had no idea how long it would take them to find the Gate, and they would need to be awake and alert when the sun rose once more.

FOR TWO DAYS they trekked across the lush earth of the region. There was no sign of a camp, and no indication that anyone other than themselves had passed that way for some time, which was no surprise. They knew from experience that the Gate could camouflage a camp better than any other tribe or group they had come across, and they knew that the tribe was also adept at covering its tracks. And yet it seemed that this land had been unspoiled by human habitation for some time.

The first day was uneventful. The trek wasn't difficult, and it was merely a matter of covering the territory and keeping alert for danger. The fact that there was no sign of anything except small mammals and birds made it hard to keep their alertness on triple red.

Perhaps that was why the events of the second day caught them unawares. It was a double disaster that caught them off guard.

Since daylight on the first day, they had been aware of a hill much like the one that they had emerged from when leaving the redoubt some weeks before. It was right in their path on a southwesterly course, and from the first they had marked it as a possible Gate camp. Certainly it was wooded enough to provide cover, and its raised sides would enable the tribe to scout the land for miles around. So when they finally reached the foot of the hill, they ascended with caution. There was no sign of any human life, but this was, after all, the Gate tribe. Anything was possible.

"Of course, it does strike one quite forcefully that perhaps they are camped on the far side of the hill," Doc commented as they climbed.

"Well, we'll find out soon enough," Mildred said, looking back.

The gradient of the hill wasn't particularly steep, but it did have a few signs of soil erosion, and in places parts of the rock and soil had fallen away to form sudden ledges. They were passing just such a point, and as Mildred's foot came down on the spot where Ryan, Jak and Krysty had just walked, the soil and scree beneath, holding the earth onto the rock, began to move.

Mildred didn't even have time to register the shift of the earth beneath her feet before she was pitched sideways by the sudden space that appeared underneath her. She felt herself turn in the air, as if in slow motion, as she began to fall. The sky and the hillside turned around her, and she was aware of her companions appearing at the corner of her vision, jolted from view by the crack of her head against the rocks, barely cushioned by their covering of soil, as she turned head over heels, her thick coat providing some protection from the impact of her body on the rocks.

"Millie!" J.B. yelled from above, moving forward to see her tumble over down the side of the hill. He edged closer, testing the loose surface as he watched her body hit the hillside like a rag doll.

Dean's hand restrained him. "Wait! Any closer and you'll bring the rest of it down on her!"

J.B. stepped back quickly, suddenly snapped into an awareness that the younger Cawdor was right. The soil, scree and rock along the path where they had just walked was loosened to such a degree that it could tumble at any moment.

Below them, Mildred had come to a halt. She knew that every bone and muscle in her body ached, but at the same time that nothing was badly damaged. She had been lucky, but this luck was holding only by a tenuous thread.

The disturbance of the falling rocks had roused a flock of birds that nested in the dwarf elms on the summit of the hill. They rose, large and dark against the sky, with a deep cawing and croak of a call. Looking up, Ryan could count about twenty of them, and they didn't look friendly.

Krysty had also observed them.

"Somehow I don't think we'll find the Gate here, and I think I know why."

"Me, too," the one-eyed man agreed. Glancing down quickly at where Mildred lay—conscious but dazed and unmoving—he added, "She's easy meat for them right now, if they want."

It was a shrewd assessment of the situation. The birds—the like of which they had not previously seen in this seemingly peaceful area of the land—were obviously hostile, circling and forming to dive down on the companions below.

"Ryan, would I be correct in assuming we must draw their fire in order to prevent the good Dr. Wyeth becoming a target?" Doc shouted across the gap in the hillside to his leader.

"Got it in one, Doc. They're mean-looking bastards, and Mildred's still out of action. We can get her after we've got rid of them. Wait till they swoop."

The companions didn't have long to wait. With one circling motion up above, the flock turned and dived on the waiting companions as they stood on the hillside path. Ryan raised his Steyr, Jak had the .357 Magnum Colt Python ready, Dean raised his Browning Hi-Power and Krysty steadied her aim with the .38 caliber Smith & Wesson Model 640. Doc raised the LeMat percussion pistol, deciding that the shot charge would do most harm, and he would use that first, while J.B. raised his Uzi, set to Rapid Fire, with which to sweep blasterfire across the flock.

It was at that point, as they were about to begin, that Mildred began to move on the hillside below. She, too, could see the flock of birds above, and although she couldn't see her companions preparing to fire, she was well-enough aware of the wildlife across the land to know that the birds were hostile—and she was vulnerable. She pulled her Czech-made ZKR target pistol from its holster, but was painfully aware of how slow her fall had made her. As she struggled to raise the pistol, all she did was make the flock aware of another—and relatively defenseless—piece of prey.

As the flock descended, some of the birds suddenly veered away from the main group and began to dive toward Mildred, who was still slowed by her injuries and was only just drawing the ZKR.

"Dark night!" the Armorer cursed, seeing them break away. He changed the angle of his Uzi, so that he could fire into the group of birds as it passed him. As the birds drew level with the path on which he stood, he squeezed gently on the trigger, pressuring until the machine blaster kicked with the white heat of rapid fire, spraying almost molten death into the middle of the birds. He moved the Uzi side to side, trying to take them all out in one blast.

He was almost successful. Most of the birds were ripped apart in midflight, their calls harsh among the chatter of the machine blaster as their chilling rattled in their throats. A rain of feather, blood and flesh fell upon the side of the hill, splattering the rocks and earth and covering Mildred in their stench.

But not all the birds were dead. Two of them had managed to avoid being chilled by the expedient of being on the far side of the group, and so protected from the majority of the Uzi fire, which embedded itself in the rest of the birds. And as the two homed in on the struggling Mildred, she had a chance to see how big they were. Looking like eagles, they had bodies the size of an average dog, and a wingspan that kept them flying far enough apart for her to have to adjust her aim rapidly if she were to take out both of them.

Something she didn't feel possible as all her muscles protested. She took aim at one of the birds, and the shell from her ZKR flew straight into the creature's head, blurring it into a spray of blood, feather and bone. The lifeless corpse kept coming, and hit the ground near her with a sickening thud. She tried to readjust her aim, but her injured arm failed to respond.

The bird had to surely land on her, beak and talons tearing at her weakened and unprotected body.

And then the bird changed trajectory, veering sideways to hit the ground near her, a trail of blood and intestine pouring from the hole ripped in its side. Looking up, she saw Doc staring down, the LeMat aimed in her direction, the ball charge having taken out the danger.

Doc's previous shot, spreading grape shot charge among the flock that had headed for the path, had done much damage. Judicious shooting from the others had chilled individual birds, leaving only the falling corpses to endanger them.

J.B. looked across to Doc.

"Damn fine shot," he said thankfully.

Doc grinned. "One endeavors to do one's best, my dear John Barrymore. Now, shall we try to rescue poor Dr. Wyeth?"

AFTER THEY HAD PICKED their way down the hillside and collected Mildred, Ryan decided that they would travel around the bottom of the hill until they reached the far side. It was obvious that the Gate would not have set up camp where there was such a predatory flock—at least, not without neutralizing the danger. It wasn't worth risking another earth slide like the one that had nearly chilled Mildred, who was bruised and aching, but otherwise unharmed. It took her the best part of a day to get back to speed, and so their progress was slow, but at least she was alive, and without any major injuries.

It took the best part of the following day for the companions to get beyond the shadow of the hill, and they had just entered a patch of wooded land when Krysty stopped them.

"What is it?" Ryan asked, but the question was unnecessary, as one look at her hair, curling protectively around her head and neck, told him all he needed to know.

"I'm not certain exactly what, but there's a need to be wary here," she said slowly.

Ryan nodded. "Okay. Blasters ready, triple red. We'll stay in formation, but keep it tight and real frosty."

The words were unnecessary. The companions knew that Krysty's mutie sense acted as an early warning, and whatever was ahead of them, they would be ready…or so they thought.

The trees were more of the dwarf elms, and what they lacked in height they made up for in the density of their cluster. The roots were aboveground, making the floor of the wood uneven, and a trap for less than cautious feet to catch and break among the rock-hard wood. There was no direct path, only an uneven trail that wound through the trees. The light was poor as the overhead canopy of leaves was thick, and cut out most of the light from the sun. They were groping their way through in this semidarkness, and were listening intently for any other sign of activity.

Jak suddenly stopped. "Others," he hissed, "coming from left, right—mebbe six, seven—and quick!"

Ryan strained his ears and stared hard into the gloom. It was almost impossible to see or hear anything, except...

"Fireblast! They're almost on us," he yelled, raising his SIG-Sauer.

"Where the hell are they?" Mildred shouted. "I can't—"

She was cut short as a slender figure dropped from the trees above and onto her shoulders with a bloodcurdling and deafening scream. It was the cue for other warriors to drop from above. Their opponents had managed to travel through the branches of the trees without disturbing the foliage enough to be visible to any except those with Jak's highly developed senses.

The albino had looked up as his enemy had fallen, and had palmed a knife with which he now engaged his opponent in combat. Falling with her—for he could see it was a woman—he pulled her to him and then used the momentum to part them, turning to come to his feet before her with the knife held in the palm of his hand, blade outward. She did likewise, and it was only when they were in such close proximity, and easily visible, that their mutual identities became apparent.

"Tammy!" the albino exclaimed with shocked surprise.

"Jak! Shit, who else could it be but you who'd nearly get the better of me with a blade!" the Gate warrior exclaimed, a smile of surprise cracking her face.

At the sound of this exchange, the fighting came to a surprised halt, as Gate warriors recognized those they had attacked, and the companions pulled back from their sudden line of defense. Warrior faced warrior, glad that combat had not proceeded further.

"Well, well, by The three Kennedys," Doc said wryly. "We were just saying how nice it would be to bump into you once again."

Chapter Five

Astonishment on the part of the Gate sec party was matched only by relief from the companions. They had found their quarry after several days where it seemed as though they were wandering without aim. For the Gate, however, there was none of this relief, only joy.

"Just you wait until we get you back to camp," Tammy said excitedly. "They won't believe it... especially Gloria," she added, with a glance at Jak.

"Then let's get moving," Ryan agreed. "Mildred got caught in a landslide, and she needs as much rest as possible."

"Hell, it ain't that bad, Ryan," Mildred protested, but as she flexed her still-aching muscles and they, too, protested, she added, "Then again, maybe it's not such a bad idea."

The two groups picked themselves up, dusted themselves off, and Ryan and his people followed the Gate sec party as they began to weave a way through the dense woodland. They seemed to head toward the heart, where there would surely be little room for a tribe the size of the Gate to camp, particularly if they wanted to erect camouflage barriers like the ones they had used before the mat-trans jump.

"By the goddess," Tammy said to Jak as they moved, almost gabbling in her excitement, "I thought we'd lost you guys forever. What the hell happened back there?"

"Long story," Jak said simply. "Talk later."

"Yeah, guess so. The main thing is that you're all here, right? And we can get those fuckers now."

Even though Tammy and Jak were at the front of the sec party, the companions and the rest of the sec patrol were close enough to hear this exchange.

"You mean the Illuminated Ones? You've seen them around here?" Ryan asked urgently.

"Hell, yeah—more than that," Tammy replied. "But wait till we get back and celebrate your arrival. Gloria will tell you all."

Ryan was about to press the matter, but was stayed by a hand from Doc. Panting a little from his exertions in keeping up with the fierce pace set by the Gate, he said, "I know you are impatient, friend Ryan. We all are. But you know that these women cannot be hurried."

Ryan nodded. He knew that Doc was right, but all the same he felt a mounting sense of impatience as they continued their journey at a rapid pace.

A journey that was over before any of the companions had a chance to realize it. Tammy let loose a whistling call, followed by a series of guttural whoops, and it seemed as though a bank of foliage opened up before them, revealing a clearing where the Gate had set up its camp. Although all their camouflage, most of their wags and a lot of the tents had been left behind—from both haste and necessity—during the flight after the Illuminated Ones, the armory had been intact, and the tribe had obviously used its trading opportunities and skills to acquire more tents and materials and construct another set of camouflage shields from the materials around them. Certainly, they had disguised their whereabouts as adequately as when the companions had first encountered them.

As the sec party and the companions entered the camp, there was considerable interest. Obviously, they had been intercepted by a routine patrol that should have found nothing, and should not have returned this early. However, the interest soon turned to a buzz of excitement as Ryan and his people were recognized by the Gate members who could catch sight of them. They found themselves greeted by shouts and joy and disbelief, and it was almost impossible to return the greetings that started to flow. Dean, in particular, was looking out for Jon. For a second, he almost hoped that Pietor would be in among those greeting them, even though he could recall only too clearly the grief they had shared at the chilling of their friend. Suddenly Jon appeared from among the throng, the disbelief fighting for space with the sheer joy in his expression.

"Dean! How the fuck—?"

"Tell you later," Dean cried, "but it's good to see you again!"

There was no time for any more words to be shared before he was swept on by the tide of the Gate people, now propelling the companions toward the tent where Gloria—the queen of the Gate—held court.

"Wait till she sees you, man—she'll be so pleased, sweets," Tammy whispered to Jak, a big grin splitting her face.

Jak's visage was as impassive as ever. It was rare for him to let pleasure or pain show on his face. But although he was about to encounter Gloria once more, it wasn't joy that filled his heart, rather, it was dread.

The nightmare of the mat-trans dream still haunted him, and a part of him was on triple red for the Gate queen to come from her tent and try to rip him to shreds, her body covered with the open sores of the pox.

He stood, all activity around him tuned out, waiting for Gloria to emerge. It was as though the Gate, his compatriots, the camp, the woodland—indeed, the whole world—were blotted out, and there remained only himself, face-to-face with his destiny.

The tent flap parted, and he could hear the husky, sweet tones that he knew so well.

"What the fuck is all this stupidworks noise about? Has everyone gone plain stupe or—" Gloria emerged into the open, straightening and staring the companions full in the face. She stood silent for a moment, her mouth open in surprise. She was still the same Gloria: whip thin, muscles glistening under her tan, the cut-off denims and shirt showing much of her taut skin, her eyes liquid under that mane of flowing red hair...and not a blister, pockmark or sore anywhere on her body. Jak breathed a mental sigh of relief, and relaxed, the pleasure at seeing her again now flowing through him.

Gloria broke the silence that had fallen over the tribe with a wild whoop.

"Glory be to Gaia! I never thought we'd see you again—any of you, but especially you, babes," she added, throwing herself into Jak's arms and kissing him full-on, her tongue expressing things that words couldn't.

A cheering broke out from the Gate, and Gloria stepped back. "This is truly a miracle! Now then, this we've just got to celebrate!"

Ryan stepped forward. "Gloria, glad as we are to see you, we've been searching for you for a reason. We—"

He was stopped by a raised hand from the Gate queen, who—despite being tiny next to the one-eyed warrior—had the authority to silence even Ryan Cawdor without question.

"There is nothing so pressing that we can't party down when the need arises. Tomorrow we will talk of what we've done and where we've been and even of what we have to do, sweets. But right now, we chill out and celebrate. Remember, honey, chilling out can stop you being chilled."

Ryan stared at her for a second, but as her face cracked into a grin, the one-eyed man found himself following suit.

And so the celebrations began.

ALTHOUGH THE CELEBRATION didn't end until first light, such was the restorative powers of the tribe that the companions found themselves roused shortly after noon, and while the rest of the tribe went about its business, Tammy and Jon joined their queen outside her tent in discovering what had happened to the companions after they had made the mat-trans jump. But first, Dean congratulated Jon on becoming the new Armorer of the Gate tribe. After Margia was chilled— albeit by her own stupidity—during the battle in the redoubt, it had been important for someone to take over the running and maintenance of the armory. As Jon had been Margia's assistant, it seemed an obvious choice for Gloria to make, even though a male had never before been awarded such status in the tribe. The young man was almost bashful as he was congratu-

lated, and invited J.B. to check the armory later and
give him any advice he had to offer.

Getting to business, Ryan outlined to Gloria what
happened to the companions since they had been
parted by the mat-trans jump. He put forward the theory that the old comps had a fail-safe mechanism that
changed the destinations of jumps, and told of how
they had left the redoubt and traveled to Crossroads.
He neglected to mention Jak's dream, and a glance at
the albino confirmed that Jak, too, had been reticent
to mention this to Gloria. Perhaps it was as well. At
this stage it could be counterproductive.

He did, however, talk at great length of the disease
they had encountered in Crossroads, and how they felt
it related to the Illuminated Ones and their sightings.
Mildred and Doc told of the incidences of smallpox
before it had been eradicated long before the nukecaust. They wanted to drive home just how devastating
it could be, in case it was hard for the Gate to imagine.

They shouldn't have worried. Gloria could quite
plainly see the importance of such a disease spreading
across the land.

"None of us have been in the ville long enough to
see such a thing," she began when Ryan had finished,
"but it seems to me that the baron is some kind of a
stupidworks fool who'd rather hide his head than face
facts. If they're hiding it away, then it'll be the chilling
of them. That's their choice, but not when it affects
the rest of the people across the land.

"I knew our paths would cross again," she continued, "as it's in our fate. As to your notion that the
old tech would send us to different places from the
Illuminated Ones, then it's either a wrongheaded notion, or that tech really is fucked by time…because we

ended up following them right into the belly of their beast.''

The Gate queen paused before continuing. ''I know that you'd warned us about travelling through the chambers, and how it could make you feel, but I don't think any of us were really prepared for that feeling of being torn up into tiny pieces and then flung through the air before being shoved back together by someone with a heaviness of hand. None of us was really ready to fight, and the fact that we had to get it together and face whatever was outside the chamber only made things harder.

''But I guess that they were feeling the same way— or else they didn't expect us to follow them—as no one came to attack us when we were at our most vulnerable...for which I give thanks to the goddess.

''We were soon ready, and we came out into a room like the one we had left. It was deserted except for a few of the Illuminated soldiers, and we were able to chill them real easy, as they were taken totally by surprise. I guess they were able to raise an alarm, 'cause a whole load of others were ready to meet us when we hit the corridors. Trouble was, they knew exactly where they were, and we didn't—shit, we had no way of knowing if that redoubt was the same design as the one we had left behind. And we were wondering where the hell you were! 'Cause we knew you'd jumped into the other chamber, and the second chamber where we'd landed was empty when we got the hell out, we kinda figured that you'd gotten chilled along the way, and that made us all madder than ever, I guess...

''There were more of them than us, and they had those laser blasters, as well as normal ones, but fuck it. We were mad and ready to chill any fucker that got in our way, and you know that they might have the hardware but they ain't no good at firefighting, so we were able to drive them back and make some kind of dent on their numbers. We lost a couple, but a lot less than you'd expect when we were supposed to be the ones up against it.

"We were making progress, but suddenly it changed. They pulled right back, and we were chasing them rather than fighting them. I guess it was a tactic to make us chase and run where the hell they wanted us. Not the first time they tried that, but this time we were so blood fired that we were blinded, and let them push us exactly where they wanted. They sealed off some corridors so that we were going exactly where they wanted. Then it happened.

"Ahead of us, the corridor was sealed with a sec door, and as we went through, before we had a chance to double back they brought the door down on our tail. We were trapped in a section of corridor, and as we started to try and break out, they started soaking us with water, for Gaia's sake! Yet it wasn't like the trick they tried on us before, to soak us into submission. This was different. It wasn't water like ice, and it was too fine to really get in the way, so we were able to keep hammering at the door with battering rams, and trying to lever the door or blow the mechanism. We were too hemmed in to try any plas-ex or heavy-duty blasters on the door, which was the fucker of it."

While Gloria had been talking, J.B. had noticed a sudden expression of surprise and then rapt concentration come over Mildred's face when the queen had mentioned the fine mist that had been rained upon them; and he had also noticed Mildred glance at Doc, and the almost imperceptible nod that the old man had given in acknowledgment.

Meanwhile, Gloria was finishing her story.

"It seemed like we were there for hours, and then suddenly the sec door lifted and there was the outside world. We got the fuck out, away from the rain, as we were all soaked through and it was starting to finally have an effect. Oh, sweet goddess, it was good to see the outside world. There was no way they were going to let us back in, so we left to make camp and wait. Since then, we've done some trading, some hunting...but not the one thing we want to hunt—those Illuminated scumfuckers. Our people have heard stories of them coming out, too, but we haven't caught any of them yet...yet," she added venomously.

"So you know where they are?" Ryan asked.

Gloria looked at him as though the one-eyed man were a stupe child.

"Of course we know, stupidworks," she said slowly, as though spelling it out. "Why d'you think we're here? It's because it's near to their redoubt. And I'll tell you as much as this, too—we're going to get back in there and chill those fuckers once and for all. For us—for the Gate—it's part of our destiny. We've come this far, and we're near the ultimate goal. There's no way they're gonna stop us. But now it seems that's there's even more of a reason. If we don't stop this disease, then there won't be any land worth our inheriting when our destiny is fulfilled. No riches have meaning without people to use them."

"Glad you feel that way," Ryan commented.

"Speaking of that," Mildred said carefully, "have you had any problems with the way you're all feeling?"

Gloria eyed her suspiciously. "In what way d'you mean that?" she asked sharply.

Mildred kept her gaze level with that of the Gate queen. "The mat-trans jumps can have a bad effect on the body. It isn't supposed to go through the stresses it does with each jump. Jak always suffers very badly, and most of your people have the same type of body build."

Gloria considered this. "Some of the guys have got little blisters, and feel like they've got some kind of bug. You know, like a winter sickness or bad food. But that's it, really. None of the women felt anything."

Mildred forced a smile. "That's good. We all need to be a hundred percent for this."

"Too right, honey," Gloria replied, "and you need to rest a little more after that landslide. We should take a few days—recon the redoubt with both us and yourselves. That way we can really work out a strategy."

"That sounds good. We should get that together as soon as possible. But first we should rest," Ryan said.

Gloria agreed, and the companions were shown to a part of the camp that had been prepared for them. Ryan was relieved when Jon and Tammy left them alone, as he needed to question Mildred urgently, and did not wish them to overhear.

But it was J.B. who spoke first, as Tammy and Jon moved out of earshot.

"What is it, Millie? I saw you and Doc look at each other," he said in an undertone.

Mildred shook her head, plaits gently shaking around her. "I can't be sure. It was when Gloria mentioned the Gate being trapped and then being soaked by such a gentle rain. It sounded to me like some use of a saturation technique—"

"No, back up a little," Ryan interjected. "Run that one by me again."

"It seems to me likely that the Illuminated Ones used the virus in a solution of water to soak it into the Gate, and try to spread it that way. There were too many of them to inject or infect individually, as they seemed to do with the baron's daughter. This way they hit the whole tribe in one go."

"Except that it doesn't seem to have affected them," Krysty added. "But why, if that was what the Illuminated Ones intended, hasn't it worked?"

"Perhaps they have some kind of immunity," Doc posited. "After all, I can remember when I was young that there were always cases of a disease spreading over a whole community, and yet some remained untouched."

Mildred assented. "It's possible that the Gate has some kind of immunity built into their genetic code, and it's stronger in the women than the men. It sounds like some of the men have developed mild initial symptoms but no more."

Ryan nodded slowly. "So you're saying that mebbe they have it, but it just doesn't affect them?" And when Mildred nodded, he added thoughtfully, "But it's still in them, so they can still give it to others, right?"

"Yeah." Mildred sighed softly. "Which makes the Gate more deadly and dangerous."

"And makes it more imperative that we get into the redoubt and find the cure," Ryan stated.

Mildred agreed, adding, "That's if they actually

bothered to cook one up. They seem so crazy they might just have forgotten to do that...."

IT TOOK the companions no time at all to renew their ties with the Gate. Having rested, they renewed old friendships and fell into training with the warriors. J.B. inspected the armory, and was impressed with the work Jon had been doing. Jak sharpened his knife work with the Gate warriors, and Ryan talked tactics with Gloria. Krysty and Dean worked on their marksmanship while Mildred did some body work on rebuilding the muscles bruised in the landslide. Which just left Doc, who wandered around brooding about the past. The sudden reappearance of a disease, the like of which he had thought eradicated by the nukecaust, made him think about the life from which he had been dragged kicking and screaming by the horrors of Operation Chronos and the time-trawl that had taken him from the nineteenth to the twentieth century, and then beyond to his present state.

While the others were occupied, Doc grew more morose, and so was glad when the chance came to go out on a recon patrol with some of the Gate women. It would be the first chance any of the companions had to view the redoubt where the Illuminated Ones had their base, and Doc was determined to bring back a full report for the others.

Apart from himself, there were three others in the patrol: a brown-skinned, haughty warrior named Dette, a blonde named Nita who was taller than her compatriots and stood out because of that and her mane of flowing blonde hair, and Cat, who was perpetually nervous and whose hair had been hacked back close to her head, which would have made her look like a boy if not for the obvious assets of womanhood she possessed.

The patrol was to set out in the late afternoon, as the sun began to move down in the sky. That made Doc anxious.

"Will we be able to reach our destination before the dusk makes it too hard to define the area?" he asked as the sec patrol left the camp, the camouflage screens moving back into place behind them.

"Say what?" Nita asked with a frown.

"He means will it be too dark before we get there," Cat explained, adding to Doc, "She's not the brightest of the bunch, you know what I'm saying here?"

"Ah," Doc said simply, not wishing to offend anyone at this stage.

"You saying I'm stupe?" Nita asked in a peeved tone.

"I don't really have to say it, do I?" Cat replied.

Dette turned on them, her large brown eyes flashing anger. "Will you two shut it? Why the fuck I get sent out with a pair of stupes like you I'll never know. Keep the noise down and let's just get moving, okay?"

The brown-skinned warrior turned away without waiting for an answer. Doc cast an eye over all three of the Gate warriors, and wondered why he seemed to have been landed with the three women who seemed to be the most disagreeable of the tribe.

Despite his doubts, the rest of the trip to the redoubt area was uneventful. After their initial spat, the three women worked together well, each one taking a turn to scout ahead for the rest of the party, reporting back so that they could move safely. In deference to Doc's comparative lack of agility, they traveled on the ground across the woodland, rather than using the tree-tops in the way the sec party had when the companions had been discovered. It made progress a little slower, as the territory had to be secured more assuredly, but there was still full daylight when they emerged at the edge of the woodland.

"Here's where it gets tricky, my old bud," Cat said to Doc as they hit open land. "There's not a lot of cover, and we're only a mile or so from the entrance to the redoubt. So it's got to be triple red from here."

Doc nodded slowly. "I appreciate that—and I do also appreciate that my comparative age and the fact that I am not one of your good selves does make things a trifle more complex than would be usual."

Cat grinned. "You do like your own voice, don't you?"

Doc shrugged and returned the smile.

"Come on, then," she said, punching him playfully on the arm. "Let's get moving."

The territory was sparsely covered, and if the Illuminated Ones had sec vids surveying the area, then the chances were that they would be spotted—especially with Doc in tow. However, Dette, always going on ahead, chose a route that maximized the potential of the cover, and they made it to the edge of the land without any apparent detection. From the brow on which they stood, the earth fell away into a small valley, much like the one that the companions had found themselves in when leaving their own redoubt some weeks before.

"Down there, hidden into the side of the earth, that's where the entrance is," Nita explained.

"I figure he could have worked that out himself," Cat prodded.

The blonde looked at Cat with a fiery anger, and Doc feared that they were about to start a fight at the most inopportune time. However, a whispered imprecation from Dette halted them.

"Shut it—movement."

The four explorers stayed silent and watched as the sound of a sec door rising came from beneath them, followed by the low rumble of a wag, which then came into view.

"Usual?" Doc whispered.

"'Bout every fourth time they're recced," Cat replied with a shake of her head.

Doc kept his eyes fixed on the wag. It didn't go far—about five hundred yards before coming to a halt. The doors opened, and three Illuminated Ones left the interior. While one kept watch with a laser blaster, the other two proceeded to take samples of the air and the soil, marking the containers before getting back into the wag, the watcher taking point.

The wag rolled off into the distance. The land was flat, and the light still good. The wag traveled in a straight line for about two miles, and was still visible when it halted again and the same procedure was repeated. Still the Gate patrol stayed silent and still, observing. The wag started up again and disappeared into the distance.

Doc looked toward the women. Dette met his eye and shook her head. Doc assented his comprehension and settled down to wait.

The dusk was falling as the wag returned to the redoubt. The Gate warriors waited until the doors had ground shut and into silence before moving.

"That's the action for today," Cat said softly.

"They probably won't break cover again for a few days."

"But what the fuck are they doing?" Dette said, almost to herself.

"Taking samples," Doc replied in a flat tone. "They wish to see how far their pernicious poison has spread. May we leave? They make me feel a little ill…."

DOC'S REPORT on the activities of the Illuminated Ones gave both Ryan and Gloria pause for thought.

"Those triple-sick bastards," the Gate queen spit. "We should go and blast the fuckers into infinity."

"Yeah, I agree," Ryan said a little more calmly. "But we're so close, it would be a waste to blow it. Not after we've waited so long."

"But sweetie, you were the one who was pressing me to fight," Gloria said, a little confused by what appeared to be a sudden change of mind.

"And I still am," the one-eyed man assured her. "Thing is, that redoubt will be a bastard to get into, and just the act of busting in will give them time to get their defense ready. We need to hit them when they're on their way back from one of these missions. Hit them as they enter and the way is free. That way we can stream in and take them out before they have a chance to hit back."

"I can see the sense in that," the queen replied. "But how the fuck do we get our forces in the right place at the right time without being spotted?"

Ryan smiled. "That's why I want us to wait. We establish their routine, then fit in behind it and hit them when they're at their most vulnerable."

Gloria returned the smile, her crooked grin lighting

up her face, her vulpine teeth making her look like a predator about to spring.

"Now, that, I like the sound of...."

IT HAD BEEN A ROUTINE sec patrol. Ryan was accompanying Tammy and two other Gate warriors on a mission that took them close to the blacktop that ran in from the south toward Crossroads. It was the first time that the one-eyed man had been near the blacktop since leaving the ville, and he idly wondered what Baron Robertson thought of their disappearance. Then he remembered the speed with which the epidemic was spreading, and his face hardened.

Soon...

His train of thought was disturbed by the distant rumble of wags.

"Convoy," he whispered.

"Yeah," Tammy replied, gazing into the distance at the dust raised on the road by the wags. "'Bout four, I'd guess, two trade wags and a couple of sec, mebbe."

Ryan nodded. "That'd be about right. Let's secure cover and watch them pass. Poor bastards must be on their way into Crossroads."

The Gate party retreated from the blacktop and was hidden by scrub and stunted elms as the convoy drew level with their position.

But as they became aware of another sound, coming from behind them: the drone of two wag engines, setting up an unholy harmony as they sped across the scrub toward the blacktop.

"Illuminated wags," Tammy breathed. "What the fuck do they want?"

"Mebbe… No, I don't know," Ryan said quietly. "They don't usually want to be seen."

As he spoke, the Illuminated wags parted from the course they had followed, diverging so that one was headed for each end of the trade convoy.

"They want to stop it," Tammy murmured. "Why would they want to, unless—?"

"Unless they want to try and infect the men on the convoy," Ryan finished.

As they watched, the two Illuminated wags adopted a pincer movement, moving around to cut off the blacktop to the front and rear of the convoy, the wag at the front assuming a position across the blacktop while the wag to the rear followed up to tighten the gap between the two. The trade convoy slowed to a halt, unable to drive off the road because the wags containing the trade materials were too big and clumsy to cope with the rough terrain and the ditches along the edge of the blacktop.

The convoy came to rest. There was little ground between the sec wags at the front and rear of the convoy and the Illuminated wags that stood silent and menacing before and aft of them.

"Shit, the tension is chilling," murmured Sandy, the dark-haired woman who was squatting beside Tammy in the undergrowth.

"Part of the plan," Ryan commented. "If it's chilling you, think how the sec on the convoy must feel." He could remember his own days riding shotgun for Trader, and yet it was this memory that enabled him to keep his cool. He could remember Trader telling him about ambushes such as this. The older man had said, "They say, 'Don't shoot until you see the whites of their eyes.' I say, 'Don't shoot until you can shoot the whites out of their eyes.'"

It was a maxim worth pondering. The convoy sec had nothing to aim at except an armored wag. They had no choice but to sit and wait.

Not true. They had a choice. They could either sit tight, or they could do totally the wrong thing. Unfortunately for them, they chose to do the wrong thing.

From the front and rear of the convoy, the sec men tumbled out of their wags, some rolling across the blacktop to the ditches at the sides, where they would provide covering fire for their comrades who followed, attempting to mount an attack on the Illuminated wags.

"Fireblast!" Ryan swore. "The stupe bastards are walking right into it."

In the semiexposed ditches, and on the blacktop, the sec men presented an easy target for the laser blasters of the Illuminated Ones. Coming from the back of their wags, and using the doors as cover, the Illuminated war party was able to pick off the convoy sec with a minimum of effort, the laser blasters slicing through clothing, skin, flesh and bone with a precision that the machine blasters of the convoy sec could not hope to match.

"Fuck it, we've got to get in there and sort it out," Tammy cried as they witnessed the carnage. She began to move, but Ryan stayed her with a hand on her arm.

The woman looked at him, and with the fire of battle on her eyes it seemed, for one moment, as though she may just lash out at him if he tried to stop her. On either side of him, Sandy and Stef—the other warriors who comprised this sec patrol—stiffened, as though ready to chill him and follow their leader.

"Just say the word," Stef muttered in a deceptively gentle tone, her jet-black hair falling into her eyes, her small bosom heaving as she kept her viciousness barely in check. "We'll take him and follow you down."

"No." Tammy shook her head and relaxed. "Ryan's right."

But it was difficult for the one-eyed man to even accept his own judgment as they watched what followed.

With the convoy sec now wiped out, there was only the trader and the crew on the two trade wags to be dealt with. The wags offered little protection against the laser blasters, and the Illuminated Ones advanced on the wags with an air of confidence about them.

"Oh, fuck, it'll be a massacre," Tammy breathed.

"We can't interfere. We can't let the Illuminated Ones know we're in the area," Ryan reminded them.

The trader and his crew spilled out of the two wags. They were prepared to go down fighting, as they came out with blasters blazing. But it was obvious to the Gate recon party that the trader and his crew were doomed.

They caught one of the Illuminated Ones with their fire, the bizarrely clad and helmeted figure crumpling onto the blacktop. But there was only time for the one casualty. The laser blasters cut down the crew until there were only two left standing. Advancing quickly, choosing those two who wavered in directing their fire and so presented the least threat, the Illuminated Ones used the butts of their rifles to drive the two men into the ground.

It seemed that the two convoy members were unconscious, but from their startled screams when one of the Illuminated attackers produced a syringe and injected them, they were obviously still conscious.

"What are they doing?" Stef asked, perplexed.

Ryan's face was grim. "They're infecting them. The bastards are giving them the disease, and then they'll set them free in the direction of Crossroads."

The prophesy of the one-eyed man was proved correct as the two men were bundled into the front sec wagon, and the engine fired up. The Illuminated wag at the fore of the convoy drew back, and the two survivors—distrustful but not prepared to think about it until later—hared away from the scene of the massacre.

As the convoy wag disappeared along the blacktop, the Illuminated Ones collected their fallen member and withdrew from the scene of carnage, leaving the chilled and their wags behind.

"I feel like shit for doing nothing," Tammy whispered as the Illuminated wags returned from whence they came, almost passing the recon party in their cover.

"I know," Ryan said simply. "But there was nothing we could do without blowing our chances of getting into the redoubt. I'll tell you this much, though—those scumfuckers aren't going to get away with this. No way are they going to spread that disease across the land."

Chapter Six

It was a dispirited recon party that returned to the Gate camp. Despite the anger that they felt at the Illuminated Ones, and even though all the members of the party knew that Ryan had been right to stay them from intervening, there was still an overriding sense of despair that they hadn't been able to prevent the massacre and, more importantly, were powerless to do anything about the infection of the two survivors.

The outrunners of the party led the way while Ryan and Tammy proceeded at their rear. Thus, by the time that the one-eyed man and the Gate warrior had reached the camp, Gloria had already heard the bare bones of a report, and so was waiting for them to explain themselves.

When they entered the camp, they were both aware of the change in atmosphere, and Tammy muttered to Ryan, "I reckon you were right, thinking about it, but Glo's gonna be steamin' at this, and you'll have to talk fast to calm her down."

Ryan didn't speak, but acknowledged this with a brief nod. He could see the Gate queen coming toward them across the camp, and her flaming red hair seemed to be matched only by her temper.

"What the fuck is going on, eh?" she said without preamble as she approached.

"You've had a report, then?" Tammy spoke quietly, trying to communicate an air of calm to her queen.

It wasn't working.

"Too right, I've had a fucking report, lady, and I want to know why you let those triple-bastard scum spread the disease further. We could have that, missy—"

"So you've been talking to Mildred," Ryan interjected as calmly as possible.

Gloria assented. "That I have, sweetie, and it's a good thing I did, right? Because otherwise I wouldn't have known. You weren't going to tell me, were you, Ryan?"

"But if you've been talking to Mildred, then you'll know that she thinks—"

"I know what she thinks, but she could have told me that, as well. Mebbe we have got some kind of immunity, and mebbe that makes us just right for taking these bastards on." Her tone changed slightly, becoming less agitated as she continued. "Mebbe that's what our destiny is all about, and that's how we attain our goal. Did you not think of that, Ryan Cawdor?"

"Yeah, I did," Ryan said firmly. He could see Gloria had the faraway look of a queen in her eyes, focusing on the destiny and legend of her tribe. He wanted to bring her back to the present, and reality. Adjusting his tone so that it was softer, he continued. "Gloria, if I had let Mildred tell you that she thought you'd been infected and proved immune, then you would have taken it as this omen, and wanted to take on the redoubt that very night. We can't do that. We have to find a way to get past their defense to make sure we hit them quick and hard, getting all the advantage we can out of surprise. They hold all the cards in there. Look at how they were able to force you out without even having the guts for a fight. Who's to say that they wouldn't be able to do that if we didn't have some kind of plan?''

"Who's to say that they won't do that anyway?'' Gloria replied. "Even if we get in, how do we insure that—?''

"We can't,'' Ryan cut in brusquely. "I know that just like you. But we have to load the odds on our side as much as possible.''

"He's right,'' Tammy chipped in. "It's like weighted dice, right? And only we know about it. They don't—that means that we can hit them hard and where it really hurts. Y'know, I fucking hated leaving those poor bastards to die out there, but Ryan was right. Mebbe those scumfuckers don't know we're here, mebbe they do. They mebbe think we've moved on. But I tell you what, Glo—they sure as shit don't know that Ryan and his people are here. And that's where we've got a handful of aces when it comes to a firefight.''

The flame-haired Gate queen pursed her lips. She wasn't used to Tammy speaking to her in such a manner, and the very fact that her second in command was prepared to sound off in such a fashion made her stop and think.

"Look, mebbe you're right,'' she said grudgingly, "but if what these bastards want is to wipe out the whole population and then come up and take over whatever the fuck is left, then we've got to stamp them out as soon as possible. Otherwise it'll be too late.''

"It'll be too late if we can't get our hands on an antidote that we can spread around in the same way,''

Ryan pointed out. "Mildred seems to have told you everything else, so surely she's made that point."

Gloria was silent for a moment, before saying, "Mebbe you're right. I just hate the fact that you had to let them do that today."

"So did I," Ryan said flatly, trying to keep his own boiling emotions out of his voice. "But it had to be that way. For the long haul."

THE VERY SAME AFTERNOON gave the one-eyed man, Tammy and the rest of the recon party a chance to vent their feelings and exorcise their self-loathing for the events of the morning. Knowing that, even though they were still on recon status, an eventual confrontation with the Illuminated Ones was only a day or two away, Gloria had told her people that they would concentrate on sharpening up their hand-to-hand combat skills, as not only could these prove useful but they would also tighten reflexes for firefighting.

While the usual sec parties patrolled around the camp, everyone else within split into groups. Jak and Doc found themselves up against a group that included Cat and Nita, while Dette found herself with Dean and Mildred. J.B. and Ryan were grouped with Tammy and Gloria, which Ryan felt was the queen giving herself a chance to even a score and work out her temper, while Krysty found herself in a group that included Jon.

The red-haired beauty was first into practice, against Jon, and found herself momentarily distracted as she realized that he was the only male Gate member to be taking part in such training.

It was a slip that she regretted when he took advantage of her distraction to get her in a headlock and then flip her so that she was over his knee in a back-breaker.

Realizing that such distraction had cost her face—and that it proved she was rusty and needed to get her reflexes back to their usual highly tuned level—she dug into the soft ground with the heels of her silver-tipped Western boots and flexed her fingers, reaching for a handhold in the earth behind her head. Her back was now beginning to protest at the strain the hold had put her under, but she replied to this by tautening and tensing her frame so that her spine formed an arc that spread the tension throughout her body and used it as a springboard for her own move.

With a cry that was partly exertion and partly exultation, she tightened her calf and thigh muscles and flipped herself over, the sheer force and sudden explosive violence of the move loosening Jon's grip and throwing him backward. The young man sprawled back on the earth, and Krysty came out of her back flip to throw herself forward, pinning him to the earth.

She was breathing hard, and he could feel her breath on his face. In turn, she could see into his eyes at the fear and wonderment at the strength of the move.

"That wasn't bad," Krysty said, letting him go slowly. "But I reckon you've got a lot to learn."

"Too right," Jon agreed. "Men don't usually get a chance at combat, so I'm way behind...but mebbe you could teach me?"

Krysty smiled at him. "You're not so bad. We can work something out."

In the other groups, Ryan and J.B. were finding Tammy and Gloria tough going. It was no surprise to them that out of their group, the Gate queen and her number two had chosen to take on the one-eyed man and the Armorer, as they represented the resentment that both felt about their lack of action during the morning.

J.B. took on Tammy, and it was like wrestling with a greased stickie. Every time he felt that he had a hold on her, she wriggled out of his grasp, leaving him clutching at air. Her own attacks were on the counter, when he was just marginally off balance, and they were swift, jabbing blows that battered his ribs and kidneys. If he wasn't careful, she would cause him some damage before they even had a chance to go into battle against the real enemy. So he had to end it here. As she moved in on the counter for one more jab, the Armorer allowed himself to receive the blow, moving with it to absorb the pressure, ignoring the pain. Instead, it allowed her to overjab, her arm moving across his body and letting him grab at wrist and elbow. He took hold firmly, his fingers biting so hard into her sinewy flesh that the blood ceased to flow. Her elbow came down on his knee, and he pulled the blow at the last moment, so that instead of snapping the joint, it merely paralyzed it. With this out of action, it was easier to go for the knee on the same side, her balance disturbed by the useless arm. Kicking and catching her behind the knee, J.B. brought her to the ground, and took her free arm in an armlock.

"And I'm not letting you go until you calm down," he muttered in her ear.

Which was something that the one-eyed man needed to say to Gloria, as the queen came at him with a speed and ferocity that had him permanently on the backfoot. She was smaller, but compensated for that with her incredible speed, and he found himself parrying blows from her forearms and feet that left him no time to attack himself. She had a point to prove to herself, and aggression to work out, and Ryan was her punching bag.

Stepping back all the time, Ryan found himself moving out of the circle of combat and knew that he had to fight back quickly.

A half chance came when Gloria attempted a flying kick at his head. For the fraction of a second that she was airborne, he had time to do more than just parry. The one-eyed man stepped around the blow and used her momentum against her when he brought his arm up underneath her leg, flipping it up and causing her to turn in flight, so that her landing was awkward. It was hard for her to keep her balance, and in that extra moment of time, Ryan landed a kick to her chest that threw her backward and followed this by landing on top of her and pinning all her limbs beneath his, using his weight advantage to keep her on the ground.

There was hatred and fire blazing in her eyes as she struggled.

"Fireblast! For fuck's sake, Gloria, it's me!" he implored.

The blood lust faded in her eyes as she realized where she was and whom she was fighting.

"Shit, I'm sorry Ryan," she husked softly. "I just—"

"I know," he said simply. "I want them, too."

But the hand-to-hand didn't prove so good for some of the others. Although Dean felt fine after his bout—indeed, the young Cawdor had used his combat to sharpen himself—Doc, Jak and Mildred weren't so happy.

"I know that I am older, and therefore somewhat more prone to aches and pains than the rest of you, but I must confess that even without the bounds of such, I feel like a three-week chilled stickie," Doc said as he settled himself on the ground.

"Don't feel so good myself," Mildred said. "I took a hell of a beating out there. I just couldn't get it together. What's wrong with you, Doc?"

The old man winced. "I have a terrible burning in my kidneys, as though I were to micturate acid. And along my chest bone is tender, although I cannot recall taking any punishment in that area."

"Doesn't sound so good, Doc," Mildred commented. "I don't like the sound of that at all." She looked from under her plaits at Doc, who gave her the briefest of nods.

"I know. I was thinking much the same thing," Doc said, keeping his tone level. "And your symptoms are…?"

"I feel like I've got flu coming on very rapidly. In fact, a little too rapidly for my liking. I ache all over, feel hot, and my reactions are foggy, to say the least."

"You know what this may mean?" Doc asked, although he knew it was a rhetorical request.

Mildred nodded grimly. It was then that she noticed Jak, who was hugging himself. "Jak?" she asked, having to repeat herself in a louder voice when the albino failed to respond first time. When he looked up, she asked, "What's the matter? You feeling okay?"

Jak shook his head, and the very act made him grimace. "Feel like shit. Don't know how got through that. Mebbe you should take look," he said, moving toward her.

Jak stripped off his jacket and shirt, revealing his highly muscled and slender white torso.

"Oh, shit…" Mildred whispered as she looked at

him. Contusions and weals topped with small blisters were starting to sprout on his body.

The chron was ticking faster.

THE KNOWLEDGE THAT his people had started to contract the disease meant that Ryan felt more impatient than before for something to happen—but was also more determined to get his timing exactly right. It wasn't just the life of his friends that was at stake, or his, for if they had begun to contract the disease, it was surely only a matter of time before the rest of his party, and indeed himself, also fell prey to the disease. More than that, it was the future that they, or anyone else across the land, might have that was finely in the balance. When he had reported the beginnings of the pox among the companions to Gloria, she, too, had been keen to spring into action.

"Ryan, honey, we can't just leave it. Not when you're in danger...not when Jak's in danger."

The albino had accompanied Ryan, for the reason that the one-eyed man had foreseen that the Gate queen would have trouble separating her own feelings from a general view of the situation. As she spoke, he stepped forward and took her hand. Her fiery, flashing eyes met with his red yet cold orbs.

"You, me...we not important," Jak said to her in a soft, gentle tone that Ryan had never heard him use before. "Bigger things think about. Need get this right, not rush and fall."

The queen paused for a moment before answering.

"You're right. I thought I'd lost you once before, so I guess I can grit my teeth and get past this one."

But once again, fate was to step into the breach quicker than any of them could have hoped. For the very next morning, the regular recon patrol brought news to the queen as she breakfasted with Tammy and the companions.

"Two wags from the redoubt have left," Dette said breathlessly and without preamble as she approached them. "Headed toward Crossroads and not stopping like before."

"Any convoys leaving or entering?" the queen asked.

Dette shook her head. "Nothing planning to leave that we know of, and nothing seen in the other direction."

"Looks like they may be going to hit the ville like they did that convoy," Tammy said, cold fury etched in her face and her tone.

"Could be," Ryan agreed, "but we need to be triple sure. Anyone following?"

Dette nodded. "Cat and Nita. They may be triple stupe, but even they can't fuck this one up. As soon as they reach their destination, one of them will come."

"What if it's not Crossroads?" Krysty asked.

"Then I told them to follow for an hour and report back on the wag's direction. Leave it to them and they'd follow the fuckers forever and forget where they were going. If they turn off and head past the ville, an hour puts them well out of our range anyway, and they'd probably come back the same way."

Gloria grinned crookedly. "I'm gonna have to watch you, lady. You're too damn full of the smarts. In the meantime, we'd better get our shit together, 'cause it looks like we're going out to play today."

Ryan nodded. "You need any help?"

"If you can spare J.B., then I reckon Jon'd appreciate some help," Dean chipped in. "He's been working on those laser blasters, and he showed me the other day what he's been doing. He took one to pieces and studied it to see how they worked, so they could be used and maintained. But I figure he'd like you to give it a quick once-over."

J.B. agreed. "Glad to. The boy's a natural, though, so I'll soon be back." With which the Armorer immediately departed, galvanized to his task.

While Gloria and Tammy raised their warriors, Ryan turned to his companions.

"So how are we doing, people?" he asked. "J.B. and me are okay, and so are Dean and Krysty—" he looked to them to check, and they affirmed this "—but it's you three I'm concerned about. How are you gonna be in a firefight?"

"Slow," Mildred said wryly. "But you think any of us are going to miss this?"

"No," Ryan said slowly, "but I want to know how we're going to handle this. If—"

But he was cut short by the arrival of Cat at the camp. She ran straight to Gloria and gasped out her message before the queen turned and approached the companions.

"It's settled. The scumfuckers are attacking Crossroads. We can't just let that happen. Those are good people—and shit fighters."

Ryan shook his head. "They were good to us, too. But more than that, if there are two wags, then this may just be the break we've been looking for."

"How?" the queen asked.

Ryan smiled mirthlessly. He spoke in a murmur, but with a chilling passion: "Just wait and see."

GLORIA RALLIED the Gate warriors, who formed up for the journey to Crossroads, the companions joining them. Tammy recruited scouting parties to travel ahead and scout the ville to plot the movements of the Illuminated wags.

Although the companions had taken several days to find the Gate, the camp was situated so that the tribe was able to make the journey in only a few hours. They were able to use routes and homing instincts that gave them an unerring sense of direction where other groups would falter.

To make the journey even quicker, the Gate used their horses and wags, the men working hard to dismantle the camp and have it ready to move while Jon worked out of the armory wag, making sure that the women were ready for the firefight ahead. He handed out laser blasters among the conventional blasters and ammo.

J.B. joined him as Tammy received her weapon. She was favoring a Smith & Wesson Airlite .38 Special, and noticed the Armorer look at her askance.

"I know, I know," she said, "The last time you saw me with one of these, I nearly chilled Jak with a stray shot. But that was when Margia had tampered with the stock to make it kick sideward. It's a good blaster, really."

"And there's no chance of me trying to chill Jak," Jon added.

J.B. allowed himself a small smile and nodded. "How are you handing out the laser blasters?"

"Some of the women have been using them for a little while, getting used to the way they feel and fire. It's kinda weird at first, but after you've used them for a while…the only problem I've had is working out how long the charges last, 'cause one hasn't run out yet to give me some kind of indication.''

"Problem is, even if it did, you wouldn't know how long it had been in use before it was taken by your people,'' J.B. pointed out.

Jon agreed, adding. "I've made sure all those with the laser blasters have others weapons, as well, just to make sure. Anyway, you can't use those damn things safely in a confined space.''

"Too true.'' The Armorer nodded. "Need a hand?''

Jon grinned. "Yeah, sooner we get these handed out, sooner we can go, and no blasters are leaving this wag unless they're checked.''

"Good man,'' J.B. said, joining Jon at his task.

By now, Tammy and her scout parties had departed on horseback, leaving the packhorses to be loaded and reined, and the now-equipped Gate warriors to mount the wags ready to depart.

"I hope Nita doesn't get spotted or get herself chilled before Tammy gets there,'' Gloria said to Jak.

"Why should she?'' the albino asked as he checked his blaster.

The queen looked up from her own blaster, the lightweight Vortak Precision Pistol, and fixed the albino with a stare.

"You are kidding, man,'' she said. "You've seen her—big, blond, all arms and legs and shit clumsy. I swear someone must have left her outside the camp one night, 'cause she don't fit with the rest of us.''

Jak laughed, a rare thing. Gloria felt her spirits rise at seeing her lover laugh, as she was acutely conscious that under his camou jacket, more weals and blisters were starting to rise.

Which made speed of the essence.

Ryan was waiting for Gloria on the lead wag as the queen finished her final round of the wags, sparing a few words for each of the groups of warriors, and indicated to her that they should leave. She assented as she mounted the wag, and the convoy took off for the ville of Crossroads.

Traveling in wags spread across the convoy, each of the companions marveled at the manner in which the men driving the wags were able to pilot them through the narrowest of channels in the woodlands, and scout around the hill where the landslide had taken place. A journey that had taken them days on foot was shaved to a few hours by the extra speed of the horse-drawn wags and the innate sense of direction of the tribe's men.

Mildred was on a wag about halfway down the procession, as far as she could tell. Doc was with her, while Dean and Jak were traveling ahead. J.B. was on the armory wag with Jon. Krysty wasn't travelling with the wags. She had joined Tammy in the advanced recon party that had gone ahead on horseback.

"Tell me, Doctor," Doc began suddenly, breaking into Mildred's reverie, "do you honestly think that we have a chance?"

"Of stopping the Illuminated Ones or saving ourselves?" Mildred countered.

Doc shrugged. "Either, or, neither, nor..."

"I don't know," Mildred said after some thought. "I reckon we can whip their asses, frankly, but I really couldn't call it over whether we survive."

Doc nodded, almost to himself. "I would have said the same. I just hope that, at the very least, we can be in at the kill...as it were."

In an attempt to make this deadline, the recon party

had now reached the edge of the ville, where Nita came to meet them.

"What's happening?" Tammy asked without preamble.

The tall blonde looked at the small warrior and shrugged. "A lot of nothing, by the looks of it."

"You fuck wit, don't talk in riddles, just say it," Dette screamed at the blonde from another horse.

"Look, get off my back—" Nita began before Tammy cut in.

"Shut it, both of you. Save that shit for if we ever get time." The Gate number two raised an eyebrow toward Krysty that spoke volumes, before continuing, "Now tell me what's happening in the ville, and keep it brief."

Nita nodded slowly, taking a second to compose herself before beginning. "Okay, well, the sec posts have either been deserted or wiped out this end, as the wags just swept in. I dunno about the other three roads. But the wags are in the center of the ville, down the main drag. They're just sitting there at the moment, picking off the enemy and soaking up the Crossroads fire."

"What about the ville sec and the inhabitants?" Krysty asked.

"Far as I could tell from where I was, they've just all grouped together along each side of the drag and are trying to blast the wags without realizing that they can't hurt them."

Tammy thought about this for a moment, looked up at the position of the sun, then turned to the others.

"Okay," she began, "by the time that the main party gets here we'll have a couple of hours of sun left before nightfall. They shouldn't be that long, but

I want a full report ready for Gloria. We need to know the full situation for all the sec posts around the ville, so we'll split into four and take each point of the compass. Report back here soon as can.'' She then divided the recon party into pairs to take each sec post position on the four blacktops before adding, ''Nita, saddle up with Dette…and you put up with it and keep your mouth shut, lady.''

She turned to Krysty. ''That should keep those two quiet. Now let's do it.''

The recon party split and headed at a gallop for the sec posts that were situated at the edge of the ville on each of the four blacktop roads. Leading by example, Tammy headed for the farthest, whipping her horse into a gallop, closely followed by Krysty. At the point where they had met Nita on the road, they were about half a mile from the sec post on that particular blacktop road, and so traveled around the ville at a half-mile radius to the sec posts at each point in and out. It gave them a degree of safety lest anyone be manning those posts, but made the journey longer. It also made it hard to tell what was happening in the ville, the distant sounds of blasterfire that drifted across the empty arable pasture being drowned out by the sound of the horses' hooves.

Krysty felt her hair blow free, billowing out behind her as the horse galloped toward the sec post. The very fact that her hair was so free-flowing at this point suggested to her that they would find no one present at the post, and nothing to suggest any danger about to befall them.

''It's over there,'' she shouted toward Tammy, pointing across the empty fields toward a clump of vegetation where the signs of a sec post were clearly visible. The fact that the camouflage was so poorly disguised at this stage suggested that it was deserted. Nonetheless, both women slowed their horses and drew their blasters, ready for any eventuality as they approached.

But the post was deserted. There were no chilled sec men, nor was there any sign of a firefight. But the deserted post did look as though it had been vacated in a hurry, and a single tire track, suggestive of a motorbike, led away toward the ville.

"Looks like someone came for them in a hurry," Tammy commented.

Krysty agreed. "I figure they wanted all hands— and all blasters—back on that main drag as soon as possible. Let's hope they've done that on all the posts."

"Yeah," Tammy agreed, "it makes it a lot easier for us if they're all in the one place—provided we can actually get something done before they run out of ammo, or get themselves all chilled."

Krysty assented. "I'll second that. Let's get back there and find out."

With which they turned their horses and headed back toward the point where they had agreed to rendezvous. When they came in sight, they could see that the other recon pairs had returned from their nearer targets, and were waiting for Tammy and Krysty to reach them. Looking toward the distant hill, Krysty could see the Gate convoy approaching.

"Listen up," Tammy said as she drew near to the others, pulling up her horse. "Our sec post was empty, and it looks like they were pulled back rather than getting into a firefight and retreating. No chilled, either. Reports?"

The other pairs relayed that they had found a similar situation on all the posts bar the one that lay on the road immediately before them. There, three of the four sec that regularly manned the posts were chilled, with no sign of the fourth, who may have managed to retreat and warn the ville of the approaching danger.

"Okay, so we're clear on all points, and all our action is concentrated down that main drag," Tammy said in summary. "Guess Gloria and Ryan will have a few ideas about that."

Krysty, without pondering the matter or speaking up, was sure that Ryan already had a germ of a plan in his mind. And she suspected that she knew what it might be.

The first of the convoy wags rolled up, with Ryan and Gloria dismounting before the horses had even come to a halt. The Gate queen demanded a report of Tammy, who gave it concisely. Gloria then turned to Ryan.

"That's how it stands, then. Two sides of Crossroads, with the scumfuckers in the middle, waiting for them to run out of ammo. Any ideas on how to stop the wags?"

"Yeah," the one-eyed man replied with a grin on his face. "We play this right, and we can help out Robertson and his shit-useless sec, as well as getting ourselves a way to get into the redoubt."

Gloria raised an eyebrow. "This had better be good, Ryan."

"It is," he replied, "but we really need to get our shit together and quick. Gather everyone around."

And when the warriors had dismounted and were gathered, Ryan outlined his plan.

Gloria laughed. ''If we don't get ourselves chilled first, it might just work.''

''It'll have to,'' Ryan answered, '''cause if it doesn't, we're gonna run right out of time.''

THE GATE CONVOY SPLIT into two sections, with the mounted recon party riding beside them. They were well briefed on what they needed to do to get into position, and from there they would be able to communicate on some manner. But first they had to attain that position. Heading off in opposing directions, the split convoy headed out to the blacktop roads that ran at right angles to the one on which they had stood. To travel out and then loop in past the empty sec posts, they would approach the ville from either side of the main drag, and arrive at the rear of the bars and gaudies that lined the street and from which the Crossroads dwellers were mounting their defense.

They knew for a fact that the Illuminated wags had approached alone, and that there were no scouts to let them know of reinforcements approaching. So their only danger lay in an overzealous defense from any Crossroads sec that may be guarding the backs of the bars and gaudy houses.

The wag with Ryan and Gloria headed one way, accompanied by the wag that included Mildred and Doc. Dean, Jak and J.B.—still on the armory wag with Jon—headed for the other side of the main drag, with their sec outriders including Tammy and Krysty.

There was little chance for any immediate communication as the wags and horses ate up the distance between their original arc of travel and the outskirts of the ville. As they entered the ville itself, it was like a ghost town. The plowed fields and the residential dwellings were deserted, and it was only as they approached the main drag that the sounds of activity began to assert themselves.

As they passed the hospital, Mildred thought of Hector, and wondered how he had been coping, and if he had succumbed to the disease himself. Come to that, was he even there now, or was he with the others trying to protect their ville.

"Couldn't cover a fart with a tin can," J.B. commented to Jon, unconsciously echoing Mildred's thoughts as the armory wag approached the rear entrances to the main drag.

On the opposite side, Ryan felt the same. "They've left the rear totally exposed. If we'd wanted, we could have come and mopped them up before they even knew it."

"Shit, they really do need our help," Gloria commented.

At the last, a token defense was offered. A few desultory shots rang from the rear of some of the bars as those inside realized that they were being approached from the rear. But the blasterfire was so spare and inaccurate that the convoys were able to take cover with ease, and incur no casualties.

"Stop firing, you stupe bastards," Ryan yelled from cover. "We've come to help you, dammit!"

"Ryan? That you?" Yardie waddled from the rear of one of the buildings and came over to where the one-eyed warrior and Gloria were sheltering. His expression as he saw the Gate queen would have been worth a laugh under different circumstances. "Where the fuck did you all come from?" he asked in a small voice.

"No time to explain," Ryan replied briefly.

"There's more of us on the other side. Listen, we have some weapons that may disable those bastards, but we'll need your help to make it work."

ON THE FAR SIDE, J.B. was outlining the same plan to Robertson, the baron leading his people by example.

"But I don't understand why you want to try and take one of the wags," the baron said, confused. "Shit, with those blasters like theirs, surely you can just whomp shit out of them."

J.B. shook his head. "Not that easy. For one, we can only fire at the unprotected parts of the wags. The lasers'll just whizz off the rest of the wag like any normal shell. You think they wouldn't protect their own wags against weapons like theirs? And for two, we need to take one of the wags so we can carry out the next part of Ryan's plan."

"That's what I don't get," the baron began, but the Armorer cut him short.

"Doesn't matter right now. If we don't get this bit right, then there won't be the next bit. Are you with us?"

Robertson nodded. "Like we have a choice?"

YARDIE HADN'T even bothered to argue with Ryan's plan, and the Gate warriors and companions were in the middle of spreading themselves along the bars and gaudies, using the back entrances to slip in and explain the plan of action to the defenders while adopting offensive positions.

"Think the others are in position?" Gloria asked Ryan as they watched the Illuminated wags sit malevolently in the street outside.

"Should be," Ryan answered. "Let's find out."

The one-eyed warrior slipped out the back way to the bar, and ran to the end of the drag. There, beyond where the wags sat, was an alleyway. He arrived and looked at the alleyway opposite.

It was empty.

"Shit," he muttered, and settled to wait. Within a few minutes, J.B. arrived in the empty alleyway. He signaled to Ryan that everything was set. The one-eyed man pointed to his wrist chron and held up five fingers.

The Armorer nodded, then disappeared. Ryan watched him go, then ran back toward his own post, poking his head into each back door and yelling the countdown to those within, knowing that J.B. would be doing the same. All the while, he noticed that the constant stream of blasterfire from both sides of the main drag was answered only by intermittent laser fire that took chunks out of walls, but wasn't directed to chill.

Mebbe they want to run us dry and then take us out to use for the disease, he thought. He shuddered, all the more determined to beat the Illuminated Ones.

He reached the last of the bars and gaudies. The task accomplished, he returned to his post next to the Gate queen.

"Okay?" she asked.

"All set." He checked his wrist chron. "We go in three and a half minutes...."

Chapter Seven

"Now," Ryan Cawdor said under his breath as his wrist chron clocked up the fifth minute. Along the main drag, the firing from the bars and gaudies ceased, a sudden silence reigning along the road.

He counted under his breath, giving his wrist chron the barest of glances as he watched the two Illuminated wags sit in the middle of the street, dark and oppressive in their silence. By his reckoning, the longer the cease-fire continued, the more jumpy the fighters inside the wags would be getting—and the more likely to make mistakes. From past experience, he knew that the Illuminated Ones weren't fighters, and could imagine that the silence was playing heavily on their nerves inside the wags. They would have no idea what was gong on.

He kept counting....

As soon as firing had ceased, the Gate warriors with laser blasters had relinquished some to the companions. Of the remainder, some had detached themselves from the bars and gaudies and headed out the back way, moving swiftly on each side of the drag toward its northern end. As they did this, the companions also moved out—Mildred and Doc moving slower because of their symptoms, Jak's speed as yet unimpaired—and headed toward the alleyways at the southern end of the drag. Ryan was the exception; he planned to stay until the last, launch the attack and then retreat to join his people.

Those Gate warriors who still had laser blasters positioned themselves so that they could get a clear shot at the wags from the windows and doors of the gaudies, the barrels of the laser blasters—with their distinctive rounded snouts housing the laser jewel—being held back until time was up.

At each end of the main drag, looking across the roadway from the facing alleys, the groups of Gate warriors and companions faced each other, gesturing their recognition and checking their counting off of the time until the first offensive.

Ryan kept counting through clenched teeth, his attention fixed on the two wags in front of him. He didn't look across at Gloria, but knew that the Gate queen would be likewise absorbed in her task.

The count was over. Ryan reached the limit he had set, gave his wrist chron the briefest of checks and nodded almost imperceptibly to himself. There had been more than enough time for the two offensive groups to reach each end of the main drag, and more than enough time for the Illuminated Ones cocooned inside the wags to lose whatever nerve they may have.

Ryan raised his Steyr and took aim at the underside of one of the wags. The laser blaster he had been given was still on his shoulder. Time enough for that when he had raced to the end of the drag. The Steyr was to be the signal shot.

He gently pressured his index finger, depressing the trigger until the rifle kicked back and unloaded the first shell of the attack. In the silence of the late afternoon, with the tension that hung heavy in the air, the shot seemed to echo around the room, around the drag, around the ville. There was a whine as it ricocheted off the metal protectors that covered the tires of the Illuminated wag, but this was lost in the melee of sound that suddenly engulfed the bar in which he stood. Not just that bar. From every bar and gaudy along the drag came a volley of conventional blaster shots and the hum and heat of laser blasterfire.

Ryan drew back from the window and headed toward the rear of the bar, running to join his companions for what he hoped to be the next stage of the offensive. Gloria turned briefly to him as he moved.

"Give them hell," she yelled over the noise of firefighting within the enclosure of the bar.

Ryan didn't shout back, but gave her an "okay" gesture and left.

As the one-eyed warrior hit the street and alley that ran along the rear of the drag, it suddenly seemed to quieten from a deafening volley to a dull roar, the blasterfire partly dulled by the pounding of his own adrenaline in his ears as he ran toward the alleyway that marked the end of the drag, shouldering his Steyr and swinging the laser blaster to hand in one fluid motion as he moved.

The plan was simple. The only parts of the Illuminated wags that weren't entirely protected were the chassis and axles on the underside. Direct fire at them, and there was a chance of disabling the vehicle, as well as forcing the inexperienced Illuminated fighters into moving. And that was exactly what Ryan wanted: to separate the two vehicles. Not only would it make them easier to deal with if they had no backup, but it also increased the chances of capturing one.

And the one-eyed warrior wanted to take one of those wags very badly indeed. If he could capture one, then he figured that they would have a better chance of gaining access to the redoubt by using a principle that he would have called the Trojan horse—if not for the fact that the legend had been one of many lost forever in the nukecaust. Nonetheless, the principle behind it was one that had never been lost.

Ryan arrived at the alleyway and turned to find Mildred and Doc waiting for him. Looking across the divide formed by the road, he could see J.B., Jak, Dean and Krysty ready in position. The Armorer signaled that all was set on his side, and Ryan acknowledged. Then he turned to Mildred and Doc.

"How you doing?" he asked, having to raise his voice to be heard over the blasterfire along the main drag.

"Not so bad," Mildred replied. "Feeling a little weak, but not so weak that I can't lift and fire this," she added, tapping the barrel of the laser blaster she was holding.

Ryan turned to Doc. The older man was looking pale, his skin ashen. And although he was holding a laser blaster, he was only using one hand, barrel pointed down; he was leaning heavily on the silver lion's-head cane that housed his swordstick, with a rapier blade of finest Toledo steel. Usually, the can was a camouflage for the blade. But at this moment, it seemed as though Doc had a greater need for it as support.

Doc managed a weak and yet still wry grin. "I have felt better, dear boy. My kidneys feel on fire and my chest appears to have a ton weight heavily upon it…but my hand is still steady, and my eye—if not keen—is still in focus."

Ryan acknowledged the older man. "Just do what

you can, Doc. And you, Mildred. If the wag gets driven back here, then there's a good chance of nailing it. It may already be damaged.''

"One would hope so," Doc agreed, turning toward the drag, "but we must never forget that there is nothing more dangerous than a wounded beast.''

Looking at Doc, Ryan felt that the older man's words could as easily be applied to himself as to the wag that would be heading their way, but held his peace.

Like the Gate warriors at the far end of the drag, the companions assumed combat positions, laser blasters readied for attack, ears straining for an indication of movement from the wags in among the roar of combat that engulfed the main drag.

RYAN'S INITIAL SHOT had presaged a volley of blasterfire, and the first of several volleys of laser fire at the two Illuminated wags. In every bar and gaudy the Crossroads dwellers and the Gate warriors had directed their fire toward the undersides of the wags. The upper body of each vehicle was made of an alloy the likes of which hadn't been seen in the Deathlands since before the nukecaust, and although the tires of each wag were of the same pervious rubber material as any other tire, they were protected by a metal shell made of this alloy that exposed very little of the tire itself. There was only a thin band of the tire that was visible, at the very base of the wheel where it would touch the road surface. However, the underneath of the vehicles, although Ryan could only assume that they were made of the same alloy, had vulnerabilities. If any shells or laser fire could damage the chassis or axle systems, or by a ricochet take out one or more of the tires, then the wags would be disabled.

And whatever else, Ryan had been pretty sure that the Illuminated Ones within the wags wouldn't relish the idea of being trapped in the outside world with means of transport for getting back to the redoubt. Soaking up pressure from fire directed at the impervious body, they could sit there quite happily all day until the ammo was exhausted, and then do as they wished with no opposition. But direct fire at their weaker spots, and plant the seed of panic in their mind, and then it may be possible to push them into the action that you wanted.

Taking Ryan's position at the window as the man departed, Gloria directed the attack on the wags as much as possible on the noise and confusion. Blaster and laser fire rained down on the wags and the road around, kicking up clouds of dust and chippings from the old tarmac patches.

"Hey, give me the grens and the launcher!" the Gate queen yelled. On the far side, her shot was echoed by Tammy, whose task it was to act as opposite number to her queen.

The engines of the two wags had fired up, and could be heard over the blasterfire. Before leaving the camp, Jon and J.B. had primed the old gren launchers that the tribe had in their armory, the legacy of a trade that had taken place during their time in the wood. It was an irony that they had made the deal in the very ville where they were about to test their new toys, but the irony was lost when there was no time to consider such things.

On each side of the road, Tammy and Gloria loaded the gren launchers and primed the grens. Shouldering the heavy weapons, each warrior directed the nose of the launcher downward, and toward a spot in the center of the road and between the front of one wag and the rear of the preceding wag.

Counting to ten and steeling herself for a recoil of whose strength she had no real idea, Gloria fired. On the opposite side of the road, Tammy also let loose with a gren.

The explosion as both grens hit the road and detonated simultaneously was deafening, and drowned out all other sounds. An immense cloud of dirt, tarmac and dust was thrown up as the grens gouged a great trench from the road.

''Motherfucker!'' Gloria yelled as the air began to clear and she could see the damage that had been wrought by the grens. It was a cry that mixed surprise and exhilaration as she viewed the sight before her. Where there had once been a road, there was now a large crater that still smoked. It looked several feet deep—certainly too deep for even the four-wheel-drive wags to cope with—and extended across about half the width of the road. The wags had pulled back a few yards as the explosion had hit, and had halted again, unsure of what to do. They were covered in dirt, and some lumps of tarmac had made small dents on the bodywork, but they were otherwise undamaged.

Both Gloria and Tammy reached the same conclusion after surveying the damage they had wrought. It was obvious that the wags wanted to stay close, as they had only withdrawn rather than fleeing, and there was still enough room across the road for either one of the wags to skirt the crater and join its twin.

On each side of the road, the two women loaded up the gren launchers and took aim once more. Both directed their fire at an acuter angle than before, so that it would take out the road directly in front of them, in effect making an impassable trench that ran the width of the road. The only problem in this being the danger that they faced from flying debris as the grens hit. Before each fired, they yelled at the other inhabitants of the room to hit the floor, and then let fly with the grens.

A moment of intense silence followed the detonation as the grens hit close to the windows, the blast followed by a cone of silence that accentuated the rushing of their own blood in their ears. Then the heat and force of the detonation hit, throwing both Tammy and Gloria backward to hit the floor of their respective bars with a force that would have knocked out lesser people. But the Gate women had an innate wiry strength that enabled both to scramble to their feet and view their handiwork.

Ignoring the aches and bruises that had been caused by the impact, both were satisfied with their work. There was now a trench where there had once been a road, and it was impossible for the wags to cross to each other. They were effectively separated, and on their own. And there was only one direction for them to go: each would have to head for the end of the drag, where the ambush awaited them.

Gloria caught Tammy's eye across the divide. She gestured her pleasure at what had happened, and Tammy acknowledged this before each woman picked up her blaster and continued to harry the wags, joining their comrades in firing at the undersides of the wags.

On each side of the trench, the wags tentatively drew back a couple more yards before halting, as though the drivers of the wags were weighing their options. There was no way that either party could cross the divide, and so they exercised their only option. One wag began to accelerate toward the north end of the main drag, while the other slewed into a turn so that it wouldn't have to tackle exiting the main drag in reverse.

This was unfortunate for the inhabitants of the wag, as the very act of turning gave the Gate tribe and the Crossroads dwellers another angle from which to fire at the underside of the wag. An opportunity that they seized with both hands. While the wag that was heading north was able to escape toward the end of the road with minimal damage to the underside of its chassis, the increased angle of fire offered by the wag heading south yielded a positive result. A blast of laser fire caught at insulation on the cable for the wag's electrical system. The laser cut through the insulation with ease and severed the cable. The wag coughed and spluttered as the engine cut out before the emergency backup system for the onboard comps refired the ignition motor. But that wasn't all. At the same time, a stray shell ricocheting off the alloy of one wheel guard flew diagonally across the underside of the wag and penetrated one of the wag tires, causing it to veer dangerously across the road before the driver was able to right his course and pilot the vehicle straight down the drag.

AT THE SOUTHERN END of the road, Ryan and J.B. were keeping watch on the activity, ready to cue their companions when the wag was near enough to commence shooting.

"Got you," Ryan muttered between clenched teeth as he saw the wag stutter then veer on its course.

"Wounded heading this way," he called to Doc and Mildred. "We can take this one."

Both Doc and Mildred took heart from this and drew on inner reserves of strength, the like of which had kept them alive before in situations where they should have succumbed. For, like Jak, this time they truly were fighting for their lives as at no other. If they could capture the wag and use it as a means of getting into the redoubt, then they stood a chance of conquering the disease. If not...

They shouldered the laser blasters, ready to swing out and face the oncoming vehicle at Ryan's word.

ON THE FAR SIDE of the road, J.B. turned back to Dean, Jak and Krysty, who were waiting for his word.

"One coming—damaged and slowed up, too. This is our best shot."

"I hear you," Dean said, while Krysty nodded and Jak said nothing. He didn't have to. The look on his face said it all, the scarred white visage set grim. He felt the same way as Mildred and Doc. There were no second chances.

Ryan and J.B. stood watching. The wag seemed to take an eternity to approach. For both men, this was a familiar combat situation, and the familiar feelings flooded through them. The icy coolness that marked a survivor from one who would be chilled; the rush of adrenaline pumping through the veins; the exhilaration as every nerve screamed for action; the way that time seemed to slow so that every second took an hour, enabling their combat-trained minds to analyze the situation and plan a response—a mixture of cool intelligence and gut instinct that was born of cold, hard experience.

For both—as, in lesser degrees, for their companions—this was a way of life, and something that had molded them into what they were, as well as defining every situation with which they had to deal.

It was why they had won more times than they had lost, and why they were still alive when others were long since worm fodder.

And it was something the Illuminated Ones heading toward them couldn't possibly, by the very nature of their existence, possess.

The black, faceless visage of the wag became larger and larger, filling the field of vision of both men. As it progressed, desultory laser blasts came from portholes at the side, directed at the bars and gaudies lining the drag—random fire that hoped to score some kind of hit and give them a moment's relief from the ceaseless and intense fire.

The sounds of the battle retreated as both Ryan and J.B. dug deep within themselves.

The wag was now almost upon them. It had no front window to speak of, just a narrow grille with tinted armaglass behind it, making the vehicle oppressively opaque. There must be a camera on the front somewhere, Ryan mused, to enable the driver to get a better view. If only he could see where, he could knock it out and effectively disable the wag.

No matter. It was time.

"Now!" he yelled to Mildred and Doc at the same moment as J.B. echoed with an imprecation to Krysty, Jak and Dean.

The one-eyed warrior and the Armorer ran from cover, dropping to the sidewalk as they came out into the open, firing as they fell. The laser blasts hit the front of the wag full on, and although it was unlikely that they did any physical damage, the shock that they gave the wag driver was invaluable, as he slewed the vehicle sideways, braking suddenly in a reflex move and throwing the wag into a spin. As the other companions came out from the alleyways and took up firing positions, they could see the portholes on the side turned to them, offering the smallest of gaps in which to fire at such close range.

Would they be able to effect any damage by doing this? It was a debatable point, but there was the slimmest of chances. Moreover, it was almost certain that by firing at the open parts of the wag they could prevent the Illuminated Ones inside the wag from returning fire by making the ob slits unsafe for use.

Dean, Krysty and Mildred went for this option. Both Dean and Krysty were good target shots, and Mildred—despite the onset of the disease, had never lost the skills that had made her a Olympic sharpshooter in her now almost forgotten predark life.

Laser fire rained in on the side of the wag. With fifty percent of their options for returning fire already reduced by the fact that the wag was showing a side elevation, the Illuminated Ones now found themselves limited by their own weapons turned back on them.

This left Jak and Doc to join Ryan and J.B. in concentrating on disabling the vehicle. From their ground-level elevation, the two men were sending long strings of laser fire that picked at the metal covering on the underside of the wag. Smoke issuing from beneath the chassis indicated that some damage had already been done. They had no way of knowing that the maintenance cover had been sheered, and the electrical system had been blown, but it was certain from their vantage point that some damage had occurred.

And where there was some, then there was the potential for much more.

"One tire blown," Jak yelled into J.B.'s ear as he dropped near him. "Blow one more, they fucked."

"Go for it," the Armorer yelled in reply, unwilling and unable to divert attention from his task.

"Need better position," Jak said in a quieter voice, as though to himself, before starting to crawl along the sidewalk, circling around the Armorer as he continued firing. The prolonged bursts of fire on the ob slits had restricted the return of fire from the Illuminated warriors within, but even so it was a danger for Jak to advance even closer to the wag. The companions were all within a radius of a few yards, and it would only take one snapped-off blast to chill one of them.

But this had to be done: knock out another one or more of the tires, and the four-wheel wag would find it hard to progress. It would be effectively stopped for good, and this was the objective. Those inside would have no option but to disembark and fight on a more equal footing. And the only way to knock out one or more of the tires, getting past the metal alloy guards on the wheel arches, was to get closer, and get a wider angle of fire.

On the far side of the road, Doc could see Jak attempt this move, and understood his intent. He could also see that his fellows were engaged in a defined pattern of fire, with no one to cover Jak as he moved.

Ignoring the pain that shot through his chest and back as he moved, the older man also began to move forward, firing at the wag.

"Doc! What the hell do you think—?" Mildred began, before Doc cut her short.

"No," he snapped, "do not question, just fire. Jak

needs cover, distraction…." Doc dropped to a crouch, the movement and strain of his muscles ironically countering the pain in his chest and back for a moment, and giving him a renewed strength. He moved forward, firing at the underside of the wag, and obliquely at the front. He was determined that any attention given to Jak should at the very least be split, giving the albino a better chance.

It worked. The desultory fire from the interior of the wag started to strafe the sidewalk where Doc advanced, causing him to take cover in a doorway. His fire, and the fact that Jak had been able to keep low and move with much more speed, had enabled the albino to slip past the Illuminated defenses seemingly without them noticing.

Jak had now moved around to an angle where he was able to sight the two front wheels of the wag with ease. One was already blown; the other followed swiftly with one burst of laser fire, the rubber burning and melting as the air exploded from within.

Two wheels would make it almost impossible. But if it was a four-wheel-drive vehicle, then Jak also needed to take out a back wheel. He moved in closer, so that he was almost underneath the vehicle. In a sense, this made him both more at risk, and also safer at the same time. Although he was closer to the Illuminated Ones than any of his companions, he was also at such an angle that it might actually prove impossible for them to get a clear shot at him.

None of this mattered to Jak. The only thing he could focus on was disabling the wag and drawing the Illuminated Ones out into the open. He positioned himself and fired a short, controlled blast at one of the back wheels. He was so close that he could feel the blast of air as the tire melted and the air forced its way from the wrecked tubing. The stench of melted rubber filled his lungs, choking him.

It didn't matter; three tires were blown. Now they would have to come out into the open. Jak crawled backward triple fast, for the first time noticing that he hadn't been fired upon. A glance toward Doc, holed up in a doorway and drawing fire, told him why. Time to return the favor. Jak rose to his feet and started to fire on the wag as he retreated, drawing the sparse Illuminated fire in order for Doc to come out of the doorway and also back his way to safety.

The wag fell silent. Although the companions kept firing, there was no return fire. Ryan ceased and held up a hand to indicate the others should follow suit: but there was little need for him to do this, as his fellows had also noticed the sudden cessation and had stopped.

Now it was a waiting game. The companions retreated to the cover of the alleyway. The Illuminated wag was out of commission, and those inside had two options—they could stay there indefinitely, or they could come out and fight, in an attempt to reach the other wag and so gain safety and a return to the redoubt.

The wag engine had been cut, and it sat, dark, malevolent and silent.

What next?

IF THE COMPANIONS had been able to halt and disable their wag, the Gate party who had effected an ambush at the other end of the road hadn't been so fortunate. The wag that had headed in their direction hadn't been damaged, and so had been able to maintain and build speed and momentum as it tried to escape the grens and the continuing fire.

Tammy had been delegated by Gloria to lead the attack party, and she watched as the wag approached. Her tactics were simple, and almost suicidal. As the wag approached, she yelled bloodcurdlingly loud and leaped into the path of the wag, followed by her warriors from either side of the road.

With the wag coming head-on, there was little chance of any initial fire in their direction, and so they were able to fire off volley after volley of laser blasts, peppering the front of the wag. They knew that they would be unlikely to penetrate the alloy covering, but the intent was to try to shatter the armaglass with the lasers, or at least make it so hard for the driver of the wag to see what he was doing that he would veer off the main drag and crash into one of the buildings, enabling them to mount an assault.

To an extent, their tactic was successful. The wag veered, the driver blinded by the laser fire hitting the armaglass shield and ducking at the wheel instinctively, throwing the vehicle off track. It slewed sideways, and some of the Gate warriors dropped, firing at the underside and trying to disable the wheels.

The return fire from the side of the wag was instant and claimed two Gate warriors, the laser burning raw weals in their flesh, the smell rising with their screams as they fell.

"Cover, cover," Tammy yelled, imploring her team to protect themselves while still trying to attack. While her warriors sought cover, Tammy stayed upright in the center of the road, directing her fire in an arc along the ob slits on the side of the wag. She ignored the returned fire that cut trails in the earth and tarmac around her, her face grim as she continued to fire, ignoring the rising bile and fear in her guts as she waited for those under her command to get clear.

Fear could be a good thing in battle, if it hit a person right. Sometimes fear inspired heroic acts. Tammy knew that if no one covered the Gate women as they made for cover, then all would stand a good chance of getting chilled. But if she stood and fired, then most would make it, and it would be harder for them to pick her off.

Even so, she was relieved when the warrior in cover began to fire, covering her so that she could reach safety.

The engine of the wag whined as the driver crashed gears, trying to right his vehicle and, panicking, making the whole process more complicated. The vehicle moved backward and forward, trying to hurriedly right its course while still being fired upon from cover. Laser blasts tried to knock out the tire and hit the underneath of the wag while still peppering the sides to prevent return fire from inside.

"We're not doing it," Tammy cried in despair. "We haven't damaged the bastard at all!"

Seemingly impervious to the blasterfire, the wag finally managed to right its course and drove through the hail of fire set up by the Gate attackers. It broke past them and picked up speed as it hit the blacktop that led away from the main drag. The Gate warriors kept firing until Tammy gestured them to cease.

"No good," she said, seemingly to herself. "Fuck it, I hope Ryan's doing better...."

THE AIR WAS ALMOST crackling with tension. The fire-fight taking place at the far end of the drag only accentuated the silence as the companions waited in cover for the Illuminated Ones to make their move. They had to, as they were presented with little option except to come out and fight.

There was only one variable, as far as Ryan could see. The wag was fairly spacious, and there was no way of telling how many sec may be inside. They would be on equal terms as far as weapons, and Ryan was pretty sure that his people were better fighters by far. But would they be outnumbered?

They could only wait and see.

The back of the Illuminated wag opened, and the soldiers within emerged. Two came first, running sideways to take cover in the doorways and lay down a covering fire with their laser blasters. They were followed by three groups of two: eight fighters in all.

The companions returned the fire and cut down two of the Illuminated Ones before they had even reached cover, the laser fire cutting across their bodies and making their one-piece suits smoke as the material smoldered in the heat. The lack of sound—their screams muffled and contained within their helmets—made their chilling an uncanny sight, as they seemed merely to crumple to the dirt.

The remaining six found themselves clumped together in two doorways, with little cover for all of them, and no way of safely firing at the companions.

They were so hopelessly inept that for one moment Ryan hoped that they would surrender. Chilling them would be like chilling defenseless children, and if they lived then at least he stood a chance of learning something from them about the redoubt.

But any such hope was fleeting. They may be tactically inept and have no experience of combat, but their courage couldn't, at the moment of truth, be doubted.

Two of the soldiers fell flat, laying down a covering fire while the others charged forward, headed for the alleys where the companions were firing from cover. They kept firing as they ran, the laser beams raking the head of the alley. Their hope was that they could stop the companions from firing by making it too hard to take aim, and perhaps hit some of them by chance.

It was an insane, suicidal tactic, and they were picked off with ease. The combat was over in a matter of seconds, and the Illuminated Ones lay scattered across the road, their chilled corpses zigzagged by lines of burned flesh and charred cloth where the laser blasts had claimed them.

The companions emerged from cover and surveyed the charnel house before them.

"They did not have a chance, really, did they?" Doc asked, a tinge of sadness in his voice.

"Shouldn't feel sorry for them," Mildred said sharply. "Look how ill you are, Doc—they're part of the problem."

"Ah, but is it really that simple?" the old man mused. "Consider, dear Doctor—they have spent several generations underground being fed a doctrine that leads them to act as they do. Granted, that is not our concern. But can we not spare the briefest of thoughts? After all, if we had been born where they were, would we be any different?"

"Probably not," Ryan replied before Mildred could answer. "But the harsh truth is that it's not our problem."

Any further reflection was stopped by the arrival of Gloria, with Tammy close behind.

"The other wag escaped," Gloria said without preamble.

"We tried, but couldn't do any damage to stop it," Tammy added.

Ryan nodded. "It's okay. This one was already damaged enough to slow it when it got this far...gave us a better chance. And we only need one, if we act quickly."

Without further explanation, Ryan strode past the Gate warriors and the chilled Illuminated Ones, and climbed into the back of the wag. J.B. followed him, and found the one-eyed man examining the comps and control panel of the wag.

"What do you reckon, J.B.?" Ryan asked without turning.

"Three tires out—that should be easy to fix if we raid some ville wags for spares," the Armorer commented. "Some damage underneath by the look of the smoke—mebbe electrics, as the main chassis system seemed to be working okay. Give that a check. If it was the electrics, then mebbe the comps don't work."

"Let's see," Ryan said, flicking a switch. The console lit up. "They've got an emergency system, at least. Radio's shot to shit, though," he added, attempting to get some life out of it.

"That's good. No way of telling who's in the wag, then."

Ryan agreed. "Otherwise, it looks like an ordinary wag. As long as there's a stick shift, a wheel and some pedals, we can ignore the rest of the comp shit." He stood back, thought for a moment, then nodded decisively. "Yeah, it'll do."

The Armorer took off his spectacles and polished

them. "Let's get to it, then. Quicker we move, less suspicious they'll be at the redoubt."

"Right," Ryan agreed. "You explain to the others and to Gloria. I need to talk to Robertson. We'll need his help, and it's about time he was put in the picture, considering what those coldhearts have done to his ville."

J.B. didn't bother to answer. With a brief nod he was already about his task before Ryan's last word had died away.

Chapter Eight

"Ryan, you wanna tell us what the fuck that was all about, and how come you got some of those fancy blasters that those coldheart bastards had? And another thing, what the fuck is going on here with all these naked women running about beating the shit out of everyone and what the fuck does this have to do with the fact that my ville is getting shot to shit by that ugly bastard disease that Hector can't stop and—"

"Whoa, slow down, there!" The one-eyed man held up his hands in an imprecation of surrender as the baron continued to talk loudly and at a rapid pace. The normally laid-back Robertson was highly agitated and animated, which, Ryan had to admit to himself, was hardly surprising after the events of the past few hours. But now it was Ryan's task to try to calm him down so they could talk rationally about what was going on.

"You don't tell the baron to slow down when you've just shot the fuck out of the main drag," Yardie raged. The fat man waddled across the room, his face flushed and angry, eyes bulging, until he was right in Ryan's face and the one-eyed warrior could smell the man's bad body odor and spirit-soaked breath.

"And you don't do that to me," Ryan answered with an icy calm and a voice so low that it was barely audible. "If you want to talk about this in a reasonable manner, then we will. I came here to put you in the picture, after all. But if you want to play it hard, then I'll break your fucking neck before talking to the baron. Do you understand me, Yardie?''

The fat man wilted visibly before Ryan, his eyes registering the cold look on the man's scarred face.

''Yeah, well, I suppose you should have a chance to explain what's been going down,'' the fat sec man mumbled, backing off.

''Good,'' Ryan said. ''Now, if you'll let me explain without butting in, then I can tell you the whole story, and what we need from you in the way of help.''

Robertson nodded. ''Okay, you always seemed kinda straight, so I guess the least I can do is hold my tongue till you've finished.''

Ryan began to tell the baron and the fat sec man about the Illuminated Ones, and how his people and the Gate had ended up in the vicinity of Crossroads. He was, as ever, careful to avoid mentioning the redoubts and the mat-trans. He did, however, sketch in as much background detail as possible about the Illuminated Ones and their plans to take over the land. Much of this was still guesswork, but he presented it as fact in order to gain the ear of the baron.

Not that it seemed necessary. Robertson's daughter—the first to contract the disease after being taken by the Illuminated Ones—was dead, and her corpse, along with all the others that had amassed since the disease had taken hold, had been burned on the advice of Hector, who had obviously taken in all that Mildred had told him about such diseases. The baron was still carrying the pain from this, and it had cut him deeper than he was willing to admit. Whatever it took to end this horror, he was willing to take his part.

"So, you tellin' me that you can get into their strong hold and wipe these motherfuckers out?"

"Got to."

Robertson sat back, shaking his head, for a moment lost in his own thoughts. Finally, he spoke. "You reckon this plan of yours will actually work?"

Ryan shrugged. "It's our only chance. If we act quickly, then they may well figure that the damaged wag took a little longer to limp home. Me and J.B. had a look at the comps and electrics on the wag, and the radio system is shot, so they won't expect a radio response if they call us up when we get near. I figure they'll have sec cameras around the entrance to the redoubt, and they'll see the wag come up alone, and want to let us in. The Gate and anyone else who wants a firefight against these bastards—" he directed a glare at the now less-belligerent and still-silent Yardie "—will come up at a distance, using cover. The Gate know that land by now, and they'll keep everyone out of sight."

"And you'll just get out of the wag, say hi and open the doors to everyone?" Despite his lack of hostility, there was still a skeptical note to the baron's voice.

Ryan smiled. "Yeah, weird as it sounds. Listen, you've got to remember that we've fought these cold-heart bastards before, and we know what they're like. They've spent too long underground, and although they had better blasters and a lot of working old tech, they couldn't hold their own in a firefight. You must have seen how the ones in the wag acted when they got out to fight us."

Yardie broke his silence, his voice sounding uncertain, although the words were, "Yeah, I figure he's right, baron. I saw them, just like a bunch of kids learning the basics of fighting. Come to that, I figure that a bunch of kids would have more suss than that.''

Baron Robertson nodded slowly, biting his lip. ''So they'd be so stupe as to just let you in?''

''Yeah, I figure so. And we'll be wearing the uniforms, so they won't be expecting us to suddenly turn on them when we get out of the wag. By the time they've gathered themselves, then we'll be at their throats and have the main sec doors open.''

''How you gonna manage that?'' Yardie asked, but this time there was no sneer of disbelief in the sec man's voice, rather a genuine interest.

''Seen it in their last place,'' Ryan lied, unwilling to divulge further information. ''They always scratch the code for the door above the keypad. Mebbe it's so they don't forget if they panic. It was all over the last place they were at. I can't see that this would be any different.''

The baron sighed heavily. ''This is all too weird. Weird fuckers who come out of the ground and try to chill everyone with some old disease so that they can take over and rule a land where everyone else has taken the last train west... I mean, shit—a disease that goes back beyond the nukecaust?''

''It may be hard to believe, Baron, but it's as near to the truth as any of us can make out,'' Ryan said evenly. ''I don't understand why they're doing it any more than you do. But it doesn't matter—the only thing that actually matters is that they are doing it. Just ask Hector if you don't believe me or Mildred. We've got a chance to stop them. And if we don't take that chance, then...'' Ryan shrugged, leaving the baron to make his own conclusion.

''Hell, Baron, I'd rather die in a firefight than from

that disease," Yardie whispered, almost visibly quailing at the thought.

Robertson seemed lost in thought for the moment, then suddenly shook his head. "No, you're right. We always try to keep out of trouble, here. You never know who might pay you jack, right? But this is more than that. Yeah, you've got our help, Ryan. Just tell me what you need."

Ryan grinned. "Time, but there ain't shit you can do about that. Otherwise…"

"KEEP IT STEADY. The last thing we want is for more chilling before we even start," J.B. muttered through clenched teeth as the Illuminated wag was jacked up a little higher to enable himself and Dean to gain a greater access to the underneath of the chassis.

"No real damage," Dean commented. "These wags are real good pieces of work." He tapped the metal casings with a wrench. "If we could find out what this metal's actually made of—"

"I know, I know," the Armorer said sharply, cutting him off, "but right now I just want to get this done before it falls on us."

Dean followed J.B.'s gaze, and understood his feelings. The jacks that were holding both ends of the wag off the ground were old and rusty. Whether it was real or not, J.B. felt that he could almost see them buckling under the strain. Jak and two of the Crossroads dwellers had already changed the tires that the albino teen had shot out, unbolting the wheels from behind the alloy wheel guards and replacing the exploded rubber with worn but still serviceable tires plundered from wags around the ville. The four-wheel-drive vehicle had a large wheel radius and girth, and it had been a struggle to find wheels that would match. Eventually, a pair of old tractor wags had been located in one of the field barns, left to rot when their engines had given out and replacement parts couldn't be found. Both had rear-wheel drive, and on both the tires for those rear wheels had been still in good order. They had been rapidly plundered and placed on the Illuminated wag.

With tires in place, it was J.B. and Dean's responsibility to check that no damage had been done to the systems, and to this end Mildred was in the wag, operating the drive and braking systems, the engine whining and roaring as the wheels rotated, turning on their axles as she turned the wag left and right and put it into reverse.

It would seem that the alliance of Crossroads, companions and Gate were in luck. All the essential drive systems of the wag were in working order. The wiring that had fired and fused was involved with the comp systems alone. The wag had cut out because the on-board comps appeared to act as a pilot, with a course-plotting program—to judge from the maps Mildred had found—that would assist the driver. However, there was a fail-safe device on the dash that enabled the driver to switch over to manual, which was perhaps how the wag had fired up again during battle.

What it meant, more importantly, was that the wag could be fully operational as transport without using the comps. The sec devices on the wag wouldn't be of any use, but as there were notably few other wags in the Deathlands that had anything even approaching such a sophisticated system, this was hardly something that would bother the attack party. The important thing was that the wag worked, and could be used as the decoy to gain access to the redoubt.

Especially as the braking and drive systems were in full working order. J.B. and Dean had now ascertained this, and were quickly checking the casings beneath for any other damage, as a safety check lest the vehicle suddenly give out on the way to the redoubt.

"Everything's A-OK here," Dean yelled over the engine noise.

"Yeah, same here," J.B. gritted, sweat spangling his brow. "Let's get out from under here."

Even though he spoke almost too softly to be heard over the roar of the engine, Dean was able to ascertain his meaning, and was as swift as the Armorer in scrambling out from underneath the wag.

"Kill the engine, Millie," J.B. yelled, wondering if it would be possible for Mildred to hear him over the wag noise.

Obviously, it was possible for her to hear him. Mildred turned off the wag's ignition, and the vehicle shuddered on its jack supports so violently that the wag shifted, the weight redistribution proving too much for the rusty jacks to support. With a creak, and the sharp snap of breaking metal, the jacks gave way under the wag—first two at diagonal corners, then the other two rapidly following as they found themselves unable to adjust to the sudden sharp increase in weight that they were forced to bear. With a crash that made the wag vibrate violently and raised clouds of dirt and tarmac-riddled dust, the vehicle crashed to the road.

"Hot pipe, that could have been us under there," Dean breathed.

"Good thing it wasn't," J.B. returned, "but Millie's still inside."

Without waiting for an answer from the younger Cawdor, the Armorer rushed toward the wag. He reached it as the side exit door opened, and a visibly shaken Mildred climbed out.

"You okay?" J.B. asked anxiously, grabbing her as she stumbled and nearly fell.

"Yeah, I think so, John," she replied slowly. "I think I might have picked up a little whiplash, as I wasn't ready for that, but otherwise…I feel like I ache all over."

"It wasn't that bad a crash," Dean said, approaching her.

Mildred looked at him and laughed. "Could have put that a little better, but you're right. Normally I could have ridden that without blinking. But I'm getting weaker all the time. Jak and Doc must be, as well. It's this damn disease. The sooner we get after the redoubt the better."

Ryan and Yardie had heard the crash as they left the baron's house, and came running.

"Fireblast! You okay, Mildred?" Ryan asked.

"Sure. What did Robertson have to say?" she returned, not wanting to dwell on her own problems and keen to make progress with the objective.

Ryan filled them in as Yardie arrived, puffing and blowing hard. The sec man agreed with Ryan that his people would help in whatever way they could, although he was quick to point out that the Gate and the companions were far better equipped for the task. It may have seemed like cowardice on first hearing, but there was little doubt that the sec chief was correct. The Crossroads dwellers had spent too long living a relatively danger-free life to really have any grasp of serious combat.

"So, what now?" Dean asked when his father had finished.

"Round up the others. I've got to find Gloria and Tammy. We need to get the plan into place so we all know what we're doing." He looked up at the sky. Twilight was fast turning into night. "The dark will help us, if we can move in the next hour or two, then we can reach the redoubt and get in before sunrise, which'll give us better cover. But we'll have to move it."

"Leave it to me," Dean said. "If J.B. and Mildred stay here, I'll find Jak, Doc and Krysty. I figure I know where they may be, anyway."

"Okay," Ryan said grimly. "Let's go to it. There's no time to lose."

While the one-eyed man headed off to the area where the Gate appeared to be gathered, Dean headed toward the hospital. Along the way, he detoured toward the barn where the two-wheel-drive tractors had been found. The barn was on the edge of town, and was silent and dark as he approached. But he had a notion that he would find Jak still there, as the albino hadn't returned with the salvaged tires.

Dean approached openly, using what little light there was so that Jak would be able to see him and not mistake him for an attacker. At all times, the albino was always on the defensive.

"Jak, you there?" he called softly as he reached the open doors of the barn. There was no answer, and as he peered into the darkness, it was impossible to make out any shapes within. "Jak?" he repeated a little louder.

A white wraith, like a shadow in negative, rose from the recesses at the back of the barn.

"Dean? What want?" Jak's voice was small, like

one roused from sleep. At the same time, he sounded weary.

"We're meeting to plan the attack. Got to round up Doc and Krysty, too, but I figured I'd find you here."

"Why?" Jak was still at the back of the barn, moving slowly as he dressed.

Dean shrugged. "Figured you'd need some rest, and mebbe you'd find the quietest place."

"Figure right," Jak replied, moving forward, now fully dressed. "Tired easily. Pox eating me. Clothes hurt on skin, needed to let it breathe. Mebbe try relax totally. Need quiet for that."

"Damn—sorry I had to disturb you," Dean said, the concern in his voice showing as Jak came out into the twilight. His white hair and pale skin seemed—if it were possible—to be more ashen than usual.

"Okay." Jak shrugged. "Need rest but know no time left. We need move. What now?"

"Now we get Krysty and Doc, and I'm pretty sure I know where they are."

"Then let's go," Jak replied, setting his suddenly frail frame to move onward. "Where?"

"I figure the med building. Mebbe they'll get an idea of how bad the disease is spreading."

Without bothering to answer, Jak nodded and joined Dean as they moved back in toward the center of the ville.

The closer they got to the center, the louder the hum of activity and the more bodies could be seen swarming around, looking busy. But there was one oasis of complete calm and silence—almost, it seemed, deliberately and completely ignored. It was toward this oasis that they headed, for it was here that the med building was located.

"Really funny how everyone's avoiding this part of the ville," Dean commented with some sarcasm as they approached.

"Not really," Jak replied, ignoring the wit as he thought of his own reasons for wanting to block out the idea of the pox.

Dean said nothing more. They covered the last few yards in silence, and Dean carefully opened the door, making as little noise as possible.

As he and Jak entered, he was taken aback at how the building had changed since the last time he had set foot in it. Before, Hector had managed, with the help of his workers, to keep the small block clean and fresh smelling, even though it was beginning to become overcrowded.

Now, it was bedlam. The smell of the charnel house permeated the air, cutting through even the few measures that he had the time to take against the odor of chilling and decay. Every bed was full, and there were pallets in every available space, each with its own patient slowly fading. It was quiet within the four walls, but not silent. Low groans of agony, the murmurs of delirium, and the hushed talk of those who were still aware and of the ville healer himself mixed together in a low-level burble of anguished sound.

It looked as though the ville women who had previously aided the healer had either succumbed or opted out of helping, as he seemed to be coping almost by himself. The only assistance he had right now was that of Doc and Krysty, who were doing their best to fill the breach, even though the old man himself had begun the first stages of the disease.

"Shit," Jak whispered softly to himself, getting an unwelcome picture of what was ahead.

His distinctive voice cut through the burble and caused both Krysty and Doc to turn and face the door.

"My dear lad," Doc began, "are you here to assist, or because you yourself have taken a turn for the worse?"

Jak didn't answer—seemingly didn't hear—as he surveyed the carnage spread across the beds and floor space of the med building. But Dean was quick to reply.

"I've come to round you all up—found Jak, now you two. We're going to get the plan of action."

"We're ready to move already?" Krysty asked, not looking up from the patient she was tending.

"The Gate are assembling, and we're all getting a full briefing."

Krysty smiled crookedly, and said wryly, "Probably the sort of language those coldhearts use about planning a fight."

"Yeah, but if we're gonna best them, then what better way to think of it?" Dean replied.

Krysty turned to Hector. "Reckon you'll be able to cope until we get back?"

"You think you will?" Hector looked at her, his eyes deep into his head, shot through with red and lined with black and discolored skin. He had the initial stages of the disease, and was still working himself harder than his sick body could cope. He knew that his time was limited, but he was determined not to give in to the pox until he had no choice.

Krysty shook her head. "Mebbe, mebbe not. I don't want to give you a false hope. All I know is that we'll fight to the last one of us to try and get out of there with the antidote, and with any disease they have in there completely destroyed. Because if we don't, then we're all chilled anyway.''

Hector's face creased into something that may once have been a smile, but in his weariness and illness came out as more of a grimace. "Well, if you're going to do that, then I guess the least I can do is try and keep it together here until you get back.''

"Good man. Now we'll have to move,'' Krysty replied, bidding him farewell as she and Doc joined Dean and Jak, leaving the hospital and making their way rapidly toward the center of the ville. As they went, Dean explained that the wag was ready, and told them that J.B. and Mildred were waiting while Ryan went in search of Gloria and Tammy.

RYAN CAWDOR WONDERED what Gloria and Tammy had been up to when he had left J.B. and Mildred, heading toward the north end of the drag. After the firefight that had resulted in the chilling of the Illuminated Ones, and it was clear that the battle was over and won, the Gate had massed in the center of the drag, waiting for word from their leader. Gloria had come and surveyed the chilled, and had then disappeared toward her people. They had moved up toward the north end of the drag, and—Ryan assumed—Robertson's people had taken away the corpses of the Illuminated soldiers when they cleared their own chilled.

It was only when Ryan approached the cluster of Gate people that he realized that something else was going on. He could hear the crackle of flames, and from the center of the group a light began to rise and illuminate the area around, silhouetting the warriors as they stood. There was also a low mumble, like a chant he couldn't understand.

Ryan pushed his way through the throng, the Gate people giving way easily when they saw who was trying to move through them. The one-eyed man reached the center of the gathering, which had circled around a rapidly built fire. Gloria and Tammy were in the middle, leading the chanting. In front of them lay a pile of corpses. From their pale skin, mixed sex and the tightly cropped hair, Ryan guessed that these must be the corpses of the Illuminated Ones. But where were their uniforms?

Gloria was still chanting, almost in a trance, but Tammy was aware enough to see the one-eyed man as he emerged at the front of the crowd. She left her queen for a moment and approached him.

"What's happening?" Ryan asked, indicating the fire and the pile of corpses.

"You know our tradition," Tammy replied. "We burn the chilled, as we're always on the move. And although these people were our enemies, as they enter the next realm they are warriors stripped bare of allegiance, just like ourselves. It's the least we can do to give them a noble departure."

"I appreciate that, Tammy, but we can't waste time. The wag is ready to roll, and we need to all know what we're doing triple fast if we're going to move and be in place before sunrise."

Tammy nodded. "It'll be okay, Ryan. We're nearly through."

Ryan cast his eye over the corpses. "Yeah, I don't want to fuck with your ways, but what have you done with their uniforms? We're really going to need those."

Tammy grinned. "You don't need to be dressed to enter the next realm, for fuck's sake. We stripped them 'cause Gloria figured you'd need them. I'll get them for you."

"That would be good. Then I'll leave you to finish in peace. But tell Gloria we can't waste time."

"She won't want to," Tammy answered before departing swiftly to collect the uniforms. Within a couple of minutes, she had returned from the other side of the circle and handed a pile of clothing to Ryan.

"Now go. We'll be with you soon, and we'll bring the headpieces with us. They're too many for one to carry, and besides you need to figure who'll fit these," she said.

Ryan nodded, then left the Gate people to their ceremony.

"What the hell are those women doing?" Yardie asked as Ryan passed him with the uniforms.

"Something that's none of our business," Ryan snapped, "so leave them until they're done. Then we go over the plan. Everything set?"

The fat sec man nodded. "We've handed as much of our ammo and blasters over to J.B. as we can spare—we have to keep some kind of sec for ourselves, just in case—and any wags or other transport that you need has been readied."

"Other transport?" asked the one-eyed man, baffled.

The fat sec man nodded. "We've got a few horse-drawn carts, and the horses for them. I know the Gate have theirs, but I figure they may be useful. Some of us want to volunteer to go with you, as well."

"But you said—"

Yardie held up his hands. "I know what I said, and

I wasn't wrong. You and the Gate are far better fighters than we'll ever be. But that don't matter. We can help, and if we don't, well, that might be the margin between winning and losing. Between us all having a future or not. And that's a gamble I ain't willing to make.''

Ryan grasped the fat man by the arm. "Shit, you got more balls than I thought, and I'm sorry I doubted and misjudged you.''

Yardie gave a short laugh. "Dunno about that—I got more balls than I thought!''

Ryan grinned. "Okay, you gather everyone from Crossroads who you can, and we'll meet at the south end of the drag as soon as the Gate have finished. I mean everyone, too. Even those who'll be staying here. I want everyone to know what's going on. It's not a difficult plan, but so many people involved makes it that way.''

Yardie nodded his understanding and left the one-eyed man as he went to gather any of the Crossroads dwellers who were still standing and fit enough to take part in some way in the action ahead.

Ryan headed back to the wag, where he found Mildred had been joined by Jak, Dean, Doc and Krysty.

"Fireblast! Where the fuck has J.B. gone?''

"Armory,'' Mildred answered. "They're turning guns and ammo over to us, and John wanted to see what we had before we started.''

"There isn't time. When everyone else is preparing—''

"—I can check the weapons and get them working then,'' J.B. finished, coming up as Ryan spoke. "I just wanted to get an overall idea of what we had.''

"Which is?'' Ryan asked.

The Armorer shook his head. "Not much. But the Gate have enough of an armory as it is, and we'll be okay. Plus there are some more laser blasters from the chilled Illuminated Ones."

"Speaking of which," Mildred interjected, "what are we gonna do about those?" She indicated the uniforms Ryan was carrying.

"That's a good question," the one-eyed man said softly. "I figure we can only divide these up according to who they fit. They won't notice anything at first, as long as the uniforms fit."

"What about the helmets?" Krysty asked.

"The Gate will bring those. They're not so important, and I'd guess they're all one size but adjustable, if they're anything like the ones we've come across before."

"Okay," the red-haired woman agreed. "I guess we'd better get these fitted up if possible, then."

She took the uniforms from Ryan and began to hold them up, one by one. They were marked by the burns of the laser blasters that had chilled their original occupants, but the biggest problem was their size. Some of them were large enough for Ryan or Krysty to fit into, but a couple of them were too small for Dean or Doc.

"Shit—I really didn't want to leave any one of us out of the wag," Ryan said. "Any of the Gate may be able to cope with the wag and keeping up the deception until we can get those sec doors open, but..."

"But you would rather have people around you that you can trust totally, and who you know will cover your back?" Doc queried.

"Guess that's it," Ryan agreed. "After the things we've been through, I can second-guess what any of you will do in a situation and back you up. And every single one of you could do that for me. For any one of us.''

"Well, it just ain't gonna work that way this time, however we might like it," Mildred mused, "and just maybe that's for the best."

"How d'you mean?" Dean asked.

Mildred leveled a gaze at all of them, moving from one to the other as she spoke in an equally level tone. "The fact of the matter is, Doc, Jak and myself are buying the farm. Even as I speak, we're creeping nearer. That's just the way it is, and right now we can't do anything about it. The disease seems to be affecting us to a lesser degree than I've seen it in any of the Crossroads people who've been infected, and I can only guess at why this may be. Whatever, it seemed to have delayed and slowed the progress of the infection, but it certainly hasn't chilled it.

"I'll be honest with you guys—I feel like shit, and I'm acting like it. Everything is slower, more difficult. I'd guess it's probably like that for Jak and Doc, too. But that makes it dangerous to trust us totally in a firefight situation, because we're not the same people right now. Maybe if you have to have Gate warriors, you won't trust so much on instinct, and that may be better."

There was a pause while Ryan considered this. Finally, he said, "Yeah, mebbe you're right about that. It's not something any of us want to face, I guess, but if we're gonna stay alive and smash those bastards, then we've got to think about it."

"Okay," Krysty murmured, seeing the concern on her lover's face. "Mebbe the best thing to do is wait till we've run through the plan, then pick who comes with some of us.''

"Yeah," Ryan agreed reluctantly, "that seems the easiest way. Meantime I guess we'd all better get acquainted with the wag's comps, seeing as any of us may or may not be in the wag now.''

It seemed like a good idea, and there was time while the Gate finished their ceremony. That they neared completion was made obvious by the thick smoke that rose from the fire at the far end of the ville, rising into the rapidly darkening night air, filling it with the sickly sweet smell of roasting flesh.

There was room for all the companions to fit inside the wag, and Mildred and Dean quickly ran over the contents of the comp board. Much of it was no longer operational due to the shorting out of the electrical cable beneath the chassis, but some parts were still in operation. The interior lighting and directional controls were intact, operating on the emergency system, but the parts of the comp that were linked to the redoubt were dead, as indeed was the radio that had kept them in contact with the redoubt and with the other wag. Dean and Mildred—who between them had the entire system figured—gave the others a crash course in how to turn off the operational systems, and also how to use them if it became necessary. They also made sure that the nonoperational sections were completely detached from the working parts.

By the time the friends left the wag, the Gate had moved down the drag, led by Gloria and Tammy. Two of the warriors were carrying the helmets that accompanied the uniforms, and they laid them down by the wag, where Ryan and Krysty had left the uniforms ready for allocation. The Crossroads people had gathered with the Gate people, and they were facing Ryan and the companions, waiting to see what would transpire.

Ryan spoke. "I don't need to tell you the importance of what's going to happen. We believe that the disease that's infested this ville, and which these people we know as the Illuminated Ones plan to spread throughout the whole of these lands, has its root in an underground base not far from here. We want to break into that base, chill every last one of those people before they can do any more harm and wipe out all traces of the disease that's there. We also believe that they have an antidote. They'll have that to make sure they didn't get it.

"We know where this base is, and we have experience in fighting these people. You Crossroads people who join us are taking a risk, and we appreciate that. If we leave soon, we can reach the base before sunrise, and that'll be the best time to take them.

"My plan is simple—some of us will use this wag and the uniforms taken from the chilled, and we'll attempt to enter the base as the missing wag crew. The radio was shot out, so they won't know that we're fakes. The rest of you will follow at a distance, keeping to cover. They have sec cameras around the entrance to the base, so in order to maximize cover and lull their suspicions we need to act swiftly and take advantage of the darkness.

"We can get in, and once there we need to stall them long enough to open up the doors to the base so that the rest of you can get in and help us. They're not good fighters, but they may have better weapons, and we have no idea at this stage of how many we face.

"Your task is to drive them back into the heart of the base—Crossroads people, let the Gate lead. Like us, they have an idea of how these places are constructed. Others of us will set out to find the disease cultures and the antidote. We know what we have to look for. We need you to help us fight against the numbers.

"Basically, those of us in the wag will seek the disease. The rest of you, keep to cover until we can open the sec doors. Then follow us in and blast those fuckers into oblivion.

"There are no guarantees of success, but this is a one-shot chance, so we need to have clear heads and chill anyone who does not belong to us. Is that clear?"

There were murmurs of understanding and approval from the crowd.

Ryan nodded firmly. "Okay. We know what we have to do—let's get ready to move."

Chapter Nine

J.B. wasted no time in linking up with Jon to get an overview of the combined armory. The young Gate Armorer had gathered the cache of weapons from the Crossroads armory with his own and was checking them with the aid of Cat and Dette.

"How's it going?" J.B. asked, noting the looks of concern on their faces.

"Shall we just say that these people are kinda triple stupe when it comes to keeping their weapons in good condition?" Dette spit without looking up from the Sharps rifle that she was attempting to clean. "If some poor fucker actually fired this thing, it'd be more likely to blow up in his face than chill some enemy."

J.B. bit his tongue and caught Jon's eye, barely suppressing a grin.

Jon shrugged. "She's not choosy with her words, but she does have a point," he admitted. "I guess they don't get much of a call for combat around here."

"I don't think they do," the Armorer agreed. "Mind, they're brave enough to join us when they know they're shit at firefighting."

"Either brave or really, really stupe beyond belief," Cat remarked.

"Whatever, they're with us and they've given us these weapons. So let's stop bitching and try to get this sorted, okay?" Jon snapped.

There was a moment's tense silence as the two Gate women stopped and glared at their Armorer. There had never been a man taking such a position within the tribe before, and they were still unused to the concept of a man wielding authority. J.B. waited, interested to see how Jon handled the situation.

"You can stop that shit, too," he directed at them. "Gloria put me in charge, and we've got work to do. Who do you think's doing the right thing here?"

"You, I suppose," Cat said grudgingly. "Guess we do need to knock these into some kind of shape and triple fast…and I suppose arguing about it don't do any good."

"Exactly," Jon replied. "So what about you, Dette?"

"If you say so, I guess," the woman answered, still with a hint of hostility in her tone. "I suppose we should get this done."

Satisfied that the situation was under control enough for him to speak without interfering, J.B. moved over to where Jon sat, loading a Walther PPK handblaster that he had just cleaned.

"So, if you need to get these done triple quick, a helping hand could be useful."

Jon looked up. "I'd appreciate that, J.B.," he replied simply, indicating the pile of blasters and ammo still to be checked. "Just grab one and get checking."

With the practiced eye and hand of the Armorer to assist, the four of them soon cleared the backlog of Crossroads blasters, ignoring the sound and movement around them as the warriors prepared for battle. When the Crossroads armory had been cleared, it was time to move on and check the Gate armory.

Despite it being more than twice the size of the

ville's armory, it took a fraction of the time for the four of them to run through the handblasters, grens, plas-ex, machine blasters, gren launchers and laser blasters that the Gate had amassed. The condition of the armory, and the inventory, was so well kept that all they really had to do was to check the laser blasters used in the earlier firefight.

"They seem okay, but I sure as shit wish that I could tell how much charge they had in them," Jon said ruefully when they had finished.

J.B. shrugged. "Trust to luck. They're not our main weapons. We really rely on our usual blasters. And we picked up a few more after the firefight."

"Yeah, I know," the young Gate Armorer replied, "but they'll be a useful weapon when we get beneath ground, especially if we need to get through some of those sec doors."

"Then we use them sparingly and only bring them out when they're really needed." J.B. shrugged again. "I know what you're saying, but the fact of the matter is that we can't keep wishing and hoping. We have to build the shack with as many bricks as we've got, and no more."

"Guess I still need to learn that."

"That's experience. Just stay frosty and alive long enough," J.B. told him. "We're set here. I need to check our own inventory right now."

Jon bade the Armorer farewell as J.B. headed back toward the companions in order to fulfill his duties on their blasters.

FIGURING THAT SHE wouldn't be needed urgently, Mildred slipped away toward the med building, determined to see Hector before they set off.

When she entered the building, she was appalled by the overcrowding and the conditions, even more so when she saw Hector tending to one of the pox victims who was close to the end.

"Lord save us, man, you'll be gone before anyone else if you don't rest," she said quietly.

"If I try and rest, every time I close my eyes all I see is the suffering," he replied in a flat tone without turning to face her.

"And you'll be better off buying the farm that bit sooner?" she queried in return.

"Mebbe it'd be better to go out quicker trying to make it better for some than just hanging around a bit longer to see a few more poor stupe bastards in agony."

"You don't think we'll make it?"

Hector didn't answer immediately. He finished tending to his patient, then turned to face her. Mildred was shocked by the change in his appearance. It wasn't just where the tiredness and the disease had started to take hold of him; it wasn't just the dark under his eyes. It was the dark within them. Just a few days, a week or so, earlier, Hector had been a man who had belief in his task. He had tried his best for the people of Crossroads, and was willing to try more in the efforts to overcome the mysterious disease that had hit the ville. But now his eyes were dark pits of despair, holes in the earth that had seen into the abyss and echoed this with their own empty caverns of dark.

He had given up hope, but his basic humanity and devotion to his task wouldn't let him give up until he himself had dropped from the disease and exhaustion.

Finally, after what seemed a painful eternity, he

answered Mildred. "I don't see how any of us can make it."

"You don't think we can make it in and out in one piece, let alone find the antidote?"

Hector looked at her blankly. "What?" he asked simply.

Mildred shook her head, plaits feeling heavy as the disease took more of a grip on her weary frame. "You mean to say that you haven't heard of the attack plan?"

Hector shook his head, but there was a vague glimmer of something that may just have been approaching hope deep within his eyes. He stepped forward, hesitating as though unsure what to do or say next.

"I just knew there was a firefight, and that you and the women arrived in time to drive the wags away. Krysty and Doc were here, but—"

"Ryan and Gloria have a plan of action, and Baron Robertson is backing it. It's not much as hopes go, I guess—all ifs and buts—but it may be all we have. Take a rest, man—just for a few moments—and I'll tell you about it," Mildred said rapidly.

Hector allowed her to lead him to the rear of the med building, where there were a few chairs pushed to the wall to make way for more pallets. Sitting him down, Mildred explained the projected campaign to the bewildered and exhausted medic, who had trouble taking it all in—particularly when she had to go back and explain how both her companions and the Gate tribe knew so much about the underground base. She was sure that Hector had been told this before, but it all seemed new to him, possibly the disease and exhaustion were leading to short-term memory loss. Certainly, as she spoke part of her ran a professional appraisal on the medic. She was sure that, unless they were able to fulfill the plan rapidly, it would be too late for Hector. He was working himself to death, and nothing would make him pull back.

"Do you understand what this means?" she asked as she finished relating the details of the forthcoming attack.

He nodded slowly. "Yeah, I think so. If we can just keep it together here, then we may be able to stop the spread."

Mildred assented.

"But if we can't…" He shook his head. "Guess there'll be nothing to do except work till I finally keel over."

Mildred allowed herself a wry smile. "Guess not, and I guess I'd do the same in your position," she concluded.

Hector paused, lost in thought for a moment. Then, with a surprising suddenness, the rangy healer rose to his feet. "Best to get going, then, Mildred."

As she rose, he grasped her by the shoulders and looked her in the eyes. His gaze was now fiery and intent, the previous blackness now illuminated by a light of hope.

"Look, if we should never meet again, for whatever reason…" He trailed off, not sure how to continue, before taking a deep breath. "Listen, I realize that there's a lot about you that I don't understand and never will, like how you and Doc seem to know so much about what happened before the nukecaust, and how come you know stuff about medicine that seems, well, why that is I don't know, and I don't really want to. All that matters is that I learned more about being a healer from you in a few days than I ever had, and it's helped me more than I can say over the last few weeks. And if you don't get the hell out of this with the cure, it won't be for the want of trying. I guess all I'm trying to say is that I'm glad I had the chance to learn from you before all the shit hit the wall.''

Mildred hugged the man. ''Keep hoping we get back, and for God's sakes keep yourself alive until we do. It'll only be a day or so if we're coming back,'' she said as she held on to him.

She let him go and stood back. ''Keep yourself alive—we'll be back. And get some rest! That's from one doctor to another.''

''I'll try, but you know how that is.'' He shrugged.

Mildred shook her head. ''Damn fool.''

Hector stood at the back and watched as she left, answering her departing gesture with a small wave of the hand.

As soon as the door of the med building was closed, he forgot all idea of rest and returned to his patients.

THERE WERE SEVEN SUITS and helmets from the chilled Illuminated Ones that would be worn by those who would travel in the wag and make the initial entry to the redoubt. Not all of the companions would be able to make the cut, partly because of the problem of matching available suit sizes to the individual, and partly because of the possible failing health of Mildred, Doc and Jak.

Yet the argument for noninclusion because of health was that the infected companions would be slower, and not so reliable and quick to react as usual. Therefore, the usual—and almost psychic—level of cover between them may be broken. However, it occurred to Ryan that if some of the Gate traveled with them, then this reliance would already be broken, and perhaps the infected companions would be able to make the trip— or, to be more specific, one of them: Mildred.

The companions had gathered by the wag and were making their own preparations for battle, checking their weapons and restocking on ammo and grens from the traveling supply that J.B. always carried with him. Mildred had joined them and was shocked when she heard Ryan state that she should travel in the vanguard of the attack.

"Why? I'm in no fit state to be trusted. God alone knows I would gladly go if I felt— Ryan, my reflexes are shot to shit and I'm slow."

"But you've got something much more important that that," the one-eyed man said calmly. "You're the only one among us who would be able to tell the disease cultures and the possible antidote in the Illuminated Ones' laboratory."

"You're right, of course," she stated. "But you could bring me in on the second wave, and I could lead the search when they've been driven back. I just don't trust myself in combat, the way I feel right now."

"We can't take the chance that they would destroy everything as they pulled back. Whatever else they may be, they aren't stupes. They'll know that one of the reasons we've come is so that we can try and snatch the antidote from them. Chances are that they'll try and get rid of it before we can get it. That's why you need to be in the front line. We have to increase our chances to the max."

Mildred bit her lip, thinking hard. She tried to tune out the world around her and listen to her body—to assess the degree to which the disease had taken hold of her so far, to see how much she was aching, to see how slow it had made her.

Finally, she nodded to herself and then at Ryan. Fixing the one-eyed man with a steely glare, she said, "Okay, You're right on the reasons. I figure I may still just about have it together enough to hold my own in a firefight. I'll do it."

Ryan clapped her on the back. "Good. I know you'll be okay, because you have to be."

"I wish I could share your confidence in me," Mildred replied.

"You'll be all right, Millie," J.B. said. His face was as impassive as usual, but Mildred could see in his eyes that he was worried about her. A worry tempered by the fact that they had no choice in the matter, the struggle had to go on. The Armorer looked away after their eyes met, and directed his attention to Ryan.

"Okay, so that's one of the uniforms taken," he said laconically, "and I'd guess that you take another—" he looked for the one-eyed man to affirm this "—so what do you want me to do?"

"I'll need you to take overall charge of the ground operation that follows the wag," Ryan told him.

"Won't Gloria be in charge of that?" J.B. asked.

Ryan shook his head. "It's best if she and Tammy come with us. They're good fighters, and they'll rally the Gate from the front when we get the sec doors open. They can then lead different branches of the attack from within, as I figure that we'll have to split into factions once we get down past the second level. If this redoubt is anything like the one they left, then it'll be even more of a maze than they are usually."

"That's four of the suits gone," the Armorer said. "Three to fill."

"Not me," Jak said suddenly, shaking his head as he looked at the uniforms. "Two things—feel shit to be in lead, and too small for these."

The albino lifted two of the suits. They were the smallest, and were obviously the ones that would be taken by the Gate queen and her second in command. The other suits were all much larger and would swamp the wiry Jak.

"Good point," Ryan agreed. "I figure you'd be better helping J.B. anyway. It'll take two of you to keep an eye on this amount of ground forces."

"Okay, three suits left, then," Mildred murmured. "Who else?"

J.B. broke in before Ryan had a chance to speak. "If I'm not going to be in the front line, then I reckon you should take Jon."

"Jon? Why?" Ryan queried. From the surprise in his voice, the name of the young Gate Armorer was the last that would have occurred to him.

"He'll be invaluable in assessing the weapons they're bringing up on us…and he knows those laser blasters better than any of us, me included. I tell you, Ryan, you'll need someone with the touch who can make a quick decision about which weapons will do the job. Especially if you need to get through sec doors without causing too much damage to the structure or the people in an enclosed space."

"Okay—he's in," Ryan agreed. He had known J.B. too long, and trusted his old friend's ability to judge another Armorer too well, to argue with the choice.

"So who gets the final two places, lover?" Krysty asked.

"I figure you and Dean," Ryan stated. "You're good fighters, I know you, and between you there should be no problem with any of the onboard comp equipment, or taking over driving the wag if either me or Mildred have to be away from the wheel. I don't know if Gloria, Tammy or Jon have ever driven a motorized wag, let alone one like this," he added. "We can't find ourselves fucked because they don't know how to put a wag into reverse!"

"That's a good point," Mildred noted, adding, "but mebbe you should put it a bit more delicately when you tell Gloria."

"Yeah, mebbe avoid fight before start," Jak said with a rare glint of humor in his cold, red eyes.

Ryan agreed. "Okay, but you get the point. So we now know where we are. If we get ourselves together and wait for Gloria and Tammy to—"

"We are, perhaps, not quite as ready as you think, friend Ryan," Doc piped up. He was leaning heavily on his cane, and looking down at the ground as he spoke, but there was a hardness in his tone that none of them had heard for a long while.

"What's up, Doc?" Mildred asked, feeling suddenly and inappropriately absurd at her turn of phrase.

Doc looked up at all of them, not answering her directly but sharing his gaze with all of the companions. "I am not content with the arrangements," he began. "In fact, I think it would be fair to say that I have an intense displeasure at the manner in which any claim I may have to be a part of the initial bridgehead has been summarily dismissed without my even getting a hearing."

"Doc, what are you taking about?" Dean asked, studying the old man's face. It was pale, spangled with a sheen of perspiration and the mane of hair that fell about his face only accentuated the darkening patches beneath his bloodshot eyes. He seemed more lined and pale than usual, and he resembled someone who had long since bought the farm but refused to lie down. Which, perhaps, was exactly what he was at this time. His eyes blazed into the companions, driven by some inner fire that was consuming him, even though his body was racked with agonies.

"I will tell you, my dear young Cawdor, to what I refer," Doc stated, the words coming low and harsh, seemingly forced from the back of his throat. "I refer, quite simply, to the manner in which I have been seemingly dismissed from the plans of your father, as though I were a feeble old man who no longer had any worth…or, indeed, any existence."

"Doc, what the fireblasted hell are you talking about?" Ryan asked, confusion written across his face.

"I refer, my dear boy," Doc snapped, "to the way in which everyone has been assigned their tasks, and yet I was not even spoken of, let alone considered for the bridgehead party."

"Doc, you've got the disease, and you've been hit hardest by it," Ryan said, trying to keep his voice level and calm. "You are the most vulnerable of all of us. You know that as well as I do, as well as any of us. And by keeping you back I was giving you a chance to fight while maximizing the range of fighting ability in the wag. Mildred is only with us because—"

"Because she is a doctor! I know that—I am not a fool," Doc raged, quivering with a barely suppressed anger that was quite unlike anything that any of the companions had seen from him before. "But I have a reason to be there, too."

Mildred studied Doc. He was touchy and oversensitive because of how sick he was, she was sure of that. Certainly, a fit and well Tanner would never over-react in such a manner. But she also knew Doc well enough to know that under the hysteria there was a reason struggling to be heard.

"So tell us the reason, Doc," she said quietly.

He turned to her. "Madam, my reason is quite plain enough to see for those who have eyes. These appalling specimens of a bloated and distorted humanity, these dregs of filth that chose to live underground and operate in such a cowardly and callous manner, they are the last embodiment and manifestation of the evil and depraved imagination that led to us living in such a wasteland...a wasteland that will be eradicated beyond any further recognition by their sordid little schemes. They are the last in a long line of those who 'felt they knew best,' and who would seek to impose their perverted logic upon the rest of us, an unsuspecting populace.

"I have been dragged from the bosom of my family and taken through an experience that no one should have to face, to be finally left here, in a time and world completely alien to me, that is about to be eradicated by their last, perverse turn of the cards.

"If anyone has the right—nay, the imperative—to be in the vanguard against these coldhearted scum, then it is myself. Who but I has the knowledge of these whitecoats and their distorted vision of the Totality Concept? Who else among us has the firsthand experience of their ways? Who else has met with them face-to-face as people, though it pains me to dignify such scum with the same genus as the rest of us. I am close to my own end, with the clock ticking away precious seconds. I have the right, dammit, to attempt an act of vengeance before that most grim of reapers finally casts his shadow upon me, and takes me to his lair.''

There was a silence following Doc's words. It was an emotion that was exacerbated by his current condition, but nonetheless one that had an undeniable validity.

Finally, Ryan spoke, choosing his words with care. ''Doc, none of us can ever understand what you've been through. If not for the things we've seen, then it would be easy to dismiss it as the ravings of an insane man, as it seemed when we first met. And you're right—if I was you, I'd want to go in with all blasters blazing and take revenge. But this isn't just about us. It isn't just about the Gate, or about Crossroads. It's about whether we're going to have a future. So however good your reasons, I can't let them get in the way of what I know is the right thing to do. And if you stop and think, you know that, too. Look at how ill you are, Doc....''

The old man said nothing, his body quivering with a barely suppressed rage. Tears of frustration and anger welled in his eyes.

''Dammit, the worst of it is that, no matter how much I would wish to deny it, I know in my heart that you are right.''

He turned on his heel and marched away from them.

''Want me follow him?'' Dean asked.

Ryan shook his head. ''Let him work it out. He'll be ready when we are.''

''Not blame him being cranky,'' Jak said, watching Doc disappear into a crowd of Crossroads dwellers. ''This ache drive mad...'' He winced, suggesting that the disease was making greater inroads into his body and mind.

"All the more reason to get it right," Ryan commented.

From out of the crowd, Gloria and Tammy strode over to the wag, the Gate queen going straight to Jak.

"Hey, honey, how you feeling?" she asked, hugging him. "Let's go get those fuckers."

She turned to Ryan. "We're ready, and the Crossroads guys are as ready as they'll ever be. So let's get the plan sorted."

Ryan told her first about the allocation of Illuminated uniforms, and the manner in which he wanted the attack to be led. He was concerned that the Gate queen would be unhappy at leaving her people in the charge of J.B. and Jak while she, her second in command and her Armorer all traveled on ahead. But Gloria had an instinctive tactical sense, and could see Ryan's reasoning.

"That's fine. My girls like Jak and J.B., and they trust them as if they were of us. We trust all of you as if you were of us."

"That's good. We need that complete trust if this is going to work," Ryan said. "So now we need to plot a course that will take us all close to the redoubt without being spotted by sec patrols or cameras."

Gloria chewed on her bottom lip as she considered this. Finally, she said, "As to patrols, we know from watching them that they don't come out that often. I guess they may send some out to try and scout for this wag," she said, slapping the side of the wag they were to use as a Trojan horse, "but I don't reckon they're that brave. We can send scouts on ahead to report back, as we always do. Give them enough advance and there's no reason why the wag should be spotted anywhere near the rest of us. Sure as shit easy enough to hide ourselves."

"What about cameras around the redoubt?" Krysty asked Gloria and Ryan.

It was Tammy who interjected. "We need to find a route that'll keep us close to the wag and give us cover. Wait…"

The Gate warrior fell to her knees and began to trace a semicircle in the dust, marking a point within. "That's the hill where the redoubt is, yeah?" she said. Then, drawing a small circle some way away, she added, "And that's where we are now, right?"

"Agreed," Ryan murmured. "So it's the problem of how we get from there to there—" he indicated the two points "—without running the risk of being spotted."

"Right," Tammy said. "Well, I've been on a lot of recce patrols around there, and I reckon there is a way of using the cover we've got."

And as the companions and Gloria watched, Tammy sketched in the wooded area where the Gate had originally camped, the hill where Mildred had encountered the landslide and the crops of scrub and trees that lay between.

"If we use the outriders to make sure we aren't spotted along the way, then we can use the cover until we reach this point," she said decisively, indicating a line of scrub and sparse woodland that ran almost parallel to the slope of the hill where the redoubt entrance was located. "From here, the wag can carry on down to the redoubt alone, and get let in—that way, we can use this cover and the darkness to remain hidden. No way will any cameras pick us up in the dark and at that distance."

Ryan looked at the crudely drawn diagram in the dust. "Still some distance from the entrance, though. When we get the sec door open, we won't be able to hold them long unaided if we're heavily outnumbered. And if we're wiped out and the door is closed again, then the whole mission is fucked. You'll have to be able to move everyone pretty damn quick," he said to J.B.

"I figure me, Jak and Doc could do it," the Armorer stated. "And I'm pretty sure that the Gate can." He cast a quizzical glance at Tammy and Gloria.

"Honey, you don't even have to ask," the Gate queen said with a smile. "To get a crack at those scumfuckers, my girls would crawl over broken glass and walk on fire. A few hundred yards of flat land sure ain't gonna stop them."

"That's what I was hoping to hear." J.B. grinned. "I figure that as soon as the sec door starts to rise, we just go hell for leather. The light will give us an early warning for when it's starting to go up, leaking out of the redoubt. And they'll be too busy with you guys to try and stop us," he added.

"That's the idea, sweets," Gloria agreed. "So are we ready to move out?"

"Soon as we get these damn suits on, and your people are up to speed," Ryan answered.

With the briefest of nods, Gloria and Tammy went off to give the Gate and the Crossroads dwellers their final briefing, including handing over the chain of command to J.B., Jak and Doc.

While Ryan, Mildred, Krysty and Dean struggled into the uniforms of the chilled Illuminated Ones, J.B. and Jak went in search of Doc. They found him seated on the porch of a house, only a few hundred yards from the main drag.

"Good evening to you, gentlemen," Doc said as they approached. "I fear I must apologize for being a cretin."

"I reckon I'd take that apology if I knew what the fuck you meant," J.B. replied, "but right now I'm just glad we've found you." The Armorer briefly relayed the final plan of action to Doc, ending, "I know you feel like shit from this pox, but me and Jak need you if we're gonna pull all these people together."

Doc rose to his feet, much more composed than when last they had seen him. "Gentlemen," he said slowly, "I allowed my rage and frustration to overtake me. I am in no fit state to be in the vanguard of an attack, but if you think for one moment that I shall be found wanting in my moment of trial, then you are very sorely mistaken. Lead on, my dear John Barrymore. If I do not help attain a cure, I shall at least buy the farm with my own coin."

"That mean yes?" Jak asked J.B.

"Resoundingly," Doc replied.

The three companions returned to the center of the ville to find Tammy and Gloria squeezing themselves into the clinging material of the Illuminated uniforms. It was hard to get the suits to fit, as they were made of a stretchy material, and so had to be molded to the body in a way that clothes usually weren't, particularly for the Gate women and Jon, who hardly wore any clothes at all. In fact, the only one to slide into the uniform with ease was Mildred, who had worn such types of uniform in her predark sporting days.

"Are we ready?" J.B. asked.

Cursing the uniform, Gloria half turned to him.

"Sure thing, sweets. Everyone knows the plan, knows who's in charge. The only thing stopping us now is these motherfucking clothes," she added, trying to get her arm into the material without it twisting and becoming constricting.

J.B., Jak and Doc moved to join the convoy that would follow the Illuminated wag, mounting the horse-drawn wags that would carry the armory and some of the Crossroads dwellers. The Gate warriors would either ride the back of the wags, go on foot or, in the case of the outriders, were mounted on swifter steeds.

The fake Illuminated Ones donned their helmets, securing them so that they lost all identity. Seeing them standing there, about to embark in the wag, it seemed to J.B. that his friends no longer existed. The only giveaways were the scorch and burn marks, and subsequent holes, that scored the uniforms. Hopefully, when they entered the redoubt and disembarked from the wag, these could be put down to superficial injury just long enough for the vanguard to take the initiative.

Without a word—after all, speech would be almost impossible from behind the dark visors of the helmets—the advance war party got into the wag, the door closing behind them and sealing them off from the outside world. The engine of the wag was fired up, and the vehicle began to move slowly forward, turning so that it could head in the right direction. Directed by J.B., the wags and horses of the following war party parted to enable the wag to pass through unimpeded, and lead the way. As soon as it has passed through, the convoy closed behind it.

As the war party began to move, J.B. suddenly became aware of someone calling his name. Looking around, he could see that Baron Robertson was coming from his dwelling. He looked pale and drawn, and was coughing, hawking onto the ground as he walked across.

"We're moving off," J.B. shouted, stating the obvious so that the baron could see that he could not wait.

"Good," the baron said simply. "You've got the best we can give you, and I just wanted to wish you luck."

"Certainly need that—always helps," the Armorer replied.

"Look, it's too late for my daughter, and I reckon mebbe for me, as well," Robertson said, walking beside the slow-moving wag and gasping for breath as he tried to talk and keep up. "Look..." He pulled open his shirt and showed the Armorer a network of pox and scabs that hadn't yet reached his face.

"That's tough," J.B. said. "Mebbe we can get back in time."

"Not for me," Robertson cut in. "Weird thing is I don't give a shit about me. Never given a shit for anything, really. Tell you what, though—I look at the way this ville has been ripped up, at the amount of people that have bought the farm, and are sick and suffering, and suddenly I find that I do care somehow. I want those coldheart bastards to suffer, and I want my people to get better. So give the fuckers hell—you got our best, 'cause we won't need it if you don't come back."

"We'll just see," he said dryly. "Now we've really got to move."

Aware that the wag was starting to pick up speed, J.B. twitched the reins on the horses drawing the wag, and it began to pick up speed to match, leaving the baron gasping for breath as it pulled away from him.

Leaving the main drag behind, the motorized wag and the convoy behind began to pick up the pace, heading down the blacktop until it could turn for cover and head toward the redoubt. As the speed increased, the outriders let rip with shrieks that ripped across the quiet of the night sky, spurring their horses to a gallop as they headed off to recce the territory ahead.

The chase was on.

Chapter Ten

It was as the Illuminated wag turned off the blacktop road and started to roll across the fields toward the beginnings of the wooded areas that inspiration struck Dean. The younger Cawdor had been keyed up, like the others in the wag, and while the others had made little attempt to alleviate their boredom, he had been moved to tinker with the section of burned-out comp that was near his seat.

At first, they had tried to keep the Illuminated helmets in place, to acclimatize themselves to the constriction so that it wouldn't prove a handicap when they had to assume their disguise entering the redoubt, and wouldn't slow them unnecessarily when it came to a firefight. But the heavy metal shells and the Plexiglas visors were too irritating to the wag's inhabitants to be endured for long.

Gloria removed hers first, shaking loose her long, flowing red hair, and scratching her itching scalp.

"Gaia, I don't know how they put up with that," she spit.

"I'll go for that," Ryan agreed, taking his hands off the wheel long enough to remove the encumbrance before correcting the wag's course once more. "If I kept that on for the entire journey, I'd be too triple crazed to think straight in a firefight anyway."

They continued, the tension of imminent battle putting paid to all conversation. All would be glad when the journey was over, and the battle about to begin. Each fighter was wrapped in his or her own private world: Mildred concerned with the virus; Gloria and Tammy thinking about the Gate, following close behind; Krysty concerned with the health of her friends; Jon, the first Gate male to really take part in such an action, wondering if he was up to the challenge ahead—Ryan concerned with whether his plan would work; and Dean...

The comp near him was the communication and directional system. He was seated where the Illuminated One who operated the system would work, the swiveling seat turning to face the now-dead control panel and screens.

To alleviate the tedium of the journey, and so as not to dwell on the firefight ahead, Dean began to take an interest in the comp. Losing himself in the old tech, he began to tinker with the panel. Beneath the desktop arrangement of the comp was a maintenance panel inset into the desktop itself, lying flush. Running his fingers along the smooth metal, Dean found a catch that enabled him to spring the panel open. Sliding off his seat so that he was kneeling on the floor and was therefore able to see the underneath of the desktop, he pulled down a series of fiber-optic cables that connected the dead system with the electrical supply cable that had been shot out beneath the wag during the earlier conflagration.

Tammy, noticing what he was doing, came over and knelt beside him.

"What are you doing, sweets?" she asked him.

Ignoring the sudden rush of feeling as she referred

to him thus—and that made him almost forget what he actually had been about to do—Dean concentrated on the cables and pulled at the loosest. A long stream of cable came out from beneath the desk until it spooled on the floor around them, ending with a burned-out and severed end.

"See this?" he asked her. "This is the cable that powered up the comp and the radio. It got shot out when the wag was in Crossroads. But I reckon that, if I reroute the emergency into here, then mebbe we can get the comp working again."

Tammy gave him an askew glare. "Okay. And why would you want to do that?"

Dean shrugged. "'Cause I'm bored, and it'll take my mind off things. That's all."

Tammy smiled. "Good a reason as any, I guess."

Then, while the Gate warrior watched, Dean took one of the other cables, which he had traced by feel to be running toward the front of the wag, and pulled at it.

"Watch you don't blow the wag's backup power," Krysty said with some concern as she watched from the front of the wag. "We don't want to get stranded while you have to patch up your own mistakes."

Dean grinned ruefully. "I wouldn't risk it if I thought it might do that. This cable'll just allow me to tap into the power, it won't make the engine cut out. I figure they'd have more than one outlet from the backup as a kind of fail-safe."

"Yeah, remind me of that if Ryan has to stop and reroute it all again because of you," Krysty replied, wincing as Dean tugged and snapped the cable, a shorter length of it coming out from beneath the desk, so that there were now two spools of cable around him and Tammy.

"Tammy, you take this for a moment and keep it out of my way," Dean requested, handing her the shorter length. Then, while the woman was holding the cable aloft, he took the useless, burned-out cable and pulled it loose from the desk. Discarding the long loop of redundant fiber optic, he took the cable from Tammy's hand and stripped the covering back, so that the loose strands of fiber optic sprayed out in a fine mist of substance around his hand. Selecting some of the ends, he delved beneath the desk and attempted to connect them to the junction from which he had ripped the useless cable.

"This'll either work or give me something to think about," he muttered as he tried to make the two pieces connect.

"Shit, it's actually working!" Gloria said as the desktop comp spluttered twice, the lights flaring up briefly before dying away once more.

"Do we actually want it to work?" Mildred asked Ryan, who so far had said nothing, concentrating on the dark terrain ahead, barely lit by the wag's headlights, one of which had been shot out, the other of which was only on the emergency power supply.

"Why not?" the one-eyed man queried.

"Because if the redoubt has been trying to contact the wag, won't they think it a little suspicious if it suddenly springs back into life when it's headed toward them. Won't they want to ask questions about what happened, and why it's been silent for so long?"

"Not necessarily. They may just be glad to be back in touch. They may assume that their own people have just done exactly what Dean's doing—sorting it out when they're safe away from the ville. And anyway, even if they can contact us, will they know it's up and running again unless we answer? We're not being forced to respond, after all.''

"No, that's true enough," Mildred pondered. "But what if there's an automatic tracker that comes to life when the comp is booted up? That'll betray us, sure as shit."

Ryan furrowed his brow, considering this. Finally, he said, "Assuming that it does come up functional, and assuming that they contact us, we can use it to our advantage. A confused message, saying something garbled about injuries and damage, and they'll be prepared to receive a group of incoming injured, rather than an unknown quantity."

Krysty interjected, "Okay, lover, but how the hell are we supposed to disguise our voices?"

Ryan chuckled. "Okay, okay, but let's just see if it actually works first."

At that point, it didn't seem likely. After its brief flowering, the comp had stayed dead while Dean groped under the desktop in an effort to get it going.

He was, possibly, more surprised than anyone else when the comp suddenly spluttered back to life, beeping as the safety scan began to run. Even more so when a disembodied voice came from the radio.

"Evan, what the hell are you guys doing still out there! I thought your beacon flashed a few minutes back. You're still alive? Respond, dammit, respond.''

THE CARAVAN OF horse-drawn wags that made up the Gate and Crossroads war party followed the wag as it progressed down the blacktop, then followed it with an equal ease as it left the road and traveled across the fields, using a turnoff to access the field areas and avoid the treacherous ditches that ran alongside the blacktop itself.

"Been easy so far," Cat said to J.B. as they sat at the front of the armory wag.

"Make the most of it," the Armorer replied quietly. "It sure ain't gonna be that way for long."

"I know that. Think I'm stupe or something?"

The Armorer looked at her, taking in the indignant note in her voice, and opted to refrain from reply.

"Oh, shut up, you asshole," Cat said huffily, turning away.

"I didn't say anything," J.B. teased. Like the Gate warrior, he was reveling in the laid-back atmosphere that seemed to permeate the caravan. There would be enough tension later, without adding to it at this early stage.

On the wags behind, Crossroads volunteers for the war party were getting to know those they would fight alongside, and the prospect of making new acquaintances had lightened the grim atmosphere that had permeated the ville. The fact that most of the Crossroads fighters were men, and they lusted after the lithe Gate warriors, was certainly a help.

"Make merry while you can, children," Doc murmured to himself as he watched from another wag. "The real work will come soon enough."

The Illuminated wag passed the hill, and was soon at the edge of the wood. From here it would take less than an hour to reach the redoubt using the route mapped by the Gate. It would be hard for the motorized wag to go this route—through the woodland it-self—so it had been arranged for the wag to drive around, slowing to give the Gate and Crossroads fighters enough time to make their way on foot through the woods.

The last thing J.B., or anyone, expected was for the wag to come to a complete halt.

"Dark night, what the fuck could have gone wrong already?" the Armorer breathed.

"SOMEBODY HAD BETTER SAY something," Mildred remarked as the disembodied voice on the radio spoke again, requesting information on the condition of the wag crew.

"They'll know it's not the real crew as soon as someone does speak, though," Tammy said.

Dean shook his head. "Not necessarily. Hang on…"

The younger Cawdor found the transmitter-receiver mike and speaker on the comp desk, and rapidly unscrewed the cover. Underneath were the wires, boards and chips that controlled the mike. Loosening a connection, Dean caused the reception to go slightly awry, so that the urgent voice was no longer clear, but distorted. He then tapped the board to which the wire was attached, causing the transmission to cut in and out.

"Should work," he muttered before switching the radio to transmit and speaking in a louder, strained voice, as though he were in pain. "Problems with the electrics…hard to get away…some injured…"

He winked at Tammy as he switched off the transmission.

"Evan? That you, son? You sound like shit... Look, save the explanations till you're back. You're going a weird course, boy. What's happening out there? Has the direction finder been off-line, as well?"

Dean switched back to transmit and adopted his sore-throat voice. "All off...just managed to get back online...electrics shot out, had to reroute power..."

"That's a real award-winning performance you're giving," Mildred remarked as Dean switched back to receiver. Any other comments were cut off by another interjection from the receiver.

"Evan, listen to me. Bear north-northeast, and you'll be fine. I don't know what visibility's like right now, but it's sunup in about an hour, so if you haven't sorted out your direction by then, we'll send a wag to collect you."

"Fireblast and fuck it," Ryan swore. "That's the last thing we need—an escort that'll realize we're not the real thing before we get into the redoubt."

"But they won't be sending anyone out until sunrise, and we were planning to mount the raid before then, Ryan," Gloria said. "So what's the problem?"

"The problem is that we no longer have any slack, and we've really got to move. We also need to let J.B. and Jak know what's going on, so they can spread the word in case the wag comes out to find us before we put the plan into action. We've got to stop soon, before we part company with them."

"Better do it soon, then," Krysty commented, taking a look out of the armaglass windshield at the terrain ahead. "We'll be past the woods soon, and they'll be in there."

"Okay," Ryan said, pulling up the wag. "Let's hope they haven't already gone off on another path."

AS THE WAG HALTED, and J.B. dismounted from his own wag, the outrider patrol came back to report.

"Why's everyone stopped now?" Dette asked, pulling her horse around to trot alongside J.B. as he headed for the Illuminated wag.

"That's just what I'm hoping to find out," he replied. "Stick around and we might both learn something."

"Make that three," Jak muttered as he sidled up to them, even in a nonthreatening situation able to move with an uncanny invisibility.

As they approached the Illuminated wag, the back opened and Ryan climbed out. In a few brief words he filled them in on recent events. When he had finished, J.B. shot a glance toward the horizon.

"If they really do leave it till sunrise, then we can just about do it. You head off now, and me and Jak will get the Gate and the others to move it some. Keep up your current speed and head straight for the redoubt. We'll be behind you. And another thing, when you head for the entrance keep to the track."

"Why?" Ryan questioned.

J.B. shrugged. "Dunno, just a feeling. I could be wrong, but what if the area around the track is booby-trapped?"

Ryan pondered this for a second. "Could be. That would explain why they never really send out sec patrols, even though they must've been aware that the Gate were close by."

He turned to Dette. "Did any of your recce riders ever go near the entrance?"

"Hell, no," the brown-skinned warrior replied. "We're not that stupe. We always stayed up around the back or took the cover that there was."

Ryan nodded. "Yeah, we can't be sure, then."

J.D. agreed. "You take the track, and we'll work a pincer movement to try and come round the edges of the hill. Still gonna be a problem getting that far, but what the hell." He shrugged, acknowledging that it was a necessary risk.

"Okay, you spread the word, and I'll get the wag into position," Ryan said decisively. "See you on the inside of the redoubt."

"Count on it," J.B. answered.

DETTE TOLD THE OUTRIDERS about the amendment in the plan, and they rode off to scout the area for the war party, which was now dismounting the horse-drawn wags and readying themselves for battle. There was a change in the atmosphere. A tension crept into the party that spoke of the danger to come. There was also a sense of camaraderie that had been fostered by the first stage of the journey, and as J.B., Jak and Doc—who had been rapidly informed of the changes by the Armorer—moved amongst the war party, bringing them up to speed, they were aware of the feeling of determination that had spread among the warriors.

The forest became alive with the movement of the war party as it moved over the tangled roots and rich soil, any light filtering through from the moon above drastically reduced by the canopy of foliage overhead from the stunted dwarf elms. The small mammals that inhabited the forest and roamed it by day hid from the imminent danger as the Gate skipped over the obstacles with ease, the Crossroads dwellers following a little less surefooted. The outriders scouted the far edge of the woods, where it emerged onto the open ground leading to the hill and the ingress in its side where the entrance to the redoubt lay.

J.B. and Jak led, with different sections of Gate following varying routes through the wood that would enable them to flow smoothly, without engendering a jam of warriors in some of the narrowing paths. Their progress was rapid, and the leaders of each faction soon reached the edge of the woods, where they were joined by the outriders who were lurking just within cover.

"All clear everywhere," Dette reported. "The motor wag is on its own out there."

J.B. chewed at his lip. "Good. We wait till it starts up the trail, then move each section to cover there and there—" he indicated small crops of shrub and tree that took an arcing path around the lower slope of the hill "—so that we're spread along as near as possible, still in cover, and we avoid the open area. When the wag gets to the redoubt, we wait until it's in, then prepare to move as soon as it starts to open again."

"What if it doesn't?" Dette asked.

He shrugged. "We think about that when it happens, 'cause that'll just be a full-frontal assault. No other options."

The sound of the Illuminated wag approaching the track leading up to the redoubt could be heard.

"Here comes," Jak said. "Go, yeah?"

J.B. agreed, and the group leaders returned to their

warriors, relaying the Armorer's instructions and taking their people forward to the farthest reaches of available cover.

As the wag rumbled up the path toward the redoubt, the sky began to lighten where the morning sun began to rise above the horizon. The groups of warriors, spread out along the side of the hill in their makeshift cover, settled to wait. There was nothing more they could do right now.

The next move was firmly in the hands of the seven warriors in the wag that now reached the entrance to the Illuminated Ones' redoubt base.

Chapter Eleven

Inside the wag, Ryan turned to his fellow warriors.

"Better cover up now. We know what to do if we have to be the chilled ones?"

"Keep as quiet as possible, and keep these damn helmets on," Mildred muttered with disgust in her voice, adding, "And I'd better hope that they don't look at the rips in this suit too closely. There weren't any black sec among the chilled."

"We'll just try not to give them time to look," Krysty said with a determined manner.

For a second, all the inhabitants of the wag took a last look at their companions before the large black helmets, with their impenetrable tinted visors, were put in place. A last look to confirm who they were, before their identities were erased and replaced by the threatening blandness of the visors.

As they became Illuminated Ones, the wag radio crackled into life again.

"I'll be damned. You actually managed to find your way home before sunup—and without the comp," came the distorted voice that had spoken once before. Ryan frowned as he heard it. Was there a subtle difference in the tone of that voice? He glanced around unthinkingly to check with Krysty, but found himself staring at the empty visage of a black visor.

Damn and fireblast. He'd have to trust his own instincts, which were screaming at him to be triple red right now, and hope that the others would catch the inflection of the voice.

Because—and he didn't know how—something seemed to have gone wrong.

There was no more time for reflection, or for any kind of consultation, as the outer sec door began to open. The light from inside the redoubt—a fluorescent strip that was garish in the outer, predawn atmosphere—spread across the wag and the surrounding ground. Ryan had to squint as the light penetrated the windshield of the wag, and for a moment he was unable to see clearly into the tunnel of the redoubt. He blinked quickly, willing himself to be able to see into the tunnel.

The sec door opened to its full extent, and the light from within lit the area, extending to the edges of the cover where the Gate and Crossroads warriors waited. J.B. cursed the extent of the light, as he was sure that there would be sec cameras scanning the immediate area, and the light would make them more visible than he would have wished. But the Gate were experts at making the most of any cover given, and as he glanced around, he felt sure that their security had been maintained.

In the wag, Ryan's eyes adjusted to the light, and he could see that the corridor ahead was clear. There was no welcoming party, hostile or otherwise, and the empty corridor extended for a couple of hundred yards before coming to a close at the next set of sec doors.

Thinking rapidly, Ryan considered it likely that this would be a regular precaution: to not open up the rest of the base until the outer doors had been secured. But something still didn't seem right. He was distracted by a tap on his arm and turned to face Dean, who was gesturing toward the radio speaker.

Ryan listened. The distorted voice was hard to understand, even though the earpieces on the helmets did allow outside sound to filter through, amplifying it to allow for the layer of metal and insulation between the hearer and the outside world. The problem was, they seemed to be individually adjustable, and there hadn't been enough time to set the level as each of the companions in the wag would have wished. Ryan had to strain to hear.

"Evan? What the hell is wrong with you people? Am I supposed to keep the doors open all damn day? Get your asses in here!"

Unable to voice his feelings or canvas opinion, Ryan swore softly and put the wag into gear and advanced into the corridor of the redoubt.

STILL OUTSIDE, watching the wag enter and the outer sec door close, bringing the darkness of predawn down upon them once more, Yardie turned in his hiding place to face Doc and Nita, who were waiting with him.

"Shit, what do we do now?" he asked.

"We wait until they get the door up again, and then we fight," the blond Gate warrior replied.

"But what if they don't?" the fat Crossroads sec chief asked.

Doc smiled slowly and without humor. "Then, my dear sir, we have a conundrum to which we have to find a solution within a very small time frame."

"Eh?" An uncomprehending Yardie looked pleadingly at Nita.

"I think he means we have to move triple fast and work it out as we go along," the blonde replied.

"Succinctly put, my dear," Doc said with serenity. "Now let us keep watch, so that we may not miss any opportunity."

PULLING UP just inside the main sec door, Ryan kept the engine ticking over and waited. He felt the need to keep the wag near the main sec door so that one of them would be able to key in the sec-door code and open it up as quickly as possible. He also had a knot of tension in the pit of his stomach that told him not to get too close to the menacing blankness of the next sec door. He had a feeling that his battle plan was about to throw a loop. His instincts were telling him that the Illuminated Ones had tumbled to their true identity, though he couldn't work out quite how they had given themselves away.

The seconds crawled past with an agonizing slowness, the tension in the wag making it seem all the more oppressive. Cursing to himself again, louder this time so that it could be heard—albeit muffled—by the others, Ryan pulled off the metal and Plexiglas that had been stifling him.

"Fireblast, that feels better!" he exclaimed.

"Something's wrong, right?" Krysty asked as she removed her helmet, shaking loose red, sentient hair that refused to unfurl and uncoil. It was obvious that her mutie sense had picked up some danger, and it only confirmed Ryan's own suspicions.

"Reckon so," the one-eyed man replied. "Why aren't they here to greet us, if we're the long-lost wag crew?"

"Hot pipe, it's my fault," Dean said bitterly. "If I

hadn't got the radio going again they wouldn't have had the chance to get in contact, and they wouldn't have figured out that we weren't the real deal.''

Ryan shook his head. ''No, I figure that mebbe that didn't matter too much. Without the radio, they still could have been suspicious about us. Blaming yourself is just going to waste time and energy. We're here, we need to get the sec door open again and we need to cover our backs while we do it.''

''One thing,'' Tammy said in a small voice. ''Even if we get the sec door open again, what's to stop them shutting it like they did when we came in?''

''She's got a point,'' Mildred said. ''If they're using a remote system, we need to keep the door up once it's up.''

Ryan turned to Dean. ''Would a remote system and the manual keypad be on the same circuit?''

The younger Cawdor, who had learned some pre-dark electronics at the Brody school, pondered this for a brief moment. ''Mebbe, mebbe not. Even if it isn't, you shoot enough of a charge into the hardware and you'll blow out all the circuits. Get it up, then use the laser blaster on the keypad and the resulting charge should short out every piece of fiber optic or wiring in the system.''

Ryan nodded. ''Okay, so we know what to do when the door is up. Let's get to raising it.''

''Wait! What the fuck are they doing now?'' Gloria asked, staying the one-eyed man with a hand on his arm.

While he had been speaking, Ryan had been facing away from the windshield, with the other occupants of the wag watching him. Only the Gate queen had been watching through the windshield, keeping her eyes on the sec door that lay a couple of hundred yards from them.

At her words and her touch, Ryan swung around, bending low over the dash to get as wide an angle as possible on the area in front of them.

The sec door was beginning to rise. For the first couple of inches, there was little that could be seen through the narrow gap that made any sense. But as the door rose higher, the one-eyed man was able to discern several pairs of legs, and also the wheels and undercarriage of what seemed to be a small wag...not a personnel carrier of any sort, but rather some sort of attack wag, possibly heavily armed and wheeled for ease of transportation.

It was not a sight that boded well.

"Shit, we've got real problems," he said quietly. "It looks like they're bringing up some heavy hardware."

"And we're sitting targets in here," Gloria added. "Guess it's time to check our own hardware."

"You got that right," Ryan agreed as he checked the laser blaster, and also his SIG-Sauer and Steyr, which had been sitting on the floor of the wag. All those in the Illuminated uniforms had brought their own blasters with them, keeping them in the wag. The original plan had been to exit the wag with the laser blasters and with the helmets in place, apparently the returning Illuminated crew. Only when they had opened the sec door and begun to establish the bridgehead in the redoubt would they collect their own blasters, with which they felt much more comfortable in battle. But now, if they were going to stand any chance and come out fighting, then the only thing that they could do was to load up with their own trusted weapons and hit the ground firing.

It was as they were checking their own blasters that the voice came to them, blaring and distorted over a loudspeaker from beyond the opening inner sec door.

"Whoever you are, come out without your weapons and you won't be harmed. We have no wish to chill you, only to expel you from our base."

"Yeah, right," Mildred muttered, "maybe you do, but only when you've dosed us with your foul pox so that we can spread it."

"I'd rather go out fighting than let them do that," Tammy agreed. "They've tried that shit on us already."

Ryan looked at the warriors gathered around him. His face was set and grim. Were they ready? He turned to look out of the windshield at what they would encounter. The inner sec door was now almost fully raised, and he could see that there were twelve Illuminated soldiers lined up against them, with the center of the corridor taken up by a motorized blaster that was on wheels because of its sheer size. Like a laser cannon, it stood imposingly dead center, manned by two Illuminated Ones, making a total of fourteen adversaries that the companions on the wag were facing.

Ryan was aware of a presence at his side and inclined his head to see that he had been joined by Jon. The young Armorer was appraising the laser cannon, and although he had been silent up to this point, he now felt on territory where he had a right to comment.

"See that giant bastard?" he asked rhetorically. "If that has power in relation to size like these—" he patted the laser blaster he was holding "—then we are in deep shit if we stay in here."

"Even with the strength this wag has?" Ryan queried.

Jon nodded curtly. "I've tried and tested these fuckers to see what they can do, and if that works on the same principle, with it being that size, it'll either cut through us like a panga through mud, or it'll heat the metal so much that we'll fry in here."

"Not much of a fireblasted option either way," Ryan gritted. "There's only one thing that we can do."

"Sweets, I think we've all gathered that," Gloria said. There was a resignation in her tone that was belied by the flush on her cheeks as she turned and kicked open the back of the wag. "When there's no chance, honey, then there's nothing to lose," she yelled as she jumped out of the back of the wag and dived for cover behind one of the reinforced concrete buttresses that held up the roof of the redoubt. They were positioned every few yards, and had often been of use as cover in a firefight.

Never more so than now. The Gate queen was in position before the Illuminated Ones had a chance to register her action, and she moved from cover long enough to loose off a couple of laser blasts in their direction.

There was no time for her to take aim, but the Illuminated soldiers were so densely clustered on either side of the laser cannon that it was inevitable that a double blast in the general area would do some damage. One soldier was chilled as he was taken unaware by a blast that hit him directly in the middle of the chest, burning a hole in his uniform and flesh that caused a plume of smoke to rise from him as he fell, his scream high and anguished. Inside the redoubt, although still in the one-piece uniforms, the Illuminated soldiers were without the protective helmets they wore on the outside, and so it was easier to see which were male and which female.

It was a woman who escaped a little more lightly with the second burst of fire. Realizing that Gloria's aim was restricted, and therefore more likely to be in the same area each time, the other Illuminated Ones who were clustered on her side of the laser cannon began to seek cover, either falling flat or running to dive behind a concrete pillar. It was while attempting to find this cover that the Illuminated woman was injured. Tall and heavily built, with long blond hair that was tied back in a tight ponytail, she was slightly slower than her companions, and as she dived for the cover of the concrete, she twisted awkwardly in the air. Although that didn't save her from great pain and injury, it did possibly save her life, as Gloria's second laser blast cut through the air and scorched across the woman's shoulder as she twisted. If her passage had remained straight, it would have burned through her ribs and barbecued her internal organs. As it was, her scream and subsequent sobs as she hit the floor told of an injury that was painful, but not fatal.

Gloria's covering fire was the cue that Ryan needed to rally his troops.

"Tammy, other side, yeah?" he yelled. The Gate number two assented and dived out of the back of the wag, throwing herself in the opposite direction to her queen so that she could take the other flank of the Illuminated Ones. She rolled and came up firing indiscriminately, three sharp bursts that went over the heads of the soldiers as they took cover, but nonetheless prevented them from firing on her as she gained cover.

The Illuminated soldiers on the laser cannon directed the nozzle toward the wag and let loose a burst of laser fire. The air seemed to become dry and charged as the cannon prepared to let loose, and in that fraction of a second Gloria yelled, "Jump!"

In the interior of the wag, none of those left needed to be told that an exit was imperative.

"Go! Go!" Ryan yelled, pushing toward the rear of the wag.

Mildred and Dean were nearest the rear. The young Cawdor leaped out, landing on the run, keeping to his feet and turning to fire a covering charge from the laser blaster as he sought cover. It diverted fire from Illuminated soldiers who were aiming at himself and Mildred—they pulled the shots upward as they dived to avoid Dean's blast, and their charges hit the ceiling, bringing down a layer of concrete dust and plaster on Mildred, who wasn't so fortunate as she left the wag. Her reflexes and balance upset and slowed by the onset of the disease, she landed awkwardly, stumbling and falling on her side, her elbow twisting inward to knock the breath from her. She seemed to have no energy as she tried to rise to her feet, everything seeming to happen about her in slow motion.

She was vaguely aware of the strong hand that gripped her upper arm, hauling her up and flinging her against the wall behind Tammy. Panting heavily, Mildred focused on Krysty, who had followed her out of the wag and had grabbed at her as she passed by.

"Thanks," Mildred gasped. "Told you I wasn't up to it."

"I'll cover you. You're the only one who can find

the antidote,'' Krysty replied, snapping off a couple of bursts at the Illuminated Ones, who were now also safely in cover.

Jon followed Krysty and dived to the other side, coming up behind Dean and Gloria, firing as he arrived in cover.

Which only left Ryan. The one-eyed man was last out, and was reaching the rear of the wag when the air ceased to crackle and hum, and the brilliant laser burst of the cannon was loosed on the wag, the air split by a high-pitched whine and the singing of over-heated metal as the charge hit the wag full-on.

''Holy shit—look at it!'' Mildred yelled at no one in particular, shocked at the way the charge affected the wag. Jon had been right in his supposition that the laser charge would either split the wag in two or cause it to act as some kind of superconductor, heated beyond belief by the charge that coursed through and across the alloy shell of the vehicle. The metal glowed red then white, the heat making the air around them shimmer, causing minute blistering on any exposed flesh on the arms, legs and torso, and making their faces red and burned, singeing hair.

''Ryan!'' Krysty yelled, unable to tear her eyes away from the sight, even though her eyeballs felt as though they were dried out by the suddenly hot air around her.

For a fraction of a second, in the brightness of the glowing wag, it seemed as though there was no way that the one-eyed man could have escaped. But only for a fraction of a second.

As the charge was loosed from the wag, Ryan was but two steps away from diving out of the wag and hitting the concrete floor at the rear. His intent, knowing that the others were safely out and covering their positions, was to head directly for the outer redoubt door, hit the code and then short-circuit the system once the door was fully raised. He knew that it would leave him exposed while he was at the sec-door panel, but figured that the others could cover him, and any stray fire that hit him would be down to fate.

Fate had something a little more convoluted in store for him. As the charge hit the wag, he was preparing to throw himself out of the back, his muscles tensed to make the leap. He was suddenly aware of a cone of silence that enveloped him, as though he were at the eye of a storm. He felt an immense heat grow rapidly, the metal under his feet and around him seeming to expand as time itself seemed to slow. The inside of the wag glowed red through to white, spreading along the length of the wag interior, and as his last footfall hit the floor of the wag, it seemed that his sole and heel burned red-hot and painfully through his heavy combat boot. The expansion of air, like the metal, that had spread along from the front of the wag hit him as he started to leap, carrying him out of the back of the wag as though a giant hand had taken him and shoved hard in the small of his back, propelling him in a manner that left him with no control over his final destination.

The heat and force drove the air from his body, his lungs sucking painfully for what they could extract from the superheated air surrounding him. He shot across the concrete, landing heavily and coming up with a sickening thud against the door of the redoubt, the concrete and metal somehow strangely soothing to his burned and heat-sensitive flesh. His ribs cracked and strained at the impact, having no air to drive out, but not allowing any more to enter.

Such had been the momentary brilliance of the blinding light that none of his companions had seen him leave the wag and land so badly. But neither, also, had the Illuminated Ones who opposed them.

Expecting a hail of fire to hit his exposed position at any moment, Ryan fought against his own body to try to pull himself to his feet. His skin was hypersensitive and his muscles ached. His ribs protested and his knees refused to unbuckle, but still he persisted. There was no fire directed toward him, and he had to use every last moment he had to try to get the door open.

There was no fire for the simple reason that the Illuminated Ones were as blinded by the laser cannon fire as their opponents. Until their eyes had adjusted to the sudden diminution of light, there was no way that they could see the wag as it went rapidly back from white to red to black, let alone see Ryan struggling to his feet and moving toward the sec-door panel.

Too shocked to scream at the thought of losing Ryan, Krysty was the first to spot him, willing herself to see through the red mist of dots that speckled her vision postblast.

"Gaia," she whispered as she saw Ryan moving toward the sec-door panel. She turned her head, her skin sore from the burns, and could see that the Illuminated Ones were as blinded, and in no position to fire on Ryan.

Which meant that they were also in no position to see if anyone was ready to fire on them. If she got everyone to move triple quick, the companions could turn this to their advantage.

"Mildred, we've got to move on them now. They can't see!" she hissed in her friend's ear.

Tammy heard, as well, and replied, "I can't see them, either, but fuck it. If we come out blasting they won't have a chance to return it, will they?"

"Go, girl." Mildred grinned. "As long as we blast in the right direction..." She left the rest of the sentence unsaid. In the first place it wasn't necessary, and in the second her throat felt red raw as she tried to speak in the still hot and dried-out air.

With a hoarse whoop, Tammy began to advance, reeling off blasts of laser fire in the direction of the opposition. She was followed by Krysty and Mildred, who also began to fire in the general direction of the Illuminated Ones.

Tammy's whoop and the sounds of laser fire acted as a galvanizing influence on Gloria, Dean and Jon on the far side of the wag.

"Hey, the wee one's going for the big one," the Gate queen yelled at the men with her. "Our Tammy's going forward. Let's get in line and get after her."

"I still can't see too well," Dean said urgently. "How the hell can I aim?"

"I can't see too well, either," Jon answered, "but we just need to keep firing in the right direction. Try and keep it low. We need to put that fucking big bastard blaster out of action, and there's no way we'll do it any damage unless we can knock out the tires. If it can't move, or if we can get it to pitch over, then it won't be of much use to them."

"Okay, let's do it," Dean said, following Gloria and Jon as they progressed. They had no idea that

Ryan was trying to open the sec door, but figured that one of the other party had to be trying, as there would be no sense otherwise in a forward push.

Back at the sec door, Ryan had pulled himself upright, and was painfully aware of how vulnerable he was. He stood by the keypad that accessed the door code, squinting to try to read the numbers that were scratched on the metal plate in which the keypad was housed. The fact that human nature didn't change, and that worried sec footsoldiers still found it a fail-safe to scratch the access codes on the interior plate of every door, was something that the one-eyed man felt thankful for as his eye began to return to its normal vision, and he was able to read the numbers as he keyed them in.

The sec door began to open, groaning into action, and he leaned heavily against the concrete pillar that framed the door. His heart was still pounding, but he could feel strength begin to flow back through his limbs as he began to breathe more normally, the oxygen reaching muscles filled with lactic acid that could now disperse, the shock of the flight and impact beginning to lessen as his resilience took over.

Blowing hard, he turned to watch the light flood the immediate outside area. The question was, how long would it be before the remote was activated and the door began to close again? For he was sure that it would, and it was playing percentages to see if it would rise enough for the oncoming attacks to gain access before the remote kicked in.

The door, seeming to rise with an infinite slowness in his impatience, reached the height of Ryan's head. Let it rise a foot or two more, and that would be all that was needed.

His attention was distracted by the furor occurring farther down the redoubt tunnel. The onrush of the six people dressed in Illuminated uniforms had taken the actual Illuminated Ones by surprise. Their vision and reactions hadn't recovered as quickly as those of their opponents, and they had been completely caught out by the sudden barrage of laser fire. To this was added conventional blasterfire, as Gloria and Tammy clutched their laser rifles in one hand, and used their free hands to take pot shots at anything they could see.

The Illuminated soldiers were unable to compete with this sudden onslaught, and were thrown into confusion by the attack. Unable to return fire, other than the desultory blast as they pulled back, the Illuminated Ones were driven farther into their own lair. Jon and Dean, keeping their blasts low, were able to blow the tires on the cannon's wag, and as the first tire went the wag tilted, throwing off the cannon crew. They didn't bother to try to remount, scrambling backward to escape the oncoming war party.

Three Illuminated soldiers went down, injured or chilled, as laser fire cut through their flesh and bone. There was little blood, as the heat of the beams cauterized the flesh as it cut through. The others pulled back to the next sec door, taking up defensive positions as the companions advanced. Once they were safely behind the sec door, it began to descend.

There was no way that the advancing party would reach the door before it closed, and no way that they could open it from their side…and if they did manage to get beyond, they would be at the mercy of whatever reinforcements were being sent along, having to defend their position while reopening the sec door for the Gate and Crossroads warriors who would follow.

"Fireblast," Ryan cursed softly to himself as he tried to reason the best course of action. He had to make sure that the advance party didn't get trapped, and also keep this sec door open. His mind raced. There was only one chance, but it depended on a long shot.

Looking up, Ryan saw that the sec door was at an optimum height. If Dean's theory proved correct, he could shoot out the circuits now and freeze the door open. He stepped back and turned, leveling the laser blaster at the keypad. How would he know if it worked or not?

The question was answered for him as the door shuddered and then began to descend. A remote system had been used to reverse the door. Now he had no choice. He leveled the laser rifle and fired a charge into the keypad. Sparks flew as the circuit shorted out, but Ryan's eye wasn't on his target, but rather on the door. For a fraction of a second it kept moving downward, but then, with another shudder, it stopped. The one-eyed man breathed deeply, willing the door to stay put. When it remained, he let the breath out with a sigh. The light from the redoubt spread out over the territory beyond, lighting the way as dawn broke.

The next move from outside would have to be left to J.B. There were more-important matters to attend to. Ignoring the pain that still seared through the muscles along his ribs as he ran, Ryan sprinted back to the wag and jumped in through the open rear door. Inside, the circuits on the comp looked blown, blackened around the grilles and keys. The electrical starter system was probably blown, as well, which may ruin everything. Would he have time?

Ryan seated himself behind the wheel. If the alloy

shell had acted as a conductor for the blast, if it had acted in the same way a normal wag shell acted when lightning hit, then it may be that the engine systems had escaped, and the comp systems had blown independently because of the break in the maintenance ducts beneath the chassis.

No time to try to figure it out. He could only to hope for the best. Ryan hit the self-starter.

Once more, fate was on his side. The engine caught at the third attempt, firing into life. Ryan put the wag into gear and eased the vehicle forward. The wheels, now tireless after the jolt it had received from the laser cannon, ground on the concrete floor, sending up sparks as the wheel rims bit into the redoubt floor.

Ahead of Ryan, through the shattered armaglass shield splintered by extreme heat, was a clear run through to the closing sec door…at least in terms of his companions, who were taking cover as they fired at the Illuminated Ones, and were almost at the point of making it past the closing sec door. The only thing that lay in his path were the few corpses and wounded, and the laser cannon itself, deserted and standing at an oblique angle, still in the middle of the corridor.

Ryan ground his teeth as hard as he went through the gears, picking up speed rapidly as the wag's powerful engine gunned into full life, the axles protesting against the battering they were taking from the twisting wheels as they bit into the concrete floor, the contrary twists of the angles at which they cut into the concrete stressing the axles until it felt as though the four-wheel-drive were taking the wag in four different directions, pulling the steering almost out of the one-eyed man's grasp as he tried to keep it on a straight course.

The cannon was a big weapon, but nothing against the gathering speed and momentum of the wag as it hit it full on, battering the chassis of the cannon to one side, the barrel flying off in the opposite direction. The power source of the cannon ignited and blew on impact, almost blinding Ryan as he covered his face with one hand, the wag veering to the left as the steering pulled at the hand left grasping the wheel. The armaglass may have been shattered, but it was still just about strong enough to protect him, and he was able to get past the cannon without too much loss of time or speed.

"What the fuck is Ryan doing?" Gloria yelled as she heard the wag gun into life, turning to see it advancing rapidly.

"Blocking the sec door to stop it being closed," Dean snapped breathlessly. He added, "Drive them farther back until he gets there!"

The warriors continued to fire on the Illuminated Ones, who were now also entrenched in defensive positions, and were returning fire. The tactical blunder in leaving the cannon behind was amplified for them as the blasterfire from the laser rifle bounced ineffectively off the alloy of the wag body.

Ryan urged as much power as possible from the wag as it headed for the ever-narrowing gap between the bottom of the descending door and the concrete floor. It was a race against time, and measured in a matter of seconds. If the door descended too far, then the wag would just hit it and be crushed in the impact. Ryan had to get the wag underneath the descending door before it was too late. That was the only way that he could jam the door and maybe short the mechanism—certainly keep it open until they could secure the position and raise it from the other side of the sec door itself.

The door loomed large across the armaglass windshield, the vista of the door and the corridor beneath—itself a narrowing band of vision—filling the whole of Ryan's vision.

"Fuck!" he yelled in shock and surprise as the front of the wag squeezed beneath the door, beating the descent by a fraction of a second. It was also a cry of adrenalined terror—a declamation of being galvanized into action as he realized what had happened. The wag had jammed beneath the door as it fell, but the momentum of the wag had been arrested as the descending door halted the vehicle in its tracks, making the wheels scream and squeal as they bit into the concrete, forced lower by the descent of the door as it pushed down, squashing the front of the wag.

Ryan leaped from his seat, fighting the jolt caused by the wag's halted momentum, and threw himself backward, barely keeping his balance as he reached the back of the wag.

The sec door crushed the roof of the wag at the front, shattering the armaglass windshield beyond all recognition, driving metal onto the seat where the one-eyed man had sat a few moments before. The sec door squealed and scraped like the metal it crushed, its momentum halted by the mass jammed underneath.

Grabbing his laser rifle—the other blasters already secured on his person—Ryan leaped from the back of the wag and raced back to cover, where he joined Krysty, Tammy and Mildred.

"Glad you could drop in, lover," Krysty said dryly.

"Just had a few things to do," he replied. Looking ahead, he could see that the crushed wag—driven down with such force that the rear wheels had left the ground—held the sec door open for a gap of three or four feet. There was little indication of whether the Illuminated soldiers beyond were still in cover, or whether they had retreated.

Looking back, he could see through the open outer door, into the dawn light beyond. The larger war party was advancing.

Chapter Twelve

J.B. watched the door rise from his position of cover. All around him, in the semicircle around the recessed entrance of the redoubt, he could feel the tension rise, and the anticipation of the warriors for battle. And yet, it still nagged at him that there seemed to be no defenses between the covering foliage and the entrance itself. The wags always seemed to follow a well-worn track, which had to, by necessity, be free of traps. Yet it would be folly to send their entire force down that track. It would make taking them out just too easy.

J.B. turned to Dette, who had ended up beside him.

"Listen," he said urgently, "I want you to run and pass this on. I want Jak to lead a party down the wag track, moving triple fast and keeping triple red for any attack from the redoubt—the sec cameras will see them easily. I'm taking a group around this side, and I want Doc to bring his side around in the same way. I'm pretty sure that there'll be booby traps of some kind, so we may take casualties. The only thing is that no one do anything stupe, and move up as quickly as possible, but taking precautions. Test the ground ahead as much as possible. Got that?"

Dette smiled, her eyes flashing excitement at the thought of the battle ahead. "Sure thing. Give me just a couple of minutes to get there, yeah?"

"Do it quicker if you can," the Armorer advised her.

"You'll know if I have, 'cause we'll be moving up."

J.B. allowed himself a smile. "Okay, go."

He didn't watch the Gate woman disappear into the early light of dawn, turning instead to the warriors around him.

"We move in two minutes max, mebbe sooner if we see a party start for the track. Don't take stupe chances. We need all of us to fight in there. I figure there'll be mines of some kind, mebbe wire traps hidden beneath the topsoil. Use sticks and stones, prodding the ground for wire and throwing them ahead to try and find mines. Last blaster check now, and gather stones, as well. Then we move on the signal."

The group around him indicated their agreement, and as the Armorer ran through a last check on his Uzi, the M-4000 with its load of barbed metal fléchettes, and checked his Tekna knife was secure for any close combat, his mind was racing. He picked stones from the soil, ready to begin pitching them to test the way ahead, and wondered what was happening in the redoubt. There were so many possibilities, it would be a question of thinking on their feet when they got inside.

He wondered if Dette had delivered her messages yet....

JAK NODDED his understanding, his impassive visage belying the attention he paid to Dette. When she had finished, he looked around at the group of warriors he headed, and asked, "Everyone get?"

There was a murmur of agreement, and Jak's red eyes glittered as they searched the group around.

"You know what do," he said simply. "Give Dette time, then go fast, triple alert. Get ready."

The warriors around checked their blasters and prepared themselves mentally for the charge.

It depended on Dette reaching Doc's group and relaying her message in time.

DETTE WAS SWIFT, slowed only by the need to keep cover as she traveled from group to group. She had time to spare when she reached the cluster of warriors on the far side of the arc, where Doc was waiting for word of action, his LeMat percussion pistol loaded, primed and ready.

"How charming of you to drop in," he said smoothly when Dette arrived in the clump of foliage where they were concealed. "I presume you bring word from John Barrymore?"

"Eh?" Dette gasped, momentarily nonplussed.

"Don't worry about it," Cat said easily from her position by Doc. "Just tell us what you've got to."

Dette relayed the message from J.B. Doc checked on his old chron.

"Time to spare, as well," he commented. "I would say that you've done a fine job. Pray take a second to get your breath back while we finalize our preparation."

"Shit, how do you ever get your breath back, the amount of words you use," Dette panted.

"Don't worry about that, either," Cat said slyly. "You got any intelligence, you soon get used to it."

The two women exchanged glances of mutual loathing. Doc picked up on the atmosphere and said, "Save that for those we are about to face. I would say, from your expressions, that if you transferred that to the enemy, then you could eradicate them on your own.''

JAK LOOKED toward the area where he knew that Doc and his group were hiding. In the dim light he could see no sign of Dette. There was sparse cover between the two areas, and he knew he would be able to spot her moving among the undergrowth. Not many could have been so sure, but Jak's eyes were better attuned to the dim light, and his almost preternatural hunter's instincts could spot things that a lesser mortal might not.

So the Gate warrior had to have reached Doc and imparted her message. The door of the redoubt had been opening as she arrived, and was now still. By his estimation, there was still a little time before the limit J.B. set for the woman would be reached. But he was certain she had reached her final destination, and was also certain that the Armorer and Doc would lead their parties out on a cue from the albino.

Inside the redoubt, he heard the roar of the wag engine cutting across the sounds of blasterfire, both laser and normal.

There was no time to waste. Jak made a decision and turned to his group.

''We go,'' he said simply.

Leading from the front, the albino broke cover, moving rapidly across the land between their cover and the track that led to the redoubt. He hit the compressed earth of the track, feeling the uneven surface hard beneath his feet. He was moving at speed, the .357 Magnum Colt Python clasped in his fist. He could hear the movement of others behind him, some dropping back, others keeping pace. Without bothering to look back, he could tell from the footfalls that it was the Gate warriors who were with him.

Suddenly, from all around there came the sound of exploding mines, showering the runners with earth and small stones. Jak didn't flinch, knowing that they were safe from such devices as long as they kept on the track. He didn't dare to think of his friends and the other warriors, trying to traverse the booby-trapped area. Instead, he could only focus his attention on the redoubt door ahead.

J.B. SAW Jak break cover and lead his people forward. The albino was setting a rapid pace, and the Armorer signaled for his group to move.

But first he took a handful of stones and threw them in a sweeping arc over the land ahead. Some pattered onto the earth with only a small puff of dust to mark their landing. But two of them drew results. The first mines to be encountered went off, the sudden noise almost deafening in the dawn, clouds of dirt and stones being thrown up. Other stones flew from the hands of warriors as J.B. began to move forward, marking his own personal path by sweeping the area immediately in front of him with a long branch taken from the trees surrounding.

The first wire trap was found, tripped by the branch and springing up viciously in a loop of fine steel that would take off a foot at the ankle. One thing was for sure: the Illuminated Ones had guarded their redoubt well, for the mines and traps were well hidden. The Armorer just hoped that those following him would be as careful in plotting their path.

The screams from behind him belied that belief....

Like the Armorer, the Gate warriors were too wise in the ways of warfare to take anything for granted, and were making their own paths forward, following the direction dictated by their sweeping sticks assiduously. But the Crossroads warriors, being unused to the ways of combat, were a little more slack. They would throw the stones to try to find mines, and would attempt to sweep the oncoming path, but they had trouble sticking to that which they had tested, and it wasn't long before a stray foot encountered the edge of a snare trap.

The man who had previously been attached to the foot felt a pull that, at first, didn't hurt. This was delayed by the initial shock, and it was only when he saw the snare snap back, throwing a severed foot, still booted, across the earth, that he realized it was his own foot that he was watching. Suddenly ashen gray with shock and pain, he let out a strangled scream as he fell to the ground, the area about his legs staining dark with the ebb and flow of his blood.

At least he was still alive. A fellow Crossroads dweller taking part in the charge wasn't as lucky. Like his fellow, his straying foot had caught in a snare, cutting him off at the ankle. But as he fell, he landed on a part of the ground that hadn't been swept, and his head found another, barely hidden, snare that wrapped itself around his throat, biting through his flesh with ease. His screams were strangled and choked in his throat as he felt the world darkening around him. Veins and arteries were cut and severed, and the wire was sharp enough to slice easily through the vertebrae, leaving the head cleanly cut from the rest of his body. The tension of the wire, as it met with a sudden lack of resistance, catapulted the head across the ground, throwing it in front of the leading pack. It smacked to earth with a dull thump that was inaudible over the violent explosion it triggered as it hit a mine.

J.B. looked up momentarily to see how far ahead Jak's group was. It was a given that they would be first to the redoubt, as they weren't slowed by the necessity to plot a safe path. However, the Armorer was concerned that the other war parties should not fall too far behind. So far, his group was keeping pace fairly well.

He spared a glance to see how Doc's group was faring.

"BY THE THREE KENNEDYS!" Doc exclaimed. "If this does not bring any opposition out of hiding, then nothing will!"

"Let's hope that Ryan and Gloria have got them too occupied, then," Cat returned.

The small, dark-haired woman had been sticking close to Doc since the charge had begun. She had noticed that Doc wasn't faring as well as some of his compatriots, and she knew that—like Jak and Mildred—he had contracted a form of the pox that they were seeking in the redoubt. She liked the old man, and although Dette had been publicly dismissive of her intelligence—as well as that of her friend Nita— she was smart enough to know that Doc was more vulnerable than the others, and despite his fighting spirit may need some help along the way. So she had decided that she would be that help, and was in the vanguard of the charge with Doc, helping him forward.

As on the far side of the beaten track, Doc's war

party had been sweeping the ground and using the stone-throwing method to try to clear their own personal paths. Doc had already been outpaced by a few of the Gate warriors, but was still near the front because of the help from Cat. She could see that Doc had difficulty moving and breathing as the disease took a firmer hold on him, and so she swept ahead for him, as well as for herself.

"Come, my dear, we must make more speed," Doc implored, looking across to where J.B.'s party was advancing. "We cannot be left behind. Our strength is in depth, and we cannot let our friends down under any circumstances."

Yet, even as he spoke Doc was gasping for breath.

Cat took his arm. "Don't worry, Doc. You stick with me and we'll get there," she said.

JAK SLOWED as his war party reached the door of the redoubt. An incredible sight greeted them. The wag had just intercepted the closing door, and as the warriors arrived at the entrance to the tunnel, they were stunned to see the wag being crushed under the descending door and Ryan leaping to safety.

Taking the situation in at a glance, Jak made a snap judgment.

"We go in now. Keep close to wall, keep in cover. Push up, support Ryan and Gloria soon as possible," he said rapidly, moving to one side of the tunnel himself and pushing a Gate warrior toward the other, in this manner setting up two chains of warriors to feed into the redoubt.

The two strands advanced rapidly toward the point where the vanguard force had established a position, firing at the Illuminated Ones through the gap in the

jammed sec door. The advancing warriors didn't fire.
Until they were in position, there was an outside
chance that they may hit their own people, and the gap
through which it was possible to fire at the Illuminated
Ones was restricted by the bulk of the wag, jammed
in the center of the corridor.

"Hey, Ryan we here," Jak yelled as the first of
the war parties moved up to join the advanced party.

"What about the others?" the one-eyed man asked,
noting that there were comparatively few warriors behind the albino.

"On way," Jak replied.

OUTSIDE THE REDOUBT, both J.B. and Doc had brought
their war parties through the hidden obstacles with a
minimum of casualties. There were numerous abra-
sions and small cuts from flying stones, but only five
people had fallen prey to the snares, and none had
been in the direct blast of the mines. It had been a
much more successful assault than either could have
hoped for thus far, and it was with some degree of
optimism that they headed their groups as they con-
verged on the redoubt entrance, coming off the booby-
trapped sides and onto the safety of the track.

Ahead, they could see that the way was clear until
the point where the wag sat jammed beneath the sec
door. They could also see the two groups of warriors
taking cover in the area directly to the rear of the wag.
There were only a few desultory exchanges of fire, and
both J.B. and Doc could figure that the attack was now
stalled, waiting for the reinforcements to arrive.

The Armorer turned to the united forces.

"Go in quick, take cover to the sides—be a shame
to be caught by a stray blast—and await further or-

ders." He waved them in, and the attackers began to feed into the redoubt, flowing past him. He turned to Doc.

"I figure we should see what Ryan and Gloria have to say about this. Looks good for a full assault, but—"

"But it has been a tad too simple thus far, would you not say? Only a few traps to traverse? I would have expected more, which suggests that they have something in reserve."

J.B. nodded. "Yeah, I'd reckon on that, too." He stopped and peered intently at Doc, who was breathing with some difficulty and being partly supported by Cat. "Doc, how you feeling? I mean, honestly."

"In truth, I feel as though I have a horde of stickies with those loathsome suckered fingers crammed into my lungs, trying to prevent me from breathing. I fear that the pox is finally taking a hold on me. My skin feels chafed and sore, and look—" Doc held open his shirt to reveal a network of pustules and scabs that were starting to spread across his chest and stomach. "I may not have long, John Barrymore, and while I will fight to the last, I fear that I may not be as reliable as I would wish."

J.B. nodded once. There was no way he wanted Doc to get this far and then fall at the last fence.

Before the Armorer had a chance to say anything, Cat broke in. "Don't worry about old big mouth, here," she said, punching him playfully on the arm. "I'll keep him on his feet and fighting until we get through."

She looked at Doc, saying, "You buy the farm, I have to buy it first, yeah?"

Doc inclined his head graciously. "I appreciate your concern, madam."

"Fine, but let's cut the words," J.B. said urgently. "Doc, you and Cat get to the front on one side, and I'll go for the other. We need to get the game plan sorted quickly."

"Agreed," Doc affirmed. "Let's go...."

"JOIN, GLAD YOU COULD make it and join the fun," Mildred said as the Armorer reached the front of the vanguard party.

"Sorry, I was a little detained," he commented wryly. "What's going on?"

"Not as much as we'd like, I guess," Mildred began before outlining briefly the situation as it stood.

When she had finished, J.B. scratched his head, pushing back his fedora, before taking off his spectacles and polishing them, a habit that indicated he was now deep in thought.

"So the number-one priority is to push them back and move down into the redoubt, which we can only do if we drive them back far enough to get access to the other side of the sec door and bring it up fully. Otherwise we're sitting targets trying to squeeze through that space."

"That's about it," Mildred agreed.

J.B. put on his spectacles and pushed them up the bridge of his nose, his eyes shining as he viewed the way ahead.

"Leave it to me," he said simply before darting across the corridor, using the wag as cover and keeping low.

"Ryan, I think I've figured a way to drive them back and keep the next sec door up while we secure this one and get it up for a full assault," he said in a rush.

"Tell me," Ryan replied simply. J.B. outlined his plan, and Gloria looked at him in astonishment.

"You think that'll work?" she asked.

The Armorer shrugged. "If not, we're fucked anyway. We have to get past them and get that door opened. I figure this is worth the risk. It can be done if you give me enough cover."

Ryan nodded. "Try it. You're the only one I'd trust with such a crazy idea."

J.B. swung his canvas bag off his shoulder and began to mold a small lump of plas-ex, which he extracted from the interior. "I hope to hell that I've judged this right," he muttered as he molded and added a timer fuse to the small bomb. "If not, I'll bring down the whole tunnel."

"We'll just have to trust to luck. It's got us this far," Ryan said as the Armorer completed his bomb and set the fuse.

"Ready," he stated. "Keep me covered. I'll keep low, so just fire over me and try to stop those coldheart bastards firing back!"

Ryan nodded. "Good luck."

J.B. gave him a wry grin, then dropped to the floor, the M-4000 in one hand, the bomb in the other.

Laser fire heated the air above his head as he crawled past the door stanchion and into the no-man's land beyond the trapped door. Following their cue, the war party on the other side of the wag began a heavy barrage of fire, keeping the Illuminated Ones pinned in their cover.

Climbing to his knees, J.B. raised the M-4000. He knew instinctively that some of the Illuminated Ones would break cover to fire on him. As they leveled their laser blasters, he fired at them, then dropped and began to crawl again. He was already flat by the time that the barbed metal fléchettes from the shotgun charge had ripped into the Illuminated soldiers, chilling some instantly as vital organs were ripped to shreds, wounding others as they were hit in the arms and face.

This and the laser fire from the war parties caused the Illuminated Ones to drop back.

Acting as fast as his prone position would allow, J.B. rolled against the wall so that he was covered by the buttresses, and righted himself so that he could inch along the wall until he was up against the door stanchion. Taking a deep breath, and noting that there were only seconds left on the timer fuse, he pushed the plas-ex against the stanchion, pushing the soft, puttylike explosive into the groove that ran down the length of the stanchion to allow the door to fall.

He was never closer to buying the farm. Any Illuminated soldier with fast enough reflexes or who was close enough could easily have taken off his arm with a laser blast.

But they were in ignorance of J.B.'s plans, and so were in no position to react. The Armorer was able to place the plas-ex, turn and fling himself to the ground, huddling close to the wall as the plas-ex blew, hoping that no flying rubble would injure him.

"Damn."

Mildred was the first to react after the explosion. The corridor was filled with a choking dust as the stanchion blew out, buckling the metal runners so that the sec door couldn't be lowered, and causing the Illuminated soldiers to pull back in a panicked state. Meanwhile, Mildred keyed in the sec code scratched on the key plate. When the door had risen, she blasted the circuitry with the laser rifle to prevent it being closed again by remote means. Thanking the consistency of human nature, she turned and made her way to J.B., who was huddled against the wall, coated in a layer of dust and concrete chip.

"John! Are you all right?" she yelled as she reached him.

Taking his arms from over his head, where he had flung them to provide whatever protection he could from the blast, he grinned at her.

"You know, for a moment there I thought I might have got the amount wrong and arranged my own burial," he said matter-of-factly.

Chapter Thirteen

As the Armorer dusted himself off, Ryan and Gloria had already sped past him to the damaged sec door, taking cover and scanning the corridor that lay beyond. It was empty up to the point where the dog-legged descent into the bowels of the earth began. There would be elevators and an emergency staircase that they would have to check out, but it would seem that their best and safest option—both from the point of view of sticking together and also affording themselves the best protection—would be to keep taking the main tunnel downward.

"For fuck's sake, where the hell have they all gone?" Gloria asked.

Ryan surveyed the empty corridor. Unless there was a sec squad lurking around the bend in a primitive attempt at ambush, then they were on their own. Certainly, there seemed to have been no attempt at establishing a defensive block on the corridor. It was as though the Armorer's actions had driven the Illuminated Ones back to a core defensive position.

Perhaps it had. That would certainly make progress easy. Ryan outlined this possibility to Gloria, ending, "Though why they'd want to pull back so soon is something that worries me."

"Why? They know they're not that shit hot as fighters, so mebbe they really see that as their best option."

Ryan shook his head. "No, it still doesn't add up. There's too much tech along the way—assuming they've pulled right back to the kind of chambers we saw before…the ones you were stranded in when you landed. They must know we're after the lab, and where they keep the disease."

Gloria shook her head. "Why? Why would they assume that? They might think we're just carrying on the fight from where we left it. Why would they assume that we're going to add two and two and make four? Bet you thought I couldn't do that, eh?" she added with a sly grin. And when Ryan didn't answer, she continued. "You see? If you don't think that far about me, then why should they think that far about us? They think we're triple stupe. They think everyone is compared to them. So why would they think we're after anything other than a firefight and a chance of revenge?"

Ryan grimaced. "You could be right. Can we afford to think that, though?"

Gloria shrugged. "We can afford nothing, honey. We've just got to go for it and hammer these motherfuckers as much as possible. Hit them hard and fast, before they have a chance to think."

Ryan agreed. "But we need to divide up, so that a search party can try and find the labs where they're brewing up the pox. Mildred's not up to speed. It's taking hold on her, Doc and Jak more and more. She'll need good backup."

"Then I figure we send Tammy and Dean with her, mebbe a couple of others. They're both hard and fast, they work well together, and Dean seems to know more about old tech than anyone except Mildred."

Ryan nodded. "Good call." He scanned the area

ahead once more. "They must have sec cameras internally—most of these places do, even if they long ago gave out. Got to figure that theirs are still in operation. We want someone to keep watch on the tunnel while we brief the others."

Gloria agreed, and the two warrior leaders returned to the area where their forces were gathered. J.B. was now fully fit, having recovered from a bout of the shakes brought on by the aftereffects of being so close to the explosion. Tammy, Mildred and Dean were with him. Ryan beckoned to them. Gloria pulled Nita and Dette from the pack of impatient warriors, and put them on watch by the ruined doorway.

"Looks like they've pulled right back," Ryan told them as they approached. "I figure they'll keep an eye on us, and mebbe put a few obstacles in our path, but it's time for the main party to head on and take these coldheart bastards out of the game."

"What about the lab?" Mildred asked.

"I was getting to that," Ryan told her. "We want a smaller offensive for the lab party. Hit hard and fast. Now, you've got to be part of that, Mildred, but—"

"But I'm not on the ball," Mildred cut in. "Yeah, I know it, and that's what worries me."

"Don't worry too much about it," Ryan assured her. "I figure—Gloria, too—that we keep your party small, mebbe a half dozen at most. You, Tammy and Dean. Perhaps two, three others."

"Two max," Tammy interjected. "Those are small rooms, off smaller corridors. Too many of us and we'll just get in each other's way—mebbe even blast the fuck out of each other in the confusion."

"I'd go with that," Ryan agreed. "You pick the two you want, okay?" And when the Gate number two assented, the one-eyed man turned his attention to the Armorer. "That was damn fine work, J.B. How are you feeling?"

"Had the tremors where the explosion set my nerves jangling, but that's gone now," J.B. replied off-handedly. "I'm ready to go."

Ryan nodded, clapping his old friend on the shoulder. "That's good. Let's get this show going."

They joined Gloria, who had been briefing the war party on what the situation appeared to be and enlightening the Crossroads people on what they might expect in the redoubt.

The Gate and Crossroads party numbered around seventy, the Gate men waiting outside with the wags for their warriors to return, as was their tradition. Running his eye over the assembly with as much detachment as he could muster, Ryan wondered whether the Crossroads fighters would be up to the task if they had to face ambushes and laser fire in a close-combat situation. There was no doubting their intent and passion, as Yardie had demonstrated before leaving the ville, let alone their display in getting past booby traps the like of which were alien to them. But being hard about it, was it practical to rely on them in this situation?

Mebbe fifty percent, Ryan figured. Which meant that the bulk of the action would be down to the Gate warriors and to his own people. Looking at them, it was disheartening to see how Mildred, Doc and Jak had been affected by the pox. All three were now showing visible signs, and all had made it clear that they were aware of diminished capabilities.

Weight of numbers were good, but how many Illuminated Ones were there in the redoubt? If he had some way of knowing, or guessing, then he would feel much safer in making combat judgments.

Gloria turned to him, interrupting his train of thought.

"Next step, Ryan?"

The one-eyed man clicked into battle mode and began, "You know how the redoubts are usually laid out, from what you've just been told and from what some of you have experienced. You've also been told that the Illuminated Ones appear to have pulled all their sec right back, giving us what could be a clear run of the redoubt. A party of five will be heading for the area where the labs are usually located in order to try and find the source of the disease, and also the antidote and cure. The rest of us—our task is to wipe these bastards off the face of the earth before they can do more damage. In order to do this, there will be an advance party that will scout ahead, with a runner reporting back. The main bulk of fighters will follow when the area ahead has been recced. Those of you who will be in the advance party know you have the hardest task of all—you'll be the ones who run into danger first, so we need people who can stay frosty and triple smart, keep triple red.

"For that reason, the advance party will have to be Gate women. This isn't to belittle those of you from Crossroads—you don't have the battle experience necessary, is all. For the same reason, myself and J.B. may go, but not Doc or Jak. Like some of you Crossroads people, they have contracted the pox and know that their reflexes are slowed.

"The aim here is to keep calm, keep it under control and risk as few of us as possible until we're in full-scale combat. Is that clear?"

There was a muttering and a murmur of agreement.

"Okay, then it's time to pick the scout party and get moving. We've wasted enough time already."

A six-woman scout team was picked, including Nita and Dette. Cat elected to stay with Doc.

"Don't worry, my old friend, you'll be all right with the Cat," she whispered to him. And, in truth, Doc was glad of the support as his labored breathing and aching back and ribs made it hard for him to move swiftly.

The six-woman team set off, followed by Mildred's party. They would move directly behind the scouts and then branch off when they reached the area where the lab was situated.

Or at least, that was the plan. It soon became apparent that the Illuminated Ones had other ideas.

As the scouts and the med group rounded the dogleg of the tunnel and moved downward, they noticed that some of the corridors leading to dorms, sec-camera monitor rooms and storage bays were cut off, their sec doors closed. Rooms that led directly off the corridor were also firmly closed.

Mildred called the scout party back.

"Problem?" Dette asked in an edgy tone. From the way she was looking around, Mildred guessed that the warrior was unhappy with being stuck beneath ground.

"Could be," Mildred replied. "Nothing ahead, I know, but what about these corridors and rooms?"

"What, you figure there could be warriors waiting behind them to spring out on us?"

Mildred shook her head, pulling back her plaits. "That would have already happened. Besides, it's too close to the surface for them to do that. That'll happen farther down, when they feel we have a false sense of security."

"Then what's the problem?" Dette countered.

"I just want to see if any of these doors—corridors or rooms—open when we try them," she replied.

"You are kidding, right?" Dette said sharply. "They'll be booby-trapped, and blow us away if we're not careful."

"Then we'll be careful," Mildred said coldly, not caring for the woman's tone.

"For fuck's sake, we're supposed to be making an advance—" Dette began, before Tammy cut her short.

"We're not doing that, either, the more you stand here arguing," the Gate number two snapped. "Let's try some of them, yeah?"

Dette nodded, seething but keeping herself in check. The two parties then backtracked to a sec door leading to an ancillary corridor. Mildred checked and could see the code on the scratch plate above the keypad.

"You keep back," she said softly to the others.

"Hang on," Dean interrupted, staying her hand as she was about to punch the first number. "You stay back. You're the one we need to keep alive right now. Let me."

Their eyes met for a long moment, until Mildred looked away, acknowledging that Dean was right. She stepped back and joined the others, who were taking cover behind a concrete buttress.

Dean stared at the code and then at the keypad. He felt a trickle of sweat, cold in the small of his back. His finger trembled as he punched the first digit. Nothing happened. He closed his eyes, took a deep breath and punched in the second. Again, nothing happened. He continued this for each digit until the last, when he hesitated for a moment, feeling a cold gnaw of fear in his gut. If it was going to go, it would on this—

He hit the last digit of the code, flinching as his finger made contact with the keypad.

Nothing.

Nothing at all. Not the explosion, ripping him to shreds, that he had feared, but neither was there any movement from the door.

Dean frowned and with a renewed confidence punched in the full code for a second time.

Again nothing happened.

He turned to the others, backing away from the door. He still kept watch from the corner of his eye, and had his Browning Hi-Power to hand, in case something should suddenly occur.

"I think they've put a lock on by remote control," he said as he drew near. "Try some of the others."

He and Mildred then worked their way back while the others kept watch, trying both the ancillary corridor sec doors and the closed doors to ancillary rooms. All were locked and failed to respond when their codes were punched in.

"We've got a real problem here," Mildred said, shaking her head in anger as she and Dean returned to the rest of the scout and lab parties.

"In what way?" Nita asked.

Tammy gave her a withering look. "You stupe bitch," she began.

"I've been saying that for a long time," Dette observed quietly, but was stopped dead by Tammy's glare.

"Cut that shit out," she hissed before explaining patiently to the tall blonde, "It's like this. They shut off all these exits, and then we have to go exactly

where they want us. Like when we arrived here, remember?''

''Well, yeah, I know that,'' Nita said, ''but couldn't
we blast open some of these doors, like J.B. did back
there?''

Mildred shook her head, answering before Tammy
had a chance to speak. ''John blew the door stanchion
to stop the thing from closing. The amount of plas-ex
you'd probably need to get through a door would risk
bringing the tunnel down with it.''

''Well, what about jamming the circuits like you did
to let us in?'' the blonde countered.

Again, Mildred had to answer in the negative.
''That just blew out the remote when the door was
open—but it also blew the manual. I'm afraid that one
only works when the doors are already open.''

''Shit,'' Nita cursed. ''So what do we do?''

Tammy jabbed her in the chest with a long finger.
''You, lady, get your ass back to the main part and let
Ryan and Gloria know what's going on here, then get
back. We'll keep going on and see what's ahead,
yeah?''

Nita turned and began to run back to relay the message. Tammy watched her go, then turned to Mildred.

''What the fuck are we gonna do about getting to
the lab?'' she asked with a despairing tone. It seemed
that the woman was, for once, less than optimistic
about their chances.

Mildred shrugged. ''We do the only thing that we
can—we get going and see what these assholes have
in mind for us.''

The scout party and the lab party, now resigned to
being together on the same course regardless of intent,
moved off as one, gradually stringing out until they

were in formation, with Dette in the lead and Tammy bringing up the rear. They maintained distance between each member of the line, so that they wouldn't present a clustered target, but were still in close contact with one another.

"What are we looking for?" Dette asked.

"You'll know when we hit it," Dean replied.

The nerves of the invaders were stretched as taut as their formation, strung out and on edge.

"Hope something happens soon," Dette whispered. "I'd rather face buying the farm than endure much more of this."

It was almost as though the Gate warrior had prophesied her own doom.

The corridor curved sharply, and the line took the curve without closing, so that sight of Dette was lost to Tammy. So it was that the first the Gate number two knew of any trouble was when she heard the crackle of blasterfire and heard the young warrior scream.

As they rounded the corner, a side sec door opened suddenly and two Illuminated soldiers sprang from cover, crouching low to clear the door quickly as it rose, both clutching laser blasters and firing from the waist. The deadly light beams were wide of the mark, but as the two Illuminated soldiers moved across the corridor, and the front half of the advance-party line—those who had taken the curve in the corridor—sought cover behind the buttresses along the wall, Dette found herself in no-man's-land, with nowhere to take cover. She dived to the ground, seeking to go low and avoid the laser blasts that flew high, but she wasn't quite quick enough. No matter how fast her reactions, they couldn't compete with the speed of light. As she fell, the beam cut down the line of her spine, burning the flesh and opening a cauterized weal that ran the length of her back. She screamed, high and piercing, and hit the concrete floor in a state of shock.

Mildred was slow in making for cover. Her reflexes had slowed with the onset of the disease, and her legs felt leaden, refusing to move as she directed. When she heard Dette scream, she twisted, bringing up her Czech-made ZKR and using the reflexes that hadn't suffered too many ravages: the accuracy of her eye and the ability to exert gentle pressure on the delicate trigger mechanism of the precision blaster.

Two shots in such quick succession that they sounded as one, took care of the immediate threat. One of the sec men was caught in the throat, the bullet ripping out his jugular and carotid in one explosive blast as the shell hit yielding flesh. The other sec man, a few inches shorter, took the bullet in the middle of his forehead, a clean, precise hole being drilled at the point where the bridge of his nose moved between his eyes.

"Mildred! Get cover!" Dean yelled, darting out from his position behind a buttress and grabbing her by her free arm, tugging her with him as he made cover once more. "Good shooting, by the way," he added as they hit the wall, Mildred gasping for breath and the younger Cawdor turning his head to view the open sec door once again.

"Is Dette chilled?" Tammy yelled from the rear of the line. The Gate second in command had rushed forward on hearing the exchange of fire and the screams of the brown-skinned warrior; she was now close to the rest of the group, and could see her woman lying in the middle of the corridor, only a few yards from where the Illuminated soldiers chilled by Mildred also lay.

"She's still moving," Kass called. She was small and compact with long, tawny hair and oval eyes that gave her a dangerous feline air. Next to her, standing with her back to the wall and her blaster poised for the slightest movement, Jan was a more slender, slightly taller presence, lithe and willowy, with her shoulder-length dark brown hair pulled back severely into a ponytail, her eyes large, dark and focused.

"We could try to retrieve," the taller woman whispered, her voice deep and strong even though she tried to keep it low. "You cover, we run. Figure if we take a leg each we can still have one hand on our blasters."

"Good call," Tammy replied. If there was a chance Dette was still in this world, she didn't want to leave her. The Gate were fiercely loyal to their own, and to leave a fellow warrior to slowly buy the farm would be dishonorable. "On the count of three, take her. We'll cover."

She didn't bother to wait for assent from the two women. Instead, she trained her eyes on the open sec door, watching for any sign of life. Were the chilled Illuminated soldiers the only ones involved in the ambush, or were there others, biding their time, waiting for the assault group to make the first move?

"One, two, three, *four!*" she yelled, judging that the moment had been stretched enough to make as sure of safety as possible, yet not so far as to overpitch the nerves of the warriors who would make the run.

All those left in cover trained their blasters on the open door, ready to fire at the slightest sign of life. The only worry was that any Illuminated soldiers who may be in the corridor beyond would be able to find an angle of fire from beyond cover, and so blast Kass and Jan as they advanced.

Keeping low, and with one eye on the open sec door, Kass and Jan broke cover and ran the few yards to where Dette lay. As they closed on her, they could hear her whimpering, barely conscious but feeling agony with every drawn breath. The laser burn down her back, ugly and raw, appeared to have avoided ripping through to any major organs. Her major problems seemed to be dehydration from the burn, shock and the damage caused by the searing heat.

Squatting, both women took hold of Dette by the ankles, one each, and began to back toward cover on the double, keeping their eyes firmly on the open door.

They attained cover with no further fire, and while Jan kept her eyes on the open sec door, Kass turned over the barely conscious Dette and pulled up her eyelids. Her eyeballs were turned into her skull, but the whites were flickering where her eyes rotated in the sockets.

"Bad burns, looks like shock. We need to get her back soonest, or she'll buy the farm," Kass said, loud enough for it to carry down the line to Tammy.

"Shit," cursed the Gate number two. In this advanced position, she could ill afford to be a warrior down, let alone two or three. Nita hadn't yet returned from her runner's mission, so to send Dette to the main party on the back of another warrior would lose her valuable numbers.

"Let me take a look at her. I may be able to do something," Mildred said softly, snaking out of cover to move around the buttress and toward the area of cover where the two women had the injured Dette.

Mildred crouched, ignoring the lights in front of her

eyes and the swimming sensation in her head as she moved too quickly. Her own blood pressure was beginning to suffer as the pox took a firm hold, but at the moment this was as nothing. Her only concern was to check whether or not she could do anything for Dette.

Giving herself a second for the lights to clear, she looked over Dette, checking her vital signs and examining the wound with a practiced eye. Pursing her lips and hoping she was right, she started to reach into a pocket. As her hand met thin air, she realized that she was wearing a discarded Illuminated Ones uniform.

"Goddammit," she cursed before thinking rapidly. Dette needed to be rehydrated and kept warm. The burn would also need dressing. Back where the Gate wags were waiting she'd left her coat and the backpack containing her med supplies. If Dette could be taken back there quickly, if a warrior could be spared... She whispered this urgently to Kass, who darted back to relay Mildred's opinion to Tammy.

The Gate number two moved forward to join Mildred and Jan, leaving Kass to keep point. She cut straight to the chase. "When that triple-stupe slow bitch Nita gets back, then she can take Dette and relay your instructions. Fuck it, she should be back by now."

From afar, it was possible to hear the beating of bare heels on the concrete, so quiet had the corridor fallen. The sound grew louder as Nita closed in.

"She's not being triple careful," Tammy breathed, casting a glance toward the still open sec door. There had been no sign of any activity, but...

Nita cornered and approached the warriors, who

were still in cover. She, however, was still in the middle of the corridor, and would present a clear target. It now became obvious that Dette's low opinion of her was in some way justified, as the blonde stopped dead and stared blankly at the party in cover, a puzzled expression crossing her face as she tried to add up the seeming calm with the defensive positions they had adopted, and the obviously injured Dette.

"Wha—?" she began loudly—too loudly. The very sound of the syllable seemed to fracture the calm air that had descended on the corridor, and was a signal for an unwanted interruption. As she stood, staring triple stupe at the scene before her, two more Illuminated soldiers suddenly appeared in the doorway, visible at an oblique angle as they tried to keep cover while still angling for a clean shot at the newcomer.

Mildred saw them appear and yelled, "Cover! Incoming!" toward the startled blonde.

The air crackled with a blast from the laser rifle, and the concrete floor at Nita's feet was suddenly scored by a ray of light that made her jump back, yelling incomprehensibly.

"Shit—triple-stupe bitch," Tammy hissed as she turned her attention to the open door, trying to sight the Illuminated soldiers and fire on them. She opted for the Smith & Wesson Airlite rather than the laser blaster, and pulled a shot so that it rang off the metal of the sec door frame.

Mildred saw immediately what the woman had intended, but Tammy hadn't been using the blaster long enough to be at one with it, and wasn't a natural target shot.

"Get her in, I'll take over," Mildred murmured,

raising her voice then to call to Dean, "Aim for the frame—get a ricochet."

"Sure thing," the younger Cawdor replied, having made the same snap assessment of the situation as Mildred.

Nita suddenly realized what was going on and dived for cover, landing heavily behind a buttress that afforded her shelter. Her trajectory had been mapped closely by further blasts, and it was only her speed that had prevented her from being injured. However, the fact that the attention of the Illuminated soldiers was focused on the one Gate warrior meant that Mildred and Dean were able to aim carefully, and without the interference of returned fire, in order to try to achieve their aim.

Which was, quite simply, to try to put the soldiers out of action by use of a ricochet. The oblique angle of the defender's stance left no clear shot for anyone who was to keep cover, so it was up to the sharpshooters to try to angle a deflection from the metal of the door frame and hit their targets from an even more oblique angle than the targets themselves were firing.

It was an almost impossible task. The odds on such a ricochet being perfect, under all circumstances, were astronomical. But it would be possible to attain a degree of accuracy using precision blasters and the judgment and talent of Mildred and Dean. They might not chill their target, but they could quite possibly wound, and certainly make it so difficult for the Illuminated soldiers to return fire that they would force them back.

The two sharpshooters set up a continuous volley of fire, the carefully measured shots sounding loud in the quiet of the corridor, the sharp crack of metal and whine of the ricochets providing additional notes to make a symphony of sudden death. The blasts of laser fire from beyond the door grew less and less frequent, as the soldiers sought to evade the ricochets, and were forced to retreat down the corridor, stepping up to quickly fire a blast before moving back once more to safety.

While this occurred, Tammy beckoned Nita, who snaked her way around the cover until she was with the Gate number two and the injured Dette.

"Sorry—" she began breathlessly, but Tammy cut her off brusquely.

"No time," she snapped. "Dette needs treatment back at the wags. You carry her back and tell the men what happened. On the way, get Ryan and Gloria. Time's come to move forward, I'm thinking."

Nita, keen to atone for what she saw as her error, nodded briefly and picked up Dette without another word. She slung the brown-skinned woman across her shoulder, the extra height and muscle bulk that had made her stand out among the other Gate women now coming into its own. Dette was like a rag doll on the larger woman's shoulders, and Nita carried her easily, snaking back around the covering buttresses until she was beyond range of the fire that was still occurring. Once she had cleared this, she took to the center of the corridor and ran swift and true, ignoring the occasional whimper from the semiconscious Dette as she sought to stop her buying the farm.

"LISTEN," Jak said suddenly. "Blasterfire."

The keen hearing of the albino had picked up the volleys of fire from Mildred and Dean, and picked them out against the murmur of background noise as the main war party made ready to advance. Ryan and

Gloria had them forming into groups, with each having a chain of hierarchy so that they could operate as small units within the greater force. This would have been impossible if not for the fact that the Gate warriors often operated in this manner, and the people from Crossroads were more than happy to follow the lead of the more experienced fighters, willing to take their part but also acknowledging their own failings. They were in the middle of weapons checks and brief strategy discussions when the albino hunter was alerted to something happening ahead.

Ryan turned his head, trying to tune out the sound around. He didn't doubt the word of the albino, but wanted to make his own assessment. Yes, there it was, distant but audible. Sounded like two handblasters. By the change in pitch between the shots, and their frequency, he was almost sure it was Mildred and Dean. The smaller, lighter precision pistols had a distinctive sound when set against Krysty's blaster, or most of those carried by the Gate women.

The one-eyed warrior turned to Gloria. "We should move," he said simply.

The queen was about to answer when Jak cut in once more.

"Nita coming—something not right," he added, furrowing his brow as he listened.

Both Ryan and Gloria turned their gaze to the tunnel ahead, following the line of vision that Jak was taking. They saw Nita take the bend at a rapid pace, Dette securely slung across her shoulders.

"What the fuck…?" Gloria whispered, her immediate concern for her injured warrior. She ran forward to greet the scout.

"Need to get her out to the wags, get treated," Nita

gasped before drawing a breath and, as briefly as possible, informing her queen of what was happening in the tunnel ahead. Ryan joined them in time to hear what was occurring.

"We go now," Gloria said, turning to him. The light of battle was in her eyes, and Ryan knew that already the woman was fired up by the need for vengeance against her wounded subject.

The one-eyed warrior assented. "If they're opening up corridors for ambush, breaking into one of those may be our only chance of not being directed exactly where they want." He turned back to the clustered war party and briefly told J.B. what was occurring, while Jak—who had also been listening—informed Doc. Word of the action spread rapidly among the warriors, and when Ryan signaled for them to move, all were ready.

The war party set off down the tunnel on the double, the small units falling into place one after the other, giving space and allowing for a flow of bodies. Meanwhile, Nita headed through the open sec door to the outside world, and ran along the track toward the woods where the Gate wags were waiting, knowing what she had to do to try to save Dette. The brown-skinned warrior might always be railing against the blonde and her friend Cat, condemning them as triple stupes, but part of this abuse was based on the fact that the three had somehow formed a strong bond. The thought of Dette going out like this was something that Nita refused to even consider...even as the tears coursed down her face while she ran.

THE FIRST of the war parties, led by Gloria, rounded the final bend toward where the advance patrol was in cover, still firing on the open sec door. With a whoop of exultation at the battle about to begin, and a fire of anger, Gloria broke into a run, followed by the rest of her team. Behind, the war party increased pace to keep up with the leaders.

Tammy looked around at the sudden sound. "Good, now we should see some action," she said, satisfied.

"Yeah, but what?" Krysty countered. "If the approach is too strong, then it may... Shit!"

The red-haired beauty swore as she could see the very thing that had concerned her occurring. Hearing the approach of the war party, the Illuminated soldiers ceased fire. The sec door began to close.

"No, dammit," Krysty yelled, taking a chance. Grabbing a laser blaster, she broke from cover and ran toward the door. She raised the rifle as she ran, firing at the keypad and metal scratch cover on the corridor side of the sec door. She knew that the door would be secured by remote once it had closed, and they would have no chance of getting past it unless they used plasex and took the major risk of blowing out the tunnel and trapping themselves—something she knew that J.B. would rightly counsel against. So this desperate action was her only chance of keeping the door open.

Realizing what she was doing, the Illuminated soldiers on the far side of the door fired a few blasts into the corridor. Already the door was too low for them to fire straight, so they had to drop down to angle their blasts, which scored the concrete around her silver-tipped Western boots. The woman ignored it, and kept on coming, firing all the while. If she could short-circuit the sec door mechanism before it had closed, it would give them access to this corridor. That wasn't what the Illuminated Ones had planned, and so they would have to make more ambushes, which could in turn give more opportunity for the war party to spread out into the redoubt. This would undoubtedly disrupt the plans of their opponents, who, as Krysty had seen, weren't so hot at thinking on their feet.

Knocking out the door mechanism could change the course of the battle, which so far had amounted to little more than a war of nerve and bluff.

The door dropped lower, and the area around the keypad and scratch plate became scored with laser fire. Krysty was now almost at the door, and she braced herself, stopping dead and leveling the laser rifle so that she was able to take one last blast.

Her aim was true. The laser blast crackled and hit the door mechanism head-on, shorting out the control with a plume of smoke, a crackle of singed circuits and a crack as the power supply was severed and terminated.

But it was too late. The door had dropped to a level where it was impossible for anyone to get through except on his or her belly, and two at a time. To even try and use this access would be tantamount to throwing lives away.

Krysty swore loudly, knowing that she had failed. No one would blame her, as it was a slim chance at most. But it had been the only one, and she felt that she had blown it.

So what was before the war party now?

"I'VE JUST GOT THIS REAL nasty feeling that we're not in charge here," Gloria muttered as the war party made its way through the central corridor of the redoubt, winding down farther and farther into the earth.

"That's because we're not," Ryan returned. "We're going exactly where they want us."

"And that is?"

"Mebbe where they had us in the other redoubt—rerun that and then get rid of us through the mat-trans," Ryan mused. "I don't know. Usually you can try and second-guess strategy, but these guys... The way they think is not like anything I've come across."

"Me, neither," Gloria said sourly. "Stupidworks bastards who want to get rid of everyone so that they can run the show without anyone else around. Why? What the fuck does that achieve? And what would getting rid of us through a mat-trans do?"

"Spread the pox even further, when we got aboveground," Ryan pointed out.

Gloria snorted and shook her head. The Gate queen was ready for a firefight, and felt irritated beyond words by being both denied her fight and also manipulated.

"The only thing we can do is keep trying the sec doors and keep out of the big mat-trans chambers, if that's what they're trying to do," Ryan said. "We've got to keep it calm, here. That's our only hope."

However, the one-eyed warrior felt nowhere near as cool as he tried to sound. Inside, he was boiling over with frustration. They were being herded toward an objective that was totally on the agenda of their opponents, and they were being given not the slightest opportunity to fight back. Their own objective was also being denied to them by the tactics of their opponents. And there was nothing they could do except play the waiting game.

The danger inherent in that was that when the action exploded, the pent-up frustration and rage would lead them into error. That was something that Ryan was aware of, and why he was stressing the need to stay calm.

And yet, when the action came, it was unexpected and explosive.

Strung out, the units of the war party were moving at a slow pace, hoping for a break. Suddenly, all logic seemed to be denied as the sec door in the main corridor ahead came down.

"What the fuck is that about?" Gloria whispered.

"I don't know, but I really don't like it," Ryan whispered. "If they want us to go back, then why didn't they do it before? And if they want to guide us to the mat-trans, then why do it at all? Unless..."

Ryan's brain raced. There was little reason he could see, unless it was a move to hold them until the Illuminated Ones had positioned soldiers to— His thoughts were sharply curtailed by the door beginning to rise. Ryan's hackles rose, and the adrenaline pumped up his reflexes.

"Cover, now!" he yelled, throwing himself to one side of the corridor and pushing Gloria toward the other.

The war party as a whole had no hesitation in following this command, their reflexes as honed by the adrenaline rush as those of Ryan.

Before the door was even halfway up, the group of soldiers behind the door had begun to fire, spraying the area with laser fire. From their cover, the war party began to return fire. Two soldiers went down immediately, and the others began to draw back, taking refuge behind the buttresses and then laying down covering fire as they retreated in pairs.

"Stupe bastards, we've got them," Gloria yelled

exultantly, coming out from cover and leading the charge.

For a moment, it did seem as though the Illuminated Ones had made a serious miscalculation, the war party moving forward in waves as they pulled back. But a worry nagged at Ryan, and it was reinforced by Krysty, who reached him through the onrushing army. Her hair was tightly coiled around her head and neck.

"Bad feeling, lover," she yelled over the melee.

Ryan agreed. "Too easy."

But they had little choice except to follow the flow of the war party. There had been a couple of casualties among the leading throng. Ryan caught sight of J.B. and Jak, trying to calm down foot soldiers who were excited by the sudden release of tension, but they were swept along with the tide.

More of the Illuminated Ones went down—over half the original force had been chilled, and the others pulled back farther along the corridor until they passed through a sec door that led into a vast chamber beyond.

As the war party swept in, Ryan and Krysty toward the rear, still trying to pull them back, the remaining Illuminated Ones melted into the walls, leaving the warriors firing at thin air.

The heavy sec door closed with a clang behind the last of the war party. The room was in virtual darkness, and the lights were gradually raised to reveal a large hangarlike chamber.

"Oh, for fuck's sake," Gloria yelled, realizing what had happened.

Ryan's face was set grim. As he had feared, they had been led—willingly, as it transpired—into the very place they had wished to avoid.

Two large mat-trans units stood in the chamber. Set high in one wall was an observation port. The armaglass windows were dark and opaque.

They had played right into the hands of the enemy.

Chapter Fourteen

Ryan felt the fires of frustration and rage boil up within him to the point where he felt that he would explode if he didn't vent them in some manner, however futile that might prove to be.

Gazing up at the armaglass ob port that gave an unseen observer a full panorama of the war party below, Ryan felt that the opaque wall of armaglass was almost mocking them. He could imagine some of the Illuminated Ones—perhaps even the commander of the redoubt, or their overall leader—standing, poring over the people gathered below, examining them as though they were nothing more than insects. Not as human beings who were fighting for their survival, but rather as specimens who could be used in some experiment.

Ryan knew it was a futile gesture even before he began, but it was something that he felt he had to do. Both to vent his anger, and also in some way to galvanize an army that had been deflated with the realization of how they had fallen so easily into a trap.

Taking the Steyr from his back, the one-eyed warrior strode through the throng that clustered miserably in the chamber and took aim at the ob port. He fired a round and watched as the bullet clattered harmlessly against the armaglass, not even pitting or scarring the surface.

It may have been, in that sense, futile, but it did serve to change the mood of the army. Whereas, scant moments before, they had been reflective of the tone set by Gloria in her exclamation when she realized how her enthusiasm had trapped them, they now felt lifted by the defiance of the one-eyed man.

Ryan's blast was the first of many.

"C'mon Doc, my old beauty, let's show the bastards we're not chilled yet," Cat said, grinning as she raised her laser blaster and firing at the ob port. Her charge hit the armaglass, and although it made a faint scorch mark but little else, it was the cue for more of the warriors to fire.

As the laser blasters, rifles and handblasters went off around them, the companions sought out one another among the throng of the warriors.

"Is there really any point in joining them?" Mildred asked rhetorically as they gathered.

J.B. shook his head. "Not a hope of breaking through, even by sheer weight of numbers."

"Yeah, but at least it's got everyone on the up again," Ryan commented. "That was really the only reason."

Krysty eyed the throng. "It's certainly worked, lover. They're fired up, all right, but what the hell can we do to get out of here?"

"More question of what they do get rid us," Jak commented with a twinkle in his ruby-red eye.

Dean was puzzled. "What do you mean?"

Doc coughed, partly as a prelude to speaking, but partly because the pox was taking a stronger hold of his system. "Allow me, perhaps, to explain and expound upon our friend Jak's point. Observe, if you will, that we have been guided into the vast chamber where they keep their mat-trans units. We all, do we not, either have the disease or are carriers of such. Now, if you were in the position of the Illuminated Ones, what would you choose to do? Chill us all? Take issue and battle with us? Or would you, if you had the opportunity, not disseminate us all to the farthest corners of the land, thus achieving the rare treasure of chilling two birds with but the one stone? After all, they would not only have disposed of us, they would also have spread their foul calumny.''

''Is that what you meant, Jak?'' Dean asked with a wry grin.

The albino shrugged. ''Bigger words, but yeah.''

''Point is, it's vital to get the hell out of this chamber as soon as possible.'' Mildred shivered. ''The more time we waste here, the closer some of us get to buying the farm. And I hate to sound self-important, but if I go, then will I have time to tell the rest of you what you need to look for?''

''Don't worry, Millie,'' J.B. said softly, laying a hand on her arm, ''it's not going to come to that. They've got other plans for us, I figure.'' There was a light in the Armorer's eyes as he spoke that told of a deeper feeling, one that he wouldn't express so publicly, but which Mildred could acknowledge.

''Let's hope so, John,'' she replied simply.

The barrage of fire on the ob port was beginning to lessen as the warriors realized that it was doing little in the way of any practical good. There were still those who were pouring fire and anger on the only visible symbol of their enemy, but most had acknowledged that there had to be an alternative.

Gloria and Tammy fought their way through the throng toward the companions.

"Ryan," the Gate queen said, "that was triple stupe of me. I've just led us right into the shit, here."

"It's not your fault," the one-eyed man assured her. "They set it up so that we had to follow, in order to wipe out the threat of the sec force."

Gloria looked at Ryan askance. She knew that he was only partly speaking the truth. She had, she knew, acted rashly, but dwelling on that would do no good, and Ryan was trying to tell her to move on from it. The important thing now was what they would do next.

"Listen," Tammy said rapidly, "we need to get these stupidworks to stop firing. They'll waste valuable ammo that we may need when we figure out how to get out of here."

"If we get a chance," Gloria added.

"Will," Jak said firmly. "They need us in mattrans. We not going by choice. So they need sec to push, right?"

"Yeah, I'd figure that," Ryan agreed.

"And if they need to send sec in, then they need an opening to come in through, right?" Krysty smiled with understanding.

Ryan agreed. "We just need to wait and see. Have some patience but don't let our heads drop."

"Can't afford too much patience," Mildred muttered, shaking her head slowly. "Have to hope they don't have much, either."

J.B. looked at Mildred, concerned, then focused his attention elsewhere. "Let's get this firing stopped," he said brusquely.

The Armorer left them, moving among the masses with Tammy, trying to persuade the warriors to cease firing. Indicating that she should take one side of the area, while he took the other, they fanned out, weaving among the war party and stopping to speak with those who were still taking potshots at the armaglass ob port, imploring them to save ammunition for a possible escape maneuver. While Tammy was seriously concerned about running short of ammo, the Armorer's trained ear could tell that there weren't enough shots to warrant any real concern about stocks running down. As for the laser blasters, they were an unknown quantity, and they could run out of power at any moment, so couldn't be regarded seriously as part of the stockpile. The Armorer's reason for wanting to move away from the companions was rooted much closer to home. He could see how ill Mildred had become, and her comments on not making it through alive had alarmed him. John Barrymore Dix was by nature a taciturn man, not given to showing his emotions. But his relationship with the ailing woman was deeper than the other companions might have realized, and the prospect of having to watch her slowly expire before his eyes was one that inspired feelings he did not wish to share with his friends and compatriots. So he busied himself with this task until he could get a better grip on his feelings.

The meaningless act of dissuading the others to fire enabled him to focus on something other than his inner feelings, and let him return to some sort of equilibrium. He knew his strength, and realized that he was better equipped to deal with practical matters of combat—things for which he needed a clear mind.

The firing had ceased, but for the odd shot, when something made the Armorer look up. It was a sudden change in the atmosphere, the humidity of the room suddenly dropping in temperature, the moisture in the air growing cooler—no, definitely cold. There was more of a density to that moisture, as though it had changed from mere humidity to a fine mist or spray.

"Dark night, they're spraying us," J.B. said softly, as he looked up, the lenses of his spectacles becoming spattered with ever larger drops.

"Shit, they're going to soak us," came a voice from somewhere within the war party. Although he couldn't see the speaker, J.B. was able to identify him as Jon, the Gate Armorer, who had been absorbed into the main body of the army during the charge. "Cover your blasters, and try and keep warm!"

It was good advice, and couldn't be bettered by any of the companions, or by Gloria or Tammy. The army as a whole covered their weapons as best as possible, and also tried to cover as much exposed skin as possible with their clothing. For the Gate women, who made a habit of wearing as little as possible in order to move as freely and take as much of the sun as possible, this was a difficult task. As the atmosphere moved from a mist to a spray to the equivalent of a shower of rain, some of the women began to shiver.

The water droplets that fell from the ceiling grew larger and heavier, and rather than fall they began to bombard, as though forced from pipes by an immense pressure, so that they rained down heavily on the army below, the shower of rain now becoming like a monsoon.

The water was extremely cold, almost like little blocks of ice that stung as they hit exposed skin, leaving it numb from the extreme cold. The Gate warriors were the worst hit, their skin a mass of gooseflesh and small bruises from the impact of the water. They huddled together for warmth, trying to cover one another.

Doc offered Cat his jacket, and although the small Gate huddled closer into him for warmth and shelter, she refused to take the heavy cloth coat.

"Nice of you to offer, sweetheart, but you're ill, and you probably need it a whole lot more than I do," she said through chattering teeth.

"For fuck's sake," Gloria breathed, each syllable taking effort as her body spasmed with cold, "what's this all about?"

"Trying to soften us all up," Mildred commented as pain and cold racked her body, the air like ice as she tried to draw it into lungs that refused to obey under the stress of the cold. "Not trying to infect us, like before. That's already done…this is to make us weak, so we won't be able to react with any kind of speed or accuracy."

"Which means we'll need to," Ryan spit. "Fireblast! They must be about to take some kind of action."

The one-eyed man was correct in his assumption. After a few more minutes of the water treatment, by which time the fighters were numbingly cold to the bone, and the Gate warriors were almost unconscious on their feet from something approaching hypothermia, the water suddenly ceased to fall. The floor surface of the chamber was covered in a thin film of water that spread around everyone's feet, seeking holes and seams in boots, creeping in to numb feet and make the warriors ache in their bones with the cold. The surface of this film was no longer pitted with the consistent rainfall of the water, but was slowly stilling into a reflective sheet.

"Quickly," Mildred rasped, forcing herself into action even though she was still shaking spasmodically, and every muscle and tendon was painful. Her breath was labored, and her voice hoarse, harshened by the damp and cold. "Quickly, everyone move! Just get the circulation going again, get warm. Don't let anyone else fall asleep. It could be fatal."

The floor of the chamber came alive as previously inert warriors began to move, trying to massage life back into frozen limbs, both their own and those of their fellows. Ryan and J.B., the strongest of the companions, assisted Doc and Jak. The latter two were the worst hit by the cold, as Doc's frame was already under immense stress from both the disease and the legacy of his time-trawl experiences, and Jak was suffering from the ravages of the disease, as well as a low body-mass-to-surface-area ratio, which made it difficult for him to prevent the loss of valuable body heat. Dean, who was soon functioning normally, assisted Tammy and Gloria in aiding other Gate warriors, while Krysty directed her attention to Mildred.

Gradually, the lights in the chamber began to rise, casting out the shadows that had filled the corners of the vast hangarlike room, showing that the floor space had been stripped of anything that may have been of use to the trapped army in trying to escape. The filtering of the lights meant that the increase in illumination was so gradual that it didn't at first register with the army that there had been any change. It was only when the vast emptiness of the chamber became apparent that it was realized.

"Now why would they want to light it up in here?" Dean asked.

"Perhaps so they can see just exactly what we're doing," Krysty mused. "And if that's the case, then it means that they're planning some action of their own.''

''Best to get ready, then,'' J.B. said, speculatively fingering his Uzi.

The viewing platform also became less opaque. An internal light had been ignited, filling the gallery with a dull glow that showed three people within. Two men—both in middle age, but still trim and fit by the looks of them—and a woman, who was slightly younger, with long, curling dark hair. The three Illuminated Ones wore uniforms like their compatriots, but had an air about them that suggested they were more than mere humble workers.

''The enemy,'' Doc said, his voice harsh and racked with the cold and the pox. But there was no mistaking the fire in his eyes.

So now they could be clearly seen from the gallery, and in turn could clearly see all that was happening behind the armaglass.

Ryan took a quick recce of the chamber, noticing that J.B. was doing likewise. There were three exits: one through which they had come, one that was set in the wall beneath the viewing gallery, and one that was set into the far wall, behind the two vast, freestanding mat-trans chamber units. The door through which the attackers had entered was a large sec door. The other two were smaller utility doors used by no more than one or two individuals at a time. Chances were that any large-scale action would involve the use of the main door, but anything that would entail a filtering of the attackers in some way would utilize the smaller doors.

The question was simply this: what would that course of action be? Ryan and J.B. exchanged glances.

Neither could see anything around those doors that could be used as shelter or cover, and there was nothing in the chamber as a whole that would help them.

A low hiss filled the room. Looking up and around, none of the companions could see any speakers, although they knew from other experiences that the hiss was nothing more than the sound of a public-address system coming to life. However, some of the other people didn't know that, and there was a murmur of panic that rippled through the crowd as they sought the source of this possible attack. The panic turned to dismay as the voice boomed into the chamber.

"You have already seen what we can do to make you uncomfortable. Many of you will have been weakened. Repetition of such treatment will lead to your being chilled. Therefore, it is in your best interest—in truth, your only interest—to obey our commands."

The voice was low, soft and sibilant. Despite the echo of the chamber, there was a certain dryness to the tones that made Mildred feel uneasy. It was a voice that rang a distant resonance, back to the days before the nukecaust and her years of cryogenic suspension. She could remember her days in medical school, and the voice of the lecturer during anatomical dissection classes. The same measured, dry tone, the same detachment of all emotion from the voice, as though the speaker had lost touch with their basic humanity and operated out of pure intellectual reason, no matter how skewed it may seem to anyone else.

If it could be said that anyone sharing those vocal characteristics would also share a similar outlook, then Mildred had a suspicion that the Gate warriors, companions and Crossroads people were in for big trouble.

The voice continued. "You will all discard your

weapons. Leave them on the floor of the chamber. Please do not think that you can conceal anything from us, as we will be monitoring you most closely. You have thirty seconds in which to do this.''

The speakers went silent. There was a mutter of confusion and incomprehension from the floor, arguments between those who wished to discard and those who were determined to hang on to their weapons. The Gate looked to their queen for an answer.

"Hold on to them, see what these coldheart bastards do next," she yelled. Catching Ryan's eye, she could see that he didn't agree, but she was defiant.

The thirty seconds elapsed, and another shower of icy water rained on them. It lasted for exactly the same amount of time as that given to them for discarding the weapons. Ryan checked on his wrist chron. And when the cold, shivering and demoralized people had welcomed the brief respite, the voice came again.

"Really, I would have expected a little more intelligence from at least some of you."

There was a pause, and Mildred exchanged a puzzled glance with Krysty. It seemed as though the voice were intimating at a certain knowledge. Was this possible?

"There is no escape, and neither will there be a respite. Please put your weapons down within the next thirty seconds, or we will repeat the process. Frankly, we have no concern whether you live or die, but I think that perhaps you may care about the matter."

Gloria looked at Ryan. The one-eyed man nodded almost imperceptibly.

"Let's see what they want. No point chilling everyone now," he called to her.

Gloria assented. ''Throw down your weapons—all

of you," she cried, barely able to keep the bitter note
of defeat from her voice.

All around the companions, people shed their hardware, blasters and knives. Doc kept hold of his silver
lion's-head swordstick, but discarded the LeMat. Jak
made a show of throwing down his .357 Magnum Colt
Python. The others all discarded their blasters, Ryan
and J.B. adding their panga and Tekna knife respec-
tively.

There was a pause as the last ringing sound of metal
on concrete died away. Finally, the voice from the ob
port sounded again, this time with a faintly sardonic
air that caused a shiver to run down Mildred's spine,
impressing on her all that she had previously thought.

"Good. So glad that you finally saw sense. You will
all stay where you are, with the exception of the seven
people who travel together—the one-eyed man, the albino, the old man, the black woman, the redhead, the
boy and the one with glasses. You know who I mean.
You will please make your way toward the exit door
directly beneath this port."

The companions exchanged a series of looks that
varied from confused to concerned: given time to re-
flect, it would be easy to see that even a cursory glance
at the action that had taken place at this and the previous Illuminated Ones' redoubt would have separated
them as a force from the Gate tribe and the Crossroads
newcomers. So to be singled out wasn't that surprising. However, it suggested that the Illuminated Ones
had something particular in mind for the companions.

But what?

"Come now, do not try our patience," the voice
snapped as they hesitated. "If you do not move, then
the water will be turned on once more."

With a shrug, Ryan began to move toward the door indicated. The rest of the companions followed, moving through a crowd that parted before them. Jak stopped to hug Gloria. To the viewers above it would seem to be a touching, if uncharacteristic, farewell. But as he leaned in close and held the Gate queen, Jak whispered in her ear, "Stay alert. Look for faintest chance, from them or us. Not give up."

"I won't, sweets," Gloria replied softly. She smiled crookedly as Jak pulled away, and winked at him.

He returned to the main party as they progressed toward the small sec door.

"Everyone else stand well back," the sardonic voice intoned. "The slightest sign of resistance, and we turn on the sprinklers again. And I don't think you really want that."

"And I don't think you really want the microphone jammed up your ass, but it may just happen if I get hold of you," Mildred said under her breath as they reached the door.

Looking back, they could see that a few yards separated themselves from the rest of the army.

"Please move through the door now...and quickly," the voice said as the sec door rose rapidly.

With Ryan in the lead, they passed through into the corridor beyond. As soon as J.B.—automatically taking the rear position, even though there was no real need—was through, the door dropped swiftly.

The companions found themselves in an antechamber formed by the two closed sec doors, one leading out to the mat-trans chamber, and one a regular sec door in the corridor beyond that had been lowered to contain them. It was a small space, and seemed confining and almost too quiet after the room beyond.

"What do you reckon their plans are?" Dean asked in a whisper.

"Seems that they know we're apart in some way from the others," his father replied. "What we need to know is whether that's because they just recognize us from the last redoubt, or because they know something about us."

"What could they know?" Jak queried.

Doc sighed. "Perhaps my fault, dear boy—if they were part of the Totality Concept, then records may have survived concerning me, for as far as I know I was the only survivor of Operation Chronos."

"Yeah, well, let's not jump to conclusions here," Mildred urged. "This is going to be the only chance we get, right?"

"Right," Ryan agreed. "Keep alert, and try to keep your eyes open for anything that can help us."

Any further attempt at formulating a plan was cut short as the second sec door—leading farther into the corridor and the heart of the redoubt—slid smoothly upward, revealing a group of four Illuminated sec— two male and two female—standing in the corridor beyond, holding laser blasters, which were immediately leveled at the companions.

"Out here—now," one of the men snapped. "Quick, sharp!"

Ryan led his people into the corridor. The sec force parted, so that two stepped backward to head the procession, and two would bring up the rear once the rest of the group had moved out of the self-contained cell.

"They're not taking any chances," Dean remarked as the head sec pairing began to move.

"Silence! No talking until you're asked questions,"

shouted the sec man who had spoken previously, and whom Ryan took to be the sec chief on this patrol.

"Touchy, isn't he?" Mildred muttered, almost to herself. She was at the back of the group with J.B. and Dean, and was taken unaware by the sudden blow in the small of her back as the sec woman at the rear of the group swiveled her laser rifle and drove the butt into Mildred's kidney.

Mildred yelped in pain and surprise, buckling as her weakened system received a buffet, the pain sweeping over her in a wave of nausea and faintness. J.B. caught her as she slumped toward the floor.

"No stopping, keep moving," the head sec man intoned.

J.B. looked up and glared at him, mentally noting the man in case the chance came later to chill him first.

They continued along the corridor, Dean helping the Armorer to carry Mildred and keep up the pace set by the sec squad. The callous action had determined them even more—if that was possible—to eradicate the menace of the Illuminated Ones.

Coming to a junction, none of the companions were prepared for what they saw next. Turning left, the sec squad took them along a corridor for another fifty yards until they came to a sec door. As they approached, the door sprang upward, and they found themselves walking out onto an open catwalk that was suspended over a deep chasm.

"Hot pipe! What's that?" Dean whispered as they swayed along the catwalk, which moved with the shifting weight of the party.

It was the fact that they couldn't go more than three abreast along the catwalk, and the sec squad was obviously under orders not to chill any of the companions, that saved Dean from a sharp blow with a rifle butt such as the one that had injured Mildred. For any blow or disturbance to his balance could have catapulted him off the open side of the catwalk—over the thin handrail that was the only guard—and down the chasm.

The incredible sight that had prompted Dean to break silence wasn't the chasm itself, incredible though that was. The catwalk extended for about three hundred yards across a natural cavern that stood about forty feet above them, and dropped into the blackness below. However, there was a rock shelf that encircled the gaping hole situated about twenty feet beneath the catwalk. Its edge was fenced in, forming a walkway that extended around the chasm's circumference. And on this shelf, which was twenty to thirty feet in width at any given point, lumbered a number of creatures.

The creatures were misshapen, but appeared to be humanistic or apelike. Some were upright; others dragged their knuckles almost as though on all fours. Some were covered in hair, while others were hairless, and there were those in the middle that had a soft, downy covering over their whole body, through which could be seen their pinky-gray skin. There were troughs for food and water set around the shelf, and the creatures were naked. It was warm in the abyss, and probably maintained at a constant level. They shuffled and walked without purpose, seeming to just kill time. And even though the companions were twenty feet above, they could plainly see that many of the creatures had growths and tumors on their bodies, some of which had developed sores.

"That's sick," Mildred said. Unable to contain herself, and unthinking of any further injury, she turned to the sec behind her. "What the fuck do you do that for?"

"Shut up," the woman who had hit her said sharply, "or you'll get some more, bitch. Could be you, if you're lucky."

"Quiet!" the leader snapped, turning back. His eyes burned with fury at the sec woman. "You talk too much. Leave it for the leader."

This gave all of the companions much to consider. They knew that they were being taken to the head of the Illuminated Ones—at least, the head of this redoubt—and that they could be lined up for more experiments if they allowed. Each of them knew that they and their friends would rather die fighting than give in to such treatment in the hope of a few more days or weeks of life, but it seemed that the Illuminated Ones didn't expect such an attitude. That could be an advantage.

The sec door at the end of the catwalk rose, and they passed through and into a regular corridor. They had assumed they were at the deepest level of the redoubt, but the chasm threw that into doubt. There had to be, at least, a corridor leading to the shelf. Supposing the redoubt had been built, and this feature added later? The roof of the cavern would only have interfered with one higher level, so it was possible that this geographical factor had been ignored when the base was originally constructed.

Mildred's mind raced. For her, it wasn't the redoubt layout that mattered right now, but the creatures. What sort of experiments were being carried out on them, for it seemed to be some kind of vivisection or study of infection. Perhaps more importantly, what were those creatures, and how did the Illuminated Ones get them? They bore no real resemblance to any muties that she could recall seeing, and looked horribly like the evolving stages of mankind.

She shuddered as a thought crossed her mind. Surely the Illuminated Ones hadn't degenerated to such a base level?

Any further reflections along that line were stopped by the sec squad's sudden plunge into the heart of the redoubt. The companions were led into an elevator, with laser blasters jabbing into them as the sec squad made sure that no sudden action would be taken. They were whisked up three levels by the elevator, and came out into a corridor where all the sec doors were open, and the normal life of the redoubt continued as usual. This activity had been proceeding unheeded for the entire time that they had been directed down into the mat-trans chamber, and it was frustrating to consider that the normal activity of the Illuminated Ones had continued unimpeded.

Mildred tried to look through the open doors as they passed, hoping that she would catch sight of something that she could store for future reference, something that looked like a medical lab where experimentation had been taking place. But all she could see, much to her chagrin, were weapons labs, the armory, and kitchens and shower rooms. There were also offices where comp terminals flickered and hummed, manned by personnel who took no notice of their passing. They all seemed to be busy, and Ryan wasn't the only one of the companions who wondered what they were doing. Were they keeping in touch with other Illuminated Ones in other redoubts? Or were they in some way plotting, mapping and planning for a world after the devastation of their disease?

It was a question that concerned all of them. If there were other bases, then where were those bases? How many of them were there, and how many personnel in each? Or was this the only base? On leaving the redoubt from where the Gate tribe and the companions had followed, had they, so to speak, come home?

Looking around, the base did seem to be sparsely populated for one that contained the original redoubt crew and those who had come from the previous location. Was it a larger base, with more levels in which these people were working? Or had they then traveled on to other bases?

There was one option that Mildred did not dare to consider: all along, the companions—particularly herself—had worked on the assumption that the Illuminated Ones had some sort of inoculation or antidote for the smallpox variant strain that they had let loose across the land. To unleash it without would be beyond madness; it would be a work of pure idiocy.

Yet was it possible that they had released the pox without having an adequate defense against it? If so, then it would have decimated their own numbers, which may account for the seemingly sparse population of the redoubt. It could also account for the experiments they had seen in the chasm—a last desperate attempt to beat the chron and find a cure before they themselves were wiped out.

If that truly was the case, then everything that the companions and the Gate had done was all in vain. Their efforts were wasted.

Mildred desperately scanned the faces and hands, the only exposed skin, of every Illuminated One that they passed, searching for some kind of sign, a skin discoloration, a blister, a red mark, a sign of temperature or fever....

She could see nothing. But that didn't reassure her. Those who were infected could be hidden away in some sick bay, isolated in the hope of somehow containing the disease.

J.B. and Dean could see Mildred staring at every Illuminated One they passed, but didn't understand her reasons. They were confused, and the confusion was shared by the others...except for Doc. He had reached a similar conclusion, but in Doc Tanner's mind, there was no attempt to reason for a solution. Doc's face was set like stone, grim and harsh. To him, if this was the way in which it had to end, then so be it. It made a kind of sense that the last remnants of the decadence that the Totality Concept represented would be eradicated because of its own small-minded stupidity.

The sec squad turned another corner, into a smaller corridor leading off the main. At the far end was a closed sec door, the only one in this section that had been closed.

Ryan chewed his lip thoughtfully. The fact that it was closed made it significant. Were they about to learn the truth at last?

The leading sec duo turned as they reached the door, leveling their blasters on the companions. At the rear, the two people who had been keeping watch on the tail stepped back and also leveled their laser blasters. There was no way that any of the companions could make a move without incurring a hail of laser fire.

"You're about to meet the leader," the sec chief said softly. "That makes you very lucky people. Even we do not get to be in his presence very often. He's a busy man, planning for the time when he will take his rightful place as the leader of the new earth. While the other scum in the transport section are considered expendable, for some reason you are considered important—at least, for now. Remember that you have no arms, and that we would take great pleasure in chilling you.''

The companions stayed silent, biting tongues that held ready replies to such arrogance.

''Be ready to be admitted to the presence of glory,'' the sec leader said, reaching behind and pressing the single key on the sec door keypad.

Deep inside the room on the other side of the door, they could hear a buzzer signaling their presence. What kind of a man was the leader that he had no keypad or sec code for his door? That he isolated himself from his people in this manner, so that they could only signal their presence and hope for an audience?

As the sec door finally rose in response, they knew they were about to find out.

Chapter Fifteen

The companions found themselves hustled through the open door by the sec squad, pushed through the narrow opening without a real chance to recce the room beyond before being pushed into it. Doc and Mildred almost stumbled as they were prodded by the butts of the laser blasters.

"Move—he mustn't be kept waiting," the head sec man rapped out as he cajoled the group…and was that a note of fear that Ryan could detect in his voice? The leader of the Illuminated Ones was obviously a man who was held in awe by his people.

Now inside the room, the companions had a chance to take a look at the surroundings. First thing should have been to look at the leader himself, but the room was an immediate attention grabber by its sheer opulence and grotesque clutter. It was only slightly larger than the usual office rooms found in redoubts, and wasn't even the size of a larger bunker such as the armory or a med bay. But its size was hard to estimate accurately because of the vast array of ornamentation and treasures gathered within.

They had all seen or heard of things like this. There were some barons who had the accumulated loot of what remained after the nukecaust, and for Mildred and Doc it was a reminder of the world from which they had been expelled. But no one had seen such a collection in such a small space: there were finely carved antique Louis XVI chairs; gold-and-silver ornaments displayed in fine mahogany cabinets, polished to a sheen; beautifully framed oil paintings by artists from Leonardo to Picasso; tapestries and carpets of the finest weave; and—instead of the usual military-issue desk—a large oak writing desk with intricate carving decorating the scrolled legs.

To see such predark riches in one place was unexpected enough, but to have them crammed into a relatively small space and bearing down as soon as the room was entered—in stark contrast to the bare corridor outside—was overwhelming. There was so much sensory overload that it took a second for them to notice the man seated behind the desk.

How someone such as this could remain anonymous was a marker of how overpowering were his surroundings. The man, although seated, was a giant. He had enormous girth and was squeezed tightly into his silver-gray uniform. It stuck to his more than ample form and showed rolls of fat dripping from his ribs and overhanging his vast stomach, which was wedged behind the desk. His head seemed almost too small for such a body, with dark hair short and swept back from a furrowed forehead over deep-set eyes, a thin nose and full, fleshy lips. His jowls hung as heavily as the rolls of fat on his body, and he appeared to be breathing heavily even in repose.

"So glad you could make it," he said in a cold, sardonic tone that was familiar. His had been the voice that they had heard over the PA system in the chamber. "I would offer you a seat, but you're dripping all over my carpets and frankly I wouldn't want you to stain the seats on the chairs."

Mildred curled her lip. "I wouldn't want to be soiled by anything that was yours."

J.B. moved quickly, seeing the rifle butt from the corner of his eye as it was directed toward Mildred's kidneys once more. He deflected the blow so that it grazed harmlessly off to one side, but was rewarded by the backswing, which caught him in the chest. He raised his arms and warded off the full weight of the blow, but it was enough to send him staggering backward, where he was halted by another blow across the back of his neck and shoulders, driving him to the ground.

Ryan, eye blazing, turned to help his friend, but found the muzzle of a laser blaster jammed into his face.

"Children, children, desist from this stupidity," the fat man said wearily. "I really do not wish to have my chambers destroyed by anything as sordid and petty as a fight. I have wanted you to be kept alive thus far, but believe me, I would have no compunction in having you chilled where you stand rather than risk any of my belongings. They've survived a nuclear winter, so I'm sure they can survive you."

J.B. pulled himself to his feet and rejoined his companions while the sec squad stood off.

"You okay, John?" Mildred asked. He nodded, but stayed silent. Instead, it was Krysty who spoke.

"This is all very pretty," she said with barely disguised sarcasm, "but what does it all mean? What point is there in keeping it all hidden down here, safe and warm, and never daring to venture even out of the room?" The woman chose her words carefully, watching the fat face as it reacted to her words.

Unless her intuition had let her down, she had hit

unerringly on a sore point. It would seem that the fat man was indeed confined to this room by something. Looking at the desk, she could see that there was a comp terminal and a sec monitor built in to the ancient wood. There also had to be a microphone with the terminal.

Why would he never set foot outside the room?

"Madam," the fat man began in even, measured tones that were all the more suspicious for being such, "your petty jibes may be intended to wound, but they will have no effect on me. I have greater matters to concern me."

"So tell us about them," Krysty replied simply. "They must be something incredible if they confine you here."

"They do not confine me," the fat man barked. "I stay here by choice, until such time as the world is fit for me to enter once more."

Suddenly, Ryan realized what had made Krysty dig at their captor in such a manner. For whatever reason—either physical or psychological, the fat man who was the Illuminated Ones' leader was unable to leave this room, which would account for why it was crammed with all his accumulated treasures. He had to bring them to himself as he was unable to go to them elsewhere. It also explained why the companions had been separated from the Gate. He had to have them brought to him, as he was unable to go to the chamber.

And then it hit him: the fat man's words had been "until such time as the world is fit for me to enter once more." But if the fat man was unable to leave the room, then he would never be able to leave the room. And the world would never be fit.

Was this why he was intent on spreading the foul disease across the land? If he could never go out into the world, then he had to eradicate it, make it fit for himself by destroying it?

Psychology was a dead form in the postnukecaust world. Virtually all written records of the science had been eradicated, and it lived on only in those few enclaves where the predark sciences and disciplines were kept alive...and in most of those the sciences were perverted and distorted by insanity and mutation. But as a practical form that had no name, it was still very much alive. The art of judging a man and second-guessing his intent and action were the very things that kept the companions—and many like them—alive as they tried to exist in the world above the redoubt. And the longer you survived, the better you became at this unspoken and unnamed psychology.

Looking at Mildred and J.B., Ryan could see that they had also guessed or half guessed the reasoning behind the spread of the disease. It did have a certain twisted logic: in a country that was hollow and empty, then the man confined to one room could truly be king of all, not just of what he surveyed, but of the emptiness that lay beyond.

The fat man behind the desk studied them intently. He had expected more from them, certainly, his sec squad had kept them under close watch as he was sure that they would try to escape into the redoubt and fight against him. Yet here they were, doing nothing except standing and exchanging puzzled glances.

His confidence grew, and he signaled for the sec squads to stand farther back. He rose from behind the desk, his vast bulk wobbling in the tight-fitting uniform, which seemed to barely stretch over his skin.

They could see that he was as immensely tall as he was wide, and he stepped with difficulty from behind the desk so that he stood in front of them.

"You know, when I was a younger man, before the nukecaust, there was a tradition in the entertainments of the time for the villain of the piece to stand before the hero and say, 'Now you will die—but first I must explain my plans for world domination to you.' And of course, this would allow the hero time to effect some miraculous escape. I always used to wonder why the mastermind, supposingly so brilliant, would do something that was seemingly so stupid. In fiction, just a plot device, of course, to reveal the full extent and implication of the story to the waiting audience. But would it happen in reality?

"Now, there is an interesting proposition—what would one do in reality? I had always wondered, and now I know. I am about to follow in the footsteps of my fictional forebears and relay to you my story, and why I intend to follow my current course of action. Of course, there are some differences. For instance, you will not escape, and you will be chilled...not immediately, it's true, but as the disease takes hold on you. And you will have the bittersweet knowledge of knowing what is occurring as you helplessly spread the pox across the lands above." He chuckled, high in pitch and suggestive of madness. "That rather appeals to me. The biggest difference is that in this scenario, I win. Now, that definitely appeals to me."

Mildred's mind raced. There were several things for which she needed answers, and perhaps quicker than this dangerous buffoon would supply them. What was the disease? Did he have a cure, or was he intending to wipe out even his own people? And what did he mean when he spoke of being a younger man, before the nukecaust? Mildred had lived in those days and been cryogenically frozen; Doc had been trawled from then and before; but what was this man's secret?

The companions were all lost in their own thoughts. Krysty's were running along similar lines to Mildred's. Doc, too, was pondering on the fat man's cryptic references.

But the other four had separate notions.

Dean was eyeing the comp terminal, and wondering if it would be possible to gain access to it if a fight broke out. He figured that the terminal here had to be the mother of all others in the redoubt, and from it he could control all the systems within the base, and free the Gate.

Ryan and J.B. were balancing the chances of winning a hand-to-hand combat with the sec squad with a minimum risk of casualty against the option of waiting a little longer, lest the fat man give away more about himself and his organization that would help them in their battle against him.

Jak was more decided. He was waiting for the chance to strike. He knew that Doc still had his sword of the finest Toledo steel hidden within the lion's-head cane on which he leaned. He also knew that the sec squad had been slack in not searching each companion, for he still had his leaf-bladed throwing knives secreted within the patched and metal-decorated combat jacket he wore. Although the words of the fat man might give them insight into why he was pursuing this course of action, Jak considered that this was completely irrelevant. To the albino, it was important to strike quickly. He trusted Mildred to know what she was looking for, and that their imperative was to move out of this room and look for the lab before freeing the Gate and wiping out the opposition. It was that simple. There was no time for anything else.

But he knew that he would have to bide his time. Ryan was the leader, and although any of the companions could act independently if it was necessary, in a situation such as this they would have to take direction from the one-eyed warrior. A hierarchy had to be maintained if they were to pull together.

It was just that Jak would have preferred to pull right now. Instead, he waited as the fat man began to unravel his tale. He glanced across at Doc, whose obvious distaste and disgust for this symbol of the corrupted world that had birthed the Deathlands was about to grow greater.

"THE FIRST THING you must know about me is that my name is Emile Taschen. I am not the first to serve that name, although I am the same as the others. You see, although animals had been successfully cloned in the public eye before the nukecaust, there was always so much squeamishness about the concept of cloning in human beings that the technology was kept quiet. I am the third Emile Taschen, my two previous bodies having died from nothing more serious than old age. Number four is currently being grown in the labs, where he will be kept at fetal stage cryogenically until I get older, and will then be nurtured and birthed before I die…if I can ever be said to actually die.

"I am taught my own memories and ideas, and these are absorbed into the blank state of my being. I am the perfection of science and humanity. Everything else is lesser, and I bestride it like a colossus, leaving everything to wither and die in my shadow."

So that was the answer, Mildred thought. Cloned, and then the clone kept in isolation and fed the ideas and thoughts of the previous generation so that it became a carbon copy rather than a genetic copy open to variation from social conditions. It would seem that Taschen had solved the problem of living forever, even if it did seem somewhat by proxy. And what if some of the memories fed to the clone were distorted by time and telling? How could it have a grasp of identity? Perhaps this gradual erosion of identity accounted for the creeping defects of agoraphobia and the onset of madness. She was halted in her thoughts as Taschen continued.

"You're probably wondering how someone such as myself managed to create such a structure as this without being part of the military-industrial complex on either side of the divide. The answer is simple. You become that which finances the military industrial complex. I'm sure I don't have to tell you that what you refer to as 'jack' has always been the oil on the wheels of human activity. It was the same in the days before the nukecaust—perhaps more so.

"I first became aware of the Totality Concept when I was a banker in my homeland of Switzerland. In the days before nukes, my land had always maintained neutrality, based around our banking industry. Money was the richest commodity in every way, and it bought peace, as well as prosperity. Those who controlled the jack controlled the world. But nukes made things different. Even with bunkers to hide in, there would be little to come out to—certainly not a society that we could serve any purpose within. So when the political situation of the world worsened in the latter half of the twentieth century, I knew I would have to search for a solution to my problem.

"It was then that the cabal of generals first came to me. They were from the U.S. military, and they were seeking a way to hide and increase the funds they had taken from their military budget. There were scientific and weapons projects that were being developed away from the eye of the U.S. Congress, which would either have stopped them or made their existence more open. This wouldn't suit the cabal, who took the usual military view that a civilian government was more of an imposition than a necessity. Democracy was a concept for which they had little, if any, use. Something I agreed with—you must always watch your own back, on the assumption that nobody else will be bothered.

"My own banking activities skirted around this kind of activity—what was known as the black sector, because it stayed in darkness. I had a certain reputation as a man who could hide vast sums of money, and could also increase them with speculation and the courting of outside investors, who would not necessarily be aware of the full facts relating to their investment. I confess that this aspect used to amuse me at times.

"But amusement was something that soon took a back seat to more pressing matters. The scope of the Totality Concept and the projects that were gathered under that umbrella were breathtaking in their imagination and diversity. Here was something that would ensure the winning of any conflict that may take place, and the mastery of the world. To be frank, I have never been sure if any one member of the cabal, or myself, was ever truly aware of everything that was contained under the umbrella of the concept, such was the double-dealing and secrecy involved.

"It became apparent to me that a conflict from which there would be no escape short of a total war was approaching. Call it a combination of the egos and paranoias of the men involved and their will to prove themselves the better of their fellow men, or call it just the desire to play with toys and prove that they work, and that all the expense and work were justified. Whatever it may have been, it was an inevitability."

The fat man called Taschen was obsessed with his ideas and his organization—of that there was little doubt. The companions watched him carefully, and with rapt attention. Any scrap of information may be of use, although each of them in turn wished that he would get to anything that may have relevance with haste, as they were finding his egotistical ramblings dull.

In Doc's case, it was a little more than that: the man with the complex history spread over three centuries had the utmost contempt for the thinking that had empowered the cloned banker, and the ideals that he perpetrated. So much so that he had to interject, "So tell me, O great and mighty one—how, pray tell, did you progress from being a mere money broker into such a major player that you can command this? And, if it's not too much trouble, to what end is all this frippery, anyway?"

Taschen fixed the old man with a stare that was half amusement, half hatred. It was clear that he didn't relish being interrupted, but the question in itself only acted as a prompt to the next part of his tale.

"You must, perforce, be Dr. Theophilus Tanner. I had read about you, but never thought that I would meet you. You always sounded a troublesome and obtuse man for someone who was seemingly so bright. A view that I find unexpectedly—and a little disappointingly—confirmed.''

Doc gave a mocking bow before replying in sarcastic tones, ''I am so terribly sorry to have let you down…and, indeed, to have interrupted you at such a crucial point in your narrative. Are you, in fact, about to unveil your entire plan before us?''

Taschen indulged Doc, despite the bristling of the sec squad at the old man's tone.

''Most amusing,'' the fat man stated. ''But you are correct, indeed, in the assumption that I am about to explain the whys and wherefores to you. Partly, I fear, because that old dictum about leadership and responsibility being lonely is proving to be quite true.

''However, that would be to dwell on the side of self-pity, and that is not my wish.''

Mildred closed her eyes and had to concentrate hard on staying conscious. The pain from her treatment at the hands of the guards, and the continuing effects of the pox, were beginning to weaken her. And yet she suspected that, despite his words, self-pity was the entire motivation for Taschen's activities now, and that he was soon to reveal his secrets—and perhaps give them the break they needed right now.

Taschen continued. ''The interesting thing about being a banker in Switzerland was that money was not the only commodity in which one dealt. Secrets were a much more valued and valuable commodity, in fact. At my facility in Geneva, we had safe-deposit boxes, the contents of which could easily have changed the course of history several times daily—perhaps they did. Who can tell? The point I wish to make is that money powers secrets and secrets generate money. The two are interdependent, and as a banker I was able to trade off this dependency and make for myself a power base from which to build not just my own survival, but a way of making sure that the next time around a glorious society would arise from the ashes of old order, and make a new order that would lead the world into a better era.''

"Pernicious claptrap!" Doc spit. "It has been the same throughout history. Those who wish to foist their own views upon an unsuspecting and unwilling world always seek to justify their own egotism.''

Taschen shrugged. "A small-minded view, and little more than I would expect from one such as you. When you have access to the secrets of power, then you are privy to the small-mindedness of most people. And if you have a vision, then you realize naturally that you have been chosen by the fates to shape their very existence.

"I began to become interested in a Bavarian philosopher and schemer called Adam Weishaupt, who had founded a society known as the Illuminati. There were some who believed that this secret cabal had grown in power since its founding in the late eighteenth century, and that far from being outlawed and then disbanded, the successors to Weishaupt had used this as a cover from which to recruit at all levels of world governments, forming an inner circle that actually ran the world. All I can say is that, were this true, they had made an extremely bad fist of matters. No, my friends, the Illuminati had not existed for some time, and even when they had their influence had been limited in the extreme. However, that did not mean that their ideas had been bad, merely that no one had previously acquired access to the right sources to make them work.

"Of course, now that I was in such a position, I would be a spineless fool to ignore my destiny. Such secrets as I did not have within my immediate grasp could be obtained by a mixture of blackmail and bribery, feeding the fear and greed that fuels the desires for power. I used money from my bank, and from the banks of fellow adventurers and bankers that I recruited to my cause. Naturally, I had every intention of dumping these fools by the wayside as I continued, but at this point they did not have to know that. I wished to keep them all in the dark, and in this I think I succeeded."

"So why did you end up here, and not back in Europe?" J.B. asked, hoping to steer the discourse toward matters the companions wished to explore.

Taschen shrugged, his immense bulk wobbling as his shoulders heaved. "Where else? The main players were the USSR and the U.S.A. There was little chance of cooperation with the Communists, who already had their own version of the game in progress. Besides, the vast majority of my contacts were within the black areas of the U.S. military-industrial complex, so it made much more sense to pursue this option. So I relocated my home and also my business base to the U.S.A., leaving my office in Switzerland as nothing more than a shelter from which to avoid investigation by the U.S. authorities—although given that those investigating would be those under my thumb, the only thing I truly had to avoid was the publicity that such a matter could entail. I had many of the intelligence agencies and military projects bought off, and the only reason I cannot be sure of the true extent of the Totality Concept is simply that it was so vast that I ran out of time to explore and exploit before some fool started the nukecaust.''

The fat man sighed and settled his bulk on the edge of the desk, which creaked beneath the weight.

The companions were starting to tire of his ego. Ryan and J.B. itched for action, and Jak was already contemplating the knives hidden about his person. To strike quickly would leave Mildred with time to search for the lab once they had released the Gate. The forces within the redoubt seemed to be smaller than they had feared, and could be dealt with by a determined force such as the one waiting in the vast mat-trans chamber beneath them. Mildred and Doc both felt distaste, for their own reasons, and wished the fat man would cut to the chase so that they could take action. But for Dean and Krysty, there was still something that needed an answer, something that didn't add up. It was Dean that raised the matter.

''Look, I don't get it,'' he began. ''When we first came across some indications of the Illuminated Ones—which isn't as good a name as the Illuminati, so I figure you screwed that one—it was mixed up with what Mildred told us was the counterculture, the young people who figured that the ruling sec were screwing up and wanted to build some kind of alternative. I don't see them going for your shit.''

Taschen threw back his head and roared with laughter. He stopped, looked at the expression on Dean's face and laughed again, this time louder. Finally, he stopped and explained, using the kind of tone that suggested they were more stupe than he had realized.

''That was my finest touch, I feel. I had to allow myself a little humor in what was, after all, a fairly humorless environment. It seemed a splendid jest to recruit so-called subversives and counterrevolutionaries into a movement that was allegedly opposed to the prevailing military culture, but was in fact using that very thing to manipulate it toward its own ends. Those who believed they were fighting for a freedom from such—as they saw it—oppression were in fact upholding the very ideals and complexes that they opposed. It was merely that it carried another name. My foot soldiers were the very people who would gladly have spit on my grave. And it did, of course, also serve the excellent double purpose of keeping them off my tail.''

''That's pretty sick,'' Krysty commented. ''But then again, what would I expect. Are you happy with what you've made?''

''Ah, no—not me,'' Taschen countered. ''You must remember that I did not begin the nukecaust. In point of fact, my reason for building this was in knowing that it was inevitable, and in waiting for what would happen afterward. And that's exactly how it happened. When the nukecaust came, and the long, hard nuclear winter began, I retreated to my redoubt and ordered my people to do the same. The cloning project was at such an advanced stage that I was assured of my own future. There was, over the ensuing decades, some diminution of my forces—natural wastage, and the necessarily limited gene pool have taken their toll, but there are still several bases left across the world, keeping in contact via mat-trans and comp links. The tech is still there, and so are we.''

Ryan was alarmed. How many of these bastards would they have to chill before their task was done? ''How many bases are there?''

Taschen allowed himself an indulgent smile. "You think I would really trust you with that knowledge? As with everything, only I know the true answers. Even the other redoubts are not fully aware. Nor, come to that, are they in full knowledge or contact of their true numbers or purpose. I would not be that stupid. Knowledge is power, and I aim to retain that power. When they are required to act, they are told…but the basis is strictly need-to-know. Without me, they would be survivors of another age, isolated in this new world. With me, they are a force that will run this world. Even those who came here from the redoubt you ruined, like the barbarians you are, have been dispersed among the other bases, awaiting their new orders when the time is right."

"And just when will the time be right?" Mildred asked.

"When the likes of you have fulfilled your little task, and spread my disease across the land, making it clean of scum and fit for the new order to come forth and achieve dominance."

"Over an empty world ravaged by a disease that will chill everyone, including your descendants?" Doc cannily posited.

Reveling in his supposed ascendancy, Taschen took the bait. "You surely do not think that I would leave my own people unprotected? Of course they are inoculated, so they can walk freely over the land above. Naturally, the shrinking gene pool and the encroachment of time will lead to their eventual demise, but I shall still be here, like Ubu roi—a character in fiction I always admired—cloned forever and bestriding my domain like a colossus. I believe I may have mentioned that fact before.

"But now, I have told you enough. I felt I would like to unburden to you, as you have been the worthiest opponents I have ever faced, and in a sense you have become my recruits, albeit unwittingly, as I shall be using you to spread my little disease across the lands, sending you in batches to my redoubts and letting you loose in your new locations to do my work on any you may care to meet. A plan stunning in its simplicity. You will, of course, be sent forth without weapons, as I will have to take precautions to insure the safety of my Illuminated Ones, just as I have taken precautions on my own behalf by stripping you of weapons before admitting you into my presence."

It was now that the despot's sense of overweening arrogance revealed itself as his Achilles' heel. He had finished his discourse, and Mildred was assured that there was an antidote and inoculation against the pox. Her fears regarding the lack of people resident in this redoubt were also calmed. She looked at Jak and Doc, and as her eyes met theirs, they knew that she was satisfied. J.B., Ryan, Krysty and Dean also gathered this, and from the brief glances that were exchanged, it was obvious what needed to be done.

"You know something?" Ryan asked of Taschen, stepping forward and attracting the attention of the sec squad. "You really have got too big a head—even bigger than that fat body of yours. You should get out more, you coldhearted, fat bastard."

"Hard words, my one-eyed friend, but my men will cut you down before you get near me," the fat man grated, expecting an unarmed attack from Ryan.

Which distracted their attention from Jak for just long enough. The albino had been slowed by the ravages of the disease, but even with this handicap he

was too quick for the sec squad to follow. Palming
three of his leaf-bladed, razor-sharp throwing knives
from their hiding places, he tossed two to Ryan and
J.B., hilt first, so that the two men were able to catch
them with ease. The movement of the knives flashing
in the muted light of the room confused the sec squad,
who froze. With fatal consequences.

The third knife was hilt to hand for the albino,
whose arm, despite the slower reflex action, was still
a blur as hand and eye combined in perfect alignment.
The knife sped to its target, landing in the left eye of
Emile Taschen, penetrating the eyeball, spilling the
viscous liquid down his cheek as the point cut through
the muscle at the back of the eye, and thence into the
skull cavity and the brain itself.

Taschen half fell, half staggered backward, rolling
his vast bulk over the desk, gurgling in pain and shock
as the impact hit him and the receptor centers of his
brain realized that the synapses were being extin-
guished.

"You can't do this," he gurgled in strained disbelief, his voice almost a strangled whine. "It's too
soon...I'm not ready yet...."

"Are," Jak said simply and in a neutral tone as he
vaulted the desk to where the stumbling Taschen had
come to rest, behind the comp terminal from which he
ruled his own little perverted universe. The albino followed his simple words with an even more simple action: removing the knife with a determined tug, so that
blood and fluid poured out of the wounded eye and
down the fat man's cheek. Jak pulled back his head
and finished the chilling with a swift slice across
Taschen's throat that caused blood to jet across the
room with the beat of the man's heart, diminishing in

flow as the beat lessened until the fat man was still. It had been a simple task. Jak may have been slowed by the disease, but he was still infinitely quicker than his opponent.

The sec squad was still stunned by the sudden ferocity of the action, and the chilling of their leader. Ryan and J.B. were able to overpower their chosen opponents with ease, disabling them with kicks and blows that doubled over the sec personnel, making them easy targets for the knives to find a home and buy the farm.

The two sec who hadn't been attacked had a few moments more in which to galvanize themselves to action. One of the women—the one who had been vicious to Mildred—raised her blaster, once more picking the plaited woman as her target. But she had reckoned without Doc. Assuming that he was a frail old man, she had ignored him leaning on his cane. But as she looked away, Doc unsheathed the Toledo steel blade within the cane and brought the finely tempered metal slicing through the air, chopping it down onto the sec woman's arms as they cradled the laser blaster. The blade cut through her flesh, severing nerves, as well as causing her hands to become slippery with her own blood. The blaster dropped from nerveless fingers, and she squealed in pain.

Doc completed the sweep of the blade, bringing it back up so that he could thrust the fine tip at her exposed and uncovered heart, the thin material of her uniform proving no defense against the steel. She stopped squealing as her ruptured and pierced heart jolted to a halt.

Three down, but the last one was armed, and the two companions facing him weren't.

Krysty and Dean unconsciously separated, making the distance between them such that he couldn't fire on both without changing his stance. Unsure of whom to aim for, he vacillated with dire consequences. Dean kicked out, his boot catching the man on the side of the knee. He gasped in shock and pain as the joint gave way, making him fall sideways. As he fell, Krysty was on him. The blaster was pointing downward, and her knee pinned it harmlessly to the ground, while her knuckles sought the soft area around his temple. Finding it with a short jab, she drew back her arm and smashed the vulnerable section of his skull with one blow, sending splinters of bone into his brain, and causing the vital organ to begin shutting down.

The companions were now alone in the room, surrounded by five corpses. With Taschen chilled, the Illuminated Ones were now just disparate groups of dwindling people waiting for orders that would never come. The important thing now was to find the cultures of disease and destroy them, synthesize the antidote and mop up the remnants of the base.

Arming themselves with the laser blasters from the chilled sec squad, they headed for the door.

"Let's get Gloria and the Gate out of that chamber and get down to business," Ryan said brusquely.

The chron was now almost at zero. The ticking had stopped.

It was now or never.

Chapter Sixteen

Gathered by the door leading from Taschen's quarters, the companions readied themselves for the trip back to the mat-trans hangar and the Gate.

"Everyone triple frosty?" Ryan asked calmly, gathering a series of nods from his people. "We follow the usual formation, but keep it tighter. We need to move quick and get through the redoubt without being spotted, or at least without raising an alarm. Anyone sees us, we chill them on the spot. First priority is to get the Gate out of that chamber. Then we hit them hard, and go for the med lab."

"Why don't we free the Gate from here, so they can get moving and we can devote ourselves to getting to the lab?" Dean queried. "It won't take me and Mildred more than a few seconds to crack the comp on the fat man's desk...and then they can start to wipe out the Illuminated Ones while we get to the lab."

The one-eyed man shook his head. "Nice idea, son, but there are problems. We don't know if the Gate have had their weapons taken away, and if the sec doors on the chamber start to move, the sec on guard will have the advantage—"

"—and they'll come and check here," Mildred added. "The longer fat boy buying the farm is kept quiet, the better."

Dean thought about that, then nodded. "Yeah, I see what you mean. Guess we'd better get going, then."

The group now had four laser blasters, taken from the sec squad. As Jak, J.B. and Ryan all had blades, the other four had taken the blasters, meaning that Mildred, Doc, Krysty and Dean were now equipped to face any danger head-on. They clustered in the doorway of the room, casting a glance back at the mayhem behind them.

Taschen lay at his desk, blood dripping across the surface and spilling onto the antique Persian rug that lay in front, once regally spread but now rucked and torn by the fight that had taken place. Although most of the antique furniture and priceless objets d'art that he had collected in his various incarnations still cluttered the room undamaged, Louis XVI chairs were splintered and antique display cabinets were splattered with blood.

"All that conspicuous wealth," Mildred muttered, almost to herself.

"Wealth? It doesn't mean anything now." J.B. shrugged. "It's got no real value in the real world."

"That's the problem, John," Mildred said sadly. "In his version of the real world, it still did. And it once had in the world I lived in. That was why people like him made shit like this happen."

"It's over for the Illuminated Ones now," Krysty said firmly but quietly. "Without that fat bastard, they're nothing more than a bunch of confused idiots spread across the land, waiting for a call that'll never come."

"None of which will matter a jot unless we get the little matter of the nefarious disease resolved," Doc interjected with a note of urgency in his tone. "So I

suggest that we follow our leader and begin the counterattack.''

Ryan nodded firmly, his mouth set grim and tight
in anticipation of the knife-edge journey they had to
face, and hit the sec door release with the flat of his
hand. As with the exterior locking mechanism, there
was no keypad, only a single red button. Dean was
about to ask Doc how it could be a counterattack if
there was no initial attack to actually counter, but held
his peace as the door began to rise. Taschen had obviously had the self-belief to never consider that anyone other than himself would wish to leave the room,
and so had no safety devices built in.

Led by the one-eyed man, they stepped out of the
room that stank of decadence, decay and death rooted
in the long-distant past, and moved into the bare concrete corridor of a world that was more familiar to
them.

THEY KNEW that the redoubt was sparsely populated.
That gave them an advantage in that it should, theo-
retically, be easy to avoid the Illuminated Ones and
get back to the mat-trans hangar in order to free the
Gate. But that could take a little time, and the ticking
chron was a commodity of which they were short.

The auxiliary corridor in which they found themselves was quiet and deserted, leading onto a main
corridor in which there was also very little sign of life.
Although they kept close to the wall, alert for any
activity, they were in a part of the redoubt where little
in the way of work activity took place, and so they
were able to make rapid progress down to the next
level. It was as they progressed that Mildred became
aware of the pains in her lungs, her breathing coming

harder. She was acutely aware of the wheezing that emanated from Doc, and Jak's normally ghostly pale skin was scored by a number of weals and sores as the pox burst out on his hands and face, becoming more visible.

"Ryan, slow for a second," she rasped.

The texture and urgency of her voice made the one-eyed man cease moving forward, and he looked back to her. Under her plaits, which hung limply around her face, he could see that her dark skin was darker in patches, where the disease was erupting through her pores. The whites of her eyes were bloodshot. She looked ill, and her labored breathing was alarming to him.

"Listen," she began, "I don't know if I can make it back to the bottom and then find the lab. I have a suggestion. Doc and I go for the med lab, try to find the cure, while you free the Gate and chill these fuckers."

"You be okay, just the two of you?"

Mildred smiled. "How the hell do I know, Ryan? But Doc and I are worst hit, so we need the antidote first, and we can move better as two than as three or four. Besides, you need all the firepower you can get if you're going to get the Gate free."

Ryan pondered that. In truth, it took less than a second for him to see the sense of what she was saying. Under any other circumstances, he would have been more cautious until the Gate were free. But time was of the essence.

"Okay," he agreed, "you two go for it. Know where you're going?"

Mildred nodded. "I've got a good idea. And we've got these to keep us safe and warm on the way, right,

Doc?'' she added, slapping the laser blaster she was carrying.

"It should suffice, madam," Doc told her.

So, with the briefest of farewells, Mildred and Doc left the rest of the companions at the junction of two corridors, heading toward the level where the woman believed the med lab was situated while the rest of the party headed downward, hoping to encounter as little resistance as possible.

"DO YOU HAVE anything other than a rough idea of where the lab should be?" Doc panted as he and Mildred moved rapidly along an empty corridor. "I ask not from any lack of faith, but purely because I fear I may soon run out of steam."

"You know something, Doc? I feel pretty much the same myself," Mildred commented, "but I figure the lab should be on this level. Most redoubts they're pretty high up, and I'm counting on the late and unlamented fat man Taschen wanting to keep a pretty close eye on things."

"Ah, yes, the man who invented himself," Doc mused, "That would make perfect sense."

So far they had been fortunate. There had been little activity on this level, and with luck they would not have to pass any of the comp rooms or admin rooms where they had seen Illuminated Ones at work on their initial journey through the redoubt. Which left the possibility of stumbling across moving sec. They kept to the sides of the corridors, using the buttresses as cover, but were completely unable to prevent what happened when they reached the level of the lab.

As they approached an open door, Mildred suddenly became aware of the sounds of movement from within.

He held up a hand to stay Doc, who was moving close behind her, but they were already past the last line of cover. And then she heard the voices.

"You got everything you need now?" spoke the first.

"Uh-huh. Be glad to get off this level. The lab always give me the creeps," returned a second, this one female.

"Don't let the boss man hear you say that," returned the first.

"Like I'd be that dumb," the second countered.

Both voices had grown nearer as the pair approached the open doorway. Mildred swore softly to herself, knowing that there was no way to get into cover.

She had forgotten that she was still wearing the Illuminated uniform with which she had first entered the redoubt, and as she readied to blast, she was momentarily taken aback by the friendly way in which she was greeted by the duo of Illuminated Ones as they exited the room.

"Hey, what're you doing here?" the woman asked, puzzled. "I thought we were the only ones who—"

Mildred recovered first. Their initial lack of hostility had thrown her for a fraction of a second, but despite the pox her reactions were still quicker than those of the Illuminated Ones, soft from lack of combat.

She raised the laser blaster as Doc stepped from behind her, also raising his weapon. Two short, sharp blasts from the rifles pulsed in the air before the Illuminated Ones had a chance to even bring around their weapons to aim. Both shots had been for the head, a feasible target given the close range. Both skulls were hit by the high-powered lasers, the bone crumbling and the flesh searing under the deadly ray. With no actual force of impact, the chilled Illuminated Ones merely crumpled to the ground, a sickening black charred mess occupying the space where their heads had once sat. The head shot had eliminated the risk of either Illuminated One crying out, be it in pain, fear or alarm, at the moment of buying the farm.

"That was a trifle too close to be comfortable," Doc commented mildly as he stared down at the corpses.

"Yeah, and we're too close to let it slip now," Mildred added.

Doc moved around in front of her and began to drag one of the chilled corpses back into the room. "Then I suggest we hide these, just in case they should be spotted before our task is accomplished."

"Good call," Mildred agreed, taking the other corpse and following the old man into the room.

It was a fortunate act of chance that took them there. As they stashed the chilled Illuminated Ones out of view from the corridor or a casual glance into the room, Mildred caught sight of what was contained within.

"Look at this, Doc," she murmured, leaving the hidden corpses and walking across the room to a comp display that was linked to graph machines spilling reams of computer paper silently into a collection basket.

"I believe I've seen something like this before," Doc whispered, joining Mildred. "It is, is it not, some kind of medical monitoring device?"

"On the button, Doc," Mildred muttered, scanning the comp displays and taking out a sheaf of the papers to study them. "Complete vital function, brain and

organ scan. But who are they monitoring this
closely?''

"Time enough for that in a while,'' Doc said quietly. "If this is medical monitoring, then perhaps we
have hit the home run?''

"Might just be that, Doc. Whatever this is attached
to is through that door,'' she said, indicating a closed
sec door that linked the two rooms, the cables for the
machine running through specially built wall sockets.
"I figure there won't be anything else in there, by the
look of this hardware, so we'll take a look after we've
scouted the rest of this level. 'Cause it should all be
here.''

Doc agreed, and they temporarily left the comp
setup in order to scout the rest of the level. There was
only one external sec door onto the corridor—the one
through which the two chilled Illuminated Ones had
come. But internally, the rooms were linked by a series
of sec doors that formed a chain. The first two rooms
they entered were nothing more than standard examination rooms with tables and plentiful supplies of
medications. Any other time, Mildred would have
gladly raided them, but there were more important
items on the agenda. It was in the third room that they
found that for which they sought.

"Sweet Jesus in heaven, this is a nightmare, all
right,'' Mildred whistled softly as they entered the
room.

Doc surveyed the sterile laboratory conditions. Under protective glass, with built-in arm and glove sockets arrayed along the side, a number of cultures were
being developed. The petri dishes in which the disease
cultures were being grown seemed innocuous enough,
but a closer examination of them would reveal growths

that echoed their evil intent on the ugliness of their development. At one end of the long tables on which the cultures were housed there were facilities for making solutions of the culture. It was from these solutions that the disease was being disseminated.

It did not seem, to the untrained eye, the stuff of nightmares. However, Mildred had seen enough of bacterial research and development facilities in her predark life to know what this represented. There were four long benches, one apart from the others. On any one of the other three alone there was enough of the disease being cultured to destroy the population of Earth many times over.

Mildred caught the bemusement in Doc's eye. "Believe me, my friend, this truly is the stuff of nightmares."

"I shall take your word as I have little option but to believe." Doc shrugged. "It seems as little more than a mystery to me, so I hope you have some way of differentiating between the disease and the antidisease, as it were."

Mildred immediately, walked across to the bench that lay separate from the other three.

"You know what?" she mused. "These folk are so simpleminded in some ways that I'd lay odds this is where they cultivate the antidote, and I'll bet you that they have stores of it that are even labeled as such."

Doc allowed himself the ghost of a smile. "Whitecoat arrogance permeates through the ages. Of course, no one would ever dare to encroach upon their sacred domain."

Mildred agreed. "Let's just hope we're right."

With Doc's assistance, which the older man confined to obeying her instructions alone, reasoning that she knew far better than he what to do, Mildred busied herself. The cultures in the dishes on the fourth bench were markedly different, and it took her only a little time to acquaint herself with the process for distilling the results into a solution.

By the wall-length cupboards lining the far corner of the room was a freestanding comp terminal, and Mildred punched in a few commands to access the system. There was no security code as this was a lab terminal, and the relevant information could be readily accessed. From this she was able to find a brief statistical history of the disease, and also confirm that the solution she had just distilled was, in fact, the antidote. It could prevent the disease being contracted, but there was no indication of whether the disease could actually be cured beyond a certain stage of contraction. These were the experiments that were being carried out on the subhumans they had seen in the chasm.

On opening the cupboards, she found shrink-wrapped syringes, and also a store of the antidote, bottled and labeled. Thanking God for the tidy minds of the Illuminated Ones, she turned to Doc and outlined what she had discovered.

"There's no guarantee this will cure us, or that it won't kill us any quicker," she finished.

Doc divested himself of his jacket, rolling up his sleeve. "My dear Doctor," he said quickly, "you must try it on me. At least if I buy the farm quickly, you will know not to try it yourself. It is imperative that you survive long enough to pass this knowledge onward. For my part, my work is done. The last useful task will be to fulfill this function. And if I am still alive in a few moments, then perhaps it will effect a cure."

Mildred filled a syringe and increased the dose from that outlined on the comp stats. She explained this to Doc, finishing, "You sure you want to go through with this?"

"Madam, it will just kill me quicker. Without it, I am already dead, am I not?"

Mildred pursed her lips. It was an unassailable argument. Nodding, she swabbed Doc's arm and pushed in the needle, gently pressuring the plunger so that the liquid was forced into Doc's bloodstream.

Despite everything that he had seen and endured over the years, Doc still found himself grow faint at the sight of the needle—an irrational fear that even time couldn't conquer. He looked away as the liquid from the syringe flowed into his arm. The solution was the same consistency as blood plasma, but felt corrosive and hot. A wave of nausea swept over him as he felt the solution travel around his body, heating him so that his skin turned red and his face was awash in perspiration.

"Doc, how you doing?" Mildred asked in concern, still holding the older man's arm and feeling the muscles spasm beneath her fingers.

"I have felt better," he gasped, trying hard to catch his breath between the clenching of his gut and the weakness spreading to his legs. He tried to relax, counting inside his head and conjuring up pictures of his beloved wife, Emily, and children, Rachel and Jolyon—all long since departed from the world, many years before even the nukecaust—nurturing the thought that if he didn't recover, then at least he may see them before too long had elapsed.

It seemed to be forever, but in truth must only have been a few seconds before the waves of heat and the muscle spasms subsided, leaving Doc slumped against the wall of the lab, Mildred still holding his arm.

"Well, at least I am still alive, so it will be worth trying to inoculate yourself and Jak, at the very least," Doc commented wearily as he straightened himself. "Are you ready for this?"

"No," Mildred said as she prepared another syringe, "but I don't see there's any choice. Hold me, Doc—I may just need it."

"Madam, it will be a privilege, but pray hurry," Doc uttered, "for we must move."

Mildred nodded and swabbed her arm. She plunged the syringe into her vein and depressed the plunger, waiting for the sensations to wash over her. As the bile rose in her throat, she ground her teeth together to stop herself from vomiting as she leaned into Doc. The old man enfolded her with his arms, feeling the muscular contractions run through her, and knowing every step of the way how she felt.

He continued to hold her as the sensations subsided, and Mildred was able to think of something other than the fire in her blood and the sweat that made the Il-luminated uniform stick to her back. Within a short time she was able to right herself and stand apart from Doc.

"We shall continue?" he asked.

"First thing is to load up on the antidote. Get as many of the vials in that cupboard as possible in your pockets, and the syringes," she said as they carried out her words. "Then we need to fire the virus where it sits—wipe it out. But leave that table," she added, indicating the lab bench that housed the antidote cultures. "If we can get rid of the Illuminated Ones, I want that there so that I can come back and work on more antidote.''

''Very well,'' Doc commented as he filled his pockets. ''How do we destroy the virus?''

Mildred looked across at the benches. The atmosphere within the glass cabinets was maintained by a mixture of gases that were fed from mains pipes. At a guess, Mildred figured that the mix would have a high percentage of oxygen. Plastic hosing carried the gases from the outlets and into the airtight chambers housing the petri dishes.

''Leave it to me, Doc. It'll be a pleasure,'' she commented.

Doc's expression needed no explanation. ''I shall leave it to you. I shall just check out the room where the computer leads come from....''

As Doc disappeared, Mildred checked the pipes and how they ran into the glassed chambers. On the benches were dials that showed the mix of gases within the chambers. Her observations of the dials showed that she had been correct in her assumption about the mix. To fire the cultures should be simple.

''Goodbye,'' Mildred muttered simply as she fired a short laser blast at the hoses feeding the gases into the chamber. The plastic melted under the bolt of light, and the heat ignited the oxygen, the flame from the plastic and oxygen spreading into the chamber, washing over the cultures and eradicating them. The sudden ignition caused an explosion within the chamber, shattering the glass covering.

Mildred swore and turned away, sheltering herself as well as possible from the sudden shower of glass, throwing herself to the floor in order to try to take cover. She felt some of the smaller splinters pluck at her clothes and skin as she hit the floor.

When the shower had subsided, she rose quickly to her feet. The noise could attract some unwelcome attention, and she had no idea whether the Gate had been freed as of yet. The last thing she wanted was for Doc and herself to face a force of Illuminated Ones that outnumbered them. So she would have to act quickly.

Turning her attention to the other two chambers, she fired two quick blasts at the pipes on the other culture chambers, and dived for cover as the chambers exploded in glass and flame.

"Shit, why does it have to be so loud," she muttered tersely, pulling herself to her feet. She listened for any indication of oncoming sec, but there was nothing. There was only the sound of Doc, in a distant room.

"Lord save us from this abomination," he said, faint in the distance.

Mildred furrowed her brow. What the hell had Doc discovered? She raced through the lab until she was on the threshold of the room in which Doc stood. She could see him through the open sec door, stopping from his imprecations only to vomit in disgust.

She sped through the doorway and was brought up short by the obscenity that confronted her. The wires and leads led into a tank filled with nutrient fluids, and were attached to a human being that was curled into a fetal state, despite the fact that it seemed to be fully grown.

"What—" she began, but stopped when she saw the look of hatred and loathing on Doc's face. He didn't need to tell her, but spoke anyway.

"This, my dear Doctor, is the fourth Emile Taschen, the obscene blank slate, cloned for a purpose that no longer exists, with nothing to give him identity. Please, put him out of his misery."

The clone turned in the tank, eyes opening and focusing blankly on the two people on the outside of the tank.

Mildred swallowed the bile that rose in her throat and leveled her blaster. "Why didn't you do it, Doc?" she asked before firing.

"Strange as it may seem, I cannot face it. The poor creature is ultimately, at this stage, an innocent...."

The clone's expression remained blank, its eyes fixed on Mildred.

"Maybe," she said gently, "but we can't let it live."

Unleashing a blast of fire, she shattered the tank, the nutrient fluid flowing across the floor, steaming with the heat absorbed from the laser. The clone fetus opened its mouth and screamed, a formless, wordless sound as it was burned by the laser, its life ending before it had even truly begun.

Doc stepped back from the fluid flowing around his feet and vomited again as the corpse fried.

"You okay?" Mildred asked. "We need to get the hell out of here. There's been too much noise, and we need to try and get to the others."

Doc smiled crookedly. "My dear woman, I shall be only too glad to get the hell out of here—or to get out of hell, as I feel the eternal fires themselves could not be worse than this."

"That's something we'll really have to see," Mildred mused. "I just hope they got down to the bottom level without too much trouble in the way."

Chapter Seventeen

For Ryan and the rest of the companions, the journey back to free the Gate had been a little more difficult. Unlike Mildred and Doc, they had, of necessity, had to traverse areas of the redoubt that had a much denser population. It made caution a triple-red necessity, and meant that progress was slower than any of them would have liked.

It was a balancing act. If they sped down the levels, chilling any who got in their way, then it was a certainty that they would arouse the full forces of the Illuminated Ones. With the Gate free, Ryan would still have risked this...but with just the five of them, the numbers meant that it would be unlikely that the Gate would ever get free. It would also alert the Illuminated Ones to whatever Mildred and Doc were doing, and possibly scupper their actions.

So the companions continued down the levels of the redoubt, taking cover and sending scouts ahead to assess the territory. Krysty mostly took this role, as her Illuminated uniform was the least damaged of all of them, so it would be easier for her to blend in with the rest of the redoubt.

Each corridor on each level was scouted by the woman, and—when the way was clear—the rest of the party would follow her in tight formation, Ryan in the lead and J.B. at the rear.

The corridors themselves were surprisingly free of personnel for some time. Whatever Taschen had them working on besides his biological-warfare campaign, he kept them hard at their tasks, as they rarely seemed to leave their admin and science bays. On the rare occasions that an Illuminated One walked out of a room and into the corridor, they were able to take cover easily. All itched to take out the enemy and reduce their numbers, rather than skulk in hiding. It went against the grain of their being for all five of them. But they all knew that it was the right way. Get the Gate free, and the cleaning-up could begin.

As they progressed, J.B. kept checking his wrist chron.

"What's up?" Ryan asked of his old friend, noticing this for the seventh or eighth time.

"Been a while since they left us. It's hard when you don't know how much time they need."

"Harder still when you have to do things this way," Ryan muttered.

They were now at the point where they would have to cross the chasm on the narrow bridge. This was the point of the journey that left them the most vulnerable both to discovery and attack. Krysty had traveled on ahead to scout the entrance to the bridge, and she returned as Ryan and J.B. spoke.

"So what's it like up ahead?" the one-eyed man queried.

Krysty shook her head briefly. Her hair was clinging protectively to her, although whether as an expression of her feelings or as a premonition, Ryan couldn't tell.

"It could be better, lover," she whispered. "There's no one around on this side. The rooms nearest the sec door entry are empty. But I'm not sure about the other side... I couldn't risk taking a look across, in case I was spotted and blew it before we even got there."

Ryan chewed his lip. "That was the right thing," he murmured. "We're just gonna have to go for this one and hope."

Krysty fell into formation behind Ryan, and the companions moved forward at the double, down the corridor toward the sec door that led out onto the bridge. The rooms around were deserted, with no sign of any activity having taken place for some time. They reached the sec door quickly and with ease. Ryan paused before keying in the door code.

"We'll take this as quickly as possible. Anyone comes in from the other side, then I'll try and take them out with a blade. I just hope the bridge doesn't go."

He keyed in the code and the door rose, revealing the chasm and the narrow metal bridge that spanned the divide. Taking a deep breath, he began to run across, the panga grasped firmly in his hand. If he had to face an enemy, then he would rather use a blade than risk the metal of the bridge being melted by laser blasterfire. He felt the bridge begin to move beneath his feet, swaying with the rhythm of his run. On their previous encounter with the narrow metal walkway, they had been moving slowly, but now they moved at speed, and the bridge began to sway wildly at the heavy footfalls, first with Ryan's rhythm, and then with the counterrhythms of the others as they followed.

"Fireblast!" Ryan cursed through gritted teeth, grabbing at the thin rail as the bridge began to move wildly beneath him. He looked over the side of the bridge at the darkness below, which moved beneath, delineated only by the edge of the rock shelf that ran around the chasm. The shapeless subhumans that lived along the rock shelf became little more than rapidly moving blurs as the bridge swayed wildly.

"Stop! Everyone stop," Krysty yelled sharply, holding on to the rails. "If we don't, it'll pitch us right off."

Holding on to the rails, they swayed with the bridge as the momentum began to slow, and the metal walkway steadied. The only member of the party who had looked in any way comfortable was Jak, whose innate sense of balance had made it easier for him to maintain his footing. But even the albino had found it hard to stay steady as the metal snaked and twisted beneath his feet.

"Dark night, I thought we were going to do the job for the Illuminated Ones ourselves," the Armorer said, clasping his fedora to his head and fighting the dizziness and waves of sickness that still assailed him.

"Yeah, I reckon we should be a little more careful the rest of the way across," Dean added. "You know, try not to upset the balance too much."

Ryan looked around. They were more than halfway across, which was good. Although they would have to slow their progress, it would be for a shorter distance. It did still make them vulnerable, however, as they were easily visible from below.

"Okay, let's do it. Slow and easy," the one-eyed man said as he began to move forward.

The metal bridge still swayed under the combined rhythm of their walking, but the slower and lighter movement kept it to a minimum. Looking down again, Ryan could see that they were now over the rock ledge, and within twenty feet of the sec door.

It had all been too good so far. Sooner or later, trouble was going to hit them.

As Ryan looked up again, the sec door they were headed for began to rise, and Ryan could see the lower half of an Illuminated One. Narrowing his eye to get a better view, he was sure that there was only one opponent, which should make it easier for him to handle. But then again, the Illuminated One would have a laser blaster, and Ryan only his panga. And it was on the swaying bridge…

The rising door reached head level, and the astonished expression on the Illuminated soldier as he stepped under the door—obviously in a hurry—and onto the bridge before looking up spoke volumes. He was a tall, gangling man who had his laser rifle strung across his back. He gaped at Ryan, who had taken two steps toward him before he even had a chance to try to swing around his rifle.

"No, you don't," Ryan muttered to himself as he engaged with the soldier. He had to end this swiftly. The longer a fight went on, the more likely it was to raise an alarm, and the more likely it was to disturb the equilibrium of the bridge. Neither was a good option.

The panga blade glimmered in the dull light as it sliced through the air at just higher than waist level, Ryan delivering a roundhouse action that brought the blade into contact with the Illuminated One's arm, just above the elbow as he reached for his rifle. His mouth opened in a silent scream as he lost the arm, the hardened and razor-sharpened blade slicing through flesh, sinew and bone, jarring against Ryan as the resistance of the bone traveled up the blade. It cut through into his ribs and chest, slicing through bands of muscle and splintering rib edges, sending bone shards through internal organs.

The Illuminated soldier staggered to the side, carried over by the momentum of the blow, and fell heavily against the rail. The bridge swayed dangerously, and the companions had to grasp at the rail. Ryan, trying to extract the panga from his adversary, was carried after him. The blade began to move, slowly and with an obscene sucking sound. Ironically, it was the downward momentum of the man that gave Ryan the extra purchase he needed to pull the blade free...but still it began to topple him.

Ryan looked over the side of the bridge at the rock shelf twenty feet below. He could survive the fall, but what would the subhumans below do to him? And even if he could evade them, how would he get back up here?

He had time to think about that as everything seemed to move in slow motion. It seemed like forever until he felt the hands on his ribs, moving around to his chest and bracing him, seeming to pull back with an infinite slowness.

The panga came free, and the Illuminated soldier plunged to the rock shelf below, unable to scream for the blood bubbling and filling his mouth in death throes. He hit the ground with a dull thump, and a cloud of dust rose from beneath. As Ryan watched, a group of the subhumans began to run and shamble from around the ledge, headed for the dying man. They clustered around him, tearing at his clothes and flesh in a fury. The soldier was lost beneath a dense throng of half humans, venting their fury at their captors and creators on the one, chilled representative.

Ryan felt himself pulled back, and turned to find

that it was Krysty who had grasped him in his moment of need.

"Be a pity to lose you after you'd already won the fight, lover," she said with a twinkle. "And to see you end up like that."

Ryan shivered despite himself. The sounds of a feeding frenzy reached him from below, and he knew there would be little of his opponent left to give them away.

"Let's get moving. We don't need another one like that," he said shortly, turning to head through the open door.

IT WAS SIMPLE to evade the Illuminated Ones for the rest of the short journey. Although they had to pass by rooms that were occupied, they followed the same expedient as before: Krysty would scout ahead, and the others would follow when the way was clear. Once past the bridge, they were able to pick up speed again, and were soon nearing the mat-trans hangar.

"Bastard! Which way?" Ryan swore as they reached a junction.

"We came from down there," J.B. said, indicating the corridor that led to the small sec door under the viewing bay. "But we sure as hell don't want to go back like that," he added.

Ryan shook his head. "We want to get up to the level above, take out the coldhearts overlooking the Gate. Need the comps to open the doors safely and take out any kind of alarm."

Dean looked around. "It's not going to be a level up in the redoubt, so there must be an elevator or stairwell leading off one of these corridors."

Ryan agreed. "Quick recce. We take each of them,

splitting up. Meet back here as soon as possible. Triple fast, triple frosty, people.''

They separated into three—Dean and Jak took one corridor, Ryan and Krysty another, while J.B. traversed the third on his own. Within a minute they had gathered once more. Ryan shook his head and took an acknowledgment from Dean, but J.B. had more to say.

"Sec door halfway down the corridor, closed where the others aren't. From the lay of the land, it can't do anything but lead up a stairwell.''

"That's got to be it,'' Ryan said firmly. "But it's going to have to be a full assault. There's no other way we can handle it. Just the one entrance.''

"Dean, if the comps are down, could we open the main sec door to the chamber from any other way?'' J.B. asked.

The younger Cawdor considered that for a second. "Depends. I reckon we could still rewire and bypass any damaged terminals.''

"I'm thinking of tossing a shrapnel gren up the stairwell into the ob port. I'd prefer a nerve gren, but I don't have one. It's just the comp damage....''

"What about the walls?'' Krysty asked. "We don't want to bring down the redoubt around us.''

The Armorer shook his head. "The armaglass will give way, and the blast'll be directed out into the hangar. The only worry is that the people below will pick up some superficial injuries. But they should be able to take some kind of cover,'' he added.

"We'll risk it. It's virtually asking to buy the farm if we do it any other way,'' Ryan decided.

The Armorer nodded and pulled a gren from his omnipresent canvas bag. "I'll do it,'' he said calmly. Without a word, Ryan punched in the sec code on the door, and it opened. The Armorer looked up the twisting staircase that led to the ob port. He had hoped that he would only have to toss the gren up the stairwell, but the angle at which it twisted dictated that he had to take another course. He figured that if he was quick enough, he could take a couple of the steps, then toss the grenade around the angle of the stairwell and pull back before it detonated. The thing he didn't want was for any of the Illuminated Ones keeping watch from the ob port to suddenly descend the stairwell as he was on the way up.

Taking a deep breath and counting inside his head, J.B. took the stairs two at a time. Four stairs, two steps, pull the pin...count one, two, three, four... He tossed the grenade around the angle of the stairs and leaped back down to the corridor as the gren went off with a roar that shook the walls around.

"Hot pipe! If that didn't do it, nothing will," Dean exclaimed.

"WHAT THE FUCK is going on?" Tammy yelled as the armaglass above the heads of the huddled army exploded in an explosion of light and sound.

The Gate and the Crossroads dwellers had been kept in semidarkness and silence since the companions had been taken from them. Once Ryan and his people had been removed, the Illuminated Ones seemed to have lost interest and had merely maintained a watch. There had been no further communication, and the people in the ob port had dimmed their light so they couldn't be seen. In truth, the people below had no way of knowing whether they were still being observed.

There had been no more attacks with the water, and the Illuminated sec hadn't entered the chamber to collect the discarded weapons. After a period, Gloria had directed her warriors to pick up their weapons and clean them off, checking them so that they could be used despite the film of water across the floor. She had no idea if they would be able to use them, but hoped that the companions would find a way to release them and fulfill the mission. Jon traveled around, checking weaponry, and was able to report back to Gloria that the force would be ready, if and when necessary, to begin the fight.

But the question was when?

The time passed with no way of knowing how long they had been there. The cold inside the chamber, the damp from the soaking they had received, ate into their bones, making them shiver and feel that they were stuck in limbo.

So the sudden violence of the gren explosion did far more than give them hope—it jolted them out of a stupor caused by inertia and cold that threatened to lull them into hypothermia.

"Gaia! It's Ryan!" Gloria yelled. Her heart leaped when she saw the companions appear in the hole left by the shattered armaglass. Dean then disappeared to one side, while Ryan shouted down to them.

"The main man is chilled. Mildred and Doc are in search of the cure. We're gonna open the doors, then we move. Clean the place out, quickly as possible."

"I hear you, honey!" Gloria yelled in reply. And with a whoop, she turned to the fighters around her. "Check your blasters and check your brains—we're gonna roll."

Up in the ob port, Dean had picked his way over the blood-splattered corpses in the bay, and was examining the smashed comp terminals. There had been three people in the area, and the shrapnel grenade had ripped them to pieces. It had also ripped into the terminals, and Dean was examining the smashed metal to try and make sense of the fiber optics that lay loose across the floor.

Krysty came across to him. "Think it can be fixed?"

"Don't know."

The younger Cawdor crossed fiber optics, and the lights came on in the chamber below.

"It's a start," he commented, before crossing another two.

In the chamber below, the main sec door began to rise.

"Come on, let's get down and join them before the sec arrive," Ryan said quickly. The others assented and dropped down the dozen or so feet to arrive on the floor of the chamber. It was an easy descent compared to many, and they were soon with Gloria and Tammy, ready to begin the assault.

Gloria embraced Jak, holding him close. "C'mon, sugar, let's get this tidied up and get you sorted."

Jon made his way through the throng of people and handed the companions their blasters, holding back Doc's LeMat and Mildred's Czech-made ZKR. "I'll keep these for when we catch up with them," he said laconically. "You'd better check—but I've given them a thorough clean and check already."

"You're a good man," J.B. said simply, noting that the Uzi and the M-4000 were ready to fire. Jon smiled. From J. B. Dix, that was the highest of praise.

The companions took their weapons, and Gloria watched them. They were ready now for a firefight, and for the Gate to move forward in their destiny.

Despite what had happened, the Gate queen still believed that part of the legend of their tribe could be fulfilled by this battle.

The woman turned to her people, checking Ryan's expression. He gave her an imperceptible nod, and she yelled, "Let's go get those scumfuckers!"

THE BATTLE WAS SWIFT and violent. The Gate and Crossroads fighters spilled out of the opened sec door with speed, their enforced idleness now cleansed in the expectation of battle and of vengeance.

"Take the corridors—split into groups and root out the scum," Gloria yelled. "Tammy, split them like before."

"You know your task—you know how you were split. Take out the corridors one by one!"

"Will we be able to open those doors?" Yardie yelled, his dreadlocks plastered to his head, panting heavily, his dark skin gray with the cold and exertions to which his fat frame was ill-used.

"Yeah, the main comp is off, I guess," Dean replied. "Once we were locked up, there was no need to secure the redoubt, and there's no one to operate the comp now. Key in the sec codes."

Yardie read the code from the scratch plate and keyed it in. The door began to rise.

He yelled, then screamed, "We've got the bastards!"

Following his lead, other war party leaders keyed in codes and the doors began to rise along the corridor. The army split into parties that began to traverse the corridors.

They were of taut nerve, ready for action, and for the most part highly trained fighters. They were up against a force that was unprepared for the attack, and had no idea that their leader had been chilled—at any moment, they expected some kind of leadership, and none were prepared to take the lead. The explosion in the ob port had resounded along many levels of the redoubt, but without an alarm or any information to tell them what was occurring, the Illuminated Ones were easy meat.

Some were more alert and had better fighting instincts than others, banding together to try to form bridgeheads from which they could defend their positions. But despite their laser rifles, and the defensive strength of being inside the rooms that were overrun with the invading forces, they didn't have the skills of the Gate and were soon eradicated. The invading fighters suffered few in the way of casualties, with only a few Crossroads dwellers getting caught in the cross fire. For the most part, the Gate warriors mopped up resistance with ease.

The companions stuck together as they swept through the redoubt, with Gloria and Tammy joining them when their paths crossed at corridor junctions.

"Where are Mildred and Doc, sweets?" Gloria yelled over the noise of blasterfire.

"I don't know," Ryan answered briefly. "We need to find them."

Tammy soon joined the party, and they headed toward the sec door leading out onto the bridge.

"Over the other side there's very little going on, but they must have some kind of warning by now," Ryan shouted as they ran. "Can only get a few people over at a time, so we need to really hit hard and fast."

He keyed in the sec code and the door rose, revealing the bridge stretching out over the chasm.

"Sweet Gaia," Gloria breathed as she surveyed the narrow metal strip that ran across the abyss. "That's gonna be a fucker if they come out the other end."

"We'll have to get across quick and hope they don't, then," Ryan said with gritted teeth as he stepped onto the metal, not looking down at the rock shelf below. "Tread lightly," he said to Gloria and Tammy, "this bastard thing moves too much for my liking."

"Don't worry about us." Gloria grinned. The Gate warriors had spent too long moving through trees and dense foliage, balancing and picking their way across branches, to be worried by the metal bridge.

Gloria and Tammy moved across behind Ryan and Krysty, and before Jak, Dean and J.B. The Gate women looked over the side at the chasm and at the ledge populated by the subhumans.

"What the fuck are those poor bastards?" Tammy asked.

"More experiments by these coldhearted scum," Dean said softly. "Could be us, if we hadn't got the hell out in time."

Tammy shook her head sadly. "Be a better place without any of those scumfuckers."

They were halfway across when the sec door on the opposite side opened. A sec squad of Illuminated Ones was behind the door, armed with laser blasters. It was obvious that they were now aware of the battles taking place on the other side of the redoubt. Although they hadn't had time to recce fully, it was possible that some of the corridors curved around the chasm, and war parties had already reached that area, alerting the Illuminated Ones to the invasion.

Whatever the reason, the party standing on the

metal bridge now found itself at the mercy of the sec squad, with nowhere to run.

"Damn those bastards to hell," Ryan yelled as he pulled the Steyr from his back and blasted toward the gathering of sec that were clustered in the doorway. The rounds from the rifle ripped through them, scattering the Illuminated Ones. Some fell to the ground, chilled or fatally wounded. Others dived backward to get out of the angle of the shots. Others still dropped to their stomachs and began to fire back with wayward blasts of laser fire that dipped wildly about the bridge.

"Try and keep out of range," Krysty yelled, diving to the moving floor of the bridge and attempting to take aim with her .38 Smith & Wesson. But the bridge was now beginning to sway wildly as the seven people gathered on it began evasive maneuvers. Both Ryan and J.B. were trying to aim their weapons with one hand while gripping the thin metal rail with their free hands in an attempt to duck out of the way of the laser blasts and still stay on the walkway.

But it was getting harder to keep balance with each evasive move. The sway of the bridge increased, and two of the sec squad had good cover within the corridor beyond the door from which to snipe at the bridge. Either the laser blasts would get them, or the bridge would throw them off, such was the cumulative increase of its motion as they moved upon it.

Then the laser fire ceased. Sounds of battle came from within the doorway, and as the bridge steadied the people on it could hear a laser fire exchange beyond. It was short and sweet, ended by the screams of two people.

"Hold your fire, I implore you!" called a voice from beyond the silent doorway.

"Doc!" Dean yelled. "It must be Doc and Mildred."

As the companions, Gloria and Tammy moved along the bridge, they saw Doc and Mildred appear in the doorway, holding laser blasters.

"Our people are everywhere," Mildred gasped. "It's like a charnel house back there, but I think we're ahead. There's not many of the Illuminated Ones left."

"That's good, but…" Ryan left the question unsaid.

Mildred smiled. It was weak, as the disease had left her system ravaged, but there was a note of triumph in her voice as she spoke.

"The disease cultures are destroyed. So is the clone—" she ignored the look of complete confusion from Tammy and Gloria "—and we've got an antidote. It'll prevent the spread of the disease, but whether it'll cure those who have it, I guess you'll just have to watch me and Doc to see."

Chapter Eighteen

In the aftermath of the battle, it was relatively easy to mop up the last few Illuminated Ones and dispose of them. Normally, Ryan would feel that chilling the defeated and defenseless was somehow wrong, but with the Illuminated Ones he was prepared to make an exception. They wished to eradicate the remnants of humanity, and as such deserved to be treated as little more than vermin. It wasn't execution, even, it was pest control. After them, the subhuman creatures they had created had to be destroyed. The poor, shambling half humans were riddled with disease, and the war party was advancing their date of chilling, making it as quick as possible.

While Ryan and Gloria organized that, Tammy and J.B. joined Doc and Mildred in the lab, where Mildred explained her plans for inoculation and spreading the antidote across the lands. After she and Krysty had synthesized large amounts, she would leave it in Crossroads for convoys to transport. But in the meantime…

Tammy and J.B. rounded up the war party and ferried the fighters into the lab where Doc and Mildred worked in relays, inoculating them all. After Krysty had been injected, she joined them, enabling them to get through the vast number of people with ease. Gate runners were sent out to the wags and returned with the men of the tribe, who were also inoculated.

THE ARMY RETURNED to Crossroads—not in triumph, as the Crossroads dwellers were thinking of those they had left behind and who, even in the space of twenty-four hours, may have breathed their last—with a supply of the antidote, and the means to administer it to the rest of the ville.

Baron Robertson was among the first to greet them, and the first to be inoculated. Hector was among the next batch, Doc making sure that the hollow-eyed ville doctor, himself now covered in sores and breathing poorly, was treated, and making him rest until the injection had a chance to make some effect.

The ville was a hive of activity in the following days, as the Gate and the companions helped the decimated population to restore some kind of order and repair to homes that had been sundered by the action of the past few days. It would take a long time to rebuild totally, but the aim was for Crossroads to become the port of call for all convoys once more.

On the third day, Mildred and Tammy returned with a wag containing copious supplies of antidote, synthesized within the redoubt. The facility was now closed, but still operational, and Mildred met with Robertson and Hector to discuss the manufacture of more of the clear fluid in the future. It was important that the ville now act as a distribution center, sending the antidote across the lands with the convoys. The disease had spread beyond this area for sure—convoys had unwittingly carried it out. In which case, they could take the antidote along the same routes. The disease might never be truly eradicated, but it could be controlled.

What could have been a plague could now be little more than a localized nuisance. Hector and two of the ville women who had assisted him in his med building traveled with Mildred and Krysty to the redoubt, where they learned how to synthesize the antidote.

Within a few days, things were ready for both the Gate and the companions to move on. But to where?

LEAVING CROSSROADS to rebuild, the companions and the Gate retreated to the area where the Gate had previously camped, and the tribe set up there for some days. It was a rare chance for both parties to take some respite from the hardship of constant battle. With Jak recovering after his inoculation, it was a chance for the albino to spend some time with Gloria, and also for Dean to renew his relationship with Tammy. But for all four of them, it was bittersweet, tinged with the knowledge that the parting of the ways had to soon come.

By the fourth day, Ryan and J.B. were both itchy. New England made them uneasy, the memories of their exploits on the coast still too close for comfort, and both were keen to move.

So it was that they gathered around the campfire as the night drew on, cold in the woodlands—the companions and Tammy and Gloria.

"You know the time has come to part, don't you, sweets?" Gloria asked.

Ryan nodded. "We need to go. Mebbe move farther north. One day mebbe we'll settle, but for now..."

"For now we just have to keep moving, keep searching," J.B. added.

"For what?" Tammy asked.

Ryan shrugged. "I don't think any of us know, but we'll know when we find it."

"Have you found it, honey?" Gloria asked Jak.

The albino was silent for a moment, then looked her in the eyes. "Mebbe could have...but chilling follows, always. Can't be with, must always be alone. Safer for all."

The Gate queen agreed. "I can understand. I feel that way. And I'd like us to come with you, but we've got to stay."

"Why?" Mildred asked, curiosity getting the better of her.

Gloria looked into the fire, and for a moment it seemed as though she were lost in the flames, retreating into a trance state to look for an answer. Finally, she said, "Our legends have always spoken of the Gate, and the pathway to Illumination. I really thought that we'd found that gateway when we found these scumfuckers. I thought that I would be the one to lead the tribe to our ultimate destiny."

"And now?"

"And now I don't know. I kinda figure that the answer does lie with what's happened. Somehow it equates to what's in our legends. I just haven't worked out how yet. But if the answer does lie in that redoubt, then I'll work it out. It just may take some time."

She fell silent, looking once more into the fire.

WHEN THE GATE TRIBE rose in the early-morning sun, the space in the camp where the companions had billeted was empty. Before the dawn had even begun, Ryan had rallied his people, and they were already at the redoubt.

As RYAN CLOSED the door to the mat-trans unit and hurried to sit beside Krysty, he knew that none of them knew where they would end up.

They only knew that they had to keep searching.

For something—absolution, release, freedom, peace?

Just something...

James Axler
Outlanders®
EQUINOX ZERO

As magistrate-turned-rebel Kane, fellow warrior Grant and archivist Brigid Baptiste face uncertainty in their own ranks, an ancient foe resurfaces in the company of Viking warriors—harnessing ancient prophecies of Ragnarok, the final conflict of fire and ice, to bring his own mad vision of a new apocalypse. To save what's left of the future, Kane's new battlefield is the kingdom of Antarctica, where legend and lore have taken on mythic and deadly proportions.

In the Outlands, the shocking truth is humanity's last hope.

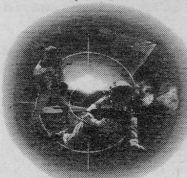